# Puffin

T. K. LOUIS

Thank you for buying Puffin,
a Frank & Hildy novel.

I truly hope you enjoy the read.

T. K. Louis

If you would like to join Frank & Hildy's readers club and receive FREE scenes and background stories for Puffin, please visit the link below.
http://www.tklouis.com/freestuff

First published in 2019 on Amazon

Copyright © T.K. Louis Aps

T.K. Louis has asserted his right under the Copyright, Designs and Patents Act 1988 to be identified as the author of this work.

This book is a work of fiction and, except in the case of historical fact, any resemblance to actual persons, living or dead, is purely coincidental. Every effort has been made to obtain the necessary permissions with reference to copyright material, both illustrations and quoted. We apologise for any omissions in this respect and will be pleased to make the appropriate acknowledgements in any future edition.

ISBN 13: 9781091013988
ISBN 10: 1091013985

Edited and Typeset by Amnet Systems.
Cover design by Amnet Systems

# PUFFIN

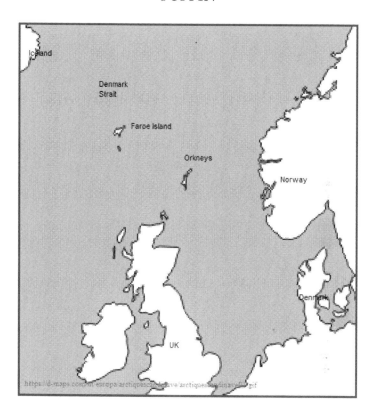

# The Faroe Islands

# 1

The CEO was innocent, not that they cared. Coming out through the hotel gates, he looked to his right and noticed a jogger a hundred metres down the road, dark shorts and T-shirt, pale legs, the man was doing stretches against a wall. The CEO turned the other way, walked a few steps and broke into a jog.

For their Easter holiday, they had splurged, taking two full weeks at the Turkish resort. It was some compensation for his many months away from his family this past year, him working on the Faroe Islands, them living in Copenhagen. He had just left their two-bedroom holiday flat after kissing his boys goodnight. His wife had been in bed, reading. She had changed into a tantalising chemise. When he returned, he would shower and then? They both wanted that third baby, and perhaps this time it would be a girl.

Feeling the heat radiating off the pavement, the CEO savoured his evening runs along the coastal Mersin Antalya Boulevard, hotels lining the right side of the road, white sands and hotel swimming pools to his left. Beyond, in the moonless night, he could hear the waves crashing on the beach as the tide came in.

At first, he ran slowly under the dim streetlights, many of the flagstones were cracked and uneven. A sprained ankle was the last thing he needed. He glanced quickly over his shoulder, a precaution only. This late in the evening, he saw no cars, but he did notice the pale-legged jogger headed his way. After crossing the street, he followed the paved walkway that ran along the Boşaltma Kanal, going inland. Thankfully, here, the surface was more even, and he could pick up the pace.

He heard the other jogger's heavy footfall and glanced once more over his shoulder. The stranger had crossed the street and was now thirty metres behind him. The other man was obviously in better shape, the CEO concluded, as he passed their regular ATM.

He veered right and followed the footbridge, which spanned the canal. Then a sharp left. He breathed deeply, enjoying the cool evening breeze on his face, a relief from that musky smell that permeated the area during the day.

Behind him, the CEO heard the other jogger's feet pounding the tarmac, and he grew irritated, the other runner was invading his space. He decided to stop and let the man pass by. There was a bench he could lean against and stretch his calf muscles, and resume his run when the other jogger was gone.

As the CEO slowed to a halt, the other man bumped into him. He felt at first a punch in his abdomen, then a numbness that spread upwards through his chest. Looking down, he was shocked to see the hilt of a knife protruding from his side. As he reached for it, falling, sensing his surroundings as if in slow motion, his head thumped into the ground, his body tingling.

The CEO closed his eyes one last time, panicking. As he let out his final breath, he thought of his lovely wife and little ones whom he would never see again.

# 2

Present Day, late March

The Sheep Islands, in old Norse 'Færøerne', situated hundreds of kilometres north of Scotland and an equal distance south of Iceland. A tiny Hawaii without the warmth, the sunshine and the palm trees. Actually, without any trees what-so-ever, or so it seemed.

I had read somewhere that the present-day inhabitants were successors of Vikings who had taken holiday cruises to acquire antics from Catholic monasteries in the ninth century AD and had decided to stay. Ever since, this native people had lived off the land or more accurately, off the land and the sea. And now from tax-free shopping as well.

Shuffling down the main aisle of the airport mall, in a scrum of fellow travellers coming off the Friday morning flight from Copenhagen, where we had stayed with Hildy's mum, I looked through the glass wall and noticed that the adjacent baggage hall was void of passengers. The single carousel stood inert with no luggage visible. Instead, the crowd of arrivals bustled about here in the shopping area, binge buying their tax-free cosmetics, spirits, and chocolates.

I wondered if the airport staff intentionally delayed the luggage to boost sales as I asked Hildy to wait for me by the doors and watch our carry-on. A few minutes later, I re-joined my wife lugging the bottle of premium gin that her cousin had suggested (£60, would you believe it?), and six bottles of decent red.

'Frank darling, your turn to watch our things,' Hildy said. 'I want to get something for the children.'

'Children?'

'Wherever we visit, there will be children. We will need a general supply.'

She reappeared some minutes later, heavily laden.

'I got six one-kilo bags of M&Ms,' she said.

Our suitcases arrived almost first on the conveyor belt. With our trolley stacked high, I turned the cart around, and as I wondered just how many children Hildy planned to visit, alternately how obese they were likely to be, I took two steps out to the tiny customs area, where a black Labrador sniffed our bags.

There was no proper arrivals hall, no line of expectant faces or bored chauffeurs holding name signs. It seemed the airport had taken all available space for the tax-free mall. Instead, passengers exited through a revolving door directly out to the pavement. The taxi rank was on the opposite side of the road, the entire pick-up and set-down area was covered by a wide overhang.

After helping the driver load Hildy's luggage into the back of the people carrier, together with our purchases and my cabin-size suitcase, I climbed into the warmth of the rear seat. As usual, Hildy had taken the front so she could converse with the driver.

'What are we waiting for?' I asked.

'If the driver can get more passengers than just the two of us, the trip is classed as a shuttle instead of a taxi. Then we do not pay the full six hundred, just four.'

She was talking of kronor, not British pounds.

Minutes later, two fit-looking men in their mid-twenties approached the vehicle and, after a short negotiation with the driver, they unshouldered their small rucksacks into the rear of the car and climbed in next to me. They smelled unwashed.

The driver climbed in, and as he got going, I studied our surroundings as we left the airport and drove east along the coastal road.

The islands consisted exclusively of hills, mountains really, which rose from the ocean surface and towered above us. Only a thin layer of topsoil covered the basalt rock and provided a tenuous foundation for an emerald blanket of grass, a sprinkling of wildflowers and little else. No trees or shrubs could be seen, nothing with deep roots. Bare-naked nature.

High up on the mountainsides, I could see black crevasses where rainwater had washed away the grass, small waterfalls cascaded down the rock. As these fissures came down the slopes, they turned into fast flowing creeks, and then into slower moving streams before entering the sea.

Where the largest of such streams met the ocean, small villages had sprung up, seldom more than thirty or forty houses. Each township we passed through had its own little wooden church and soccer field with artificial grass.

Perhaps a grocer or a car-repair, but invariably a church, and the football pitch.

The driver proved chatty. After ascertaining that Hildy and I were from England, he looked in the rear-view mirror and asked the young men about their origins.

'Ukraine,' one of them said. 'Backpacking.'

Then they clammed up.

On hearing this, I found it strange the men should have so little baggage. I mean, didn't serious trekkers typically have huge rucksacks, with heavy boots hanging by their laces?

The driver turned his attention to Hildy. He wanted to discuss family. Hildy had once explained to me that most Faroese people had between ten and fifteen cousins, sometimes more. In older times, before they had decent television, married couples often had up to eight or nine children, hence their extended lineage.

'Darling, what a coincidence,' she now said over her shoulder. 'The driver comes from the same village as my father. One of the northern islands, you remember, Svínoy.'

Swine Island. I had been there once, a quaint little place with a half hundred souls where there once had lived five times as many. The driver and Hildy knew, or knew of each other's family members, and discussed them in detail. I expected their deliberations to last all the way to Tórshavn, the capital of the island state and its only major town, a drive of some seventy kilometres. Being considerate, they kept it in English for my benefit. I listened with half an ear.

'Did you know, Karolina is having a baby, she's due in a month,' the driver said.

'But she must be over fifty,' Hildy replied.

'No, that would be your second cousin on Ionna's side, your father's sister. I mean Elna's daughter, your father's brother's wife, Kristin. Her niece, probably your second cousin, once removed or thereabouts, maybe your third.'

It was all bollocks to me. How could anyone follow what the man had just said? Seriously. The names meant nothing to me, the family relationships were pure gibberish. I did not have brothers or sisters. My Welsh father had been an only child, and the revolutionary guard had exterminated most of my mother's family after the return of Ayatollah Khomeini in 1979. All this third-cousin-this and second-cousin-that was far beyond me, but as always, I was in awe of my family-tree proficient wife.

While they droned on, I sat thinking about the family I did have. And how lucky and proud I was. The twins, Max in the Third Paras, my old regiment, and Oliver doing well at university, studying finance at Oxford. Our eldest, Sophie, was six month's pregnant, living in Toronto with her husband, an investment fund manager, and their eight-year-old Emma, his daughter from a previous marriage. There was Wilson, of course, he counted as family, my batman from the army, and my closest friend who lived in our gatehouse as a paid gardener and personal trainer, for us and the dogs.

And last but certainly not least, our second eldest, Penny, who we had not seen since the Christmas holidays. She was busy with her internship here on the islands, some oil exploration company. From our weekly Skypes, she seemed enthralled by her work. I looked forward to spending time with her, knowing it would be the pinnacle of our trip, the most appealing bit, because, let's face it, when all was said and done, nothing exciting ever happened on the Faroes Islands.

The driver caught my eye in the mirror,

'So, you're English. Now we are in the same boat, yes? Good for you. Not bound by the EU fishing restrictions anymore. Now we can trade together. And with the Russians.'

I sensed the men beside me shift in their seats. They had seemed content to gaze out of the far window, but now they took an interest in the conversation, albeit they seemed unwilling to show it. Fair enough, I knew Ukraine had a strained relationship with its northern neighbour, not least after the Crimea debacle.

'Why the Russians in particular?' I asked the driver.

'The Faroes are not part of the EU, so we are not bound by any of the sanctions. We are free to trade with them just as much as we like.'

'What do you sell? Sheep?' I asked.

'Ha! No, we export fish, all we can catch. The Russians will not purchase fish from the EU, so they buy it from us. And the prices have skyrocketed.'

'Is that all you export?' For the life of me, I could not imagine anything else the Russians would be interested in. Home-knitted sweaters perhaps?

'It's all we have, all that they want from us,' the driver said.

From the corner of my eye, I perceived the Ukrainians give each other a knowing smile, just fleetingly, and then their gaze returned to the passing countryside.

The road snaked its way along the coast until it was time to cross to the other side of the island. Our driver, his chatter undiminished, turned left and drove through the village of Sandavágur, past a white church with a red roof, it looked as if it was built from Legos. The ascending road was steep, I was pressed back in my seat.

We reached the top, a mountain pass, where we had a spectacular view of the islands to the north, dozens of mountain peaks, and the fjord below, a single fishing boat creating a wake. There was no denying it, the sights here were fantastic and unremarkable at the same time, nature at her very best, but there was just so damn much of it. Through the pass, the road wound its way down, and just when I thought the highway must level off, it plunged into the earth.

'This is the tunnel we built so we can get to the airport without taking a ferry,' the driver said.

'Why not build an airport closer to Tórshavn?' I asked.

'You British built the landing field at Vágar during the war. There is no other place on the islands flat enough. Your landing was hard, yes? Because the strip is very short. If the pilot does not put the plane down immediately and brake very hard, you go over the edge. So we built this tunnel. Now we have built many more because we don't want everyone moving to Tórshavn.'

'So the tunnels are for shoppers going to town?' I asked.

'No, they are for the children,' the driver laughed. 'There are not enough children in the smaller villages to warrant having their own schools, so buses bring them to central schools and back. In the past, accidents happened when school buses took the narrow, slippery roads, going over the mountains in the fog. So now we have tunnels.'

Passing through the undersea tunnel took seven or eight minutes. It sloped sharply down to the halfway point and then ascended. Coming out into brilliant sunshine, the mountains towering above us, we drove for a quarter of an hour through grass-covered valleys with small lakes, most no bigger than ponds, along pastures with sheep, no structures visible other than sheds and the occasional lean-to used by the animals.

As we neared yet another tunnel, the two men next to me bent low and craned their necks to study the local topography. They took it all in, something which happened again as we exited the tunnel. They studied the fjord to our left and the high ground to our right. Perhaps they intended to go hiking there, I figured. Leaving the inlet behind us, the men settled back once more to a bored gaze.

The taxi driver followed the coastal highway clockwise into the heart of Tórshavn. Passing the police station, I caught a brief glimpse of the bay on our left, before the old fort masked the view. I noticed a cruise liner and the stern of what must have been a naval vessel of some sort anchored behind the passenger ship. The men beside me said something to each other. I did not speak Ukrainian nor for that matter any of the Slavic languages.

As we stopped at the bustling 'Eystaravág', meaning 'East Basin' or 'East Harbour', the Ukrainians climbed out, paid the fare and retrieved their rucksacks from the boot. Back in the car, the driver slammed his door and then took off, up a narrow street between rows of two-story houses. He stopped at an intersection.

I asked Hildy, 'A stop light? Last time I was here, there were no stop lights.'

The taxi driver answered for her,

'Yes, we have traffic lights now. I always seem to get a red one. Unlucky, I suppose.'

I asked, 'Traffic lights? You mean you have more?'

'What do you think we are? Some third world nation?'

He pointed to his left,

'The other two are down that way.'

# 3

Moscow

The morning sunshine streamed through the tall windows as Defence Minister Oleg Ruzhkov, deep in thought, sat at his mahogany desk with its bronzed lion's claw feet, and sipped his coffee, now grown cold.

From the outset, he had told the president this was not the job for him. Mining and agriculture perhaps, but no, not the military. History had proved him right. There was not a folder on his desk requiring his attention. The only meetings on his agenda were with squabbling department heads, each pushing for a larger chunk of his dwindling budget.

He knew it was his own fault, he should have resisted, but how could he turn down the navy, when they offered to promote his one and only child, his boy, to vice-admiral? They'd made Oleg's brother brigadier-general and given him his own missile base. And finally, his nephew, that rascal Georgi, getting that lucrative job in New York where he could earn himself a small fortune and stay out of mischief. With the boy's habit of scheming and fraud, Oleg feared his conniving nephew would otherwise have got himself locked away by the FSB ages ago.

However, everything came at a price. In return, the generals had demanded full autonomy. Decentralised procurement, allowing the bribes to flow freely to the officer corps. And budgets approved for one expense, the funds misappropriated to some other cause. His job was now strictly to provide a smoke screen, to protect the generals from public scrutiny. Not from the president, surely he and the FSB were acutely aware of the corruption. However, the president did nothing. Instead, he left Oleg in place as a neutered administrator.

The red phone rang. Speak of the devil. Oleg lifted the receiver from its cradle.

'Mr President, to what do I owe the honour?'

'Ruzhkov, just checking in. You know I am relying on you.'

'Yes, Mr President.'

'I will not have another incident. They fooled us once, Almazov and his gang of idiots. Invading Ukraine, taking Sevastopol just to have a port for their new toys. But no more.'

'Yes, Mr President.'

'No ice-free harbour in the north, no new Atlantic fleet. That's what I told them, and I expect your full support. And the Baltic Sea does not count. I know what they've done for you and your family, but you are my man, I need to know I can rely on you.'

'Yes, Mr President. But sir, where will they find this new port?'

'Ruzhkov, you can be so naive. That's the beauty of my plan. They'll never do it, not in a million years. We don't want those damn ships, we cannot afford them. But outright telling that to the high command would cause a revolt. So I've given them an insurmountable task.'

'Yes, Mr President.'

'Ruzhkov, if you get any inkling they're making progress, I want to know about it, immediately. We must do everything possible to stop them. Help me on this, and in a year's time, you can choose another ministry. Within reason, of course.'

'Yes, Mr President.'

'Alright. Good talk. We'll speak again soon.'

'Yes, Mr President,' Oleg said to his commander-in-chief, who had already hung up.

He eased the receiver into its cradle and leant back in his chair, daydreaming, and thinking about the president's words. Minister of sport? No, not with all the scandals. Minister of culture then, with the grand openings and cutting red tape. That would be nice, his wife would like that.

# 4

Hildy's cousin and her husband, a sea captain on leave, were a slim couple in their mid-forties. Knud was tall and ginger-haired and Oydis an attractive brunette with a perpetual smile. I knew from my previous visits they both spoke excellent English.

They came out to greet the taxi. As Hildy paid the fare, I unloaded the luggage, the candy, and the spirits. I handed these last precious bags to our host couple knowing the Faroese had an ambivalent relationship with alcohol. It was not freely available, not sold in shops or the few existing supermarkets, only at the tax-free at the airport and in the government-owned off-licenses where the prices were purposely set high, exorbitant even. Hence many Faroese cherished spirits as a luxury item.

Once our luggage was safely deposited in the upstairs guest room, I was anxious to get to town, we were meeting Penny for coffee. I felt an excitement I had not experienced in months. With Oydis taking the lead, I followed my wife as we left the heights and housing enclaves of the Hoyvík suburb behind us.

We headed on foot for Tórshavn, which could be seen in the distance between industrial warehouses to our left, and sports stadiums to the right. As we descended, one path leading to the next, weaving between pastures and rocky outcrops, we passed the occasional farmhouse with backyard sheep bleating at us. From time to time, Hildy would turn around and give me an encouraging smile.

'Are you happy being here, dear?' I asked.

'As always,' she said, with rosy cheeks and a spring in her step. With her auburn hair and her trim waistline, she was in decent shape and the love of my life.

We entered a grassy dale. The footpath followed a gurgling creek running between rocky bluffs, the kind of rough-and-tumble place where I would have loved to play as a boy, instead of being cooped up in our house in Riyadh. As we continued our descent, isolated copses of small trees sprang up, the first real foliage I had seen on the islands so far. Finally, after passing through a cosy enchanted woodlot of evergreens with a brook, and fish standing in its waters, we walked past a row of shops, down a short pedestrian street and reached the town square. There were perhaps a dozen maple trees, which seemed to complete the Faroese forestry.

As we got to the bottom of a set of stone steps, the view opened up before us. This was more like it. To me, this was what the Faroes was about, quaintness. Pastel coloured four-story buildings on our left and the shipyard on the right enclosed a harbour, 'Vestaravág', the western basin, the 'West Harbour'. A parking lot packed with boats, a few sailing boats and some smaller motor yachts for sure, but the vast majority, perhaps a few hundred, were recreational fishing boats, most of them painted in blue and white, the Faroese colours.

'They belong to regular citizens. Knud's boat is over there,' Oydis explained, pointing. 'We catch our own fish. It is only twice a month he is allowed to go out, so when he does have the chance, he catches as much as he can. You'll see, he's going fishing in the next few days, we're running low. He wants to bring you along.'

Not for the first time, I admitted to myself, these indigenous folks were a far cry from my fellow Brits and myself. We liked to buy fish in shops or supermarkets, preferably frozen and already breaded. We certainly did not want to know where it came from.

'But isn't he a ship's captain as well?' I asked.

'He is, that is his big boat.' Oydis smiled proudly and pointed across the harbour. I was not sure which vessel she meant. There was a group of ocean-going trawlers and a dark grey naval vessel.

'The Brimil, the coast guard ship,' Oydis said.

We crossed the street. The multi-coloured buildings had ground-floor coffee houses spilling out onto the promenade. Patrons, wrapped up tight against the breeze sat among the tables braving the elements.

Immediately, my eyes were drawn to a face I had not seen in months, a face, which would normally have been happy, would usually have warmed my heart with a brilliant smile. Now, however, as my daughter spotted us, I could see there was something amiss.

After a cheek-to-cheek for Oydis and a warm embrace for me, Penny held her mother as they hugged.

'Penny darling, what's wrong?' Hildy asked.

'Mom, would it be all right if I talked to Dad for a bit? There is something I need his advice on.'

It was a proud moment in my life. In the past, Sophie and Penny had always turned to Hildy with problems at school, problems with boys, or whatever. When shopping for clothes, I was forever barred from giving my fashion advice, impeccable as it was, and often banished from the changing rooms altogether. However, now she sought my help, and I was glad to give it, although I had not the faintest idea of what it was about. Surely not money, Hildy was the wealthy one.

'Are you certain you don't want me to stay?' my wife asked. I knew she must have been bursting with curiosity.

'It won't take long, Mom. Just something I want to discuss with Dad.'

'That's fine, dearest. Oydis and I will go shopping. We'll be back in half an hour.'

'Take your time,' I called to their backs.

The women disappeared between two of the coffee houses. From my previous visits, I knew the steps led up to the old town and its wooden church.

Once seated, Penny reminded me that after finishing her degree in geology she had accepted an offer of a one-year internship with FaroeOil, the Faroese company that held a monopoly on drilling for oil in the surrounding seabed. She pointed across the harbour, indicating a building, which she said was the FaroeOil headquarters.

'Dad, I was finally getting to know the business and its activities. I was also contributing to the analysis of the drillings.'

'Was? Penny, you're speaking in the past tense.'

'I'll get to that. First, you need to understand some things. The geological activity, which once formed the Faroe Islands fifty-five million years ago, pushed the seabed upwards, resulting in rock formations, basalt mountains rising from the ocean floor. It created the topography we see today. My main thesis from university was in traps. At the base of the islands, where the slopes meet the ocean floor, are what we call 'Anticline Traps'.'

'I'm parched. Can we get a coffee?'

'In a moment, Dad, when I'm finished. So the traps are there. The question is whether there are oil deposits under the traps and if they are shallow enough so we can access them. Drilling at sea depths of a kilometre is difficult enough, drilling deeper will be more costly.'

'But if the international oil price is high, it could still be worth it, I assume?'

'Exactly. We've calculated that Faroese investments in new oil fields will be profitable if the market price is over sixty dollars a barrel. However, since prices can drop below that level, we need to be selective in our drillings.'

'Penny, what does all this have to do with your internship?'

'Dad, a year ago my boss, his name is Hans Klerk, he's from Holland, he compiled a roadmap for the exploration of the Faroese seabed. Then Wednesday, I was going over the data and made a discovery. Although someone had registered the correct coordinates on the reports, the engineers have made the actual drillings in other places. Places where there are no traps.'

I was relieved. I had feared my daughter's concerns were something serious, perhaps something personal.

I asked her, 'Is that all this is about? You don't think the company will succeed? My dear Penny, it's just an internship, learn as much as you can and move on.'

'There's more, Dad, it gets worse. I showed Hans my findings. He took some convincing, but afterwards, he went straight to the CEO and demanded to make a presentation of my results to the board of directors. Hans wanted me to attend the presentation as well. After all, it was I who discovered the discrepancies.'

'Penny, don't you think you are becoming too involved? I fail to see how all this can be your problem.'

'Dad, it's because you're not listening, you never do.'

My daughter sounded exasperated.

I found the comment unfair. I was listening, actively, but I conceded, often enough, the women in the family made the same accusation. Apparently, somehow, I did not listen *in the right way*.

'I'm trying.'

'Okay Dad, then just hear me out. The CEO said no, a board presentation was not necessary, but he wanted Hans's recommendations in writing. According to Leif Olsen, it was the lender's independent engineers who'd demanded we try these other locations first.'

'Who's Leif Olsen?'

'See? I told you, you're not listening. He is the CEO.'

'Okay, Penny, if this Leif Olsen knows his stuff, he will get this sorted, and they'll no doubt get the drilling schedule back on track. I don't see there is anything you need to worry about, or am I missing something?'

'Dad, the two of us, Hans and I, worked yesterday until past midnight. We checked and rechecked the original sites Hans had recommended, and we took into account the new data learnt from the dry wells these past six months. When we finished the report, we locked up and went home, it was one in the morning. That is the last I've seen of Hans. He's disappeared.'

'What do you mean, disappeared?'

'He didn't come into work this morning, he's missing.'

'Penny, you can hardly say he's missing, you saw him only hours ago, perhaps he overslept.'

'I knew you'd say that. When Hans didn't show up for work, I called his mobile, it went straight to voicemail. I asked the director's secretary if she had heard from him. She said Hans had quit the company for personal reasons, he would not be returning. Dad, it's so unlike him, he would at least have said goodbye. And when I returned to my desk, I logged onto my computer. Our work, every document, every study, someone had deleted it all from the server.'

'Can it be some sort of mistake?' I asked.

'Dad, online, I found Hans's home number in Holland. His wife picked up when I called. I didn't give her my name, I didn't want to upset her, so I merely introduced myself as a former colleague and said I needed a reference letter for a job application. She gave me his mobile number, the one I already have, and told me he was presently working abroad.'

'Maybe she said 'working a broad', meaning he has a mistress somewhere.'

'Dad! Be serious,' Penny hissed.

I had thought the remark quite witty. Obviously, under present circumstances, dad-jokes were not welcome.

'I walked over to Hans's flat and knocked on his door, it's not far from here. No one answered. The door was unlocked, and he wasn't there. Dad, to make matters worse, just before I left to come here, the CEO called me into his office. He told me they no longer need me at the company. He fired me with immediate effect. Instead, they've found me a well-paid job at a company, which makes studies for new tunnels. I need to correct that thing about well paid. Dad, the salary is outrageous.'

'How much?'

She told me, and I wondered whether they were in need of ex-intelligence officers such as myself.

'Dad, I'm not sure what to do. On paper, I'm a qualified geologist, but I need work experience in the oil industry before thinking about a PhD. I want to be an oil engineer, you know, just like Grandad. I should probably book the next flight back to London and start looking for something else, but I can't, not yet, it would be abandoning Hans. I'm sure something terrible has happened to him, but what can I do? Should I tell his wife he's gone missing?'

I wanted a few minutes to consider what my daughter had told me and suggested she get us some coffee and cake from the self-service counter inside the café. Once she disappeared into the shop, I leant back in my chair and contemplated the seagulls screeching, hovering over the harbour waters.

It was typical of Penny to become so engaged in her work even though this whole thing was not her problem. However, it clearly meant a lot to her, and if, in some way, I could be of assistance, I would gladly do so. Moreover, it did seem suspicious, this Hans fellow vanishing the day after he confronted the CEO. On the other hand, this was the Faroe Islands, people did not just go missing unless they foolhardily went hiking alone, then they invariably were found safe the next day.

When Penny returned with a tray, there was a decision to make.

Did I want the strawberry cheesecake or the chocolate cake with frosting? After mutual deliberation and indecision, we agreed to switch plates halfway through. I started on the cheesecake.

'Dad, it's so great you being here. I already feel much better, just sitting, being able to talk to you about it. The CEO gave me all of next week to consider his offer. I'd like to stay, I really would, I love it here. Or I could move back home and use Guildford as my base while I search for something new. If I find something in London, I might even live with you and Mom permanently. How are the dogs?'

Staring out over the boats, I considered her options. And mine. It was lonely in the big house after all the children had moved out, but now they were gone, I had begun to relish my independence, no longer being at the beck and call of my family. Hildy and I just got on with it, we did what we felt like doing. Penny moving back would mean regular meals, routines and commitments. Also, I felt she needed a place of her own, she needed to be out and about, not cooped up on Hildy's estate. My mother-in-law's comment that Penny would never marry because she took after me, with her black hair and dark complexion was of course bollocks, but it furthered my resolve that she not move to Guildford. However, telling Penny this was not an option, she needed to reach that conclusion by herself.

'Penny, what does your heart tell you? What do you really want to do?' I asked, feeling rather fatherly.

'My heart? Dad, you can be so daft sometimes. This isn't 'The Sound of Music', 'Climb Every Mountain'. What my heart tells me is irrelevant. I need a job, it's that simple. I need work experience to boost my CV. The only thing is, my flat, my lease is for a full year, but water under the bridge, I suppose.'

'Where is it?'

'Just a short walk from here.' Penny pointed up the street. 'I thought I'd show it to you both when Mom returns.'

'Okay Penny, what I suggest is this. We give it the weekend. If your boss hasn't shown up by Monday, you call his wife and recommend she lodge a missing person's report. On the work front, I'm sure it's a waste of time staying up here, but enjoy yourself for the next month or so, do your research, decide what you want to do next and begin sending out job applications.'

Penny did not acknowledge my summation, but she did agree with me on one thing. The strawberry cheesecake was better than the chocolate. As I drained my cup, Penny stood and went to get us refills.

It was then I realised she had never really wanted my advice. She had wanted my ear. To talk it through. My daughter was a strong girl, well-educated like her mother, and she would make her own decisions, no matter what I thought.

And whatever she chose, it was all fine by me, as long as she did not permanently move back to Guildford, with me as her personal chef. And her boss, Hans? That mystery would need further consideration.

# 5

As Penny returned with refills, a hush came over the other guests. Pedestrians on the promenade stopped, all eyes were on the outer harbour.

'Here comes trouble,' Penny said.

Heading towards us were two vessels. The boat in the lead was a sleek ocean-going yacht, dark grey, with white shark's teeth painted on the bow, high-speed inflatable boats hung from winches in place of lifeboats. A medium-sized fishing trawler followed in the first boat's wake, perhaps five hundred tonnes, painted in the same colour scheme. The vessels approached empty moorings further up the promenade from where Penny and I sat. As we watched the spectacle, I sensed the animosity in the people around us.

And I felt a sudden presence behind me.

Hildy and Oydis had returned from their shopping. I noticed Hildy carried only a small white paper bag. Postcards? I got up and organised chairs for the women and blankets against the chill as Penny left to fetch them tea.

Oydis leant forward and whispered venomously,

'They call themselves the Ocean Lovers. They've been in the islands for a week now, and they are not welcome here. They come from America, and are here to stop us from killing the grind, the pilot whales.'

She pronounced 'grind' with the 'd' silent, like 'grin'.

'First, those Americans kill their own buffalo,' Oydis continued, 'They destroy the American Indian, the first peoples. They destroy the market for the poor Greenlanders and Inuits whose lives depend on selling the sealskins, and now they come here. We are a native people too, and we have never done them any harm. It's so unfair. We respect the whales and take only a few, four hundred a year at most.'

'You take four hundred?' I asked, surprised. 'I would have thought just one whale could feed most of Tórshavn.'

Oydis looked at me incredulously and then giggled. She had a charming, infectious laugh.

'Frank, you think these whales are big? They are not the, how do you say, majestic blue whales. They are the size of cows or big pigs, except they live in the sea. So this whole protest is about four hundred pigs of the sea!'

Hildy added, 'They are killed on beaches, in the historical tradition and in a manner no less humane than a modern-day butchery. And there are hundreds of thousands in the oceans. Pilot whales are contrary to their much larger cousins, not a threatened species, the UN and WWF agree.'

'Whales have cousins? Second or third, and I guess four hundred removed,' I said, thoroughly enjoying seeing the women riled up.

'Frank!' Hildy hissed.

'Yes, exactly,' Oydis replied. Then that giggle again. 'Oh, you make joke. But we do not make fun, not about this. Instead of raising and killing cows in some foreign land with all the pollution problems and sailing meat across the ocean, the village men kill the whales on a beach, and share the meat equally among the islanders, young and old.'

'Yes, but what about exports?' I asked, having read somewhere this was an issue.

'The meat contains too much mercury,' Oydis giggled. 'Exports are forbidden. Besides, we use all the meat we can get from the few herds of grind who come near our shores. But there is never enough, only for perhaps a meal or two a month. But when we have it, mmm... it's our national dish, our favourite.'

Looking at the two vessels, their crews busy attaching mooring lines to the dock posts, I could well imagine they were here to make trouble.

As the women conversed about distant cousins, I savoured my coffee and sat contemplating the dilemma of whale hunts and of environmental groups.

On the face of it, on an emotional and superficial level, I found the killings disturbing, as I supposed many did in the western world. But all killings in our industrialised food chain were disturbing. I was a carnivore, most people were, but we did our damnedest to avoid thinking about how meat or fish arrived on our table. We did not want to know.

And what was the difference between the indigenous Faroese people killing pilot whales, as they had done for a thousand years, and Native Americans of old, driving buffalo off cliffs and butchering them in their mass killings? Was it because the Faroese had better technology? Then what of modern-day deer, moose and wild boar hunting? Why was that acceptable to most if grind killing was not? Was it because of the event? The beach turning red with so much slaughter all at once? Or because pilot whales were thought to be very intelligent mammals? I had a lot of questions, but few answers.

On the flip side, the footage was great for environmental groups when they could get it, good promotional material. A filmed killing was a gold mine for much-needed fundraising, way better than pictures of the other essential work these groups did, fighting pollution, supporting renewables or protecting endangered species...

Torn from my thoughts, I jumped in my chair.

Shooting, close by. Not the rat-tat-tat of automatic fire. No, the boom, boom of a much heavier calibre. A sniper rifle.

I was out of my seat in a flash, crouching, shouting, 'EVERYONE, GET DOWN.'

I was about to flip our table on its side so my family could hide behind it, instantaneously planning in my head how I would grab Penny's arm with my left hand, tumble her to the ground and shield her with my body.

'Frank, darling, sit down, you're making a spectacle of yourself,' my wife said, surprisingly calm under incoming fire.

The other customers gave me fleeting glances, they whispered among themselves, grinning.

'It's a wedding, they must be coming out of the church,' Hildy said. 'They always fire their shotguns in salute of the newlyweds.'

'How do you know?' I asked, embarrassed, dropping heavily back into my chair.

'Because we... because we... because we saw the bride arriving!' Oydis held her tummy, shaking with laughter. Penny and Hildy joined in, adding to the merriment, the hilarity spread to the other tables as the shooting continued.

I chuckled bashfully, seeing the humour, but mainly not wanting to show I was indignant over their fun at my expense. However, as the women's shrieks of laughter reached new heights with each resounding volley, I thought, enough is enough, right? A concluding salvo brought a final howl, and then the three of them slowly regained their composure and dried their eyes.

Not long after, much to my relief, finishing our hot drinks, we were ready to depart. I was thankful to escape the snickering patrons behind me. We strolled down the promenade, past the fish market stalls where one merchant was selling seabirds of some sort, hopefully not seagulls, and crossed the street, me following the still-chuckling threesome.

The street was called Tórsgøta. Penny's flat was on the top floor of a blood-red four-storey building.

'The only bother is the noise,' Penny explained as we climbed the stairs. 'Especially on Fridays and Saturdays when the town's two nightclubs next door, and the bars and the Irish pub are in full swing. But it's okay, that's where I normally hang out.'

We mounted the final flight of steps and entered her flat. The panoramic view was impressive, the harbour, the outer seawall stacked high with forty-foot containers and Nólsoy across the bay. The island looked like a giant green slab tipped into the sea and now lying at an angle. And of course, the cruise liner and the warship, the stern of which I had seen from the taxi. Penny had an old pair of binoculars on the windowsill. I borrowed them.

Seeing the full length of the warship, I realised this was no ordinary corvette or destroyer, it was massive. Focusing on the stern, its number became legible, '099'. From my time at MI6 and the ministry of defence before that, I had a rudimentary knowledge of the world's grandest naval vessels, and when it came to surface combat ships, they did not come any bigger. It was the Russian battlecruiser, the Pyotr Velikiy.

'Penny, the warship, how long has it been here?'

'It arrived a few days ago. I think it's on some sort of unofficial visit to the islands, that's what they say. The crew has yet to be given shore leave, but everyone agrees. They're gorgeous.'

'How would you know what they look like if the sailors haven't been ashore?'

'Dad, their boats are always plying back and forth. Me and my friends hang out on the quay to watch.'

'My friends and I,' Hildy interjected.

'You, too, Mom? I hadn't noticed you around goggling younger men. Is that your thing?'

Not wishing to contemplate on my daughter's or my wife's interest in sailors, I scanned the West Harbour from right to left. A small crowd had congregated next to the grey boats belonging to the protest group. The name of the first vessel, the sleek-looking yacht, was legible. 'Ocean Avenger'. The yacht partially masked the boat furthest away. I could read only part of its name, 'Nemesis' it said.

Smiling, I trusted it would not be mine.

Back at Oydis and Knud's home, it was late afternoon. The long walk up from town in the salty air had been strenuous, but invigorating. On arrival, Knud told us we had an hour and a half before leaving for the evening's party. He said we had time for a nap in our guest room.

I lay down intent on reading my book before falling asleep, a Bernard Cornwell novel. It was not to be. Hildy wanted to know about my talk with Penny. After a thorough interrogation, she confirmed that her opinions mirrored my own.

'Darling, the children have to learn to fend for themselves, they cannot be moving home all the time as if they're some sort of boomerang.'

Seemingly having satisfied my wife's curiosity, I picked up my book and put it back down again. Although feeling drowsy, sleep did not come at once. Instead, I lay awake, pondering the question that so often boggled my mind these days, the question of what to do with the rest of my life.

# 6

During the past months, I had done some research into male mortality rates, weighing the pros and cons of early retirement, the main question being: do people die prematurely if they chose to retire sooner rather than later?

Apparently, the statistics did not give a conclusive answer, not for the general population as such. Some scholars argued sooner, some said not. However, when it came down to middle-aged men, such as myself, who'd had long stressful careers, the verdict was alarming. According to the Wang study from the University of Massachusetts, after the last day of work, life expectancy for men like me was measured in years, sometimes months, but seldom in decades. Based on evidence from one international electronics firm, where retirement was mandatory at the age of sixty, it seemed I had about three years before I was due at the pearly gates.

However, the studies also showed that men with ill health often chose early retirement. It was therefore not surprising they had a higher mortality rate. In addition, men who could not afford medical expenses naturally lived shorter lives. Both these factors lowered the average life expectancy.

So how did I figure into all this? Was I average? No, at fifty-six years of age, and with a slim build and my agile five feet six, I was in the finest of health. And Hildy's dosh was adequate for the odd hospital bill, regardless of how long we lived.

All right then, if I had plenty of years ahead of me, what did I want to do with them? I had no idea. I was reminded of the four Jungle Book vultures with the Liverpool accents in the cartoon movie. 'What do you want to do? I don't know, what do you want to do? Let's do something. Okay, what do you want to do?'

I was clueless.

Because I had to face it. My background was highly specialised, not exactly private sector general manager material. I was fluent in Arabic and Farsi. I had spent fifteen years in the army, the Third Paras with a three-year stint in the SAS. And seven years at the ministry of defence, mostly negotiating procurement contracts for any number of items, aircraft carriers down to paper clips. And then, twelve years ago, I had found my calling, at MI6 as head of the Middle Eastern desk. I had thoroughly enjoyed every minute of it. That was until a year ago. When everything went tits up.

So I had plenty of experience, but nothing very useful to offer the private sector.

And having money did not help. I was not forced to work. Hildy was loaded, her inheritance from her father was humongous, not that we used that much. Frugal? No. Reasonable? Yes, if you did not count the house on the hill, Pewley Down in Guildford, also an inheritance. And you did not include the newest Land Rover model each year, or Hildy's Jaguar. Otherwise, we lived normal lives with reasonable expenses, especially now all four children had moved out. I could say 'enough about money', I guess it is easy when you have enough, but apart from giving us financial independence, Hildy's inheritance had not made us happier. Our thriving family did.

And my work had. Regardless of the stress and the everyday conflict of bureaucracy, it had been fulfilling. Having a decent group of colleagues, a meaningful job, a sense of purpose, contributing to society, and of course, to Queen and Country, call me old-fashioned. Now, however, having served my country all those years, they had chucked me out. Unfairly, not just in my opinion. I was certain C, MI6's director, felt the same. But orders from the top, from the foreign minister himself, because of my screw-ups, three in a row, which had cost the British taxpayer the tidy sum of seven million pounds plus change and had produced no results what-so-ever.

I mean, everyone has a right to make mistakes, right? Apparently not. The prize had been the Syrian dossier, rumoured to prove who, in recent years, was responsible for the unexplained influx of conventional and dirty weapons to terrorist groups throughout the Middle East. We had followed the money, cash transfers made by Virgin Islands shell companies through Estonian banks, but we had not discovered the identity of the ultimate mastermind behind it all.

After the first failed handover in Amman, I had planned the next exchange, money for documents, in even more excruciating detail. A brush-by in Istanbul. My final gambit had been Beirut. All for nought, with money gone and agents dead.

Now I would never know. I was out of it, finished, and with my narrow field of expertise, and at my age, there were few jobs on offer, fewer still the government would allow me to take, and those available were unappealing.

So again, what to do? Hobbies? Hobbies were only interesting once you engross yourself in them, once you master enough to appreciate the finer details. How to save your béarnaise sauce from curdling at a finer cookery class would not really do it for me. Besides, I already knew. Add cold water and whisk. Watercolours? Oils? Gardening and taking away Wilson's livelihood? Writing my memoirs, which would be classed top secret and never be published? Writing fiction, like Hildy was doing, with her paranormal book, soon to be published? None of these caught my interest.

What then? Perhaps I could set up shop. But sell what? Or a B&B? I could imagine myself turning into a regular Basel Fawlty, no that would not do. Get a license and start a pub? With my recent increased drinking, that would be a slippery slope, dead in three years from liver failure, a confirmation of the statistics. No, that was not the answer either.

But I knew I needed to find something. I could not just lounge around, the highlights of each day being the arrival of the morning newspaper and the evening cocktail hour.

Which led me back to the question, as it did every time I contemplated my predicament. What did I really want? The answer was simple. I wanted the impossible. I wanted MI6 to take me back. I longed for that phone call, C or operations director Michaels, preferably both on their knees, begging me to return to save the commonwealth in the nick of time. I knew it was never going to happen, not just the ambitious part about saving the country, forget that, but just being asked back would be enough. It was a dream to be sure, a dream I held onto regardless I knew this particular aspiration was hindering me in the arduous task of getting stuck in with something else, something new.

At least, during the coming days, I had an excuse for forgetting my problems. A short-term respite from making any decisions on whether to take up pottery making or bird watching. This trip to the Faroe Islands and Hildy's cousin's husband's birthday party tonight. In all honesty, I was not looking forward to the dinner. I was apprehensive with spending an evening in a crowd of people, some I hardly knew, most not at all, they were totally foreign to me.

Yawning, with yet again no progress made on deciding what to do with my life, having used my train of thought merely as a sheep counting exercise, I felt the sleep creep into my brain as my mind went blank.

# 7

In the garden, under the temporary white pavilions, Sámal, host and birthday boy, a tall, fair-haired man, took a break in his rounds of pouring snaps for his guests to come over and sit with Knud and me at one of the picnic tables. He brought with him a fresh round of beers.

It turned out Sámal was a member of Løgtingið, the home-rule assembly, which sported thirty-three part-time members, and which he proudly stated was the world's oldest parliament, dating itself back to the arrival of the original settlers.

We had filled our plates at the buffet. Knud's contribution was large pink prawns, with homemade mayonnaise. And of course, there was grind, the pilot whale, thinly-sliced, similar to carpaccio. I followed Knud's example and rolled it into a small package around a potato cube, a sliver of crunchy blubber and a shred of dried fish. Popping it into my mouth, I discovered it tasted as good as anything I had ever eaten, especially accompanied by the snaps, Norwegian Linie Akvavit. I made myself another package, mercury was on the rise.

Thinking about the afternoon's discussion with my daughter, I brought up the subject of the island state's aspirations for oil production.

It was a topic Sámal was only too willing to discuss.

'The British, the Irish and Iceland are all in the race, claiming huge parts of the seabed, although many of those areas legally belong to us. Regardless of these disputes, we are well underway in our exploration, now the financing is in place. The company awarded the license to drill is called FaroeOil.'

'And who owns that company?' I asked.

'It is a daughter of FaroeFour, which in turn is owned by four elderly Faroese businessmen, hence the name. Coincidentally, their chairman is also a member of the Løgting.'

'Why has it taken so long to get started on the drillings?' I asked, gnawing the meat off a deliciously greasy lamb spare rib.

'FaroeOil could not get financing. Oil exploration is a risky business. But last year they got a new CEO after the other one was murdered. For years, they have been searching for funding, the new man arranged it in a matter of months.'

'The former CEO was murdered?' I asked.

'Yes, but not for money. Someone stabbed him when he was out jogging.'

'Where?'

'In the belly, at least that is what they are saying.'

'No, I mean, where? As in, here on the Faroes?'

Sámal thought for a moment.

'Turkey. I believe somewhere in Turkey. He was on holiday with his family last Easter. They say he had two small children and a pregnant wife. Terrible, isn't it? They never caught the killer.'

My curiosity perked. The Faroese company seemed to be losing employees left, right, and centre. Perhaps the situation regarding the disappearance of Penny's boss was more serious than I had first imagined, something that needed looking into. The sooner, the better.

Sámal continued,

'In any case, the new director secured almost immediately this offer of financing from prominent American banks. The parliament passed the necessary law guaranteeing the loan, and now the oil exploration is progressing from a base on Suðuroy, the township of Sumba. Now, you must excuse me, I need to attend to my chores.'

Sámal stood and with a mischievous smile added, 'You'll enjoy this.'

He disappeared into the house. Returning a moment later, he held a leg of lamb in his hand. I knew what it was, having tasted it on my previous visits to the Faroes. 'Skerpikjøt', fermented mutton, hung for months in a shed, semi-dried but otherwise untreated. Rumour had it, that mites in the fat made it extra tasty, although I had never encountered any on my previous trips. I had to admit, it was not my favourite culinary dish.

Sámal had also brought with him a knife.

'This is a grind knife, forty centimetres long and razor-sharp. It is used to cut the spinal cord, killing the animals instantaneously and as painlessly as possible.'

He used the knife to carve thin strips of fatty meat as he walked between the tables and handed out slices to waiting hands. Another man, hard at work, followed in his wake, offering snaps from a single beaker to all takers. I gladly accepted and drowned the taste of the meat with the liquor, before handing back the shot glass.

'Does he normally use a grind knife to carve Skerpikjøt?' I asked Knud.

'A smaller knife is safer. You know, the Swiss Victorinox knives we all use here on the islands. The grind knife is for your benefit, for you tourists. He likes to impress.'

'I guess, whatever floats your boat,' I remarked.

About to take a swig of his beer, Knud hesitated, a quizzical smile on his face.

'Why do you ask? I have a fibreglass hull. You'll see when we go fishing, it floats quite nicely on the ocean.'

'No Knud, what I meant…'

I stopped myself, at a loss for words. An explanation would be too complicated.

I noticed that the women at the party were drinking little and had begun to congregate in a makeshift garage disco. A four-piece band struck up some 1960s pop, and the women chose other female partners, one to lead, the other to follow, and in short order, they were twirling around the cement dance floor. It was an enjoyable and unusual sight, women paired off, waltzing about, and in most cases in traditional dress to boot.

Dancing was not my thing. This seemed to be the case with the other men as well. I had also had enough spirits for one evening, and besides, I had begun to feel lonely, excluded, despite Knud and Sámal's kind efforts to make me feel welcome. These were not my friends, merely

Hildy's family. They spoke another language and had a history together of which I was not part.

I had a sudden feeling of angst, a longing to get away.

Besides, the discussion regarding FaroeOil and its murdered CEO had sparked my curiosity. I was anxious to do some nocturnal exploring, so I excused myself from Knud's company and went to find Hildy.

Once we were back at Oydis and Knud's house, I turned to my wife,

'Hildy, dear, I have to admit, I was bored. I had no idea what they were talking about with the conversation being in Faroese and getting ever more slurred. I'm sorry for dragging you away from the party, but I thought we might take a walk, perhaps into town. It's not that late.'

I knew how she loved her walks, regardless of the hour.

In our room, I changed from my Oscar Jacobsen blazer into my bomber jacket, and then stood undecided. It had been a spur-of-the-moment decision. I had chucked my retirement present from MI6's director, C, into my suitcase, it was a .22 calibre Ruger pistol, coloured green. Admittedly an unusual gift, it being illegal to own pistols in Britain. During our stop-over visit to Copenhagen, I had hoped on the off-chance to get in some open-air target practice at the shooting range I had read about, not far from the airport, the opportunity had not presented itself.

Now, I needed to decide whether to bring the gun with me. These *were* the peaceful Faroe Islands. On the other hand, night had fallen, and unknowingly to Hildy, we were headed for the secluded docks to do some investigating. Penny's boss had mysteriously disappeared that same morning, and I had just learnt someone had murdered the former CEO of FaroeOil, albeit in Turkey. I made my decision, hammered home the clip, checked the safety, and slipped it into my pocket. Better safe than sorry.

Leaving through the back door, Hildy looked fetching in a brown woollen sweater, chopsticks holding her bun in place. For the second time that day, we began the descent down the hill and headed for Tórshavn central.

'Let's take the streets,' Hildy said. 'The paths can be treacherous in the dark.'

The strings of street lamps crisscrossing between housing estates, rocky outcrops and murky slopes created the impression of a vast yellow spider web. The night sky was overcast, the air crisp, a slight breeze blew head-on from the east. Just the thing I needed after all the alcohol I had drunk.

'Hildy, dear. Regarding this fellow Hans, Penny's boss. As I mentioned, he didn't show up for work this morning, so I figured this evening would be as good a time as any to visit the area around the FaroeOil facilities, see if there's any activity. That's the true reason I wanted to leave the party,' I finally admitted.

'Once a spy, always a spy, wanting to go nosey around.'

'Dear, hardly a spy. An intelligence officer, yes, but a spy, no.'

'It always scared me so when you went on missions.'

'As was I, when you were out and about. After we'd bought the flat, when you and C were in the Service together. Remember how we first met, at the Hippodrome on Leicester Square, me asking her to dance, you bumping her aside?'

'That was when we were young, and she was much too tall for you. But remember, it was I who quit the Service so we could have a family, not so you. The army was not so bad, and I thought you'd settled down at the ministry. But the Service? The number of nights I stayed up, wondering how I would explain to the children that their father was not coming home.'

I mused over we'd never before had this conversation. Never while I was at MI6, the topic was just too sensitive. Now I had retired, everything seemed different.

'You needn't have worried, dear. Unlike your time in operations, I was only away on intelligence ops, never anything dangerous,' I lied.

'You could have been caught. I know the risks.'

'Hildy, dear. You are letting your imagination get the better of you.'

'Frank, darling. Have you ever carried a gun in the field?'

'No, no guns, not since my days in the paratroopers,' I said truthfully.

'Then why are you carrying one now? Frank, this is the Faroe Islands, for Heaven's sake.'

'What gun?'

'The thing that keeps bumping into my hip. And don't you dare say, it's just because you're excited to be with me. You are not that well-endowed.'

'Sorry, dear. About being less than adequate. You've never complained before.'

'Nor has there been any need to. I wasn't referring to that, and you know it, so don't change the subject. I assume it's C's present. How did you get it through airport security?'

'No problem. I wasn't daft enough to put it in my hand luggage, and they can't effectively scan checked baggage. They only use sniffer dogs or machines to find narcotics and explosives. And I was careful to put coffee grounds in the gun-case.'

'Well, you should have left it at home. Promise me it goes straight back in its box when we return to our room. Unloaded. You'll have to find somewhere separate to hide the ammunition.'

'Yes, of course, dear,' I replied, chastised.

'And Frank, darling. I'm sorry, but I'm not comfortable with their children sleeping right next door. The walls are so thin. We should consider getting a hotel room, perhaps only for a night.'

She said it with that mischievous smile, the one I adored so much.

# 8

We turned right on Steinaðun. I wanted to skirt the town centre and avoid bumping into Penny if she was out and about, she might want to tag along. Coming down a street called Bøgøta, we strolled arm in arm. When we reached the quayside of the western harbour, I could see the closed coffee shops off to our left, where we had met Penny that same afternoon.

A near empty road, Vágsbotnur, 'basin's bottom' it translated, ran along the northern side of the anchorage. Weak lights from the adjacent car park illuminated the area. The surroundings were quiet save for distant disco thumping. The building Penny had pointed out, the place where she worked was directly in front of us. No lights were on, it seemed deserted. Regardless, I felt the hairs on my neck stand on end. I knew I imagined it, but I sensed someone stood within, in the shadows, watching us.

We strolled past the building and passed the shipyard on our left with its vast construction hall. After passing a large warehouse, I steered Hildy onto Vestara Brygga, a descending road, which curved sharply left. As we approached the dock area, I could make out four white storage tanks, the place seemed deserted.

'The main oil terminal,' I commented in a hushed voice.

'Why are you whispering, darling?'

'Dear, if villains are out and about, it's best we are not discovered.'

'Villains? Is that an operational term, Mr Spy? I don't recall villains being in the handbook.'

A tall security fence encompassed the harbour facilities, but they'd left the gates wide open. It seemed odd to me. This community was certainly not security conscious. We walked along an elongated one-story building lined with shop windows, mostly catering to the nautical profession. Lights out, everything was closed for the night.

Up ahead, a boat's engine rumbled. Far off, an unseen dog barked, a sheep bleated from high up on the hills.

A long narrow structure stood at the end of the road, between the waterfront and us. I guessed the interior was partitioned off into individual boatsheds and imagined on the other side, towards the harbour waters, that each unit would have a set of double doors, allowing boats to be floated out or retrieved using a winch. I reasoned the row of doors on our side acted as backdoors to the individual stalls.

As if from nowhere, some fifty metres away, left of the boathouses, a silhouette appeared. The sound of the muffled engine came from that same direction. I nudged Hildy into a recessed shop entrance where we could stand invisible in the shadows. Hildy's demeanour changed in an instant, I felt her tense up. Her old training coming back to her?

The door of one of the sheds opened. From the dark interior, three men staggered out, arms linked, the one in the middle dragged his feet. One of the other men closed the door, and together, they walked over to the waiting person. Then, two of the figures disappeared from view.

'There must be a boat parked there,' I whispered.

Hildy nodded.

The two remaining men, one large and one shorter walked away, towards our left, in the direction of another, smaller, white storage tank. They passed under some fuelling hoses hanging from a metal framework and disappeared from view.

The sound of the idling engine increased.

'Come on,' I said and hurried forward, Hildy following. We turned right at the corner and walked parallel to the boat sheds, the building hid us from the harbour waters. Once we reached the end of the structure, we stopped and waited, crouching low. I checked over my shoulder, all was clear behind us.

The engine noise grew louder as the outline of a ship's boat came into view. It glided across the still waters with what looked to be three or four persons aboard and sailed past us, headed south, out through the harbour mouth. When the boat was gone from view, we turned and retraced our steps. I tried the boatshed's door, it was unlocked. I risked flipping on the light switch.

A bucket, reeking of poo, a half used roll of toilet paper, an old blanket and some cut ties lying on the ground next to a metal chair, otherwise nothing, no boat, no equipment. I turned off the light and closed the door.

We walked over to where the boat must have been moored. Looking down, I could see nothing of interest, just the waters lapping against the quay. Continuing along the quayside, we strolled arm in arm, as we passed fishing trawlers moored stern to bow on our right, industrial buildings on our left, following the route, the two men must have taken.

'Hildy dear, what did we witness a moment ago?'

'We saw some men help a person down into a boat. And a shed where the man had been held, a pail for a toilet. Do you think he was Penny's boss? Has someone abducted him? If so, we must call the police.'

'And tell them what, dear? We'll sound bonkers. That man could have been drunk, he could be anybody, and we know nothing of who owned the boat.'

'There will be DNA,' she said.

'Perhaps, but you'd need a matching sample. And even if it was him, we've no way of knowing where the boat's gone. I think the best thing is to discuss it with Knud in the morning, I don't see there is anything more we can do tonight.'

Passing the Brimil, coming around the corner of the shipyard's construction hall, we were confronted by two deep-sea trawlers in cradles, standing on a sloping ramp. There was no easy way out, we could use the ladder to crawl down and cross the slanting dry-dock, or we would have to go back.

'Let's be naughty,' Hildy whispered.

Now, I am not a prude in any way, on the contrary, I never say no to a quicky with my wife. However, under the circumstances, the suddenness of the suggestion surprised me.

'What here? What if we get caught?'

'No silly, I didn't mean that. Let's crawl down.'

Oh, Okay. I let Hildy precede me to the bottom of the steel ladder and then descended after her. We stood directly under the massive propeller of the rearmost vessel. Looking up, the whole contraption seemed truly gigantic. I could readily imagine the trawler tipping itself over and smashing us to a pulp, something, which fortunately did not happen. Regardless, we hurried to the other side and gingerly climbed across some slippery boulders before we came to a fence attached to a building on the left, the harbour waters were on our right.

'There is a hole cut in it,' Hildy whispered. 'Let's try it.'

'Why are you whispering, dear?' I asked. Now it was my turn to tease. I got no reply.

While I held the gash open for her, Hildy squeezed through the gap, and I followed her through, careful not to rip my jacket. On the opposite side of the barrier stood an ancient-looking three-story warehouse, the ground floor made of boulders, with the top two stories in black wood. Beyond it, I could see the FaroeOil building across the road.

'Darling, someone is standing there,' Hildy whispered and pointed.

The person faced away from us and stood stock-still. I looked to my left assessing our possible escape routes. A track ran along the length of the stone building, it seemed to be our best option.

'Silly me,' Hildy whispered, sounding relieved. 'It's the statue of the washerwoman.'

She was right. We walked past the stone sculpture.

A big man with hunched shoulders emerged from the shadows. With him was a smaller man with wet lips and sparse hair plastered to his dome. Wet Lips, I dubbed him.

He asked in Danish what we were doing there. I did not understand the exact words, but his aggressive tone was unmistakable. Sensing Hildy about to reply, presumably also in Danish, I squeezed her hand to stop her. Because it was obvious, these were the men we had witnessed escorting the third man to the boat, and I wanted to have the upper hand in this encounter by keeping it in English.

'Sorry old chap, but we don't speak the local lingo. You see, we're British,' I said, using my most posh accent.

'Why you here? What you want?' Wet Lips asked.

My mind raced, my blood pounded in my ears as I readied myself for any sign of violent intent. There was no way I would have time to extract the Ruger from my pocket if these men attacked us. In my mind, I practised the movements of kicking the big man in the knee and then punching Wet Lips with the heel of my hand, a technique I had learnt in the Paratrooper Regiment ages ago, and which I now practised back home with Wilson during our regular workouts. I would aim for his chin, if he took the hit on the nose, it might drive cartilage into his brain and kill him.

I stepped protectively in front of Hildy. The men moved forward, threatening. I took a step back, willing Hildy to do likewise, to give me room, and be ready to run.

'We were just out for an evening stroll. We were at a dinner, you know, too much of that God-awful sheep's meat. It seems we're a bit lost, off the beaten track, so to speak.'

'You beat track?' the big man asked.

'Just a saying, old man, just a saying.'

'Me not old.'

No, but you stupid. I thought it, I was not daft enough to say it to the big oaf. Big Oaf? A fitting nickname. Wet Lips looked around, scanning the area behind us as if checking for witnesses. I tensed my body, ready to beat him to the punch.

'You should not be out alone on the docks this late at night. Did you see anyone else? A boat perhaps?' Wet Lips asked.

'No, it's all very quiet, except for that damned disco music. Otherwise very pleasant indeed,' I replied.

Wet Lips stood for a moment, undecided.

The adrenaline was pumping in my veins. I went over in my mind the actions of pulling a chopstick from Hildy's hair and stabbing Big Oaf in the throat after kicking him in the knee, an act of desperation to be sure, since I had never actually confronted anyone in earnest in hand-to-hand combat, not since my paratrooper days, decades ago in the occasional pub brawl.

The difficulty would be in bringing my right hand up to her hair, thumb pointing down, in order to get a firm fighting grip on the improvised weapon without having to turn it over in my hand. I imagined Wilson, and I could practice the move when we returned to Guildford. The thought of my friend on his knees immolating Hildy's height with chopsticks in his hair made me smile.

Perhaps that's what did it, the smile. In any case, Wet Lips, the obvious leader, seemed to have reached a decision, and it was a sensible one. Violence on the Faroes was nearly unheard of, the main reason being, an escape from the islands was all but impossible. These men would have been imbecilic to create an incident unless they were completely sure it was necessary.

The smaller Dane bade us a good night, and then both men walked past, crowding me unnecessarily, and climbed through the gap in the fence.

As Hildy and I once again reached Vágsbotnur, having come full circle, I saw across the street a blond haired man letting himself out of the FaroeOil building. The man put his carry-on into the boot of a sedan and then drove off. I wondered if we had just glimpsed Penny's CEO. I also wondered why, if there had been someone inside the building, why had the lights been out when we passed by the first time around?

On our way home, we came through the lively part of town. The first nightclub we walked by was responsible for the resounding disco music. It had high outdoor cocktail tables, and there stood Penny amongst friends. Her face lit up when she spotted us.

Hildy leant into me and said in a hushed voice,

'In England, young people are embarrassed by having their mom and dad around, but on the Faroes where the family is everything, children are more than happy to introduce their parents to friends.'

As Penny motioned for us to join her group, the young people made room to include us in the festivities, making us feel welcome. It was years since I had experienced anything like it, the lively conversation, and the carefree abandonment of youth out on the town. Two young men were dispatched to get drinks for the group, Hildy and I asked for sparkling water. I handed over some money, a five hundred kronor note, my hand still trembling from the subsiding adrenalin.

The boys reappeared ten minutes later with sparkling water for Hildy and beers for the rest of us, informing me water was for women. There was no change. Despite a spark of irritation at being told what I was allowed to drink by some youngsters, I enjoyed their company. I did not notice the time nor the number of beers placed before me until it was time to call it a night.

Finally, after a long day and a taxi ride up the hill to Hoyvík, I staggered up to bed with my Hildy. It had been a good night out, I was thoroughly knackered.

# 9

Saturday morning, at nine o'clock, Oydis had breakfast ready. Much to my delight, her teenage children were staying with friends for the weekend, it would give Hildy and me some privacy tonight.

I could hardly believe we had been on the islands less than twenty-four hours. I was slightly under the weather but nothing compared to Knud, who nursed a severe hangover.

Oydis had fetched fresh bread from the local bakery. There were cheeses and marmalade, and a roulade of lamb, layers of meat and fat rolled into a tight, cold sausage. Smoked salmon was on the table and of course, a leg of Skerpikjøt, which Knud began to slice using a responsible knife with a serrated edge. Had the meal been served under any other circumstances, some of the items on offer might have turned my stomach, but here it all seemed so natural. I dug in, avoiding the fermented mutton.

After a sip of scalding coffee, buttering a slice of bread, I described for Knud our late night outing.

Knud sat thoughtfully for a moment.

'Frank, about the two men, how do you say, being scary. I think you imagine things. You need not fear a walk around the docks. But the boat sailing out, it is irresponsible at that time of night. The cruise ship departs much earlier so it cannot have been their boat. It could have been boys out joy riding or someone headed for the island across the sound, you know, Nólsoy, which would be equally dangerous.'

'Could it have come from the Russian ship?' I asked.

'That is unlikely. No shops are open late at night, and the rumour is the crew has yet to be given shore leave, even though they have already been here a couple of days. Perhaps the boat picked up officers. Maybe they disobeyed their own orders and came in for a drink. But why they were in the small bay over by EFFO, the oil company, I have no idea. It would have made more sense to pick them up closer to town.'

After breakfast, three cups of coffee and plenty of tap water I could only describe as pure and delicious, Hildy and I decided to go out for some fresh air. I wanted to clear away the cobwebs. As we came out into the open, with the housing enclave where Knud and Oydis lived behind us, I stopped and looked out over the town and further out, towards the bay. The Pyotr Velikiy was gone. Which gave me an idea.

'Hildy, we need to return to the house.'

'Why darling? What's wrong?'

'Humour me,' I said.

Arriving back, I asked Knud if he could find out the Russian ship's intended destination. Knud made a few phone calls.

'The Russians requested to move their ship's moorings to Sumba, on Suðuroy, which in Faroese means 'south island'. They sailed at midnight,' Knud informed us.

On hearing this, I remembered the evening before, Sámal mentioning that the town of Sumba was FaroeOil's operational base. Up in our room, I turned to my wife,

'Hildy dear, is it just me? Do I imagine things? Penny's boss disappeared in the early hours of yesterday morning. The boat in the harbour last night, we saw a man be put aboard by those Danes hanging around close to the FaroeOil building. Now the Russian ship has moved down to where the oil exploration is based. Was it their boat we saw? Or is it all a coincidence?'

'How should I know, darling? I'm not the spy in the family. However, if you want to go have a look, I have a cousin who lives there. We could visit her, I've not seen Susanne in ages. You remember her.'

I did not.

Hildy got on the phone, and in no time, she arranged for us to be on the 12.30 ferry headed for Suðuroy, a trip, which took a couple of hours. I called Penny inviting her to come along, explaining that her mother wanted to visit another cousin. We agreed to meet at the Smyril ferry terminal in the East Harbour.

There was a knock on our door.

'Frank, Hildegard, I thought we could go fishing a bit later. Would you like to come?' Knud asked.

'Sorry, Knud. Hildy has just arranged for us to take the midday boat to Suðuroy.'

'What, so soon? You just got here.'

'Knud, we'd love to go fishing, but another time. A rain check perhaps?'

'I did. The weather is going to be fine.'

I looked at Knud, perplexed, and then it dawned on me what he meant. Instead of explaining the slang, I simply said,

'Knud, could you to give us a lift to the ferry? Are you sober enough?'

Events were moving fast. A full day yesterday, the flight from Copenhagen to Tórshavn and the party, then our late night outing. Now we were off to somewhere completely different. We quickly packed our things in my suitcase, Hildy taking along only the essentials, me hiding the gun case and ammo in my reserve underwear.

In front of the ferry terminal, Penny stood waiting in frayed jeans and a raincoat, with a rucksack draped over her shoulder. A thought crossed my mind. Perhaps if she took the new job, she would be able to afford some decent clothes. I reminded myself to ask Hildy to take our daughter shopping.

'What took you so long? Come on. We need to hurry,' Penny said. 'We've only a few minutes before departure.'

However, as we rushed up the three-storey access tower to the gangway, a crewmember in dark blue held up his palms.

'No need to hurry, you have plenty of time. The ferry is waiting for a couple of airline passengers. They called ahead after landing, their flight was delayed.'

'Do you generally postpone departure if passengers are late?' I asked.

'Always,' was the reply.

I could only shake my head in admiration. It was not a service I had encountered elsewhere.

The ferry ride south was comfortable, the ocean placid and the sun shone warmly through the windows. Passing the island of Sandoy, on our right, I could see fog blanketing the far side of the island. The *dimma*, yes, I knew how much of an issue it was here on the islands.

London fog was nothing compared to the Faroes. Here, thick clouds came in at sea level, condensing further as they collided with the cliffs, and swarmed their way up the rock face. One minute you could be standing in the sun. Literally, a second later, you might be engulfed in fog so thick, you could barely see a metre ahead of you. If that.

I remembered, fifteen years earlier, we had stopped our borrowed car in a parking area, not fifty metres from a cliff. As I turned off the ignition, the girls, Sophie and Penny, and the twins piled out from the rear seat. Hildy shut her door and herded them together.

'Now Darlings, listen to Mommy. Do as I say.'

The boys were at that wild age, more Max than Oliver.

'Boys in the middle,' Hildy ordered. 'Penny, take your father's hand, Frank hold on to Max. Oliver, Sophie, you are with me. Right, now hold on tight everyone, nobody lets go of each other. We are not going to the very edge, but still, it is quite dangerous.'

'Aw mum,' Max complained. 'I want to look down, see the birds. I'm not scared. What if we crawl?'

'No crawling Max,' his mother replied. 'Either you do as I say, or it's straight back to the car for you.'

Max did not answer, but his face fell in obvious disappointment. I squeezed his hand. 'Do as Mum says, Max, this is more dangerous than you know. A sudden gust of wind, and we could be flying.'

'Cool,' my son said, looking up with a smile, stars in his eyes.

'Not if it's directly over the edge. The landing could be a bit rough. Now come on.'

Following Hildy's lead, we approached the cliff, a sheer drop of hundreds of metres. We stood well back from the very edge, but by viewing along the cliff-face from where the land jutted a bit further out to sea, we could see along the precipice to where swarms of puffins darted in and out of their nests.

Suddenly, Hildy ordered in a voice, which commanded immediate obedience, 'Sit down Darlings, sit down. Now!'

Seconds later, the fog engulfed us. Penny and Max sitting on either side of me appeared as shadows. I realised then, if we had walked about from where we sat in the wet grass, had we moved at all, we might have wandered straight over the edge.

'Hello, anybody out there?... out there?...out there?' Max called, mimicking an echo. Then, 'Olly Olly oxen free, come out come out where ever you are, you are, you are…'

'Max, just this once, listen to the wonderful silence,' I suggested.

'Can't hear it, Dad.' But my son did as I asked, until, 'No, Oliver, don't let go, no, come back, no…!'

Alarmed, I panicked, my heart jumped, I did not know what to do, Oliver was completely hidden in the fog. Should I let go of Penny and Max, get them to hold each other's hand, so I could search for Oliver?

From the shadows, I heard my wife's admonishing voice surprisingly clear, the fog muffled all other sounds.

'Max, behave yourself. Frank darling, Oliver is just fine, he's sitting here next to me.'

'Did he buy it?' Oliver, the serious one whispered loud enough for me to hear.

'Yup, hook, line, and sinker,' Max replied.

'Max, that was not funny,' I said. 'We'll talk about this when we get back.'

'Oh no Dad, I'm sorry, I truly am. Please Dad, no, not the belt, not again. Mum, Dad is taking a belt to me. Mum, tell him not to, please Mum.'

It felt odd, listening to the exchange, just hearing the voices, cocooned out here in the fog where no one could see each other.

'Max, behave yourself,' Hildy said. 'You know very well your father would never dream of using a belt on you. But I might.'

Although I knew, and Max would know his mother was not serious with her threat, her comment ended the discussion. When minutes later, stark sunshine replaced the fog, we got up and returned to the car, the girls complaining they had sheep manure on their clothes, the boys excited over their prank.

Knowing the peril we had been in, I was not impressed, but I did not let on how frightened I had been or how cross I was with Max right then.

On our way back to Tórshavn, coming over the mountains, we once more encountered the rolling clouds. I was driving, and could not see the lane ahead of us.

'There is nothing for it, Hildy, you'll have to take the wheel. I'll walk in front, but roll down the window so I can shout to you if we veer off course.'

'I wouldn't dream of it, darling. You know how I enjoy my walks,' she said sangfroid. 'Besides, I have more experience with these things. Promise me though, just take it slow.'

With that, she opened her door and climbed out.

She walked in front of the right-hand headlight, five yards ahead of the car, the beam picked out her shadow. I had never been so frightened in my life. Not by the thought of going off the road, I trusted my Hildy to save us from that. No, I feared an oncoming vehicle might not see us in time, or a car or truck might hit us from behind. However, we could not stop, there was nowhere suitable to pull over and wait.

'Dad, if you speed up, Mum could ride on the bonnet.'

'Shut up Max,' that was Sophie.

'She'd be like the mascot on Grandad's Jaguar.'

'Sophie said shut up, Max,' Penny having her say as well.

'Stop pinching me, Oliver.'

'It wasn't me,' Oliver said, although, concentrating on the road ahead, I knew it probably was.

The boys began to wrestle in the back seat, only adding to my sense of impending doom.

However, at that moment the fog lifted and the weather cleared. Hildy got back in the car. It was with a sigh of relief and a feeling of utter exhaustion I accelerated and drove down the mountain. Thinking back, I had to admit, being a father to the twins had at times been every bit as nerve-racking as when I was in the Paras.

# 10

That all happened a long time ago, but a chill still ran down my spine, each time I recalled the incident, which could have cost me my family. I woke from my thoughts as Hildy arrived back from the cafeteria deck, Penny following, balancing a tray of hot drinks.

I had withheld from my daughter my suspicions regarding her boss and the Russian ship. I had not told her of our encounter down by the docks, she would begin to ask questions for which I had no answer. Instead, I asked her,

'Penny, dear, I heard last night your oil exploration company uses Sumba as its base.'

'Who told you that?'

'Sámal Haldorsen. He hosted the party we attended. Is there any chance he's gone to Sumba?'

'Sámal Haldorsen? Dad, how would I know?'

'No, your boss, Hans.'

Penny did not need time to think.

'Yes, of course, how stupid of me. We have an office there. I should have thought of that before. We use it from time to time because it is the first port-of-call for vessels working in the drilling operations. We get seabed samples directly from the rig and can analyse them in the laboratory. He must have forgotten to turn on his phone. He does that sometimes when he is alone at remote locations with no one to remind him.'

'Penny, dear, the secretary said he had quit.'

'He's probably gone to get his personal stuff. I'm sure we'll find him there. At least we can say goodbye,' my daughter said, with remorse in her voice. I also hoped to find him there, but perhaps not under the same positive circumstances as my daughter imagined.

The ferry gave a slight nudge as it docked and after a few minutes, crewmembers were bidding us farewell at the gangway. Lugging my suitcase, I chose to take the lifts down while Penny and Hildy took the stairs. Meeting at the bottom, on the ground floor, we exited the aluminium-sided terminal into glorious sunshine and a cool breeze.

Susanne, Hildy's cousin, stood waiting with a big welcoming smile. A sixtyish woman with an elaborate hairdo, she seemed to be a competent type. On the ferry, Hildy had told me of how Susanne had lost her husband in a fishing accident some twenty years earlier. She had never remarried. As I loaded the suitcase into the boot of Susanne's car, I noticed a bright blue first-aid kit together with an old woollen blanket. The kit was the only thing new about our ride.

The vehicle, a Toyota Camry estate, must have been twenty-five years old and it showed its age. Hildy took the front seat so she and Susanne could converse. Penny and I climbed into the rear as the car settled on its springs. All the mirrors were cracked but functioning, held in place in their sockets with rubber bands. I asked myself, how exactly do you break a car mirror? Especially the interior one. The car had a radio and a novelty item, a cassette deck. I had not seen one of those in ages. The loudspeaker sockets were, however, empty.

I jumped in my seat, as the car started with a cough, then a loud bang. The clasp to fasten my seatbelt did not work. I sat back and readied myself for a hazardous mountain drive.

'We need to visit a shop first, now you are here,' Susanne said. 'Before we head for Porkeri, where I live.'

The ferry terminal stood on the south bank of the fjord. Tvøroyri, a town of perhaps three hundred houses was on the northern side. I expected it to be our destination, shops being in such short supply, especially in the smaller villages.

I was wrong. Susanne turned right, but then immediately left and drove up a gravel road, which led to the island's oil terminal, two white storage tanks with 'EFFO' painted on the sides. She stopped outside a warehouse, which had an empty parking area with room for a few cars only.

'Frank, may I ask you to do me a favour? Could you please go in and buy what is on this list? Here is money,' Susanne said, as she handed me a piece of paper and a coin purse.

Curious, I climbed out. The warehouse's barn doors were half-open, I could see pallets of beer, and to the left a glass storefront with a door. There was no sign anywhere telling me what the place sold, only a stylized R on the façade. The island's off-licence, I concluded, and Susanne wanted me to do her shopping for her.

I was happy to oblige, of course, I was. I knew that in the more remote communities and especially among the elderly, alcohol was frowned upon. The reason for this needed to be understood in a historical context. In small isolated fishing villages, feeding the family, and maintaining the house and boat was a full-time occupation. Being inebriated could mean drowning at sea or injuries, fatal with doctors and hospitals days away. A dead provider meant an added burden on the remaining township as they assumed the care of the widow and her children. Hence discouraging drinking was an act of self-preservation for the community as a whole.

In the modern day, most people did enjoy spirits, they just did it discreetly and in moderation.

The shop was near empty of merchandise. No browsing was allowed, you needed to know what you wanted. As I read from the list, Susanne had given me, the young bearded shop assistant retrieved each item from the warehouse out back, one thing at a time. In short order, he had packed for me five unmarked black plastic carriers.

When I had counted out the amount required from the neatly folded banknotes and coinage in the purse and handed over the substantial sum, I received my receipt.

I decided to get something for myself. A six-bottle beer selection in a cardboard case, the only item on show, high up on a shelf. The Faroese beer I had tasted was delicious, I suspected due to the clean water. And the labels were colourful, each showing a ram's head. However, when I paid with my own money and picked up the box by its handle, the young man informed me I would need a bag for it.

'Why?' I asked.

'If people see you are carrying beer or spirits, they gossip. So you need a bag.'

'But your carriers are all black and easily identifiable. People will know it is alcohol in any case,' I commented.

'No,' the young man replied. 'They will know the bag is from here. They have no way of knowing what is inside. It might be, you have reused it for something else,' he said with a wink, as he double-bagged the beer.

Musing over the young man's logic, returning to the car, I could see Penny in the back seat but not Hildy and Susanne. I suspected they might have gone for a walk, that is, until I opened the boot to put the purchases inside, next to my suitcase. Up front, Susanne and Hildy were in their seats, slumped down low, apparently not wanting to be recognised. It seemed silly to me. Any of her acquaintances would know Susanne's car by sight. Surely, there could be no twin rust bucket on the island. However, being too polite to comment, grinning, I merely closed the boot and climbed into the back.

Susanne fired up the car with a cough and a bang, which startled me once more. She turned onto the two-lane highway and soon had the car puttering along at fifty kilometres an hour, seemingly its top speed. After a few minutes, we rounded a small bay and entered a modern well-lit tunnel, which had not existed on my last visit. I was relieved we could avoid the high road that crested the mountain in this less than adequate vehicle. Some minutes later, we emerged from the tunnel and followed the highway over a headland. We had arrived, the turnoff was on the left.

'The island is in the shape of a banana,' Susanne explained, 'With four fjords cutting into it from the east. Down there,' she said pointing, 'is the most southern fjord with the town of Vágur. This is Porkeri where I live, we have over fifty houses, a supermarket and even a hairdresser. It's a quite popular place to live.'

I listened with an impatient ear, for although I appreciated the stunning views of the little township, partially sitting on a plateau overlooking the sea, and partially with its old black church with a grass roof, and quaint dwellings lining the tiny bay, I was anxious to get to Sumba and asked Susanne about that town.

'Sumba is the most southerly village, on the tip of the island. We get there through a tunnel similar to the one we just passed through, although much older,' she said.

'I'd like to see it. Would it be possible to borrow your car?' I asked.

'Yes. That is fine. You can leave soon, but first I would like to show you something,' Susanne said, much to my annoyance. I felt an increasing urgency to get going. My gut tightened as I realised just how excited I was. Hans's disappearance was an enigma, which needed my immediate attention. Expecting to solve the mystery in the coming hour or so had my blood pumping.

# 11

As soon as we emerged into the open from the Sumba tunnel, an extraordinary spectacle greeted us. I asked Hildy to pull over into the lay-by.

It had taken far too long to get here. In Porkeri, Susanne had wanted to show us the village sheep shearing first! When, at last, we were on the road, after delivering Susanne, her spirits and my suitcase, sans pistol, at her house, the ride had proved scary with Hildy behind the wheel. She steered dangerously close to the right-hand side, something she invariably did when driving, 'On the wrong side of the road!' as she put it. The windscreen fogged up, the ventilator did not work, and after lowering our windows to alleviate the situation, we could not roll them up again.

Now standing in an utter calm, I tried to relax as I admired the vast expanse of black rock spreading out to sea, the white surf crashing over it and receding in a continuous bombardment. Beyond, perhaps a half-mile further out, a grey jack-up drilling rig towered high.

Smack in the middle of the Sumba bay was the huge warship, the Pyotr Velikiy, it lay at anchor dwarfing the town's houses. With the air so crisp, I could see every detail of the battlecruiser as if viewing a plastic miniature from up close.

'Why is the Russian ship here?' Penny asked, a question I could not answer with certainty, although I had a premonition.

When she got no answer, pointing, Penny said,

'That's the FaroeOil building.'

A hundred metres from where we stood, was a black modern house-sized structure built on the cliffs, below the main road. There was an adjacent parking area.

We climbed back into Susanne's car. Hildy restarted the vehicle, the engine caught with a cough and a bang. This time I was ready for it. She checked for traffic. Sitting diagonally behind my wife, I met her eye in the cracked rear-view mirror.

'Hildy, dear, I'd like to get a feel for the place. Can we continue into town?' I asked.

Passing the FaroeOil building, a black SUV parked out front, I looked down to my right as the view opened up and revealed far below a massive seawall jutting out into the ocean. Four large tugboats and a single smaller craft painted naval grey lay protected by the jetty, which was broad enough to accommodate traffic. A twin black SUV stood on the pier. The place seemed deserted.

In the town, houses in typical simple Faroese style lined the main road running parallel to the shoreline. White concrete ground floors supported colourful wooden superstructures. Whereas, the other towns we had passed through sported a greater number of houses in traditional black woodwork with white framed windows, here the predominant colours seemed brighter, almost exclusively off-whites, greys, and especially yellows.

There was no traffic. Outside the town's grocery, on a corner of the main street, stood an empty blue bus at its end-stop. Further up, the road forked. Hildy signalled and turned left. If nothing else, at least the car's indicator worked.

'This is the old road,' she said. 'In the early days, before they built the tunnel, it was the only access route between Vágur and Sumba.'

Well-worn with potholes, loose gravel and broken basalt littering the surface, the narrow lane wound its way up the hillside, wide enough for a single vehicle only. Every fifty yards or so, the lane broadened for a short space, allowing vehicles going in opposite directions to pass each other. Hildy drove on until we reached a viewing area where she stopped the car, and we climbed out. The breeze coming off the sea from the west was distinctively chilly.

From where we stood, the view of the town beneath us, the warship on the ocean surface and the oilrig further out, white puffs of cloud in the sad blue sky directly overhead, grey clouds in the distance rolling towards us at sea level, it was a spectacular sight. The silence was complete save for the whisper of wind through the grass and a single sheep bleating at us from higher up the hill.

I inhaled the salty air through my nose, smelling its freshness.

The most impressive sight was on our far right, the Beinisvørð, a geological phenomenon. A mountain, which rose sharply to hundreds of metres above us, even as we stood well above the town. But the outer half of the mountain was missing. As the emerald green slope rose ever higher, it suddenly ended in a sheer vertical drop of six hundred metres, the second tallest precipice of the Faroe Islands, according to Hildy.

Studying the town below, I commented,

'It looks deserted. I see only the four boys playing soccer on the field by the church. Is it normally this peaceful?'

'Always,' Penny laughed.

There was some activity on the distant warship, a few minuscule uniforms moved about. However, there was no movement over by the tugboats or the seawall.

Climbing back into Susanne's car, Hildy negotiated the steep descent without incident and turned right. As we approached the FaroeOil building, my intuition told me not to leave the car in the carpark. I suggested we drive past and park at the lay-by facing towards the tunnel. If need be, we would be better positioned for our getaway, albeit, in this car, nothing was ever going to be quick.

We got out and walked back to the black painted building, Penny confidently leading the way. As we approached the main door, she pulled out her key ring. However, when she touched the lock, the door ghosted open. Uh-oh.

Penny turned to us with a smile.

'He must be here,' she said as she made to enter.

'Penny, would you mind if I go first?' I asked my daughter.

I stepped inside.

# 12

Listening for any sound, I realised how utterly foolish I was. A man had perhaps been kidnapped, we were in the house where I suspected he was being held, and I had with me my wife and my daughter in this precarious situation.

Too late now, we would have to wing it, I decided.

Penny followed me in, with Hildy bringing up the rear. A door stood ajar, it led to a bathroom. Opposite, on the right, I passed the doorway to a modern kitchen and then a TV den.

Next on the left was a door that looked quite sturdy.

At the end of the hallway, I stopped to listen at a door standing ajar and then pushed it open. The place was deserted. I realised I had been holding my breath and let the air out of my lungs with a sigh of relief. It was an office environment, one big room, surrounded on three sides by bay windows giving a panoramic view. Three desks stood in front of the windows.

There were filing cabinets at the back, left and right of the door, drawers pulled halfway open with documents having spilt out onto the floor. Maps and diagrams depicting geological layers hung above the cabinets, they covered every inch of wall space. Someone had stacked piles of papers and reports on the central desk.

'It looks like someone searched the place,' I said.

'No,' Penny laughed, 'This is how it always looks. Except usually, those piles are in the drawers.'

I froze, there was a muffled sound from somewhere in the building.

'He must be downstairs,' Penny said and made for the door.

'Penny, a moment, please. The SUV outside, is that Hans's vehicle?' I asked.

'No, and you may have noticed the other one down by the pier. They're used by the crews. Usually, Hans and I take the bus from the Smyril terminal, we don't generally need a car. When we need supplies, we walk down to the grocers.'

'When you stay here, where do you sleep? In town?' I asked.

'Downstairs. We have three bedrooms and a laboratory where we study the test samples. It's quite cosy, really.'

I looked at my second eldest.

'Penny, you may think me paranoid, but just to be on the safe side, you must do exactly as I say. You must stay here, upstairs, and run for the police if I call to you. I know this will seem strange, but there are some things I never told you, and we do not have the time right now.'

I took the Ruger from my pocket as Penny looked on in disbelief. I gave her a reassuring smile.

'Don't ask. It's just a precaution. Now, Hildy, dear, please follow me.'

In the hallway, I had my left hand on the handle of the sturdy door as I put my ear to it. Hearing nothing, I turned towards Hildy and Penny standing down in the office and raised an index finger to my lips, and then eased the handle down. As soon as the door opened, just a crack, faint voices were audible. I opened the door a bit further, having to take a step back, and then placed a foot on the top step of the basement stairs without putting weight on it. I lifted my foot again and gently closed the door.

'Wooden stairs, I don't want them to creak. Step only on the outer sides of the steps, not in the middle.'

'Darling, shouldn't we call the police?'

'And tell them what? We've seen nothing untoward. They may take ages getting here.'

'Darling, are you sure?'

'Do you trust me, dear?'

Hildy smiled nervously.

'No, not at this moment.'

'We'll be all right, I promise. We can always walk away.'

She nodded, conceding reluctantly.

I opened the door once more, fully this time, and placed my foot on the very left part of the top step, then my other shoe furthest to the right, pushing down on the bannisters with my hands, taking as much weight off my feet as possible. The Ruger in my right hand slid along the smooth wooden railing.

After descending ten steps in this manner, I reached a landing and turned around, motioning for Hildy to follow me. I made a U-turn and took the remaining steps. A door stood ajar at the bottom of the stairwell. Stopping, I waited for Hildy to catch up.

Holding still, I could hear the voices clearly. The men were speaking in English, one with an accent I could not place, the other had a distinctively Flemish articulation. I hoped it was Hans.

What to do?

A tremor ran through my hand, I could feel the adrenalin pumping, my blood pulsating in my ears. This was all new to me, wilfully entering into a potential confrontation at close quarters. I had no reason to expect armed opponents. I had the element of surprise, and a pistol, little as it was.

But would I use it, if need be? Only in self-defence, surely. How many would there be? Two or three unarmed adversaries? I figured I could handle that many, but anything more would mean a hasty retreat.

And if they did have guns at the ready, what then? I would have to pull the trigger, there was no avoiding it. It would be a first for me. To my knowledge, I had never actually shot someone. Had I fired my weapon on the Falklands? Yes, of course. Killed indirectly, through terrorist operations, again yes. But never like this, never up front and personal.

I turned my head and nodded, signalling my wife, telling her I was ready and then moved into the hallway, which stretched back to front. The layout was similar to the one upstairs, except the walls here were concrete painted grey. Directly opposite was an open door leading to a dark bedroom, a cot with bunched up bedclothes visible inside.

Sidestepping to my right, I checked the other rooms. A bathroom and two other bedrooms, all empty. I moved silently back to where Hildy stood in the middle of the hallway, careful the rubber soles of my Dr Comforts did not squeak against the concrete floor.

The voices came from behind the door at the end, it stood slightly ajar. I imagined the room I was about to enter had the same floor plan as the office upstairs and mentally kicked myself for not asking Penny about it. Too late now. The handle was on the left, the door hinges were on the far side. Therefore, the door would swing away from me into the room.

I held the pistol behind my back and motioned for Hildy to come over and open the door. She stepped forward. Standing next to me, I could smell her perfume. Chanel no 5? She took hold of the door handle, I gave her a nod, and in a fluid motion, she pushed the door away from us, letting it glide open, and then she stepped back to let me pass.

In front of the windows stood two elevated tables with laboratory workstations, computer screens, test tubes and various other apparatus I did not recognise. To my left, a man sat in a chair, his hands secured with plastic ties to metal armrests. A plastic bag and a roll of duct-tape lay at the man's feet.

Two men stood a meter apart, facing the prisoner. They had their backs to me. One of the men, bald in a white shirt, stood on the right, the other was dressed in dark blue. Subconsciously I dubbed them 'Baldy' and 'Blue'.

The man in the chair looked up, surprised, he stared me in the eye. The other men followed their prisoner's gaze, they turned towards me. Baldy was fortyish, Blue in his late twenties, in his hand he held a knife, which he tried to conceal behind a trouser leg.

'Hello. We were just passing by. I am afraid we are lost and in need of directions,' I said.

Baldy replied, 'This is private property, you are trespassing.'

'Please, you must help me,' the man in the chair said.

A stalemate ensued. Neither the men nor I seemed to know what to say. I was relieved I could see no guns.

'I think you should untie that man,' I said, as I stepped down into the room and sensed a presence to my right. A muscular young man. He was standing in the far corner, he'd been looking out over the bay and now turned and took a step towards me, his fists clenched, his eyes calculating. In black jeans and a black turtleneck, his hands were empty. Blackie, a good name.

'No. Stay where you are or die,' I said, as I brought the pistol up in a two-handed shooting stance. It sounded a bit melodramatic to my ear but had the intended effect. Now I was committed.

Blackie looked down at my legs, left and right. I guessed he was evaluating his options, assessing how to attack. With a kick, or maybe a tackle? He would have to traverse half the room first. Keeping my eyes on him, the closest threat, seeing Blue in my peripheral vision, I said, 'Drop the knife.'

I heard it clatter to the floor.

'Good. Now, on your knees, all of you.'

After a moment's hesitation, all three men complied. The sound of cracking joints came from Baldy.

'Good. You,' I waived the pistol at Blackie. 'Walk on your knees over to the others.'

As Blackie came nearer, I trod back up the steps to just inside the doorframe. If the man suddenly lurched at me, the narrow frame would afford me some protection against a roundhouse punch, or arms held wide in a tackle. Blackie paused when he was closest to me.

'Keep going or die.'

Again, a bit theatrical, however, it had the desired effect. It also made me sound less nervous than I actually was.

The man shuffled towards the others. The three of them now knelt in front of the seated man, Blue and Baldy facing me, Blackie with his back to me on the right, by the windows. I leant in and surveyed the room, checking to see if there were any other surprises. Satisfied and relieved there were just the three of them, I stepped down into the room once more and held the gun aimed at Blackie, whom I presumed was the most lethal threat.

'Now, the two of you, turn around. No, stay on your knees.'

I waited as Blue and Baldy scuttled around to face in the opposite direction, it looked quite comical.

'You in the white shirt, ever so slowly, lean forward and scoot that bag of ties all the way back to me. No funny business.'

Blue, kneeling on the left began to turn his head.

'Eyes forward,' I ordered.

I beckoned Hildy to enter and pointed at the bag of ties lying at my feet. She bent down and picked it up and then treated me to a questioning look, an eyebrow raised, her head tilted.

'The one on the right, hands first, then his feet. I'll cover you and shoot if there is the slightest opposition. Now, everyone put your hands behind you and stay still, not a move.'

Shaking her head, obviously dismayed with our predicament, Hildy came around behind me. She got to her knees, and crawled forward, coming in at an angle from under a worktable, allowing me a full field of fire. Good thinking. Taking her time, Hildy wrapped a tie around Blackie's hands and pulled it tight. The man leered to his left. I detected a nod from Blue and deduced he was in command. He had just given his subordinate the order to take action. Both men tensed their shoulders.

'Come back a bit, I'm going to shoot one of them.'

I said it for the benefit of the men, obviously hoping I would not have to make good on my threat. Blue shook his head, and both he and Blackie visibly relaxed their bodies.

'All right, just so we understand each other, I have no intention of harming you unless you force me to. We are just here to collect the prisoner. It is Hans, correct?' I asked, without looking directly at the man in the chair, my eyes darting between Blue to Blackie.

'Yes, I am Hans Klerk, and I am happy for your assistance. But who are you?'

I was relieved. Coming all this way, threatening the men at gunpoint, if it had been someone else being held hostage, my actions would have been difficult to explain.

'Later,' I answered, I needed to concentrate. 'Now gents, we'll soon be out of here. Just keep your hands behind you, and no one will get hurt.'

Hildy picked up the bag of plastic ties and once again crawled forward. She tightened the tie around Blackie's hands with an extra pull for good measure and then fumbled another tie out of the bag and secured the man's ankles.

I could see her hands were trembling, so were mine.

She continued her work, meticulous as ever, threading a tie between the man's bound wrists and through the tie between his ankles. 'Hogtied' was the expression, which came to mind. My wife's proficiency was astounding. I had seen her use ties in the garden for her plants. Anyone could insert the tongue into the lock and tighten it. Still, doing this to a human being who could turn violent at any moment was certainly not something she had tried before. At least I assumed not.

Seemingly unperturbed, she crawled backwards under the table, stood and went around behind me, over to Blue on the left. On her knees once more, she scooted the discarded knife back over the concrete floor, I stopped it with my shoe. Hildy then completed the same procedure on Blue. When she tied the hands of Baldy, he began to protest.

'You do not know what you are doing. You are creating an international incident. My name is Georgi Ruzhkov. I am a Russian diplomat, you will find proof in my jacket in the corner.'

I glanced over my shoulder. A beige jacket lay on a chair.

'Keep going,' was all I said.

Hildy did, I was so proud of her, I was impressed by her courage. After completing the procedure on Baldy, she returned to my side, gave me a shy smile, and then rubbed her knees. The hard concrete floor must have hurt, despite her wearing trousers.

Flipping the safety, I pocketed my pistol and picked up the knife. Cutting a length of duct tape, I slapped it over the eyes of Blue. Blackie got the same treatment. Up close, I could smell their sweat. Finally, I did the same to Baldy wondering how much of the men's eyebrows they were likely to retain when they pulled off the tape.

The trio was now secured and blinded to the events around them. I stepped forward between the kneeling men to liberate Hans. In so doing, by chance, I knocked Blue off balance. The man toppled to his side, his head smacked resoundingly against the concrete floor. I was about to say 'Sorry', but had second thoughts. Instead, I purposely pushed the diplomat off balance with my knee. Baldy tilted sideways, knocking heads with Blackie, and then both men toppled over, akin to bowling pins. Strike! I knew it was a mean thing to do.

With the knife, I sawed through the Dutchman's bindings. He stood up from the chair, unsteady at first as he massaged his wrists, and then he took my offered hand for support and stepped over the flailing legs of the men on the floor. Hildy led him from the room.

Sure enough, in the jacket in the corner, I found a green diplomatic passport, Russian. Georgi Nicolai Ruzhkov, I pocketed the document. Next, I surveyed the room and decided there was nothing more to be done.

Should we call the police? Now we had proof the Russians had in fact kidnapped Hans? It would be the Russians' word against Hans's. Three to one, and they were the ones who were tied up. They had diplomatic immunity, and I had in my possession an illegal firearm. We had what we came for, it was time to go.

There was a key in the door, I took it, pulled the door shut behind me and locked it from the outside and then chucked the key into the bedroom and made my way upstairs. As I entered the hallway, Penny had her arms around Hans, embracing him. Releasing her boss, Penny turned towards me, smiling, about to speak. I put a finger to my lips and used my arms to shoo them all out of the building.

Coming out into the open, with a deep sigh of relief, I closed the main door behind me. Mission accomplished with no casualties, so far so good, now we needed to leave and in a hurry.

# 13

Outside, Hildy led the way. Jogging up the driveway, she turned left towards where we had parked Susanne's car.

Ominous clouds were coming in off the sea, the breeze was steady, it had rained a bit.

Passing the parked black SUV, I hesitated and tried the car door. It was a decidedly better ride than Susanne's Toyota. Unfortunately, it was locked. Going back to retrieve the key was not an option. What if the men had it? Finding the basement key in the bedroom where I had chucked it would prove tricky and then searching three dangerous men at gunpoint? No thanks.

I bent down and inserted the knife's tip into the valve of the rear tyre until I heard a satisfying hiss. When the wheel was flat, and the SUV had settled, I pulled the knife out and hurried after the others. Coming up onto the main road, my pistol in my pocket thumping against my hip, I heard Penny explaining to Hans as they leisurely stood by the car.

'They told me at the office you had quit for good. You never said goodbye, I just couldn't believe it. My parents wanted to visit Suðuroy, my mother's cousin, you know how it is, and I came along. I remembered the office down here, so we came to find you.'

'Does your father always carry a gun?' Hans asked.

I caught up with them.

'What gun? Forget you ever saw it.'

Both Penny and Hans turned and gaped at me.

'It never existed, okay? I could be in trouble.'

Hans gave me a hesitant nod, while Penny just shook her head and followed her mother around to the driver's side. Hans climbed into the front passenger seat, as I got in behind him and slammed my door, hoping it would not fall off its hinges.

A roar through the open windows startled me. My nerves were still raw. The public bus passed us on its way up the incline, headed for the tunnel.

Hildy turned the key, and the car started with a bang. Hans jumped in his seat, I was getting used to it by now. However, I could feel the cold under my thighs. The breeze had blown through the open windows during our visit to the FaroeOil building. I inadvertently pushed the button to raise the window, nothing happened.

'What is this shit?' Hans said from the front seat attempting to fasten his seatbelt.

'Everyone ready?' Hildy asked cheerfully, ignoring Hans's question and his swearing. Although she seemed to be making light of our predicament, I knew she was not happy. I saw her shake her head at me and give me the evil eye through the broken rear view mirror.

'Frank, darling, tell me that was not totally irresponsible.'

'In hindsight dear, I agree. However, all's well that ends well,' I said, craning my neck, checking the highway for traffic, willing my wife to get a move on.

'You're good to go, no cars as far as I can see.'

Amidst Hans's continued battle with his seatbelt and his swearing, she put the car in gear and inched out of the lay-by. She tried the wipers. They smeared the windshield making it all but impossible to see the road ahead. Regardless, Hildy pulled out onto the road, crossed the oncoming lane and we entered the tunnel.

Hans pushed the button on his door, attempting to raise his window. Sitting next to me, Penny said,

'Hans, the windows don't work, you'll have to leave it open.'

Hans's swearing upped a notch. The interior of the car was cold, the man did not have a jacket, just a blue shirt and dark trousers. With everything the man had been through these past twenty-four hours, culminating in this freezing getaway, I felt for him.

As Hildy leant out of her window to see the road ahead, she changed gears. We heard a bang, a cough and a second louder bang, which rocked the car as the engine died, and a burnt odour filled the cabin. She must have depressed the clutch because the car kept coasting along.

'Hildy, stop the car,' I said.

'Darling, let's see how far it takes us. We need to park in a safe spot.'

'Stop the car. Now!' I shouted at my wife, something I never did. Well, almost never. With an angry sigh, Hildy applied the brakes, and the car came to an abrupt halt in the middle of the lane.

'Hildy dear, what if we cannot start it? I don't want us to be trapped far inside this tunnel. We don't know when those men will get loose from their bindings and come looking for us. We'd be sitting ducks. Now, please dear, try and restart the engine.'

'What men, Dad? What are you talking about?'

'In the basement, Russian sailors had kidnapped Hans. We tied them up.'

'Were they gorgeous?'

'Penny, now's not the time.'

'Sorry Dad, but this is all getting a bit scary.'

Hans fumed, 'What kind of junk is this thing? Who chooses a wreck as an escape vehicle?'

'Nothing else was available at the time,' I answered patiently, as Hildy turned the key to no avail. The engine did not even turn over. We sat in silence.

'I think the car has had it,' I said. 'Even a pushing start will not help if the engine is done for. Let's get out of this tunnel, we need to skedaddle, maybe we can take the next bus.'

Penny thought for a moment. 'It just passed us, Dad. It's Sunday, there's only one every hour.'

'Then we'll have to walk,' I said.

Climbing out of the car, I looked to see if we could get the vehicle off the road. Spying into the darkness, I could see no indent in the cavern wall, no emergency stopping area. It could be a hundred metres up ahead. Feeling a sense of urgency, I made my decision.

'Come on, there's no time to push the car to safety. We need to get out of here.'

As we started for the tunnel entrance, I heard the slap of Hans's shoes against the road. That would be a problem. I wore my Dr Comforts, Hildy had on her Timberlands,

Penny, Adidas trainers. The three of us were in jeans, sweaters, and jackets or raincoats. But Hans wore only dress shoes with no sweater or overcoat. The temperature was well above freezing, but with the breeze, the wind-chill factor would be an issue. Giving him my jacket was not an option, I measured several sizes smaller than the Dutchman. As far as I could see, there was no remedy for the clothing situation, Hans would have to suffer the cold.

Then I remembered the content of the boot. Telling the others to carry on, I jogged back to the car and retrieved the woollen blanket and the first-aid kit. The beers I had bought were still there, I had not wanted to do an extra run from the road up to Susanne's house. I left the carton behind but extracted two bottles of beer from the cardboard case thinking it was the only beverage available. We might get thirsty later on. Once everything was double-bagged in the black carriers, I shut the boot, turned and hurried after the others, catching up quickly. As I slowed to a walk, regaining my breath, the bottles clinking, Hans looked at me sceptically.

'Are we having a party?' he asked.

'Hans, you have no coat, it will be cold out there.'

'I hardly think liquor will help.'

I stopped at the tunnel entrance.

'Let's find out.'

Inside the first-aid kit, I found a small set of scissors and a roll of surgical tape. Taking off my jacket, I surrendered my sweater to Hans.

'It's too small, but it will stretch.'

I put my bomber jacket back on.

Hildy tried in vain to use the scissors on the blanket. I handed her the knife, it worked much better. She cut and ripped into the blanket, making a long tear in the middle of the material, and then she cut a second shorter incision at a right angle. As Penny helped Hans into the makeshift poncho, I cut long strips of surgical tape with the scissors, which Hildy used to secure the blanket around Hans's torso as he held his arms high. Finally, we taped a plastic bag around his body giving him some protection against the wind.

I put the knife, the scissors and the first-aid kit into the second carrier holding the beers. We marched out of the tunnel.

'Hildy, dear. We'll have to go up over the hills. If we're lucky, they won't be looking for us there.'

'Dad, you're doing it again. Reliving the 'Sound of Music'. Escaping from the Nazis over the mountains. How romantic.'

'Penny, this is serious. They were dangerous men, they threatened Hans. You need to concentrate.'

'Hans, is this true?' Penny asked her boss. I was annoyed that she trusted his word more than mine. He simply nodded as he adjusted his coverings to get more comfortable.

'Alright Papa, I shall lead the way across the Alps,' my daughter replied, throwing her arms up in dramatic fashion.

Penny did not take the lead, Hildy did, she kept a steady pace. The drizzle had all but stopped as we entered a pasture and began to climb the hill. Up ahead, higher up on the mountainside, I could see the old road where we had parked only a short while before. We were headed that way.

'Watch your step,' Hildy warned over her shoulder. 'We don't want anyone twisting an ankle.'

When viewed from a distance, the pastures had seemed lush and even, similar to a vast piece of billiard cloth. However, I quickly discovered the terrain was clumps of grass interceded with rock, making the going uneven and arduous.

'We wouldn't be in danger of breaking a leg if you had picked a better car,' Hans said under his breath.

I had to agree. But I'd been in such a hurry to get to Sumba. Besides, where could we have found a different vehicle?

Wire fencing supported by wooden poles divided the mountain into pastures. Fortunately, we would need to climb over just five or six fences before we got to the old road. I was happy to see the pastures were inhabited by sheep only. Getting chased and head-butted by rams was not what we needed right now.

Then, literally out of the blue, a new danger arrived. From above.

# 14

Scores of birds rose from the fields around us. Smaller than crows, I had no idea what kind they were. Perhaps if I had taken up birdwatching, I would have known. They circled overhead, and began a continuous dive-bombing attack, swooping down to just over our heads, apparently annoyed by our intrusion in their nesting grounds here in the early spring.

Up ahead, Hildy and Penny waived their arms above their heads, attempting to ward off the Hitchcockian assault. I copied their actions, as did Hans, but not before one of the birds had completed a dive, and pecked the unlucky man in the head. Swearing, Hans ran his hand through his sparse hair, I saw it come away with blood.

We continued our climb, enduring the anxiety. Both my daughter and my wife pulled their raincoats up over their heads, I did the same with my jacket. Hans's poncho, taped around his body, did not afford him the same option. He would have to suffer. I felt the cold, especially on my bare back, now I had my jacket up over my head, my arms pulling my shirt tails from my trousers, and I hoped we would not be out in the open for long.

'Hildy, dear, how far is it to the next town?' I shouted.
'About six kilometres to Vágur,' came the reply.

I did the math. Walking at normal speed on an even surface, it would have taken us about an hour to get there. In our present circumstances, over the terrain we were traversing, the birds threatening overhead, we would be lucky to do it in two. Should we have stayed in the tunnel and avoided the birds? Stop second-guessing yourself, you are where you are, live with it, I told myself.

Despite the airborne onslaught, Hildy kept up a gruelling pace, Penny following right behind her. Hans, immediately in front of me, struggled to get traction on the wet, uneven hillside while at the same time waving his arms above his head. I ran the risk of sounding condescending.

'Hans, I was in the paratroopers once. They taught us to keep our feet flared, to use the edges of our boots to gain traction.'

I omitted to mention that bird attacks had not been included in my curriculum. Hans did not reply. However, I did see him take my advice, and we were soon making better progress.

Despite the earlier drizzle, we had decent visibility. Looking back, I could still see the town of Sumba and the Russian battlecruiser shrouded in the mist, but the fog now hid the drilling rig from sight. As far as I could see, there was no activity around the FaroeOil building, the black SUV stood parked out front, and all seemed quiet.

'Hans, how are you doing, are you warm enough?'

I got no answer. Fair enough. Hans was angry with me, angry for us not having a better escape plan. But on the other hand we *did* rescue him, at least he could have shown some gratitude. Because I could not imagine what we could have done differently, save somehow finding the SUV keys somewhere in the house. However, at the time, there had been no indication that Susanne's car, a vehicle, which had worked for a quarter of a century, would choose that very moment to break down. Had we been just ten minutes earlier, we could have taken the bus. The twenty-minute ride to Porkeri would have been ample time to see us clear. I assumed it would take the Russians at least that long to get themselves untied and to be on the road. We had been unlucky in our timing, nothing more.

Hans interrupted my thoughts, mumbling under his breath. The words in Dutch, 'Auto', 'Kaput', 'Godverdomme' and 'Bus' were clearly audible through his clenched teeth.

I changed my line of thinking.

There had been just three men in the house. Baldy did not seem to be the physical type. Blue was obviously a naval man, probably an officer of some sort and Blackie was their muscle. Were the hostage-takers armed? I had seen no weapons in the FaroeOil building, save for the knife now in my bag. Unless the men contacted their ship for guns and reinforcements, something, which would take time to organise, I felt confident we would be all right.

Turning around, looking back down the mountainside, I realised my assessment was all wrong. Two figures stood by the black SUV, now perhaps a thousand metres from us. Both men were looking up the mountainside, straight at me, the man on the right pointing, as if laying out the land, describing a plan.

I marvelled at how quickly they had gotten themselves untied. As I watched, the men went to the SUV and opened the boot. One of them reached inside and withdrew something and then turned and jogged up the driveway. I expected him to head towards us. Instead, he ran back in the direction of town, before disappearing from view, down the road, which led to the seawall.

'What's happening, darling?' Hildy called. The others had stopped and were looking back as well.

'I think they got themselves untied. Keep going, I'll catch up.'

When next I looked, the SUV by the FaroeOil building had reversed and stopped. The driver stood bent, inspecting the flat tyre. He went to the boot and then jogged up to the road. The second SUV appeared, coming up the ramp from the quay. It turned onto the main road. The driver stopped to pick up his friend and then accelerated full out. Headed towards the tunnel. Our pursuers seemed intent on heading us off on the opposite side of the hills.

It was not a strategy, I would have chosen. I would have driven east through Sumba, directly away from us and then come up along the old road, the same route Hildy had taken less than half an hour ago. Thankfully, the men did not seem to know the area as well as they should have.

Watching with a hopeful smile, I saw the vehicle disappear from view, followed by the far-off thunder of a crash. Ouch! I figured the tunnel had funnelled the sound away from us. What I heard was the resounding echo coming off the hillsides. I could almost not believe our luck. I turned, grinned, and hurried after the others. Minutes later, out of breath, I caught up and told them what I had witnessed.

'Is that the last we have seen of them?' Hans asked.

'Not unless they were hurt in the crash. I expect they will come after us on foot. Hildy, what can we do?'

She thought for a minute, then pulled out her mobile phone and dialled. After a lengthy discussion, she ended the call.

'I ordered a taxi. It will meet us at the top, by the transmitter. I explained our car had broken down.'

This seemed to be a fortunate turn of events until Hildy added,

'The only taxi working today is up north with passengers, headed for Sanvík. It could take almost an hour to get here.'

'Let's keep going,' I said.

We trudged on. It began to drizzle once more. I felt miserable. The rain soaked through my jacket, and with no sweater underneath, no insulation between my skin and the wet lining other than my shirt, the cold was getting to me. I could see Hans was suffering as well. The Dutchman shivered continuously, his teeth chattering. However, we were not in any serious peril, not from the weather. Although it would soon be dark, if unchallenged, we would reach Vágar and be out of the elements soon enough.

The real danger was the Russians. That is if they were in any condition to pursue us. I looked back and concluded they were. Well, at least one of them was. Down on the mountainside, I could see a figure ascending, waving one hand in the air, the other holding something long and thin. A gun of some sort, perhaps.

'We need to hurry up. They are coming,' I said.

The going got better once we reached the old road. The birds relinquished their attack, satisfied they had defended their nesting grounds. The broken asphalt proved kinder to Hans's shoes, and the flatter surface made the going less strenuous. Hildy kept up the pace, with Penny beside her. They both had thick sweaters underneath their raincoats. Penny had her hood up, while Hildy seemed to enjoy the breeze in her face. She had pulled her coat back down over her bum, her hair blew loose in the wind. She must have pocketed the chopsticks she normally used to hold her bun in place.

Walking next to Hans, I willed him to hurry, at the same time not wanting the Dutchman to exhaust himself. We could never leave him behind, however, against rifles or shotguns, we had no defence. We needed to get a move on. I decided to get him talking, to take his mind off his misery.

'Hans, why did they take you hostage? What did they want?'

Hans did not respond immediately, and just as I concluded he would not, Penny's boss said,

'It was strange. When I left work in the early hours of Friday morning, two Danish men, one big and one very small, about your size, stopped me and took me to a shed by the harbour. The little one had a knife. They tied me up and left me for the night with only a thin blanket. When they came back the next day, I was certain they were going to kill me. The small man was evil. He kept sharpening his knife against a stone. They refused to look me in the eye. I've never been so frightened in my life.'

I saw him tremble as he recounted his harrowing ordeal.

'I got no food. Occasionally, they allowed me water, it was the only time they took the cloth from my mouth. They gave me a bucket as a toilet, and only untied me when I needed to use it. Disgusting. Then they got a phone call. Afterwards, everything changed. They were kinder and got me food. I think the phone call was the reason.'

'How so?'

'I don't know. In the evening, they untied my legs and marched me out to a waiting boat. Russians. They took me out to the warship and brought me here. They wanted me in Sumba to discuss geological formations, and to show them our paper files.'

'Was the man in the white shirt a geologist?' I asked.

'No, it was strange. I'm not sure what he does, but he gave the orders. He's also a Russian, although he speaks good English.'

'Who were the other two?'

'The one who did the talking was a lieutenant, he said. I did not catch his name. The guard's name is Spetsnaz. It was supposed to scare me, but I do not know of him.'

'He's a Russian commando. Special Forces.'

'You know this man? The one called Spetsnaz.'

'Hans, that's not his name. Similar to the SAS.'

'Scandinavian Airlines? He did not seem to be a pilot.'

'Hans, I take it, they wanted to know about the oil under the sea.'

'No, that was the funny part. Perhaps not funny, ha, ha. But the strange part. Yes, initially, they wanted my paper files about the drilling sites, my original work made a year ago. Then they showed me a document listing coordinates. Those sites where FaroeOil has already drilled, not the correct ones according to my calculations. I signed it, they forced me to.'

I saw that Hans's shivering was easing, I was happy to see the exertion of walking gave the Dutchman some warmth inside his makeshift poncho, and the discussion took his mind off his miserable circumstances. I looked back, our pursuer was gaining on us. I called ahead,

'Hildy, he might catch us, and he has a gun. Is there something else we can do?'

She pulled out her phone and made a call.

Hans continued, 'After I signed their document, they asked about the geological characteristics of the islands. They wanted to know about the archipelago of rock formations east of the harbour at Sumba. Whether it could support an extended seawall that could enclose a full-sized naval port. And about the possibility of excavating a cavern in the cliffs for a 'duikboot' base, you know, submarines. Perhaps they think the Americans will build one, I do not know. I assured them it was possible.

'Then they wanted to discuss a place called Mjoerkadalur on the island of Streymoy, the fjords to the north and south, and the mountain of Sornfelli. They took all my studies from the drawers and made them ready for packing. They needed them because all my computer files were deleted, they said. How they accessed our computers, I have no idea. Maybe we were hacked.'

'What's so special about those places?'

'From a geological point of view, nothing. However, inside the Sornfelli mountain, there is a large cavity. Sixty years ago, NATO excavated the mountain to make room for a military bunker. It was a radar and sonar station that could follow aircraft and ships over a vast area, stretching from Scotland to Greenland, even the duikboots. Now, however, it is disused. Abandoned, empty. Therefore, I have no idea why the Russians would want to know about this site. If it were active, it would be a military target, that I understand, but it is not.'

'Hans, just now you were in the FaroeOil building, being held by Russian naval personnel. Do you have any idea of a connection between FaroeOil and the Russians?'

'No, not really. I remember some talk of a Russian bank wanting to give us loans some time ago, but nothing came of it. Now that the American banks have financed the company, I do not understand their involvement, and I cannot see how they know what files we have here in Sumba. I also ask myself, why they used their big warship as a ferry, my personal taxi, to get me here and confiscate my work.'

Hildy shouted back to us, 'I called 112, the emergency number for the police and told them an armed crazy man is following us, threatening us. Because I mentioned the gun, the police cannot dispatch a car immediately, they need their whole team. It should arrive inside half an hour.'

'Their whole team?' I shouted. 'An armed police unit?'

'Only four police officers and two vehicles. It's all they have on Suðuroy,' she called back down the hill.

A chorus of bleating sheep added their opinion.

I nodded to myself as we trudged on, taking in this new information. Four police officers, armed. No doubt, it would be enough to scare off our pursuer.

'When I entered the basement, they had you bound to a chair. The man had a knife. If you were cooperating with them, why did they tie you up?'

'When we arrived here, they were very polite. Very, how do you say, pleasant? But when I answered their questions, I demanded to be let loose. Instead, they offered me a job in Murmansk. Murmansk, I tell you, that Godforsaken place. No, I said, my wife would never move from Den Haag to Murmansk. They say it is an offer I cannot refuse, and when I do refuse, things got, how do you say, ugly. Very ugly. And then you came through the door.'

'One last question, Hans. Could you have been detained on orders by the FaroeOil people? They told Penny you had quit, that you had left the Faroes, which was obviously not true.'

'No, I do not think the director had anything to do with this. Why would he? He could just have asked me these questions in person.'

Up ahead, not far from the road, a windowless structure appeared, it was painted black with white doorframes. Standing next to it was a lattice tower with an antenna on top. A signals station of some kind, I wondered what it could be.

I looked back. The man in pursuit was two or three hundred metres behind us and seemed content to hold his distance. I could make out the twin barrels of his weapon.

A shotgun.

# 15

The precipitation had all but stopped, and the breeze had softened. Standing in the middle of the winding lane, I could see we had arrived at the point where the road reached its highest elevation. To our rear, Sumba was no longer visible. To the north, I could see the town of Vágur shrouded in the mist. We were over halfway. From here on, it would be downhill going, we would be able to make better time, or so I hoped.

Hildy shouted something and then pointed. A man was coming up the hillside from the direction of Vágur, limping heavily, obviously hurt. He also appeared to have a gun. I reckoned this must be the second man, the Spetsnaz soldier. He must have struggled the two and a half kilometres through the tunnel and ascended the mountain from the opposite direction. He was now at our front, we were boxed in.

I looked at my watch. Ten minutes until the arrival of the promised taxi, not that it would do us much good with armed men about. Fifteen minutes until the police arrived.

This was the Faroe Islands for heaven's sake, a peaceful place. I could not imagine these men wanting to kill us, they could not afford to leave dead bodies lying around. I might get roughed up a bit as punishment for interrupting their little party, however, the men would be more interested in retaking their hostage, or so I assumed.

As Hans and I caught up with the women, I asked, 'Penny dear, are you alright.'

'Dad, who are they. They have guns. What do they want?'

'They're the Russians. They probably want Hans back. But with the four of us here, they shall not have him. With us as witnesses, there is little they can do without getting into trouble with the police.'

'Frank, darling, you forget something.' Hildy pointed to the west. 'Just over there are cliffs, more than four hundred metres, going straight down. Those men don't have to worry about evidence or bodies lying around, and afterwards, they can make their escape on their ship.'

Penny looked visibly shaken, as did Hans.

Hildy's phone jingled. For me it was odd, hearing the merry tones out here in the middle of nowhere, in otherwise total stillness save for the far-off braying of a sheep and the whisper of the breeze through the grass. Hildy answered.

'Frank darling, the taxi driver says he will arrive in ten minutes. We can't have him coming up here. He could get hurt.'

She did not add, 'along with the rest of us.'

'Cancel it, dear.'

After a short conversation, Hildy terminated the call.

'I explained we had gotten the car working and we were already in Tvøroyri,' she said.

Looking towards the man approaching from our front, and back down the road at the man in pursuit, I was all out of ideas. I asked my wife,

'What do you suggest?'

'Darling, I don't know.' She sounded scared, that made four of us.

I looked around. A wire fence on our left ran from the road all the way out to the cliff edge. On our side of the barrier, posts supported a sign, a warning depicting a man falling off a cliff. Not an encouraging thought.

The signals building was built of sturdy wood.

'There's no alternative,' I said. 'As I see it, we're caught between two armed men, with a cliff at our backs. We have no other option than to barricade ourselves inside the building, and hold out until the police arrive.'

'What about their guns?' Hans asked anxiously. His eyes were roving in their sockets. 'They can shoot us when we are inside the building.'

'Those walls look quite sturdy. They've only got shotguns, I doubt if the pellets can penetrate the walls.'

I said it with a confidence I did not feel, as we approached the building. However, I was proved right, the structure was indeed sturdy, as was the locked door. It defeated my attempts to gain access even using a piece of basalt in an effort to break the door handle.

All this was taking too much time. I was getting frantic. I considered firing a round into the lock but reasoned the small-calibre bullet was unlikely to do any damage and more likely to ricochet back at us. And firing the gun would give our pursuers confirmation I had a working firearm. It might cause them to shoot first and ask questions later. I looked left and right. The men continued to converge steadily, but they stayed on the road, they were equal distance from us, about a hundred metres away.

'Darling, do you still have the beer?' Hildy asked, looking out over the cliffs.

I felt with my hand the bottles inside the black carrier and nodded.

'Okay, this is not working,' she said. 'We can't get into the building. All of you, follow me and do exactly as I say. Now hold hands.'

She led the way and headed for the sign, which depicted the silhouette falling off the cliff. She held Penny's hand, who in turn reached back to hold Hans's hand. When Hans reached for mine, I hesitated, thinking linking hands was a bit over the top. We were twenty metres from the cliff edge and not likely to fall off.

I also thought, by approaching the cliffs we were making the Russians' job much easier for them if they intended to kill us and dispose of our bodies. However, I complied with my wife's instructions, feeling the soft skin of Hans's palm in mine, feeling uncomfortable as I always did when touching the flesh of another man for anything more than a handshake.

As we reached the sign, I did a double take. We were standing on the edge of a field covered knee-deep in ground-hugging mist, the occasional boulder rising from it. Then the wind stirred, and the field disappeared. With a sense of vertigo, I stared down into what seemed an endless void. Ten metres out, what had looked like a boulder in a pasture was, in fact, the tip of an obelisk-shaped rock formation, rising from the depths. I saw the finger of rock continue down, its base well hidden in the fog far below. Further out, on the other side of the rock formation was more land as the cliff we were on, crescent-shaped, curved from left to right in a half circle.

Seemingly forgetting our circumstances, proudly, as if it was his invention, Hans said,

'You see, the elements have eroded the cliff, carving out a great abyss in the rock face, leaving just the pillar behind.'

Then the fog filled the abyss once more and recreated the illusion of a rock-strewn pasture.

'Turn around and sit down,' Hildy instructed, with a no-nonsense voice.

'Oh, Mom, there are sheep droppings everywhere.'

'Penny!'

'Yes, Mom. But just so you know, these jeans are new.'

They had not looked new to me. On the contrary, they were full of holes, but I had not dared criticise.

'Now, all of you, re-join hands, and keep them that way,' Hildy instructed. I was not sure of my wife's thinking. Did she want us to be holding hands when we met our Maker? Our pursuers were now fifty metres from us. They took their time, approaching with confidence. They could afford to, we were hardly in a position to oppose them. I decided to leave the pistol in my pocket, I did not want to provoke the men into using their superior firepower.

Hildy whispered,

'The fog is coming. In a minute, you'll hardly be able to see your hand in front of your face. We are going to crawl along the edge to our left. When I pull on your hand, Penny, follow me on all fours, stay close. Hans, you follow Penny. Frank, the beer, when the time is right, you'll know what to do.'

We waited in silence, watching the men approach. As Hildy had predicted, the fog came in from behind and billowed over us, as thick as pea soup, a metaphor or simile I had never fully understood. Why would anyone want to be in a bowl of soup, especially pea soup?

As the fog enveloped me, the men broke into a slow, uneven run, as if panicking, fearing their quarry might escape them. I felt Hans tug on my hand. He released my grip and then moved away.

I decided on a plan and took a beer from my plastic bag. As I heard boots come at me, pounding the grass, I held the bottle by its neck in my right hand and with a flick of the wrist, I tossed it over my shoulder and across the abyss hearing it shatter against the rock face of the obelisk.

I pulled out my second beer.

A shotgun roared, ear-deafening, and the ground next to me erupted, where the others had been sitting only moments before. The area was peppered by pellets tearing into the grass and rock, one of them ricocheting, searing my hand.

Fooled by my diversion, I heard boots run past me, I struck out with the second bottle, cracking it across someone's shin. Then there was silence. Then a shout and finally a distant drawn-out scream.

Sneaking the pistol out of my pocket, I heard the second pair of boots stop on my right. All went quiet for a moment, an eerie silence. Then I sensed a movement, and a shadow in the fog loomed above me. I raised the gun and fired four times at the figure, hearing a heavy grunt, the man collapsed to the ground.

Leaning over the body, I checked for a pulse. The man groaned, he was still alive. In the fading light, I could not be certain, but I thought it was Blue. I would have been prepared to leave it at that, except for the fact that one of the men had blindly fired his shotgun. Had Hildy and the others not crawled away, they would have been severely wounded or worse. Had I followed the others, the pellets would have hit me.

A shotgun lay next to the man, I broke it open. It smelled of fresh cordite, which made my decision for me. The man had tried to murder us. Anger welled up within me as I clenched my teeth. I took the shotgun by its barrel and flung it over the cliff.

Next, still on my buttocks, using my feet, I rolled the shooter in the direction of the cliff edge as the man continued to moan. I grabbed hold of one of the stakes supporting the danger sign and gave it a shake. It was firmly anchored in the ground and was unlikely to budge.

Rolling onto my stomach, using the stake for leverage, I placed both my feet against the man and stretched my body full length, giving him a mighty push as I felt him feebly claw at my trouser legs. The man slid across the grass, it was hard work. Suddenly the resistance gave way.

Lying there for a moment, panting, I regained my wind and then crawled away from the cliff edge on all fours.

'Hildy dear, stay where you are. Do not move another inch. I fired warning shots. It must have frightened them off, they're gone.'

Technically, I was not lying, although my words indicated that the shots had not hit their mark and the men had left on their own accord.

'We're safe,' I concluded.

Some ways off in the fog, I heard to my relief, 'All right darling. Are you sure?' and then 'Mother, perhaps we can get up now. I'm all covered in sheep shit!'

'Now Penny, darling, language.'

# 16

We were seated in the booth surrounding Susanne's kitchen table. Hildy, Penny, Hans, and a lovely female police officer. She was Danish, her name was Ida. She had blond curly hair and light blue eyeliner. As she sat in the corner taking statements, she reminded me of a young Hildy.

Susanne was busy preparing 'Raisten Fisk' over by the cooker.

'It's cod, untreated and hung in the shed for three weeks to ferment and then boiled,' Hildy said with a mischievous glint in her eye. 'Served with a sauce made from sheep intestines. You'll enjoy it.'

Hans looked on sceptically. At least he had stopped complaining to Susanne about her car.

I was deep in thought, sad and shaken, my bandaged hand stinging. Today had been a first for me. I had killed outright. Goose Green, the Falklands in 1982 had been my first and only live-fire combat. At the time, I had fired my rifle at the shadows, but had I hit someone? I would never know. At MI6, I had orchestrated the demise of others, but never actually been present at the physical assassinations.

I asked myself if I had killed in cold blood? In his pursuit of us, the first assailant had dropped off the cliff on his own accord, albeit helped by my bottle against his shin. Nevertheless, it was the chap's own fault. The second man, wounded by my bullets, had been alive, that is until I shoved him off the cliff and he presumably hit the rocks below. No, not cold blood. There had been nothing calculating about it, I had acted in the heat of the moment, the rage burning inside me.

A righteous killing, then? I certainly thought so, the circumstances taken into consideration. But still, I kept replaying in my mind what had occurred, over and over, asking myself if I could have done anything differently. It was the first time I had caused someone's death up close and personal, a person with family, friends, a life, it felt terrible.

Of course, there was Hildy and Penny to think of. We'd had a narrow escape. The shotgun blast could have injured them both or worse, something which did not bear reflection. In hindsight, I regretted their involvement in Hans's rescue, I knew I should have taken Susanne's car on my own and gone to Sumba. I had been impetuous, reckless even. On the other hand, I could not have tied up the Russians by myself, and it was Hildy's quick thinking, which saved us, out on the cliff. Without her, Hans and I would not be sitting here at the table.

Ida had her notebook out, and I was happy Hans had stuck to our prepared story. He had agreed to say he had escaped on his own accord and had flagged down our car. I did not want to explain how we had held the Russians at gunpoint and liberated Hans, or where the bodies of our pursuers could be found.

'The car broke down,' Hans said. 'I thought it was a bad idea to walk through the tunnel, and so we trekked over the mountains and took the scenic route. Then they chased us with their guns, the Russians who held me against my will, who brought me to Sumba, I'm convinced it was them.'

'When we arrived, we saw no sign of them,' Ida said.

'No, they disappeared when the fog came in from the sea,' I said.

When the police had finally shown up, they had come in full force in their two Nissan Navaras, lights flashing from the rooftops. On seeing the four of us calmly walking down the road sharing that second beer, the police officers had come out of their cars, weapons at the ready. Once they heard our story, the police relaxed, and Ida drove us back to Porkeri. The other three officers said they would continue in their second vehicle along the old road and look for armed men.

'The bus driver saw the crash blocking the tunnel on his way back to Sumba and alerted us,' Ida said. 'The mayor is angry, he demanded we file charges against the drivers who abandoned their cars. That would be you, Mrs Llewellyn. However, after I told him your vehicle belonged to Susanne, here, he calmed down. I think he said you are his wife's third cousin on her father's side, correct?'

Ida directed this last question to Susanne who whisked away in a pot.

'Can't talk now, the sauce will, will..., how do you say it?'

'Curdle,' I suggested.

'Girdle? No, I mean burn.'

Ida continued, 'The other vehicle in the crash belonged to FaroeOil. The mayor's hoping for them to provide jobs to his little town, so apart from the clean-up expenses, it's case closed.'

'But you must investigate,' Hans said. 'I was kidnapped. You must find the two Danes in Tórshavn. You must interrogate the Russians.'

'Mr Klerk. The Russian ship left its moorings an hour ago, and even if we knew the persons implicated in your abduction, it would be your word against theirs,' Ida said.

'But you do agree they are responsible,' I said. 'Or perhaps you think they were just here to do some shopping?'

'No, the shops are much better in Tórshavn. Oh, I get it. You made a joke. But even if we accept Mr Klerk's story, we would have to charge the captain as well. I'm not sure how we could do that, but I'll ask my chief. So it's case closed, except we are on the look-out for a big man and a smaller man in Tórshavn. It's not the best description, we shouldn't expect much.'

'Unless they are together,' I said.

'Now all that remains is to clean up the tunnel and get the vehicles towed away. Susanne, what should we do with your car?' Ida asked.

'Please take it to the garage in Vágur, I'm sure they can fix it. Although how I shall pay for the repairs, I don't know. The insurance money will be very little,' Susanne said sadly, as she took the casserole from the heat.

'But Susanne, we wouldn't dream of leaving you with the bill, this was my fault entirely,' Hildy said.

This last remark startled me. Normally my wife blamed me for any accident at home or in the car. 'You should have told me about the tree, darling,' I recalled hearing. Here, she voluntarily took the blame. Or did she?

'Actually, my fault for listening to Frank, it was his doing, leaving your car in the middle of the road like that. You must promise to send him the bill for any expense.'

I wondered if Hildy intended for me, or rather us, to compensate Susanne for the depreciated value of her twenty-five-year-old heap of rubbish, or if she meant for us to pay for a new vehicle, something, which in my mind was entirely out of the question. If Susanne's car had been there for us when we needed it most, I might have felt differently. And then it dawned upon me, my wife was brilliant, of course, she was. The car saved us, blocking the road as it did, causing the accident. It had forced the Russians to follow us on foot. Yes, I was more than willing to buy something new for Susanne, anything, as long as Hildy promised to foot the bill.

'Supper's ready,' Susanne said and began to shuffle plates onto the table. 'Ida, you're welcome to stay.'

After dinner, I felt exhausted. Only the day before, we had arrived on the islands and so much had happened since. My stomach was pleasantly full after a surprisingly delicious meal and one of Susanne's beers, my own had been lost in the crash or were at the bottom of some cliff.

I had wanted to talk to Penny. I knew our trek across the mountains must have been a harrowing experience for her. I wanted to find out if she had been traumatised in any way. But she had gone to bed refusing to talk about it. Hildy told me to give her some space.

'How are you feeling?' I asked my wife.

'This is not about me, darling. Remember, I was once in the Service myself, I've seen worse. But you, I know what happened out there in the fog, I see it in your face, and you were quiet at dinner. You must stop thinking about it. Think of something else, something pleasant. And you have to realise, you saved us, you had no other choice. What happened is raw, it'll take time for the memories to fade, but knowing you did it for us will help. Now, you need to get some sleep.'

Totally knackered, physically and mentally, I had hoped Hildy would join me in bed. After all, it was she who said I should think of something else, something pleasant, right? What better way, than in bed with my loved one, this in spite of us being houseguests with our daughter sleeping in the bedroom next door and Hans just across the hallway.

However, it was not to be. The Faroese tradition of women staying up until well past midnight, drinking Typhoo tea, knitting, and discussing their extended families, cousins, neighbours and who was getting married to whom and who was expecting, all this was not a tradition to be trifled with.

I fell asleep, all alone.

# 17

Sunday afternoon, Penny served tea and oatmeal cookies in her flat. Arriving back from Suðuroy only minutes before, after the short walk from the ferry terminal, Hans went straight to the window and studied the Pyotr Velikiy anchored out in the bay. I saw a shiver run through the man's body as he stood there staring through the glass, teeth clenched, and I could well imagine the confusion the Dutchman must feel, one day minding his job, the next being kidnapped for no apparent reason, his life threatened.

The doorbell rang. Hildy went to open up and showed Sámal in, our host from the party Friday evening, she had invited him over at my request. In addition to being a member of the parliament, part-time employment at best, Hildy had mentioned Sámal was a solicitor in his day job.

'Sámal, thank you for coming,' I said. 'We have something we would like to share with you, something we think you should hear. Hans, perhaps you will begin.'

We sat on assorted chairs, no two alike, around Penny's rustic white dining table. Hans, focusing on Sámal, gave his redacted account of his experiences beginning Wednesday when he first reported Penny's findings to the FaroeOil CEO. Sámal listened attentively at first, then indignantly as Hans's story unfolded, and finally, he interrupted with outrage,

'The Faroe Islands is a place of peace and tranquillity, not of kidnappings and violence.'

Hans continued. When he ended his tale, Sámal asked,

'But what does it mean? You say these Danes abducted you, they handed you over to the Russians who used their enormous warship to play water taxi, to take you to Sumba. And there, they questioned you about your studies and offered you a job. And when you make your escape, helped by Hildegard and her family, the Russians tried to recapture you but had to give up when the fog came.'

Sámal sipped his tea, smacked his lips and then continued,

'Your story is quite unbelievable. I think anybody hearing it would find it utterly preposterous if you did not have corroboration from the Llewellyn family.'

'There's a couple of things,' I said. 'First, we have no explanation why the Russian ship travelled to Sumba other than to get Hans there in secret. What other plausible reason could there be? And second, there's this.'

From my pocket, I retrieved the green passport, the one I had pinched from the Russian diplomat's jacket, and handed it to Sámal. After studying the document, page by page, Sámal closed it and lay it on the table.

'Where did you get this?' he asked.

'Hans nicked it on his way out the door,' I said.

I gave the Dutchman an intense stare, willing him not to contradict me. Sámal leant back in his chair and closed his eyes. I smiled at Hans and shrugged an apologetic shoulder. After a full minute of silence, I asked,

'Sámal, obviously the Russians' kidnapping of Hans and the activities at FaroeOil are somehow connected. So humour me. Just suppose there is a rational explanation behind all this. What could it be?'

'Frank, there is no explanation. FaroeOil is not involved in kidnappings or with the Russians. It is a respectable company. What I don't understand is, why would the Russians want to steal your files?'

Sámal directed this last remark to Hans.

'I don't know, I was asked to recount what happened to me. I merely told you what they questioned me about.'

'Sámal, the Russians had access to FaroeOil vehicles. That must prove something,' I said, thinking myself clever for stating the obvious.

'Dad, the keys always hang on a rack in the kitchen.'

On hearing this, I could have kicked myself. I had mistakenly assumed the Russians had the keys in their pockets. Had I known they were on a hook just inside the building, we could have made our getaway in the SUV, and I would not have had to kill those men.

'Be that as it may, there must be some connection,' I said a bit lamely.

'Russians and FaroeOil? I don't see how,' Sámal replied.

'There was once, you know,' Hans said. 'Dealings with the Russians. Regarding the financing.'

Sámal thought for a moment, then,

'Those were only rumours. The company got its financing from an American banking consortium last year, hundreds of millions of US dollars. The government of the Faroes Islands guaranteed this loan, I know, I saw the documents.'

'When did the loan transaction take place?' Hildy ventured. Studying faces, she had been listening attentively until then.

'As I said, over six months ago,' Sámal replied. 'I was away on business at the time of the parliamentary vote. However, the papers, the documents were made available to all members. I saw them but never studied the wording in detail. The prime minister's office and the government's legal experts reviewed them, it was their responsibility.'

'Okay Sámal, so tell me this. On hearing Hans's story, what should we do? There must be something,' I said.

'Nothing. You must wait for the authorities to investigate his abduction and find the two men, a tall one and a small one.'

Exasperated, I leant back in my chair, hearing it creak. I understood the man's scepticism. However, I had a strong feeling everything was not as it seemed. FaroeOil's business should be of no concern to the Russians, but they were making it their business. I wanted to persist in investigating the matter, and most of all I wanted to be involved. This was the most excitement I'd had since leaving MI6. The alternative was visiting Hildy's relatives and handing out M&Ms.

'Sámal, I don't want to flog a dead horse, but there must be something going on, something we do not understand. Would it be possible to review the loan documents? You said you have a copy of them.'

'A dead horse? No, we don't have horses, only ponies, very small, like the Icelandic ones and they are protected, only about fifty left, so you mustn't beat them, but why would you want to?'

'Sámal, it's just an expression. It means doing something not needed. But the agreement, could we see a copy?'

'As you say, it is not necessary. Reviewing it would be a lot of work. But it would be possible. As I mentioned, the documents were initially circulated to the members of the Løgting, I should have a copy on my computer somewhere. The whole matter is on public record because of the government guarantee. Therefore, any Faroese person can request and have full insight into the files.'

'We're not Faroese.'

'No, Frank, you're not.'

What to do? I made my proposal.

'Sámal, will you do this then? Together, we review the loan agreement, but the documents do not leave your house.'

'But there is no need, Frank. And besides, I'm very busy.'

'Sámal, what's your normal rate,' Hildy asked.

'Two thousand kronor an hour.'

'Alright Sámal, do as Frank asks, and we'll pay your standard fee,' she said.

'No, I couldn't do that. This might be an important matter for the Faroese government. In the unlikely event, there truly is something wrong, I would see it as my civic duty, the authorities have a right to know.'

We sat waiting expectantly for him to continue.

'I'll give you a fifty per cent discount.'

'Done,' Hildy said.

I sighed, 'Okay, Sámal, now we've agreed, what I propose is this. We meet at your place in the morning. If, by tomorrow evening, we find nothing, so be it. There is no harm done.'

'And if we do find something?' Sámal asked.

'We'll dig that tunnel when we get to it.'

My witty comment fell completely flat save for an encouraging smile from my staunchest supporter, Hildy. Too bad, their loss.

Dinner with our host family was a cosy meal, the teenagers, a girl and an older boy were back home. Slim like their parents, they were obviously not into eating M&Ms by the bagful. Hans, apprehensive with returning to his flat, was staying the night at Sámal's house and had promised to help the solicitor print out the documents I wanted to review.

For cocktails, Knud served G&Ts with the gin I had bought at the tax-free, tasty indeed, but £60? Oydis served fillets of dark breast meat of fowl, accompanied by cooked potatoes, steamed carrots, and thick brown gravy.

'I would have liked to serve you boiled sheep's head,' Knud said. 'It's one of our specialities, especially the meat around the ears is good.'

'And the lips chewy,' Hildy added with a sweet smile.

Penny and the children made faces.

Knud continued unperturbed,

'But unfortunately we've run out. Instead, we are having Lomvig, guillemot you call it, which is also a favourite of ours. We take the boat out to below the cliffs to catch them. You see, they jump out of their nests high up, the fat chicks, unable to fly, and land softly in the water to feed and grow. That's when we scoop them up using a big net. A quick twist of the neck and we have the most delicious meal. A gift from God.'

'It tastes fantastic, but I'd expected puffin,' I said.

'Catching puffin is no longer allowed,' Knud said. 'They are becoming extinct.'

'Why?' I asked.

'Mostly climate change. They are not reproducing. And the rest? I'm afraid, Frank, we've eaten most of them.'

Knud said it with a melancholic sigh.

After coffee, Knud and I did the dishes, and then we retired to the dining room. From the living room, I heard the hum of gossip, Hildy and Oydis sat with their knitting.

'Where's Penny?' I asked through the open doorway, she had been quiet at dinner. I had yet to discuss with her the events at Sumba and how much they had frightened her.

'Gone home to her flat. She's fine, and she doesn't want to talk about it,' Hildy replied.

Knud brought out two bottles of whisky.

'Frank, this is my favourite, Glenmorangie. But I also have this other bottle. I've had it from the time when our youngest was born, and I can't seem to get rid of it. None of my friends like the taste. Perhaps, being English, you think differently. Would you like to try it?'

I was intrigued. I could not imagine anything, my host did not enjoy, with his all-inclusive palate.

When Knud presented the bottle to me, I sucked in my breath and then gave a short silent whistle. The bottle was my favourite Scotch whisky, in my opinion, the tastiest of them all. Ten-year Ardbeg, and by all accounts, from Knud's description of when he had acquired it, the liquor was at least twenty years old.

I let Knud pour me a generous splash in a crystal tumbler before carefully taking a sip. As the liquid flowed over my tongue, I tasted the warmth, the smokiness of peat. Yes, an acquired taste I thought, as I savoured my drink.

'Knud, it's not that bad, and it'll be bedtime soon, it's been a long day. Perhaps I should have another, just to help you out with that bottle.'

That night I slept like a baby.

# 18

We congregated Monday morning in the front room of Sámal's house. Hildy, Penny, Hans, Sámal and myself. And Sámal's adorable little black Labrador puppy who kept demanding our attention.

We sat around the coffee table in deep sofas. Contemporary and traditional paintings adorned the yellow walls, all depicting green mountains rising from the blue-green sea. I knew this was a thing here. It was the same at our hosts' and Susanne's homes, the Faroese loved sticking nature on their walls, regardless the real thing was just outside their door.

As promised, Sámal had printouts of the loan document, it was over fifty pages thick. There were a number of appendixes as well, each dealing with a specific topic.

The first appendix was a project description with a timetable, another appendix dealt with technical descriptions of the drillings. The list of intended drilling sites was appendix 3, followed by the appendix, which dealt with health and safety policies.

The text of the guarantee from FaroeOil's mother company was at the back together with a draught copy of the undertaking required from the Faroese government.

'I suggest Frank and I look at the primary document,' Sámal said. 'Hildegard perhaps you could read the guarantees, they should be straightforward, and Hans and Peggy can concentrate on the technical issues in the appendixes. We made two copies of each, so there are plenty to go around.'

'It's Penny,' my daughter commented.

Sámal handed out the copies, and we all settled down to read the legal texts, Sámal and I retired to the dining room.

I leafed through the thick pile of paper. Most of my legal experience stemmed from my time at the ministry of defence where I had negotiated all sorts of agreements. First, I went to the back of the document to check the jurisdiction clause. The governing laws had a decisive impact on the wording of the text.

European documents were short and to the point, made in accordance with civil law, meaning they abided by a civil code, a concept accredited to Emperor Napoleon. If a dispute arose, the judge could easily read the particular law enacted by parliament, and make his or her verdict accordingly.

In British and American agreements, the document itself was the law. Verdicts were made according to what other judges had ruled in similar cases in the past, interpretations commonly agreed on. Hence, it was called Common Law. The intent was admirable, to make a document which was clear, concise and indisputable. However, I had found this was seldom the case, with common law documents being cumbersome, months-long in the making, with neither party wanting clauses, which were precise. Instead, solicitors chose to create legal ambiguities so they, later on, could use the resulting chaos of words to the advantage of their clients, lining their pockets in the process.

I expected the loan document to be governed by Faroese or US law, the latter because the banks would feel more comfortable with it, although they would then have to enforce a possible US ruling through the Faroese court system. The advantage of Faroese Law was, it would make the security arrangements immediately enforceable. Once a verdict was handed down, the banks could immediately seize the assets of FaroeOil in the event of a default.

Strangely, neither was the case. I let out a groan when I saw 'English Law' and 'London'. Any dispute would therefore not only require US and Faroese lawyers but also British solicitors to do the paperwork and barristers to represent each side in the London courts.

I looked up from the document and asked Sámal,

'Have you seen the dispute clause?'

Sámal almost had tears in his eyes.

'I would never have to work another day in my life if I were chosen to represent FaroeOil. However, that will never happen. Regretfully, they use a Danish firm,' he said.

Okay, so American, British, Faroese, *and* Danish solicitors.

'I feel for you Sámal. But why British law? US or Faroese would have been my guess.'

'The Americans can't trust Faroese law with the government participating as a guarantor. So Danish or US law are the natural choices. London does seem strange. If the bank consortium were international, I could understand it, but since all the banks are American, I too find this surprising.'

I looked at the first section of the document, a typical preamble, a short story, which described who the participants were, the lenders and the borrower, and what the agreement was supposed to achieve.

Next, I checked the warranties, which were statements made by the borrower saying it was indeed a lawfully registered company in the Faroe Islands and the company had full rights to enter into the loan agreement, as did its parent company.

The commercial section set out what the borrower could do with the funds, oil exploration, and could not do, like use the loan proceeds for other activities.

'Sámal, have you read the repayment terms? When they find oil, sixty-five per cent of all proceeds goes to servicing the loan. Minimum amounts are required, sizeable, but in no way horrific. However, what happens if the income is delayed? Then they cannot afford the interest, let alone the repayments.'

'There would be a default, and the guarantors would have to pay,' Sámal said.

Before the final paragraph regarding law and jurisdiction, I found a section, which referred to the bank syndicate providing the loan.

'There is a reference here to an Appendix 8, the banking consortium. But there is no Appendix 8 attached. Sámal is that something we have a copy of? Have you seen it?'

'No, but please remember this is only a draught.'

We had studied the documents for several hours when Sámal suggested we take a break. He pulled from the refrigerator leftovers from his party and retrieved a leg of Skerpikjøt from his outdoor pantry. I made a large pot of tea.

After lunch, everyone retrieved their notes, and we sat down to discuss our findings.

'I don't understand this shit,' Hans said, absent-mindedly picking his nose.

'Harrumph,' Hildy cleared her throat disapprovingly. I was not sure if it was because of his language or his nasal excavations.

Hans continued, 'Appendix 3 shows the correct drilling sites. I know those coordinates by heart. They are good sites, but not the places they have actually drilled so far.'

'Dad, I concur. I told you about that,' Penny commented.

'Hans, you mentioned the Russians showed you a list and forced you to sign it,' I said.

'Yes, it was written in the exact same format. But those coordinates were the actual sites where drillings have taken place, the dry wells.'

'Could I see the one you have?' I asked. He handed me the page, at the bottom, it said 'Approved', and 'Hans

Klerk', but no signature was affixed. I saw, however, a smear of mucus, the Dutchman had left his mark, a sort of signature, I supposed.

'Hans, didn't your CEO tell you of the independent engineer's demands, to try those other sites first?'

'Yes, but that explanation does not fit well with the list you have in your hand. Those are the good coordinates, so something is wrong.'

Sámal turned to Hildy.

'Hildegard. This is perhaps not your area of expertise. I wouldn't expect it, but did you notice anything which needs our attention?'

'Sámal, my darling, I know how to read, I do it all the time.'

Hildy was offended by Sámal's condescending tone, and rightfully so.

'I've been through the Faroese government guarantee, and there is something peculiar. Usually, I would have thought a guarantee for a loan was just that. An assurance that if the borrower does not make timely payments when due, then the guarantor will step up and pay. However, this is not the case in the document you gave me. Can there be some mistake? Is there some other guarantee we should be looking at?'

'What's wrong with it?' Sámal asked, leaning forward.

'If there is a default, the banks don't ask for money,' Hildy replied. 'They don't really ask for anything. Just that the Faroese government respects the loan agreement and promises not to change any laws, which would be detrimental to the rights of the lenders. Is that normal?'

'May I see it?' Sámal asked. He sat reading for a few minutes.

'I have to admit I'm surprised, even happy the government will not have to pay. This is not what they told the Løgting initially, they must have renegotiated it at some point. But if it is true, then the American banks are very poor negotiators.'

I doubted poor negotiators made loans for hundreds of millions of US dollars.

Hildy went over her notes regarding the guarantee from FaroeOil's mother company called SP/F FaroeFour.

'The parent company is required to countersign the loan agreement and agree to the terms,' she said. 'As far as I can see, it makes them an indirect party to the agreement. The four owners of FaroeFour have also pledged their shares in the company to the lenders, and lastly, if FaroeOil defaults, FaroeFour has to step in as borrower but is not required to repay the loan immediately, which I also find curious.'

Sámal seemed even more intrigued.

'Please Hildegard, the document.'

When Sámal had studied the areas she had marked in yellow, he sat back in his chair, hands over his face, concentrating, as Hildy and I watched him. Hans continued to dig for gold, and Penny went to fetch more tea. Finally, Sámal sighed and looked up.

'Frank, with what we've heard, take us through a plausible scenario,' he said.

I was happy to oblige.

'All right, first they put together this bank consortium of American banks. Everything is signed, the first money is paid out, and the exploration begins. If everything goes to plan they find oil and start repaying the loan with sixty-five per cent of their gross revenue.'

'And if they do not find oil?' Sámal asked.

'Well, if none of the drillings shows results, there is no revenue when the first payment falls due. Therefore, FaroeFour steps in and assumes the obligations of the borrower. However, according to their guarantee, they do not need to pay up immediately. Speaking of which, do they have any money? Do we know what assets they have?'

Sámal thought for a moment and then answered,

'As far as I am aware, they have no liquid assets. They have recently acquired some development rights, like for the oil. Except those rights are for the Sumba harbour and two fjords north and south of the valley called Mjoerkadalur, including commercial rights for the Sornfelli mountain.'

Hans looked up, genuinely excited, he seemed to have forgotten all about his nose-picking,

'Those are the areas the Russians asked me about. They wanted to know about the structure of the seabed and the possibilities of expanding harbours and building structures. Sornfelli is the old NATO base built inside the mountain. It can withstand a nuclear strike.'

'Okay,' I said. 'Let's take it slow, one step at a time. Normally FaroeFour would sell their assets to some third person and use the proceeds to repay the loan, but not in this case. Here FaroeFour steps in as the borrower. They cannot repay the loan, so the American banks take over the shares in FaroeFour as well as its assets. They sell the property and get their money back. Does that make sense?'

'It would if those assets were worth anything,' Sámal said. 'Alas, they're not. Not unless they find gold or uranium in the mountain. Building harbours in those fjords is a hopeless venture, very few people live there, and we do not need more fish factories.'

I continued,

'Okay, so where does this leave us? Normally, the government would be forced to step in and pay off the debt. But because of the wording in the government's guarantee, they don't have to. All they need to do is sit back and watch as the Americans assume a lot of worthless assets.'

The room went quiet. I could see everyone was thinking hard. Penny, doing the rounds, pouring tea for each of us in turn, commented,

'If that is the situation, then the banks could continue to look for oil. If they drilled in the right places, the sites Hans recommended, the consortium could do very well for itself.'

Sámal looked at her for a moment considering her words, 'Yes and no, Peggy.'

'Penny.'

'Pardon me, Penny. Banks don't go into the oil business for themselves, it would require more money, like throwing good money after bad. Also, banks can never get more money than they are owed. When the loans are repaid, the shares revert back to the original owners.'

I tried to concentrate, thinking aloud,

'So, according to the scenario, the banks are now holding some worthless shares in FaroeFour. They forgot to get a full guarantee from the government. The banks also hold some worthless development rights the government cannot force them to relinquish and finally no oil was found, which was the bloody point of the exercise from the outset. It's a puzzle, we must be missing a piece or several.'

Hildy asked, 'Sámal, is this the final version of the document, the original?'

'No. It's a draught.'

'Could we bother you to ask for the original appendix on the drillings? Appendix 3, was it? The one they actually used.'

I added, 'And this agreement between the banks, Appendix 8. Can we get a copy of that as well?'

'I could try. The secretariat of the Løgting should have it. I will give them a call,' Sámal said and took out his phone. Before he could punch the numbers, it rang. He listened and then held it to his chest.

'It's Knud. He wants to know what time we are finished. He intends to take you all fishing.'

Penny shook her head, sticking a finger in her mouth, mimicking throwing up. Hans looked apprehensive as well, he shook his head.

I grinned at my wife, 'I believe it's just the two of us, dear. Sámal, if it suits him, please ask Knud to pick us up in ten minutes.'

# 19

It was late afternoon. We clumsily stepped aboard Knud's boat moored not far from where we had met Penny that first afternoon. We were dressed in orange Gore-Tex immersion suits with woollen caps on our heads. Hildy looked fetching with the cap framing her lovely face.

Once she and I were seated at the back, snuggling together and taking in the scenery, Knud untied the mooring lines, entered the one-man pilothouse and backed his boat out into the narrow channel, it ran between lines of other parked vessels. He motored slowly south until he had cleared all the walkways, then he turned to port and motored towards the peninsula, passing his command, the 'Brimil', on our starboard bow.

Looking down, I noticed how clean and transparent the harbour water was, I could see every detail of seaweed and fish at the bottom. There were no oil slicks nor litter in the sea.

Up ahead, the old town and the government buildings, including the prime minister's office, occupied the peninsula, which divided the East Harbour from the West Harbour. The buildings were wooden structures painted black with white door and window frames, their stone foundations were whitewashed, and they had grass turf roofs. Many of the structures must have dated back several hundred years. Some were undoubtedly much older. Neither the Ocean Avenger, the visiting protest group's sleek yacht, nor their trawler, the Nemesis, were at their moorings over by the promenade, below the government buildings.

Once past the stern of the Brimil, Knud spun the wheel hard over and headed towards the harbour mouth and the open waters beyond. The Ocean Avenger came into view, it had moved its moorings to the opposite side of the harbour, over by the EFFO oil terminal where we had seen Hans be abducted. I wondered if the Ocean Avenger was in need of repairs, and whether the adjacent shipyard would offer assistance with the Ocean Lovers being less than popular. The Nemesis was nowhere to be seen.

As we passed the stern of a cruise ship, this one not anchored out in the bay, but moored inside the outer seawall allowing passengers easier access to the town, we left the port behind us, and the sea became choppier. There was not a cloud in the sky.

Facing into the cold wind, I felt the breeze fresh on my face. My cheeks became numb as the fibreglass boat rode high in the water, its bow rising and then crashing into the sea. Whatever floats your boat? I chuckled, remembering my comment to Knud at the party.

I was thankful for the immersion suit. Oydis's suit fitted Hildy perfectly, while Knud's reserve suit was several sizes too large for me. This gave me the opportunity to pull my hands inside the sleeves. I held onto the safety rail with one covered hand and had my other arm wrapped around Hildy's waist.

The further we travelled, the calmer was the sea, the steadier our ride. Nólsoy, the island on the far side of the bay seemed to shield us increasingly from the elements as we crossed the waters.

The Pyotr Velikiy was anchored mid-way between the islands. I continued to be impressed by just how enormous the Russian warship was. As we passed the cruiser's stern, I noticed the trawler, its full name now visible. It was the Ocean Nemesis, not just Nemesis, and it lay tied alongside the battlecruiser, amidships, on the side furthest from shore, out of sight from Tórshavn. A crane lifted a blue barrel down onto the smaller vessel's deck where it joined several others. I pointed it out to Hildy.

Knud beckoned us both to come forward to the tiny pilothouse. Through the open door, he showed us the sonar screen, it displayed a white curve on a dark background.

'That line is the sea floor, fifty metres below us. Those white dots, that's haddock, we will stop here,' Knud said.

He turned off the ignition, and in moments, the constant assault on my senses was replaced by a deep tranquillity as the boat went from a lively, noisy, thing with its bow hammering against the sea, to a dormant floating platform gently rocking on the ocean surface. The silence was complete save for the mechanical clanking noises coming from the Pyotr Velikiy.

'We've no time to waste. We are directly over the fish we saw on the sonar,' Knud said.

He showed us how to clip brightly coloured plastic worms onto great spools of string attached to the railing, a one-kilo weight at the end. I then lowered the weight over the side to the water's surface and let go. The line ran out, the spool spinning ever faster until it suddenly stopped, the lures having reached the bottom.

'Frank, you can start pulling up right away, Hildy, please take the other side,' Knud said.

I took hold of the handle on the spool and began to crank it around slowly, as I felt the weight at the end of the line and little else. After a while, I could feel the line twitching, and suddenly, a couple of metres down in the water, I spotted silver. Two haddock broke the surface each around four pounds. Thrashing bodies, one had an orange plastic worm securely hooked in its mouth, the other, the yellow worm. Knud came over and lifted the seat of the port bench revealing a storage container and then he showed me how to lift the five kilos of fish and weight up into the boat and directly into the tank. With an expert flick of his fingers, Knud withdrew the hooks from the fish's mouths, pulled up the weight and closed the bench.

'Over the side with the hooks. We must hurry, now we know the fish are biting,' he said.

As instructed, I let go of the weight, and it plunged once more into the depths. After a hectic half hour, while I continued to work the line, Knud went to the work area behind the pilothouse. As Hildy, one at a time, passed Knud wriggling haddock from the holding tanks, he gripped them behind the gills and gutted the fish.

After observing Knud clean a few of our catch, Hildy took over, working slower but more meticulous than Knud had done. I knew she must have done it countless times, years before, when out fishing with her father.

Knud took the other line. He and I caught a few more haddock, but nothing compared to the bounty of our initial success, so Knud decided we should try a different location. We pulled up our lines.

'Hildegard, you must take a break, you shouldn't work with the sharp knife when the boat is moving,' Knud said, ever careful. He entered the pilothouse and fired up the engine.

In the twilight, as the sun dipped below the mountains to the west, I noticed crewmen on the deck of the Pyotr Velikiy cast off the mooring lines of the Ocean Nemesis.

A bald man in a tan jacket stood on the deck looking down at the trawler. He shouted some instructions. Across the waters, I could hear the man's tone of voice, but not the words. It was Baldy, Georgi, the Russian diplomat from Sumba. The Ocean Nemesis engaged her engines and pulled away, running alongside the warship, and then it turned to starboard and passed in front of the Russian vessel's bow. I wondered what the blue barrels on the trawler's stern deck contained. Had the environmental group bought something from the Russians? And if so, what and why? Perhaps the Faroese were refusing to sell them provisions.

After about ten minutes, Knud switched off the engine, and this time, total and complete quietude engulfed us. Knud turned on the radio.

'The evening church service is just beginning,' he explained.

With the peaceful sound of organ music, the singing, and the pastor's incomprehensible blessings engulfing me, I continued to fish the calm rolling sea for the next hour or so as darkness fell and the stars came out. I acknowledged to myself my deep respect for this community, which seemed to be in real harmony with its beliefs. Knud enjoying the gifts from his God and, at the same time, paying homage by participating in absentia in the church service.

Inspired by my surroundings, I knelt on the bench, my hands on the fishing line, as I stared down into the abyss. I folded my hands and did something I had not done in years. I prayed. Not to anyone, in particular, it was more a mental wish list. I asked for the awful emptiness, the loneliness I had endured since leaving MI6 to go away. I beseeched the powers that be to help me find some vocation, which could make my life whole again. I asked for someone to be there for my family if one day I could not. Not that I had imminent plans of dying.

Knud called over, interrupting my train of thought, thankfully saving me from dwelling deeper into my melancholy.

'You can pull up your line, Frank. We have what we need.'

Our catch had built up, we must have caught a hundred haddock in total, and I asked Knud what he was going to do with all the fish.

'We will freeze fifteen kilos and use the same amount to make Fiske-frikadeller, you know meatballs, but made of fish. They're very tasty. All the rest goes to older relatives and friends. And of course, about half of what we catch will go to the retirement home. There is nothing the old people enjoy more than fresh fish, it helps them stay young of mind. But first, we must clean the rest.'

Knud switched on the light over the workstation behind the pilothouse. Being out in the middle of the bay, it was an eerie sensation, standing in the cone of bright light surrounded by utter darkness.

I had a go at cleaning a fish, but after a few narrow misses with the tip of the razor-sharp knife, I let Hildy and Knud gut the remainder of our catch, demoting myself to passing the wiggly creatures over and receiving back the fillets, destined for the cold storage filled with crushed ice. During the whole exercise, more and more seagulls appeared as flashes of white, diving out of the night, fighting for the offal Knud threw over the side.

'I save only ten cleaned heads, the cheeks are a bother to prepare, but tasty when I make an effort. The eyes are nice and chewy as well,' Knud said with a mischievous wink.

'You're taking the mickey,' I said, unsure of whether to believe the man or not.

'A mickey?'

'I meant pulling my leg.'

Knud looked at me, a curious look on his face.

'Now, why would I do that?'

'Knud, it's different ways of saying you're making a joke, teasing me.'

'Then why didn't you say so from the beginning?'

The man's logic was irrefutable.

Finally, Knud opened the boat plugs at the stern, and we helped him use buckets of seawater to rinse down the work area and benches, the blood-tainted water drained down the deck and out through the scuppers. When we had washed away all the blood and fish guts, Knud replaced the plugs, and then returned to the pilothouse and started the engine. He doused the work light and turned the boat towards the lights of Tórshavn passing a half mile in front of the Pyotr Velikiy.

A soft breeze was at our backs. We sailed across a calm black sea, disturbed only by the little boat's bow-wave. The surface was so placid, it could have been oil. I commented as such to Hildy as we sat together on the starboard bench, leaning back and enjoying the sight of a million stars. At that moment, I thought 'Life is beautiful', wondering at the same time why I was unable to enjoy it more.

When we neared the harbour entrance, Knud reduced his speed, so we just made headway. The cruise ship near the entrance was still at its moorings, brightly illuminated from rows of gangway lights and from the many cabin windows. I expected it was the cocktail hour, there would be a sense of festivities aboard.

As we entered the harbour, the silence was complete, save for the 'phutt, phutt' of Knud's engine turning over slowly and the faint disco bass coming from afar.

I heard a muffled shout and a splash. A man had sworn, the sound resonated across the open waters. It had come from the direction of the Ocean Avenger on our port bow. There was a shadow of a person standing on the stern of the vessel and a reflection of metal or glass in the waters below. Another shadow climbed up the side, I could just make out the silhouette of a man. He seemed to have a diving tank on his back. Or perhaps it was a woman.

I whispered, despite knowing the pulsating sound of Knud's engine would mask my voice,

'Dear, there is something fishy going on. Look over there, the Ocean Avenger. Do you see it?'

Hildy sat for a moment staring at the vessel. I knew she had the better night vision of the two of us. She whispered back,

'Divers coming up the side, I wonder why they are out this late.'

Surveying the area to the other side of Knud's boat, off our starboard bow I saw the Ocean Nemesis, barrels on her stern, she was back at her old moorings, over by the government buildings and the old town. As we passed midway between the Ocean Nemesis and the stern of the Brimil, I smelled the sharp scent of petrol in the air, made more noticeable because the air on the islands was always so pure.

Curious, I felt in my gut that something needed my attention. There were too many strange things occurring. I disengaged myself from my wife, stood and went forward to the open door of the pilothouse where Knud concentrated on negotiating the lines of parked vessels, as he carefully took the boat in.

'I am sorry for any inconvenience Knud, but Hildy needs the toilets, could we speed it up?'

I went back to sit beside Hildy and told her what I had said.

'Why does it have to be me who needs to go? Why not you?' she asked, annoyed.

'Because, dear, if it were me, he would tell me to stand on the bulwarks and pee over the side.'

The final minutes of our approach gave me time to think. I had an idea of what the blue drums contained, but hoped I was wrong. As Knud expertly slotted his boat into its docking, I looped the stern lines over the mooring posts at the rear and then went past the pilothouse as Knud nudged his boat forward. Clumsily in my immersion suit, I jumped onto the floating pier with the bowline in hand and secured it as well. The boat steady, I handed Hildy up onto the walkway, and without another word to Knud, we turned and shuffled off.

Once on firm ground, we turned right and then right again, as we walked arm in arm along the deserted quay, and past the now-closed sidewalk cafés on our left and the public toilets on our right. I steered Hildy onto the last, most southerly floating pier. I stopped and knelt, looking through a gap between two sailing boats, sensing Hildy behind me, copying my actions.

We could see the Ocean Nemesis, its stern, and along its outward, starboard side. I could see no activity aboard.

We watched for a few moments. Trusting the boat was deserted, I nudged Hildy's arm, and we continued our walk along the promenade. As we approached the trawler, the smell of petrol became heavier. Had it not been for the blue barrels, I would have sworn the vessel had a major fuel leak. No lights showed from within the trawler.

We stopped adjacent to the wheelhouse.

'Dear, do us a favour, wait here. I want to check on something. I'll just be a moment.'

'Okay, Mr Spy,' she whispered back.

I reached across the gap between the pier and the boat's side. A thick rubber lining ran along the hull, acting as a permanent fender. I stepped onto it, tested I had firm purchase and then climbed clumsily over the railing, the immersion suit impeding my movements. I gave silent thanks for my small build, my daily mountain-bike rides in the undulating landscape of Guildford and the workouts Wilson put me through, four times a week. All that stretching, before and after, now paid off.

Sneaking over to the stern of the vessel, the stench of petrol stung my nostrils. There were ten barrels in a circle with a space in the middle. Holding my breath, leaning over the closest barrel, in the shadows, I saw a stainless steel container with a multitude of valves jutting out, a timer with red digital numbers and a black oxygen tank attached to it. The timer showed '29.31'. Then '29.30'.

Electrical wires ran from the timer and between two of the barrels to the starboard scuppers. I looked over the railing. Just below the waterline, there was something strange. With a sinking feeling in my stomach, I knew what we had to do and quickly re-joined Hildy on the quay.

'We need to hurry,' I said.

We jogged back to Knud's boat, as fast as the cumbersome suits would allow. Between breaths, I told my wife what I had seen.

# 20

Knud stood waiting impatiently, he looked relieved when he saw us returning. I stepped aboard.

'Good you are back,' he said. 'I was worried you had abandoned me. I would like your help in getting the catch to my car.'

'Knud, you must listen to me. You are going to have to believe me, this is important. When we entered the harbour, we saw divers go up the side of the Ocean Avenger. This late in the evening, I found it strange. It is too dark to be doing repairs. If they were returning from somewhere, where would that be? The logical place would be the Ocean Nemesis.'

I paused for breath.

'So we went over to check out the trawler. It's piled high with barrels of petrol, and there is a timer. There is also something strange attached to the boat's starboard side, just under the waterline. Maybe a limpet mine. Knud, I was in the army for years, I know what I saw. The Ocean Nemesis is set to blow up in less than half an hour. It could take half of Tórshavn with it.'

I could readily imagine what must be going through the man's mind. Disbelief. Was his wife's cousin's husband deranged? Insane and fantasising?

'Now you pull my legs,' he answered. 'You joke, but I do not think it is funny.'

'Knud, I know it sounds far-fetched, but did you see the barrels on the Nemesis's deck when we sailed in? Moreover, did you smell petrol? If that boat blows up, the fuel will spew all over the Old Town. The town will burn, it's entirely built of wood, hundreds could get injured.'

Knud asked seriously, 'But why would they use divers?'

'They got those barrels from the Russian warship. You must have seen that. The divers must be the Nemesis's crew. After attaching the limpet mine and arming the trigger, they swam over to the Avenger. Afterwards, when someone raises the wreckage, they will find a big hole in the boat, proving an outside force was responsible, blaming the Faroese.'

I could see Knud blink as he came around to my thinking.

'You are right about the barrels. I wondered earlier why the Nemesis took them on board from the warship. We must call the authorities.'

'Knud, we don't have time. We have to act. You are a captain, tell us what to do.'

'We must get the vessel out to sea. If we are wrong, there will be no harm done. Those Ocean people can go out and retrieve her themselves, it will be seen as a prank. But if it does explode, it will do no damage to the town. It is years since I have handled a boat like that, but I shall give it my best try. When I have sailed it out into the bay, I will need you to pick me up. Can you handle my boat?'

'No, but she can,' I said, indicating Hildy standing on the pier. I knew Hildy's dad had passed on his love of the sea to his daughter together with the skills needed to negotiate the elements.

'Knud, you need me to go with you, you might need an extra hand.'

I turned and made my way back up onto the floating walkway.

'Dear, we are going to try and get the trawler out to sea. Will you take Knud's boat and follow us? We'll have to abandon ship at some point. We'll need you to pick us up, but please, don't get too close, just in case.'

'Promise me, darling, promise you'll be careful.'

I had no answer. What we were doing was outright lunacy, but I could see no other option. With a warm kiss and a clumsy embrace for my wife, I followed Knud, as we headed for the trawler. Turning for one last look at my love, I saw Hildy blow me a kiss, then she cast off the mooring line and stepped across the gap to Knud's boat.

We made no pretence of stealth now but ran as fast as our suits would allow us. Reaching the Nemesis, Knud stopped and turned to me.

'Get the mooring lines. I'll try to start the engine.'

He stepped aboard, mounted the steel ladder to the bridge and tried the door to the pilothouse.

'It's not locked. Lucky for us,' Knud said in a hushed voice.

A locked door would have all but defeated our efforts. Our only option would have been to tow the larger vessel out into open waters using Knud's smaller craft, a hopeless and suicidal endeavour.

The red glow of the night-light came on inside the pilot-house. Smelling the petrol, knowing the danger, I whispered a silent prayer as I heard the boat's engine turn over and then start. As the vessel nudged forward, I got the loop off the mooring post and threw the line over the trawler's railing. As Knud reversed the boat, I raced back towards the stern and did the same with the mooring line there.

No sooner had I crawled aboard, amidships, did I hear the engine revs increase, and feel the vessel pull away.

On the bridge, Knud and I discussed tossing some of the drums overboard.

'It's not a good idea,' Knud said. 'It would take the both of us to lift a barrel, and I'm needed here, to steer the boat. I cannot recommend you doing it alone, using the crane, a single spark could mean the death of us both. And besides Frank, I'm not sure you know how to operate it.'

I conceded the man's point.

'But let's see if we can save at least one of the barrels. Get it over the side,' I said. 'It would be a nice touch, allowing the authorities to have some evidence.'

I leant out of the open door and saw Knud's boat trailing us, staying well behind. I willed Hildy to hold her distance. I did not intend to die, but if it happened, I certainly did not want our children to lose both their parents on the same night. At least that is what I told myself. The truth was I could not stand the thought of anything, anything at all, happening to my beloved Hildy.

Looking back towards the peninsula, I could see lights on in two of the larger structures. That would be the government buildings, perhaps the prime minister's office. Were they in a late night session? If the vessel had exploded at its moorings that whole section of town would have been obliterated. Destroyed by a firestorm in mere minutes.

Which got me thinking. Why were the Russians and the Ocean Lovers collaborating in eco-terrorism? The Ocean Lovers' purpose was obvious. They would score a major victory. They had mined their own ship, presumably with a limpet mine of some sort so the Faroese government could be blamed, as ultimately the French intelligence service had been for a similar incident, the Rainbow Warrior scandal in 1985. And the Russians? Whatever their motivation, it must be important enough for them to risk exposure as accomplices.

Enough about who was to blame. I needed to focus on the present. As soon as we exited the harbour, Tórshavn would be safe, but we would not. Could we disarm the bomb? Even if I had the training, I had to assume the timer had an anti-handling device. If I tampered with it, the whole thing was likely to blow up in my face. How long did we have? I went down the side ladder and holding my breath against the fumes, I looked over the blue barrels. '21.11'. I went back to give Knud the good news.

We had been motoring for no more than a few minutes and had just past the Avenger on our right. By now, they must have noticed the Nemesis was underway. However, as I looked over to their sleek craft, I could see no movement, no indication anyone was up and about. I smiled at the thought of them, hiding in the shadows, seeing their bomb-rigged vessel unexplainably making its way out to sea, their plans foiled. A smile, which quickly vanished at the thought of the danger Knud and I were facing.

As we passed the brightly lit cruise ship and sailed through the harbour mouth, I wondered why the passenger vessel was still in port. To my knowledge, cruise liners sailed at night and visited cities or ports during the day. I could see some activity on the wharf, they seemed to be getting underway. I willed them a delayed departure. If the trawler were to blow up now, I figured the explosion could very well destroy the big ship and everyone aboard. If that happened, thankfully I would not be around to see it.

However, we were soon a half mile from the harbour entrance heading southeast. I began to relax a bit, but only a bit, as we got further from Tórshavn and I grew confident, the town was beyond the blast radius of the bomb. Soon we would pass well astern of the Pyotr Velikiy, as we had done earlier that afternoon on our more enjoyable excursion. I crossed my fingers hoping we would make it that far.

Running back, I checked the timer once more, thirteen minutes had gone by since we had commandeered the vessel, we had ten minutes left. I hurried back to the bridge.

'Knud, it's time. We need to abandon ship.'

'We cannot just jump overboard. If we are unlucky, the timer might fail, and the trawler might wreck itself on the shores of Nólsoy across the bay. It might explode and hurt someone. Or it might veer off course and hit the Russian ship. What we must do is gain some more speed, then turn off the motor and let it drift.'

Knud flipped a switch turning on the blinding exterior lights. He spun the wheel to port, away from the Pyotr Velikiy and gave the trawler full throttle for a few minutes. Which seemed to me an eternity as I became ever more anxious to get off the boat. When, according to my calculations, there were seven minutes remaining, Knud switched off the engine, and we scrambled down the ladder and jumped to the deck.

I ran to the stern, Knud at my heals, and together we manhandled one of the cumbersome blue barrels to the port side after I had checked it was not in any way connected to the timer. We heaved it up to the bulwark, it was heavy work, it must have weighed at least ninety kilos.

As I watched the barrel tumble into the bay with a splash, I heard the sound of hissing behind me. Looking back through the gap created by the missing barrel, I saw a fine mist escaping the valves of the metal container. The rank smell of petrol intensified manifold, and in seconds, it was impossible to breathe.

'We have to go,' I coughed.

Instead of retreating to the entry port, we climbed the portside railing and swung our legs over the side. I heard Knud yell something,

'Jump head first!'

I needed no encouragement. I did as Knud instructed without knowing why and dived off the boat. The cold water hit me in the face like a hammer. The buoyancy in my suit stopped my downward thrust through the water, I imagined this was what it felt like, being hit by an airbag. Turning my body, so I faced upwards, as my face broke the surface, a hand grabbed my shoulder.

Shaking the water from my head, rubbing my eyes, I trod water and then watched the brightly lit trawler, now silent, glide away from us under its own momentum. The blue barrel bobbed next to us, petrol fumes clouded around us. Clearly, they did not stem from the barrel, they must have been coming from the stainless steel container with the hissing valves.

'Knud, that barrel could blow. We need to get away from it.'

I began to swim towards the lights of Tórshavn using long calm strokes. The immersion suit made it tough going, but I was eternally thankful for its warmth and buoyancy. My unprotected hands were, however, numb. After some minutes, we stopped to rest. Bobbing in the water, I caught my breath and then asked Knud why he had told me to jump headfirst.

'It's a precaution. If things go wrong, we might be out here for some time. When your face hits the water first, the blood vessels in your body contract, saving the warmth for your internal organs. I wanted to make sure your face got submerged. Otherwise, the heat stays in your arms and legs, which is not where you need it most.'

Luckily, help was on the way, I saw an oncoming light.
'Hildy, over here!' I called.

As she pulled up to us, Knud took command.

'We need to get around to the stern. Hildegard, please turn off the engine. We do not want to get shredded by the propeller.'

Climbing from the sea into a small fishing boat, wearing a heavy immersion suit and waterlogged shoes, was not an easy task. Using the handholds next to the motor, as I pulled with all my strength to lift myself out of the water, Hildy, from above, heaved on the shoulders of my suit and Knud gave me a mighty shove from below.

Once aboard, I got my breathing under control and then bent over the stern. As Hildy had done for me, I grabbed two handfuls of Gore-Tex, and called 'One, two, three!' On 'three' I pulled with all my might as Knud dragged himself up the handholds. I almost strained my back in the process, and I felt a twinge in my left shoulder.

Exhausted, breathing hard, we both sat down, forgetting our surroundings. Hildy had returned to the pilothouse and started the engine.

An explosion erupted, perhaps three hundred metres from us, my heart skipped a beat, or so it felt. A roar, and then a gusher of water shot skywards from the trawler's starboard side as the onboard lights went out. I had expected a much larger eruption, then I realised only the limpet mine had gone off.

I yelled, 'Hildy, get us out of here! Quick!'

The engine revved up as the boat turned hard over and headed directly away from the trawler.

Staring into the darkness, the night sky erupted in an ear-shattering explosion, a fireball ripped through the sky, shooting a hundred metres up and a hundred metres outwards. It remained suspended in mid-air, ever expanding as the wind around us momentarily changed direction, the sphere of fire sucking the oxygen towards it.

Then it began to rain fire.

As the burning substance hit the ocean, it seemed to sputter and dance across the surface, turning the waters into a sea of boiling flames, at first surrounding the sinking trawler, and then spreading outwards as the enormous dripping fireball continued to expand, coming ever closer to us.

Immediately, I recognised what it was and cursed the people who had planned for the explosion to happen within the confines of the harbour. The initial explosion was equivalent to the effects of a fuel-air bomb, a Russian invention. The valves on the stainless-steel container had emitted gasses, which formed a cloud of petrol. When ignited, it created the largest conventional weapon known to man.

As if that were not enough, what followed was napalm. Petrol and soap mixed, an explosive cocktail, the substance the US Air Force used to such devastating effect against the guerrilla forces during the war in Vietnam. As I watched, the breeze from the east pushed the fireball our way. The napalm cloud was a hundred metres away and closing as Hildy gave the boat full throttle. In the sea of fire, a smaller explosion erupted.

'Too bad. I wanted that barrel to survive intact,' I yelled above the roar of the engine, feeling the intense heat against my face, the air hot in my lungs.

'But I'd rather *we* survive,' Knud shouted back, his eyes wide, his face fully lit up by the orange flames.

As the inferno seemed to collapse upon itself, we began to gain distance from the raining fire. Knud staggered forward to the pilothouse to spell Hildy, she came back to be with me. Sitting close, her behind me, her hands around my waist, I stared at the burning sea, still feeling the heat on my cheeks.

'Did you enjoy the fireworks dear?' I asked as she nuzzled her face into my neck. I said it with a bravado I did not feel. In the back of my mind, I imagined the havoc the fireball would have made had the trawler exploded at its moorings. The devastation of the explosion was such that even the Avenger, across the harbour, would have been at risk. Was the size of the blast a miscalculation on the part of the Ocean Lovers? Or were they deemed expendable by someone else, perhaps the Russians? I had no way of knowing.

'Frank darling, thank God we're safe. That was too close for comfort,' my wife said.

Approaching the seawall, I noticed first, people crowding the balconies of the cruise ship, faces lit in orange, they looked out towards the burning sea. On our left, I saw there were shadows on the Ocean Avenger's deck staring out towards the fire.

And, as we entered the harbour, I saw hundreds of people, inhabitants of Tórshavn coming out for a look.

They streamed down from the town and flocked onto the promenade. I wondered if Penny was among them or if she was watching the spectacle from her flat, her view would be magnificent, front row seats.

Knud navigated the boat through the myriad of floating walkways to his mooring, the engine noise once again a 'phutt, phutt'.

'We must hurry,' he said when we had secured the boat, and he had switched off the engine.

'Knud, I think we are out of danger. We can relax now,' I said, despite my hands still trembling.

He treated me to a nervous laugh.

'We did good, ja? But no, you don't understand. The retirement home. They close and lock their doors at ten. If we do not make it by then, I will have fish stinking up my car all night.'

# 21

The previous day, we had agreed to reconvene at Sámal's house at nine o'clock that Tuesday morning to continue our review of the documents. However, as Hildy and I were having breakfast with our host couple, the phone rang.

It was the police.

Rumours of our involvement had spread. Could Knud and his accomplices come down to the station to make a statement as soon as possible? Last evening's events were having international repercussions, and the politicians wanted an explanation.

Knud went into the kitchen and turned on the radio. The usual morning country music program was replaced by a news broadcaster. Hildy gave me a translation,

'The Ocean Lovers' organisation says someone hijacked their boat and sank it out to sea as an act of piracy, because they protested the killing of whales. The Russian foreign minister is calling the incident a failed terrorist attack on the Russian battlecruiser, the Pyotr Velikiy, which is currently visiting the Faroe Islands on a friendship cruise. The Russian high command will meet later today to discuss the aggression, and they will decide whether it should be considered an act of war.'

Knud asked Hildy and me to accompany him upstairs, to the room where they had their television with the satellite connection. Turning on the TV, he scrolled down to the 'RTN' channel, Russian Television Network.

The screen showed a female reporter, who, based on her pronunciation, was clearly a fellow Brit. She read from a script,

'...can confirm that late last night, Faroese government-sponsored terrorists hijacked a research vessel from the peaceful environmental group, the Ocean Lovers, and used the vessel to make a suicide attack on the flagship of the Russian navy, the Pyotr Velikiy. It is an attack which rivals the 9/11 attack in New York, and was foiled at the last moment, due only to the courageous efforts of Vice-Admiral Alexander Ruzhkov and his patriotic crew.'

A slight exaggeration in my opinion, hardly 9/11. Then I mused over the name 'Ruzhkov'. Baldy, the solicitor in the white shirt, had that same last name. Perhaps the name was common in Russia, it must be a coincidence, I decided. After watching the news, we headed off to the police station in Knud's car, which still smelled of our catch from the night before, even though we had reached the retirement home with five minutes to spare.

My shoes were still soggy.

The police station was the three-story modern structure on the coastal road we had passed so often, it was prime real estate with a front row view of the bay. As soon as we entered the building, the desk sergeant asked us to take seats as he called up to advise of our arrival.

A senior police officer entered the vestibule through a secure door, he looked sternly at us one by one, introduced himself as the chief of police and said in heavily accented English,

'Thank you for coming. I must advise you that a special prosecutor is on her way from Copenhagen, she will arrive within the hour. I am also obliged to caution you against saying anything, which later can be used against you if we charge you with a crime and I advise you to get separate lawyers. If you cannot afford one, the court will appoint you legal counsel. Is that understood?'

As I wondered, whether they even had three competent defence lawyers here on the islands, Knud called Sámal.

Hildy whispered jokingly in my ear,

'They think we are some sort of terrorists,' words I later did not find so humorous.

Sámal arrived looking flustered. He asked to speak to us alone, the police officer escorted us to a bland meeting room and left us.

'Sámal. The chief told us to get separate counsel,' I said. 'Presumably, so we can start a blame-game. But if it is all the same to you, could you represent the three of us, at least until a conflict arises?'

'That would be okay. Now, Knud, please describe for me the events of last evening.'

Knud finished his tale stating we had put the trawler adrift with no other intention, than getting it out into the open sea where the explosion would cause no harm. When we had nothing more to add, Sámal left the room for a quarter of an hour, and then returned.

'Before they are allowed to question you, I have demanded they make enquiries regarding two issues. Can EFFO, our oil company, confirm the sale of an unusual amount of petrol, not diesel, to any single customer? Secondly, have any of the hardware stores recently sold unusual amounts of soap or blue barrels? They are making the calls now. All we can do is wait.'

We sat for another fifteen minutes and discussed the catch from the previous evening. The retirement home had taken over a hundred kilos.

'Sámal, in light of your services, perhaps I can pay you with some of the remaining catch,' Knud joked.

At least I hoped it was a joke. I assumed there would be little need for Sámal's representation. The alternative was we were in serious trouble with the risk of having our holiday extended indefinitely, perhaps behind bars, and not the happy hour kind. I also wondered if Sámal's fifty per cent discount applied to the criminal case as well, not only the document review.

Four persons with coffee cups in hand entered the room and found chairs. The chief of police introduced the government's tall, stooping solicitor, whom I dubbed 'Gov'. A thin, stylish young woman with bobbed blond hair was an assistant prosecutor, Anna something, I did not catch her last name. Lastly, taking a seat at the table-end, a young man with long hair and a laptop, the court recorder.

Hildy and I were asked to go out to the waiting room. Twenty minutes later, it was Hildy's turn. Knud took a seat across from me. He was downcast and seemed unhappy after his interrogation. He refused to meet my eye.

Finally, I was invited in. Sitting beside Sámal, I began by describing my military career in the British paratrooper regiment, my stint in the Special Air Service and my training and experience with explosives. Without mentioning my previous MI6 affiliation or delving too much into the fishing, I took them through the events of the evening before. Seated outside, I had decided not to mention the Russian diplomat. Explaining how I recognised him and the events of our first encounter in Sumba would be awkward.

When I finished, the cross-examination began.

No, I had no way of knowing what the scuba divers were up to when they climbed up the side of the Ocean Avenger, only suspicions and no, I did not know for certain, that the underwater object on the hull of the Ocean Nemesis was a mine, at least until it blew up. And yes, I did observe the timer counting down, on several occasions. I could therefore unequivocally state, at the time, it did seem suspicious. The timer and barrels reeking of petrol were, in my opinion, the deciding factors.

As the prosecutor continued to question my motives, I had trouble controlling my temper and concealing my sarcasm, but when she mentioned the word 'Piracy', I got angry.

'Answer me this,' I countered. 'If there was no danger, then why did the trawler explode? Our actions justify themselves. Getting the trawler out of the harbour was our duty.'

'Mr Llewellyn, we will be the judge of that,' the young prosecutor said.

I was winding myself up,

'And only seconds later, after the mine went off, the cloud of vapour erupted. It created the initial fireball, but not the burning sea, that was napalm, no doubt about it. The perpetrators mixed it purposely, it's not something you blend by accident. Why don't you do your job and get some samples from the ocean surface? That will prove what I say.'

Everyone shifted back in their chairs as the recorder typed on furiously. I felt the tension in the room, I intended to keep it there. I leant forward and pointed an accusing finger at the assistant prosecutor,

'If you were in your right mind, you would be thanking us for saving the Old Town and the cruise-liner. That fireball with the raining napalm was several hundred metres across. Thousands could have died, especially with the wind coming from the east. Do you know what napalm does? Do you know how it affects the human body? Once it touches you, it burns and continues to melt into your skin, you cannot get it off. Water only makes it burn more fiercely. Knud saved the town, the ship and the people of Tórshavn, he is a hero, and you should be thanking him, you should show some respect.'

The recorder had stopped typing. He seemed to understand that not all things should be recorded for posterity, especially when his superiors were being admonished. The prosecutor had turned pale, shaken by my onslaught, while Gov tried to hide his smile. The police chief studied his fingernails.

'Frank. Ahem.'

I felt Sámal's restraining hand on my arm. In my wrath, I had forgotten he was there.

'Frank, they're just doing their job. We all believe you, but they need to take the sceptical approach at first. So just bear with them.'

It took a moment for the assistant prosecutor to regain her composure. She asked us to wait outside. I took one of the chairs next to Hildy, and across from Knud. Sámal remained standing.

'In my view, everything has gone fine,' the solicitor said. 'It is the prosecutor's job to ask you the hard questions, there is a lot at stake.'

Before he could continue, the recorder opened the door and beckoned us back in.

'I am very sorry to put you through all this,' Gov said, once we were seated. He seemed to have taken charge.

'It's Miss Jespersen's job to make sure we get all the facts out in the open. This is a very important case. As you know, the Ocean Lovers are claiming this was piracy. The Russians are arguing their ship was the target of a terrorist attack, and the Faroese government is responsible. Why they are so aggressive is a mystery to us.'

He took a sip of water and cleared his throat.

'One thing we do know is, Knud, you saved the old town and countless of lives, you have our gratitude. All three of you have our thanks. I can tell you technicians are taking samples in the bay as we speak, they will no doubt prove your point, Mr Llewellyn, soap was mixed with fuel in the explosion. We have already confirmed the purchase of a significant amount of petrol from EFFO Saturday, pumped into blue barrels. According to invoices, the fuel and the barrels were bought by FaroeOil. The Nemesis's crew was initially observed loading them aboard their boat. Also, an unusual amount of soapsuds was purchased at a hardware store here in Tórshavn. It was paid for with a credit card, which the purser of the Pyotr Velikiy has previously used. We can only surmise the Nemesis took the barrels out to the Russian warship during the weekend to have the soap blended into the petrol. Therefore we must conclude the evidence so far corroborates your story.'

'What are the people at FaroeOil saying?' I asked.

'Their offices seemed to be closed for the day, highly unusual that,' Gov said. 'The CEO is not at his house, apparently, he is in Denmark on business. We will interview him as soon as he returns to the islands.'

'And the Russians?' I asked.

'They have yet to answer our query,' Gov replied.

'So are my clients free to go?' Sámal asked.

'Actually not. The prime minister would like to meet the three of you. Right away, if possible. He will be making an official statement to the media at noon, and he would like the heroes of the hour to be present.'

I mentally kicked myself. I should have seen this coming. I was shy of cameras, had been all my working life and rightly so. There was no way Hildy and I could be seen on television, being paraded in front of the cameras, accepting the gratitude of the nation. I turned to Hildy, gave her a knowing smile, lifted my hand to my mouth and coughed, 'Ill.'

She caught on immediately and slumped in her chair, as she coughed repeatedly, then she sneezed.

'I am afraid we need to get Hildy home to bed, it was cold last night. Also, I have a favour to ask. Hildy's family is awful with this gossiping. If possible, we would like our names to be kept out of this. Of course, if there is a trial at some later date, we would be willing to give evidence. But after all, it was Knud who took charge of the trawler and got it out to sea. And besides, we're British.'

I proclaimed this last statement with authority as if it was a self-evident fact our nationality precluded us from taking any credit. I could see Knud wanted to object, to refute that the effort had been his alone. I gave him an intense stare and continued to shake my head until I saw him relent.

Leaving the police station, Sámal drove Hildy and me back to his house.

Over tea in his downstairs sitting room, Sámal turned on the television, he found the main Faroese station. A nature program was on, he put the sound on mute.

It was again the five of us, or six counting the Labrador puppy snoring on Penny's lap. She had arrived earlier, and I had given her and Hans a brief summary of last night's events, glossing over the scary bits.

'So Mom, Dad, all this stuff about the loan contract we were working on yesterday, should we postpone? After all, you've both been through a lot, you must be exhausted.'

'No, it's alright dear. Let's pick up the discussion from where we left off,' I said.

'Before we do, I have some secret information, but I will trust your discretion,' Sámal said. 'There was a meeting last night in the prime minister's office. The government has been advised by lawyers representing the lenders that an event of default by FaroeOil is, in their opinion, imminent. They have asked the prime minister to reassure the banking consortium that the government will abide by its guarantee.'

'Sámal, as I remember it, we'd come to just such a situation with no oil, the lenders owning the mother company and controlling their worthless assets. Correct?'

I received a nod.

'Now it seems this scenario is unfolding before our very eyes. I think we can conclude there is something rotten in the state of FaroeOil,' I said, proud of my Shakespearian wit.

Hildy asked, 'Sámal, surely this whole business is quite extraordinary. Did the Løgting or its representatives ever actually get an explanation from the banking syndicate as to why they didn't opt for a standard guarantee?'

'Not that I know of,' Sàmal said. 'There are normally no discussions directly between the government and the banks, merely documents passed back and forth between lawyers, with FaroeOil's management as the go-between.'

'This Leif Olson seems a bit dodgy,' I said. 'He was undoubtedly instrumental in Hans's abduction, odds are he's in cahoots with the Russians.'

'Dad, we don't know that,' Penny said.

I continued unperturbed,

'Hans, you advised him of the drilling discrepancies. Did he allow you to present your findings to the board of directors? No. Instead, he fired Penny, after his secretary said you, Hans had quit. Something, which was blatantly false. FaroeOil bought all that petrol and the barrels, and now he is conveniently absent so no one can question him. I forgot to ask, does he have blond hair?'

'I fully agree with your summation, Frank. I never liked the man,' Hans said.

'Well I did, he was always kind,' Penny said. 'He even offered me that new job, and yes, very Nordic.'

'It's starting.' Sámal picked up the remote control and turned up the sound.

The assistant prosecutor stood at a podium looking lovely, her features much softer than in real life. She read from a statement in Danish, which I guessed was quite natural, all Faroese being fluent in that language. Hildy translated,

'She is describing what happened beginning with when Knud first smelled the petrol. He was resolute. He boarded the trawler and found it abandoned. He untied the boat. He sailed it out to sea aiming it away from the Russian warship. The government was in a late night session. He is a hero who saved the city and the politicians.'

'Too bad, he had to save the politicians,' I was about to joke, and then I remembered Sámal was one of them.

The prosecutor paused for a moment.

'Did she mention the divers or the napalm, or how Knud got to shore?' I asked.

'No, not yet,' my wife answered.

Sámal changed the channel over to the Russian television station. They were not covering the press conference. He switched back, as the prosecutor continued with Hildy translating,

'The Ocean Lover management is under investigation since the petrol was on their vessel. The prosecutor's office is of the opinion that having such a vast amount of highly flammable liquid in a public place constitutes a breach of law and they are charging the Ocean Lovers with reckless endangerment and banishing them from the islands, permanently. The commander of the Pyotr Velikiy has refused to be interviewed or give a statement as to whether he thinks his ship was at risk. That's it, darling. No divers, no napalm. No Russian involvement in buying soap or mixing it with petrol.'

'Perhaps they are saving that for later,' I suggested. 'Or they do not want to confront the Russian Federation openly. It would hurt their fishy exports.'

I smiled at my pun but noticed none of the others got the joke. For some reason, my dad-jokes were not getting the appreciation they deserved.

On the screen, the prosecutor stepped away from the microphone, as a man with incredibly broad shoulders, a large head, and dark hair took the podium. Knud stood in the background, his cheeks blushing, he beamed with pride.

'You don't have to translate dear, I get the gist of it,' I said, as I smiled back at my new friend.

Half an hour later, when Sámal dropped Hildy and me off at Knud and Oydis's house, I was surprised to see a crowd spilling out onto the pavement. Not the news media, but friends and family who had come over to congratulate Knud. Many carried black plastic bags. It was approaching one o'clock on a Tuesday, but apparently, it was not too early for a drink.

Sámal parked his car and decided to join us, having first called his wife, asking her to walk over. As he terminated the call, he said to me with a wink,

'She can be the designated driver.'

'What about Hans and Penny?' I asked, hoping to have a few moments with my daughter, alone.

'They didn't want to come.'

When Sámal's wife arrived five minutes later, I saw she had brought her knitting. Hildy turned to me,

'Darling, she has news. Her niece has just announced her pregnancy, I must hear more. Why don't you go join the boys?'

I did, unsure of how much more punishment my liver could take.

# 22

Defence Minister Oleg Ruzhkov sat in the high-backed chair he favoured. His lounge, next door to his office, was decorated in the old fashion style, with thick red carpets, gilt armchairs around a gilt coffee table, and large paintings on the walls depicting battles and famous commanders of the Patriotic War of 1812. The panelling was hand carved, the stucco ceilings magnificent in white.

Stone-faced, he was aghast with what he was hearing. There was a look of determination on the faces of General Almazov, Chief of Staff, and the admiral of the fleet sitting next to him.

Almazov continued,

'The ingenious plan was developed by your nephew, Georgi. We specifically requested his transfer on temporary assignment. This is also why the Pyotr Velikiy, with your son in command, was used. We thought it best to keep everything in the family, so if anything fails, we will know where to place the blame.'

Yes on me, Oleg thought.

'So, is everything going according to plan?' he asked.

The two military men exchanged glances.

'Not exactly,' Almazov replied. 'But we are getting there. Unexpected circumstances forced us to take action. By creating an international incident, we have damaged the Faroese government's relationships with other potential lenders. An opportunity arose, we were able to make the event look like an attack on your son's ship, and thus enhance the pressure on the Faroese authorities. The minister of foreign affairs will submit a letter of protest later today.'

'It was reported that an environmental group owned the destroyed vessel,' Oleg said.

'You are correct, Minister. However, unknown to others, we control the group in question through the GRU. They collect money from naïve American pensioners and then use those same funds to combat the American economy, and create discord between the political factions in their country. We've had them on the islands this past week to make trouble in general and as a precaution. They came in handy.'

'General, Admiral, what about the president?' Oleg asked. 'If your success is imminent, I think we should notify him.'

Almazov shook his head.

'No, we don't want his interference at this stage. He gave us a task, and we are completing it. Better to ask forgiveness than permission, and Ruzhkov, if you value your position, you will agree,' the general said with a wry smile.

'But…,'

'No 'buts', Minister.'

Oleg knew it was not just his position, which was in jeopardy. It was his life and that of his family. He nodded, feeling the sweat under his collar.

Aboard the Russian warship, the vice-admiral stood outside on the wing bridge, enjoying the cold wind in his face, as he looked out over Tórshavn. An ensign approached and handed him the envelope.

'Sir, incoming message.'

The ensign saluted, did an about-face, and walked back inside the ship. The Admiral opened the envelope and read,

> 'Vice Admiral Alexander Feodor Ruzhkov, commanding the pride of the Russian Federation, the Battlecruiser Pyotr Velikiy.
> TOP SECRET
> You are hereby requested and required to proceed immediately to North Sea coordinates 57.585N 4.331E where you shall rendezvous with four Ropucha class Landing Ship Tanks, Aleksandr Shabalin (110) Caesar Kunikov (158) Minsk (127) and Kaliningrad (102). You will take said ships under your command and escort them in convoy on a north by northwest heading. Once your convoy is east of the Orkney Islands, further orders will be forthcoming.
>
> Sent by the Admiral of the Fleet.'

# 23

Wednesday morning, I awoke with a splitting headache, a dry throat and a foul taste in my mouth. I remembered a van showing up with boxes of pizzas, the snaps being passed around, bottles of beer, and sitting with a bunch of men around the table, actually enjoying fat spread on rye bread with Skerpikjøt on top. I groaned at the thought, burped, which brought up the taste of mutton and staggered to the bathroom.

Holding my mouth under the tap for what seemed an eternity, I drank my fill of cold water, then showered, shaved and got dressed. Feeling somewhat refreshed, I went downstairs, Hildy and Oydis were in the kitchen, having tea, knitting and chatting.

'Have we heard from Penny?' I asked.

'She's having coffee with friends this morning,' Hildy replied.

I got myself a mug from the cupboard, poured from the pot and sat down with them. After a first invigorating sip of the hot liquid, I heard Knud come down the stairs. I was glad to see that my host looked far worse than I myself felt. I lifted my cup in salutation of my friend,

'Hero of the hour. Good morning.'

To which Knud grumpily replied,

'There is nothing good about it. And I'm not hung over. I'm allergic.'

'To what?'

'Leather.'

'Leather?'

'Yes, I feel this way every time I wake up with my shoes on.'

As Knud got himself a cup of tea, the landline gave a shrill ring.

'That was Sámal,' Knud said, hanging up. 'He says to turn on the television. Right now. BBC.'

He led the way upstairs, with me following, tea mug in hand.

The BBC 'Breaking News' was about the United Nation's Security Council's condemnation of the Faroe Island government, who was responsible for the destruction of the Ocean Nemesis. The United States led the charge, with several television celebrities all having their say, each a self-proclaimed expert on threatened marine mammals. A hate campaign had been launched in social media against both the Faroese and Danish governments demanding compensation to the families affected and a total ban on the killing of pilot whales.

The day before, a senior member of the United States Senate had proposed a bill, imposing severe financial sanctions on the Faroes. Rushed through Congress in a late night session, it was apparently the first piece of legislation passed unanimously in recent years. I wondered how they had gotten the wording agreed so quickly, and why the need for such haste?

The Danish government had responded by dispatching a salvage vessel to raise the wreckage of the Ocean

Nemesis from the seafloor and promised a full, independent inquiry. The anchorman, not a hair out of place, continued in the Queen's English,

'In related news, Russian owned Eurodea Bank here in London has announced, as the leader of a consortium of banks providing loans to a Faroese oil exploration company, it is in talks with the borrower regarding a possible restructuring of the company's debt. The rescheduling is necessary in light of the borrower's failed attempts to find oil. According to BBC sources, the expected US sanctions could necessitate that Eurodea Bank must take over the loan in its entirety from..., we interrupt with more Breaking News. We've just received a statement from the prime minister's office. Negotiations between Britain and the EU have stalled due to...'

'Eurodea Bank?' I said, 'A Russian bank? Why are they suddenly involved? And they say they control the credit, which means if the loan goes into default, they will control Sumba and the FaroeFour assets. Worthless rights, but still.'

Knud switched over to the Russian network. The attractive anchorwoman told us viewers, also in the Queen's English, that the Russian government demanded a seat on the salvage board, which would undertake the enquiry into the sinking of the Ocean Nemesis.

'...the admiralty states further that our proud Russian navy will not stand by passively as foreign nations show aggressive behaviour towards our peace-loving warships.

'In other news, the Russian ministry of defence has entered into negotiations with the Syrian government regarding the lease of a land area on the Mediterranean coast to be used as a recreational facility for naval personnel, government officials and their families. According to a statement from the ministry, the agreement will strengthen the friendly ties between our two great nations and provide much-needed income for the Syrian people.'

Knud's mobile jingled, he put Sámal on the loudspeaker.

'The Løgting has been called in for an emergency session later this morning. Obviously, everyone is nervous. Some members want things to run their course, let the Russian bank take over the loan, see what good it does them.'

'Sámal, it's Frank here. Something is going on. There was never any mention of a Russian bank in the loan agreement. I think the final pieces of the puzzle are falling into place. May I ask, did you get the original appendixes to the agreement?'

'I've not had time to check,' Sámal replied.

'Can Hildy and I come over? I think we should have a final discussion before the Løgting meeting.'

Oydis gave Hildy and me a lift to Sámal's house and then went shopping. Knud said he wanted to do some house painting. What with his hangover, I assumed it was therapeutic. On the way, in the car, I called Penny's number. She did not pick up.

# 24

'Sámal, so now we know. A Russian bank was the leader of the consortium,' I said, as we convened in Sámal's sitting room. Sámal, Hans, Hildy, and the puppy who lay in my lap, I stroked its soft fur.

Hans was looking a bit tired, I guessed the uncertainty of his future was weighing on his mind, and I realised I was taking for granted that he would just stick around until we had solved this mess.

I continued,

'This is the first we've heard of it. I think Hans once mentioned the Russians might be part of the financing, but you said the Americans won through. Did the parliament know a Russian bank was involved?'

'Frank, this is all new to me,' Sámal replied. 'I had the understanding the loan was arranged and managed by the American bank, IPFC.'

'The signed loan agreement and the appendix on the drilling sites, did you get them? Also, the missing consortium agreement between the syndicate banks, which was not in the draughts. I think those documents are more relevant now than ever.'

'I had to ask again. I just got it by e-mail,' Sámal replied. 'The printer is at work, we shall soon know which banks were involved and for how much.'

I sat thinking aloud,

'This thing about the Russian bank being named as the leader of the consortium, suspicious in a way with the timing. The US sanctions putting pressure on their banks to sell out, Eurodea considering taking over the whole thing. It all seems very fishy to me. I wonder if this is the last part of the equation, but if so, what does it mean?'

'Frank, if you are saying that all this, how do you put it, is connected, I think you are going too far,' Sámal said. 'The chairman of FaroeFour, Eigil Jonasen and the other shareholders are respected businessmen, he is an esteemed member of the Løgting. The documents we have seen so far are very professional. I am sure Eurodea Bank simply sees this as an excellent business opportunity. After all, there is a lot of oil out there.'

'If only someone were looking for it,' Hildy added.

'Hear, hear,' Hans commented, his finger up his nose.

Sámal went to fetch the printouts from upstairs, he returned with a stack of paper. There were copies of the signed loan agreement, each page initialled in the bottom right-hand corner and a copy of 'Appendix 3' together with the bank consortium agreement.

Hildy had made tea for us, we settled down to read.

After only a few minutes, Hans exclaimed,

'Stront!'

'Language,' Hildy said.

Hans kept looking at the sheet of paper in his hands.

'This addendum, the one used in the final edition, it is not like the appendix we saw Monday, and it is not authenticated by me. This explains what the Russians wanted.

That I sign a copy with these coordinates, knowing full well, they are the wrong sites. Now it will look as if I gave the instructions to drill where there is no oil and the loan will, how do you say, be in default, but now because of me.'

I looked up, 'Alright, Hans. Now we know, we'll not let you take the blame. Give us fifteen more minutes.'

After a time, I looked up, rubbed my eyes, careful not to dislodge my contact lenses and said,

'Okay Sámal, give us your thoughts.'

'Yes, well. The primary document is as we have seen. However, the consortium agreement gives the banks a right of first refusal,' Sámal said.

'Which means?' Hildy asked.

'That the banks cannot sell their participation to any third party, they must sell to the other members if the price is the same as they can get in the market. And there is something else. The participation by this Russian bank, they were involved from the outset and with the largest stake, twenty-five per cent.'

Sámal leafed to the relevant section.

'The wording allows any bank, with more than twenty per cent of the loan to veto any consortium decisions. There is one more thing, this IPFC, the syndicate leader. Initially, they took just fifteen per cent of the loan amount, as did four other American banks. That's very unusual. The syndicate leader always takes the largest amount.'

'So Eurodea, with its veto-power must have been the actual leader from the outset,' I said. 'That accounts for jurisdiction being London and English law instead of US. What do you think Sámal?'

Everything was finally coming together for me. Drillings in the wrong places, the loan in default, the Russians acquiring the assets. The murder of the CEO, dubious Leif Olsen taking his place. Yes, I was sure, but what could I prove? What hard evidence did I have to convince Sámal and the parliament? Not much.

'Sámal, to me it looks like FaroeOil colluded with Eurodea Bank from the outset. You say the owners are respectable businessmen. But what about this Olsen fellow, he's new, he got the job only after the murder of his predecessor. He must have played some part in Hans's abduction. And the petrol used in the Nemesis attack came by way of FaroeOil.'

'I agree, I never liked the man,' Hans added.

'Frank, are you saying the CEO designed a scheme to cause a default, expecting Eurodea to take over the loan in its entirety? That they planned this from the beginning? That is a serious allegation.'

'Sámal, do we agree Eurodea will legally gain control of the rights to the Sumba harbour facilities, the rights to the former NATO installations and the development rights to the fjords? According to you, the Løgting has given its guarantee not to infringe on those rights. The Russian bank can do whatever they want, and your government can legally do nothing to stop them. Do we agree this is where we are headed?'

'And do what? How would they make money on some useless development rights?' Sámal asked.

'Lease them to the Russian navy, like the Syrian deal RTN mentioned on their news this morning,' I said.

'Once again Frank, I think you are making too many assumptions. Why would anyone want a holiday resort on the Faroe Islands? The Mediterranean with the sunshine I can understand, but here? Although if it were the case, I'm sure we could use the tourism.'

'But what if it were proper naval installations?'

'That is far-fetched. We would never allow naval bases,' Sámal said.

'But can you stop them? You gave a guarantee.'

Hildy cleared her throat, 'Sámal, my darling, remember Hans's abduction, they used the warship, they interrogated him about the geological features of precisely those areas you say the banks have as security. The Russian navy. Surely this substantiates Frank's argument.'

'That's right,' I said. 'Thanks for pointing that out, dear. Sámal, you need to think this thing through with your friends in the parliament. Will the chairman of FaroeFour be at the Løgting meeting?'

'No, he has a personal interest in this case and is therefore excluded from participating.'

'Then perhaps Hildy and I should go pay him a visit and find out how much of all this the board of directors knew. Sámal, you mentioned his name. Eigil Jonasen? Where does he live?'

'In Klaksvík. He should be at home. During a Løgting session about a member's business, people normally leave the islands and go to Paris or Copenhagen, so they are recused from the proceedings. However, since this is an emergency session, the chairman has stayed on the islands and in telephone contact in case we need him. It said so in our official summons. But Frank, you can't go up there.'

'Why not?'

'Because this is official Faroese business. You can't meddle.'

'But Sámal, he could have vital information.'

'And we shall find out in due course, but this is none of your concern. Actually, it never was.'

Annoyed at his unfair remarks, I chose not to comment, not to commit but simply nodded. I refused to argue the matter of whether we had a vested interest after all we'd been through, and decided to change the subject.

'Then, one last question, Sámal. Are you still okay with putting Hans up? Hans, are you all right staying here for a while with Sámal? The reason I ask is, we need to consider your safety. Somehow I think you, Hans, may be the key to all this. Only you can prove someone deliberately orchestrated the bankruptcy.'

'I think the arrangements are satisfactory for the time being, he's safe here,' Sámal said. 'However, Hans, your whereabouts cannot remain hidden indefinitely. We might need you to give evidence at the Løgting. If you do, we will have to reassess the situation.'

With that, Hildy and I bade the men and the puppy farewell and walked back to Knud and Oydis's house, from one housing enclave to the next, passing a pond with a pair of white ducks and four waddling offspring.

'Dear, I'd love to visit Klaksvík again, perhaps we could stay the night,' I said, as we approached our lodgings.

'Frank, you promised Sámal we wouldn't.'

'I said nothing of the kind, I merely nodded, hardly a promise. But even so, it doesn't prohibit us from sightseeing. If we bump into the man by accident, so be it.'

A half hour later, with our necessities packed in my rolling suitcase, and a hotel booked for the night, I followed Hildy down the hill to the number '3' stop. When the bus arrived, I took out my wallet.

'No, darling. All the local buses are free.'

I tried Penny's number again, it went straight to voicemail.

'Dear, I've been phoning Penny on and off all morning, she doesn't pick up.'

'It's not the first time. I should think our daughter has the right to some privacy, perhaps she has a boyfriend.'

Hildy knew how to needle me. Her comment did nothing to alleviate my concern for my daughter but merely focused it. A boyfriend? Casual or committed? Faroese, like her grandfather? Worthy of her? Or had she spoken of the family fortunes, of Hildy's riches? Probably some freeloader, someone I would need to send packing. However, that would make Penny mad at me. What to do? Oh, the trials and tribulations of having a daughter.

I let out a deep sigh.

Arriving at the main terminal, we debarked, our bus to Klaksvík stood waiting. I stored my suitcase in the bus's baggage compartment and then climbed aboard. My smiling wife had taken seats at the back, the bus was half-empty. I took the seat next to her.

She wore tightfitting black jeans, a brown knit Faroese sweater with silver buttons in a line on the left shoulder, and her light brown Timberlands. Very sporty, very attractive, I looked forward to our stay at the hotel. Finally, we would get that intimacy I'd been waiting for.

# 25

Leaving Tórshavn behind us, the bus rounded the point of Hvítanes. The coastal highway followed the contours of the mountain. Sitting on the right side of the bus, Hildy next to me, I could see beyond the guardrail the green slopes dive into the sea. Further out, between the islands of Nólsoy and Eysturoy, the open waters stretched to the horizon. The skies were clear with only the occasional puff of cloud.

'This is the Kaldbakfjørð,' Hildy whispered, ten minutes into our journey. 'The more southerly of the two fjords where FaroeFour has land rights.'

I looked with keen interest at the surrounding terrain. Steep mountains protected the narrow bay, the rocky beach was half the size of a rugby pitch. On the opposite side of the fjord was a cluster of houses down by the sea, the township of Kaldbak according to Hildy.

A perfect place for a naval base. Deepwater surrounded by high mountains. The island of Eysturoy to the north would offer protection against low-flying anti-ship missiles, which could rise above the land but would have only milliseconds to drop down and acquire their targets. With a few well-placed surface-to-air missile launchers and some close-defence Gatling guns, the fjord would prove an impregnable fortress against anything but a nuclear strike, something the NATO allies would never contemplate with Tórshavn situated close by.

As we rounded the fjord, the road rose and entered a broad well-lit two-lane tunnel, three kilometres long, the sign said. In the event of a conflict, it would be a perfect bunker in which to store weapons and personnel if the Russians could seal off the entrances.

As we once again came out into the sunshine, Hildy whispered, 'And this is Kollafjørð, the other site. The one to the north-west.'

Over to our right, next to a cluster of houses, a concrete quay jutted out into the waters. A small walled harbour was further up the coast. On the opposite side of the fjord were five or six warehouses on a concrete jetty. If the Russian Navy set up base there, little infrastructure was needed, some security fencing and the place was fit for purpose.

Originating inland, a stream bled onto a sandy beach at the nook of the fjord, a perfect place for landing vehicles and men using amphibious landing ships. This place was even better suited as a naval port than 'Kaldbak'. The mouth was better protected by the mountains of Eysturoy directly across the waters, six or seven hundred metres tall, and because ships would need to take a sharp left-hand turn to enter the anchorage, attack from surface vessels or submarines would be impossible.

'The entrance to the old NATO bunker is up there,' Hildy said, interrupting my thoughts. 'Up that highway. It leads to the by-road which goes straight into the mountain.'

'Have you been there?' I asked curiously.

'Don't you remember? The young man, my third cousin on my grandmother's side? He took us up there. We were so frightened, he drove so recklessly.'

Thinking back, remembering the facility, I could readily imagine it as a formidable base for the Russians and a major concern for NATO.

'The bunker, Hans said it was abandoned,' I said.

'They use it as a prison, but I have no idea how that works. Perhaps there are buildings outside. I can't imagine anyone keeping prisoners inside the mountain,' Hildy replied.

Coming around the fjord, at a T-junction, the bus driver turned right and drove past the abandoned warehouses giving me a close-up view from the other side. Several of the structures appeared to be cold storage units. The metal-sided warehouses, the administration building and the concrete wharf made the port perfect for provisioning deep-keeled warships.

We drove past more houses, more than I initially had estimated, before coming to Kollafjørður, the town proper, with its walled harbour and a dozen fishing boats. Would the civilians be a problem for the Russians? On the contrary, there would be jobs for the locals, and the added income would be a Godsend for the surrounding towns and villages. The more I thought about it, the more I convinced myself, the Russians were coming. They had not gone to all this trouble for nothing.

With Kollafjørð behind us, we followed the highway, which snaked along the green mountainsides, in and out of fjords, over bridges and through tunnels, from one island to the next. During our trip so far, besides occasionally mentioning to me the names of towns and fjords, Hildy sat knitting. From time to time, she looked up to take in the view.

I knew I saw things in a different light than my dear wife. I was evaluating the lay of the land, defensive positions and avenues of attack.

She, on the other hand, saw the land with love in her heart. It was the land of her father and her ancestors. The land of the old Vikings and her modern-day, Christian, down-to-earth, and living-off-the-land people. Hildy would be thinking of her father and missing him. She had often spoken of how, when she was young, he had taken her to the islands every summer. Mobiles did not exist then. Instead, her father would call work from a landline, but only once a day. Otherwise, he would enjoy the tranquillity, the nature, being in his daughter's company, and visiting relatives. Hildy's mother had never seen the charm.

I admitted to myself, I missed my father-in-law, regardless of his gruff attitude towards me and I realised he must have been terribly lonely after his wife left to live in Denmark. He never did lose his devotion to Hildy's mother and never remarried. Lady friends from time to time, yes, but they could never compete with his love for his estranged wife or the software company he founded.

Her father had worked so hard to make it succeed and then sold off his life's achievement in the mid-1990s, just before the IT bubble burst.

Strangely, he did not move back to the islands. Inst[ead,] using a fraction of his wealth, Hildy's father had bou[ght] the big house on the hill in Guildford, not because [he] needed it, but because he could. He took up golf and [got] me interested as well, but his heart was clearly not i[n it.] Without daily challenges, bored, he once said he saw [no] reason to get up in the mornings. But what happened n[ext] no one saw coming.

He had a stroke.

I asked myself, had it been worth it? The answer [was] probably not. Living in England, working ninety-h[our] weeks, missing his wife, instead of enjoying himself on [the] islands, savouring the scenery, his people, and his cult[ure,] the way of life he yearned for whenever he was away f[rom] it. As I continued to stare out the window, my eyes we[lled] up, feeling pity. I realised it was not for Hildy's father [who] was dead.

No, it was pity for me.

Because I was lonely and felt irrelevant. As if my [life] no longer had meaning. But why? I knew the answer. [Like] many men, I had let my identity merge with my job [for] way too long, and I had spent too much time away f[rom] home, and from my family. It was Hildy, who had fo[rged] that unique bond with the children, which I felt in m[any] ways, excluded me. Simply because I came home late [dur]ing weekdays and was often distant during the weeke[nds] thinking about work.

I'd fallen into the same trap as Hildy's father, let[ting] a fleeting thing like my occupation take the place of v[

really mattered. My soul, my happiness and my love for my family. One day it would be my turn. I would leave behind my wonderful children from whom I seldom heard, and my loving, intelligent wife, who made me so proud. All that I would lose, and they would never know how much I loved them, how much I regretted having been distant all those years.

But perhaps now I was getting a second chance. If I could just concentrate on something else, turn my attention to something more positive, something completely different. The joy of living, of being with my loved ones, that's what I needed to do, that was the only thing that truly mattered. Yes, that is what I would do, and bugger to all the rest. With a deep sigh and sense of peace in my heart, having made my decision, I reached for my handkerchief, dried my eyes and blew my nose, hoping Hildy had not noticed my melancholy.

I looked over and saw to my amazement the progress she had made on the little sweater, green, we had no idea whether Sophie expected a boy or a girl.

Despite her busy hands, and the blur of the knitting needles Hildy also appeared to have been deep in thought. When she looked up, blinked and gazed out the window, I asked if she was all right.

'I'm fine darling. Thinking of my father, how he would have wanted to be here with us.'

Two souls, one mind. Well almost.

'Hildy dear, I was just thinking. Perhaps we shouldn't visit the chairman, I think we've done enough. We'll see

the town, go for a long walk and then have a good din
Leave all this mess for Sámal to sort out. What do
think?'

As the bus exited the tunnel, the one, which plun
deep under the sea floor and then resurfaced on the isl
of Borðoy, I saw to our right brilliant sunshine, which 1
rored my heart, my decision made, the clear skies exto
ing as far as I could see.

I looked to our left and saw our final destination, (
nous, overcast, in the dark shadows of the mountains.

# 26

The township of Klaksvík seemed a dismal place. U-shaped, it surrounded a harbour on three sides and rested in a silent damp afternoon gloom. The place seemed a ghost town, more or less deserted except for a small ferry that entered the waters at the far end of the inlet and the occasional car that passed by on the main road, which hugged the docks. Up towards the left, a dominating white structure stood high among the houses with a vertical sign stating 'HOTEL'.

Another large structure was the modern building standing on land that protruded into the middle of the harbour, which Hildy explained was the retirement home. With balconies and panoramic windows, the harbour's activity provided the elders with viewing entertainment around the clock. This seemed to me a splendid idea. Instead of hiding the old people away in some far-off secluded place, the retirees could continue to feel part of the community, however bleak. Indeed, they were at the very heart of it, geographically speaking.

As I set off for the hotel, the suitcase wheels rumbling over the wet asphalt behind me, Hildy headed for the tourist bureau. She wanted to get a map of the area and a brochure. She would catch up, she said. I took my time, and

strolled up the high street, passing a café, a white woo
church elevated above the main road, a sporting go
store, a warehouse-like building housing the natio
brewery, Føroya Bjór, a kiosk, a pizza place, a restaura
hair salon and a knitting shop.

Being the second largest town on the islands, I thou
this a poor showing indeed, not that I needed anyth
Except for a place to eat dinner, the restaurant served st
As I came adjacent to the retirement home, Hildy ca
up with me. We turned left and climbed a steep alley
arriving minutes later at the rear entrance of our lodgi

Hildy pointed up to our right.

'The chairman lives up there.'

'Yes, dear, but we're not going to visit him, now
we? We agreed. Let's check in, put the suitcase in the ro
and then go for a walk.'

At the dimly lit reception desk, Hildy rang the bel
the counter and received a key from a sweet, welcon
woman. We had a room on the third floor the recepti
ist said, at the top, and no, they had no elevator. As H
set off, ascending the stairs at a steady pace, I follow
lugging the suitcase, thankful Hildy had decided to b
extra clothes for one day only.

'You could wait for me, you know. You don't hav
go up like a mountain goat,' I called up the stairwell.

'There are no goats on the Faroes. Just sheep,'
called back from the floor above.

When I finally arrived on our floor, heaving for a
found Hildy had unlocked the room and thrown open

doors. Doors in the plural, one opened out to the hallway, the other into the chamber, providing the soundproofing we hopefully would require later in the evening. Hildy had drawn back the curtains wanting to surprise me, and surprise me, she did.

I stood taking in the view. The town looked quaint and spectacular at the same time. On the opposite side of the harbour, there were uneven rows of houses in a riot of colours, windows lit, and streetlamps piercing the premature dusk. Beyond the dwellings, the emerald mountainside disappeared high into the low-lying clouds, and below was the blue-green of the harbour waters. It was breathtaking. It looked like a perfectly executed miniature village. Directly opposite, the tiny ferry was preparing to embark tiny cars from a waiting queue.

As Hildy freshened up in the bathroom, I turned on the television, a forty-two inch flat screen, which seemed much too large for our comfortable room. Using the remote, I discovered there were twelve channels in all. The last three were American gospel stations with preachers grandstanding and choirs singing. Never my kind of religion, although entertaining enough.

As I turned back to channel one, one of the Faroese stations, I saw the prime minister sitting at a desk, and reading from a script.

'Frank, please turn up the sound,' Hildy called through the open bathroom door. I complied.

A moment later, she swept into the room and sat down on the bed next to me. She began to translate,

'It seems Eurodea Bank has received a verdic London. It intends to seize the assets of FaroeFour FaroeOil because the companies are in default of t obligations. The Løgting is presently taking a recess f their meeting regarding the FaroeOil situation. They l requested a review from their solicitors. Sámal has b appointed as head of the legal team. The Løgting reconvene later this evening where a special witness, chief engineer of FaroeOil will give evidence. That wc be Hans.'

'At least things are moving along,' I said.

'Also, the prime minister's office received a commu qué from the Russian government by way of the Rus consulate in Tórshavn. The Russian Federation is wil to overlook the attempted attack on its warship and v peacefully with the Faroese government in develop better trade relations. That's it.'

I went into the bathroom to get away from the vc on the telly and dialled Sámal's number, he picked immediately.

'Frank, I haven't much time. What can I do for yo

'Sámal, I wanted to congratulate you on your appc ment, we heard it on the news. I take it, you won't be ing Hildy from now on. Surely the government shoul paying you.'

'Agreed Frank, I will send my invoice for billable h in a few days. If that is all, I must be going.'

'One more thing, Sámal, just a thought. If from outset, FaroeOil and the banks were colluding to defi everyone, could the case be made that the government gave its guarantee under false pretences and that according to international law the promise is therefore void? This way, you do not rescind your assurances or go back on your word, you simply nullify it.'

A long silence ensued.

'Frank, I'm not sure how to put this. The thinking here is if we voluntarily rent the areas to the Russians, it will provide income and jobs. And we will not make them angry.'

'Sámal, you can't mean that.'

'It is up to the Løgting and, to put it bluntly, none of your business.'

'Sámal, they tried to destroy Tórshavn.'

'That was the Ocean Lovers. We cannot definitively prove the Russians were knowingly involved, and besides, in the future, if we work with them, we should be safe from attacks. But again, this is none of your business.'

'We helped save the town, and Hildy and I rescued Hans. I think we have a right to be involved.'

'I'm sorry Frank, no you don't. Knud sailed the boat out to sea, and you merely picked up Hans after he escaped on his own accord. You're here on holiday, so enjoy it. Now, I must go, we have a meeting. And then it will be dinner time, the family, you know how it is.'

With that, Sámal rang off.

I sat on the toilet lid, completely devastated. Yes, on the bus, I had decided to put family first and not visit the chairman, but I had never imagined the Faroese government simply caving in to the Russian dema[nd]. And then, being told to butt out and that I had not c[on]tributed? Whoever said life was fair?

I sat for a while, deeply disappointed. Finally, wi[th a] sigh, I rose and looked in the mirror, feeling utterly help[less]. There was only one thing for it, I needed Hildy's advic[e.]

'Have you thought of asking for help?' she asked, on[ce I] had told her of my conversation with Sámal. 'If you w[ant] I could give Catherine a call.'

No, I did not want Hildy calling C, and I refused to [ask] for help from the people who had fired me. Besides, [if I] did, I could well imagine Michaels, director of operati[ons,] saying, 'Thanks for the tip, mate, we'll take it from he[re.]'

On the other hand, according to Sámal, I was ou[t of] it anyway. I might as well make the call. Returning to [the] bathroom, I dialled the number I remembered so [well.] The young secretary, Hanna something, picked up on [the] third ring. Michaels was away on holiday. Anti-climax.

I thought for a moment. Was I overreacting? W[ould] she be interested in hearing what I had to say? Would [she] even believe me? Worst-case scenario, she would think [I'm] bonkers and fob me off, I decided to risk it.

'Could you put me through to the director?' I aske[d.]
'I can put you through to her secretary, Mr Llewel[lyn.]'
'Alright, luv.'

A few moments later, I heard the voice of a young man.

'Just putting you through, sir.'

Thankfully, C seemed happy to take my call.

'Frank, it's good to hear from you. Are you enjoying retirement?'

'Ma'am, I don't want to intrude. I know you must be busy, but Hildy and I are on holiday in the Faroe Islands.'

'I hear the food is delicious.'

'You jest, but you've no idea until you've tried it. Especially the pilot whale...'

'Don't get me started,' C hissed.

'...but also the fermented cod and the lamb spare-ribs are exquisite. However, that is not why I'm calling. It's a more serious matter. I know you must be following the events up here in the north, but there are one or two things I think you should know.'

I explained about the FaroeOil loan and the dry drillings. About the Russian bank's involvement and about the Faroese government considering working with the Russians.

'Oh my, Frank, you have been busy, I thought you said you were on holiday. However, it is fortuitous, you calling just now. Yes, we are following the events, very closely indeed, but there seems little we can do under international law. And I doubt we are prepared to use our military to stop them if the Russians have an agreement with the Faroese government.'

'I was just thinking, perhaps this might work...,' I laid out my plan. It took a few minutes.

'Alright, Frank. I'll think about it. Please keep m[e] the know, feel free to call if you learn anything more. [And] give my regards to Hildy.'

C rang off.

'How did it go,' Hildy asked when I re-entered [the] room.

'I talked to C, Michaels was away. She did not com[mit] to any particular course of action. Indeed she was not s[ure] they could do anything. 'I'll think about it,' was all [she] said. Not exactly a call to arms.'

I sat down on the bed next to my wife, thorou[ghly] deflated, feeling redundant. Sámal would do his thin[g, C] would handle it from her side, there was nothing more [for] me to do.

'Frank darling, I don't like this thing about coope[rat]ing with the Russians. I think we need to get up to [the] chairman's house as soon as possible and have a chat [with] him, find out if we can stop this.'

'Dear, it's finished, I'm done.'

'No, you're not. What harm can it do? Put your sh[oes] on,' Hildy said, as she switched off the television and [rose] from the bed to put on her boots.

Reluctantly, I did as instructed and then took [the] Ruger from its box in my suitcase, released the magaz[ine,] checked the ammunition, and then shoved the clip ho[me.] The pistol went into my jacket pocket.

Hildy had been watching, a sceptical frown on her f[ace.]

'What?'

'Frank, the chairman is old, he's hardly someone to put up a fight. I thought we agreed C's gift would stay hidden at Knud and Øydis's place.'

'I don't know, dear, but better safe than sorry.'

'Alright, whatever makes you happy. Just don't get arrested. And darling, please don't shoot anyone.'

Hildy took two white chopsticks from her toilet bag and fixed her bun. When we both had sweaters and jackets on, we left the hotel and headed up the hill, aiming for the chairman's house.

# 27

The fashionable middle-aged prime minister sat at the c[entre] of the long table with the unlit fireplace at her back. N[ext] to her sat the foreign secretary, C's boss, tall, grey, lo[ok]ing tired, he'd been to meetings in Brussels the day bef[ore]. Directly across from C was the defence minister, a bal[d] man with a paunch and intelligent eyes behind spectacl[es].

Dressed in her customary black, today accessorised [with] a white blouse and black buttons, C could smell the ingra[ined] sweat from the man sitting next to her, Britain's chief of defence staff. His uniform needed a good dry-cleaning, [she] thought. Furthest down sat the first sea lord in his magi[nifi]cent blue uniform with bullion shoulder boards and four [gold] stripes on his cuff, one thick at the bottom and three abov[e]. [She] wondered, not for the first time, how the navy always seem[ed] to upstage the other services when it came to bling.

She was glad the prime minister had not called a [full-]fledged COBRA meeting. Obviously, the PM wa[nted] to avoid the lengthy squabbling that the larger assem[bly] invariably gave rise to, with everyone wanting to voic[e an] opinion for the record.

'I am afraid I do not understand,' the defence mi[nis]ter said. 'How on earth is the killing of some whale[s by] that barbaric little island nation a concern of Her Maje[sty's] government, just because they blew some hole in the side of a boat belonging to an environmental group? Now you want to involve us. Do you want us to invade the Faroes as we did during the war? I am not sure where all this is taking us, General.'

The PM and the foreign secretary sat back in their chairs smiling, they had apparently chosen the defence minister as their attack dog.

'Minister, with all due respect, we think the issue is a bit more complicated,' the chief of staff countered. 'We have come to believe the Russian government, acting in league with a Russian bank based here in London, underhandedly, but possibly quite legally, has acquired rights to build naval bases on the Faroe Islands.'

The general paused to sip his coffee and then continued, addressing the PM directly.

'According to our intelligence, Ma'am, the Russians have plans for three new battle groups in the western hemisphere, each with a battlecruiser and an aircraft carrier at its nucleus. It is our assessment that the planned build-up in Russian naval power will only take place if the Russians can find suitable ice-free harbours other than Kaliningrad in the Baltic. A base on the Faroes could have decisive strategic importance, a fleet based there would be able to prevent the United States from reinforcing Europe in the event of a Russian attack on the eastern front.'

'How do we know, General, what the Russians intend and whether they have these legal rights to execute their plans?' the attack dog asked.

'MI6 has a man in-country, he confirms the pictur[e] we see it,' the general replied.

The three politicians bristled.

The foreign secretary spoke, 'C, correct me if I [am] wrong, but I do not recall any briefing or oversight c[om]mittee approval of a HUMINT operation on the Far[oes.] Am I mistaken?'

The room went quiet at the minister's referenc[e to] human intelligence. Several debacles in recent years, [not] least in connection with the Syria investigations, had [led] the politicians to refuse the use of spies on the grou[nd,] choosing in most instances to rely on the military's e[lec]tronic surveillance capabilities instead.

C replied, keeping her voice warm and assured. [She] intentionally avoided mentioning Frank's name sinc[e it] was he, the ministers sitting across from her had ord[ered] fired.

'We do not have agents on the ground per se. Howe[ver,] a former employee of Six, a retiree, a man who ca[n be] trusted, was visiting Tórshavn with his wife. It is a sm[all,] close-knit community, and coincidently his daug[hter] works for the Faroese oil-exploration company at the c[en]tre of this controversy. He has given us a heads up of v[hat] the Russians are planning. Six has therefore suggeste[d to] the Admiralty and the chief of staff that we take cer[tain] pre-emptive and non-provocative steps, so we do not [get] caught flat-footed.'

The defence minister looked at them, an expressio[n of] disbelief on his face.

'So you do not have agents in place. You have some old geezer who misses the action and who might be overreacting, perhaps making things up. I do not see why we are having this conversation. Not unless you have something substantial to present to us.'

The PM seemed to have heard enough of the bickering. She cleared her throat and leant forward.

'What is it you suggest, General?'

'Well, Ma'am, during the past week, the Russian battlecruiser, the Pyotr Velikiy, has been a frequent, if not a permanent visitor to the islands. The Danes observed a convoy of four landing-ship-tank assault craft, or commonly referred to as LSTs, heading through the Oresund in the early hours of this morning. Overflight photos from the Danish air force show they are heavily laden. The Pyotr Velikiy has suddenly upped anchor and left the islands. She is now on course to intercept and perhaps escort the LSTs, although their destination is unconfirmed. The Danes have sortied their command vessel, the Absalon, she is shadowing the LSTs as we speak. In light of these events, we feel that a certain naval presence of our own is warranted. Our aim would be to deter any conflict, should the Russians approach the islands.'

'But you cannot confirm the Faroes is their destination.'

'Not at this time, Ma'am,' the chief of staff answered. 'But as a precaution, we would like to order south our submarine, HMS Astute, which is presently in the Denmark Strait. Artful, her sister boat is already in the area on a training mission. The Americans are offering the USS Illinois,

a Virginia class nuclear attack submarine. We would
like to dispatch HMS Dauntless from Portsmouth wit[h]
due haste. She is about to sortie for a tour of the S[o]
Pacific. Being a destroyer, she is the only major Br[i]
surface vessel at the ready and in the vicinity. We w[o]
position her south of the Faroe Islands, just off the coa[s]
Scotland. The Winston Churchill will participate…'

The defence minister interrupted full of suspicion,

'Winston Churchill? I do not recall seeing her on
navy list. Isn't she some sort of passenger-vessel?'

The admiral spoke for the first time,

'No, Minister, it's the USS Winston S Churchill, on[e]
the Yank's Arleigh Burke-class destroyers. The Chur[c]
is on joint exercises with the Astute and the Illinois. P[r]
Minister, we are merely moving the submarines' trai[n]
area to the southeast, at least that is our cover story.
Churchill will head down and place herself south of
islands.'

'So you are asking for my permission to move the
ignated exercise area of one of our submarines and to [have]
one of our guided missile destroyers divert from Plymo[uth].
I fail to see the need for my consent.'

'Prime Minister. As the chief of the defence staff, I
it is my duty to apprise you of the possible scenarios. V[ith]
the Russian's recent sabre rattling, we believe the m[atter]
requires our utmost attention. And there *is* one more th[ing]

The politicians leant forward in their chairs. C k[new]
from experience that the general usually kept the n[ost]
sensitive to last.

'It is possible that the Russians might make a land grab of the areas they feel entitled to. We have therefore suggested to the Danes, merely as a precaution, that we in the coming days undertake a joint exercise on the Faroes between their Navy Seals and our paratroopers. Our participation would be one reinforced company and an anti-aircraft battery at the airport, but no heavy equipment. On the cheap, so to speak. The Danes have contacted the Faroese government, who has quietly sanctioned the deployment, stating that any possible cooperation with the Russians should be on their terms and by invitation only.'

'General, what is the mission statement?' the PM asked. 'If the Russians attempt a land grab, as you put it, they will come in force. A single company can hardly hold out for long, protecting the entire island group, elite troops they may be.'

'Ma'am, we are not protecting all of the islands. Our man has advised us there are three specific areas in question. By getting there first, our paratroopers can deny the Russians those beachheads, this is our assessment.'

The defence minister was obstinate. 'Why are we doing this? Why not leave it to the Danes?'

The general sighed impatiently. Not a good sign, C thought.

'Minister, I reiterate, Britain has designated the Faroe Islands as being in our sphere of interest. Most of the Danish navy is off fighting pirates in the Indian Ocean. Their army is stationed all over the place, in Kosovo and Bosnia-Herzegovina as United Nations troops. Their

Special Forces are in Afghanistan alongside our ⟨…⟩ forces, although they bivouac with the French prefer⟨…⟩ their kitchen. They are in Iraq and almost every o⟨…⟩ hotspot in the Middle East training our friends and a⟨…⟩ and acting as observers. The only troops they have left⟨…⟩ platoon of Seals who are leaving barracks as we speak⟨…⟩ unless you want them to call up the Faroese home g⟨…⟩ with their shotguns, we are all they have.'

'I am still not convinced,' the PM said. 'Let's adjo⟨…⟩ Perhaps when we know more, we can reconvene. ⟨…⟩ deployment of naval vessels is at your discretion, howe⟨…⟩ I see no need for ground troops.'

With that, the meeting ended, and the chief of ⟨…⟩ and first sea lord pushed back their chairs.

C stayed seated.

'Two comments if I may, Ma'am. According to ⟨…⟩ source, the Russians lay claim to an area on the n⟨…⟩ southern island. Coincidently, that is the location of ⟨…⟩ of the few existing Loran transmitters. Unknown to m⟨…⟩ it is a low-frequency terrestrial navigation beacon. We ⟨…⟩ not use it at present, the French do, for their boomers⟨…⟩ use GPS. But our submarines have the option of using ⟨…⟩ other system if ever the GPS satellite system crashe⟨…⟩ was taken out by the Russians using their anti-satellite ⟨…⟩ siles. If that happened and the Loran system is not av⟨…⟩ able to us, our boomers will be blind, they will not k⟨…⟩ their exact positioning, needed to target their missiles ⟨…⟩ this little shack on the mountain could be the differ⟨…⟩

between Britain having a useful nuclear deterrent or having some very expensive, useless, submarines.'

As the general and the admiral pulled their chairs forward, C continued,

'That is, of course, a useful argument for the military. However, there is one more consideration. According to my asset, the Russians are interested in establishing a nuclear-proof submarine base on the southern island, a stone's throw from the Shetland Islands. Made of basalt rock, the cliffs are uniquely suited for such a base. It might even accommodate a sub-surface entrance, making any detection of incoming and outgoing traffic impossible.'

'If there is any substance to these rumours, it would, of course, be a threat,' the defence minister said. 'However, we will have to deal with that as things develop.'

'Of course, Minister. But I was not thinking of the threat. My man has suggested an opportunity. Parliament has only recently extended the Trident nuclear ballistic submarine programme on the River Clyde for the next fifty years, with no alternative port. Scotland is opposed to having the base and Scotland leaving the Union, God forbid, would mean us losing our direct access to the North Atlantic hunting grounds.

'The Faroese economy, not least on an outlying island such as Suðuroy, needs jobs and income, that is unless they find oil, something, which is proving increasingly unlikely. Their government might take kindly to a proposal whereby Britain installs a submarine base in Sumba instead of the

Russians. Moving the base from the River Clyde m then placate the Scots, and they might rethink their in the Union.'

The politicians went quiet. Now, *this* was sometl completely different. This was politics. C could aln hear their devious little minds doing the calculations, she was in no doubt that the prime minister appreci the political implications for her and her governmen was a win-win situation.

A company of paratroopers activated an hour ag anticipation of a go-ahead, was on its way north.

# 28

When Hildy knocked, an elegantly dressed grey-haired woman answered the door.

'Her husband is not at home. He is at their other house, in Viðareiði,' Hildy translated. 'It's not far from here. The most northern township of the Faroes, on the island of Viðoy.'

'Too bad, let's go back to the hotel. Or down to town, I noticed the café does pints, I could use one right now.'

'Now, now, Frank.'

Hildy spoke to the woman again who retreated into the house leaving the door ajar.

'She says he needed to get away. He had some business to attend to, something which needed reflection, peace, and quiet. However, she is sure he will give us an hour of his time. Unfortunately, she can't go with us, she has relatives visiting. They are due to arrive any minute. The fastest way to get there, she says, is to take the bus. Getting a taxi in Klaksvík at this time of the afternoon could take up to an hour. She asked us to wait here, while she calls him, just to make sure he is available for our visit.'

'Do we have to go?'

'Yes.' My wife was adamant. 'It'll do you good, otherwise you'll just mope all evening.'

When the chairman's wife returned to the front d[oor] she confirmed we were welcome. The big dark house on the cliffs, her husband would see us at seven o'cloc[k].

But we needed to hurry, the last bus would be lea[ving] soon.

Ten minutes later, we arrived back at the terminus. [We] stood dutifully and waited next to the white outline on [the] tarmac. The only other passengers were a couple in t[heir] late sixties, what appeared to be their pregnant daug[hter] and her husband and seven blond children all seemi[ngly] under the age of five.

I turned and whispered to Hildy, 'They've been b[usy]. And still are.'

'I don't think they're all brothers and sisters. F[rom] their discussions, it seems there are three sets of child[ren] obviously cousins,' she whispered back.

I had no idea how she could tell apart the diffe[rent] groups of children, but I felt for the grandfather [who] already looked harassed. When the eighteen-seater arri[ved] Hildy and I climbed aboard.

'Remember, we only pay on the homeward jour[ney]' Hildy reminded me.

We took seats at the back, and I prepared myself [for] the enjoyable spectacle that followed, the youngsters b[eing] loaded onto the bus. It turned out the pregnant wo[man] and her husband were not joining us, only the grandp[ar]ents and the children were travelling, which gave rise [to a] lot of kissing and farewells.

For luggage, the grandparents had a large sports bag. Apparently, each child had a blue rucksack of their own. Once all the youngsters were aboard and seated, with seatbelts fastened, the young father began to hand the baggage up to the grandfather. There being no compartments reserved for luggage, the bags were unceremoniously dumped by the older man in the centre aisle, under his seated wife's detailed instruction. When the grandfather had everything stowed, he slumped into his seat at the very front, behind the bus driver. As the children waved and blew kisses to the young couple standing by the waiting shelter, the driver closed the doors and pulled away.

'The young couple are probably looking forward to some alone time,' Hildy remarked.

'When do I get some?' I asked.

She punched me playfully in the arm.

As soon as we turned onto the main road, and headed north-west out of town, a constant spatter of small, excited voices erupted. We had travelled along the coast of Borðoy for no more than five minutes when the bus turned right and entered a tunnel.

'It's one of the oldest on the Faroes,' Hildy said.

I could readily believe it. The cavern was extremely narrow, a single lane shared by traffic going in both directions. It had been crudely hacked out of the mountain, the only illumination came from feeble lamps which hung from the cavern's ceiling every twenty metres or so. Headlights in the distance, coming directly at us, cut sharply thro[ugh] the darkness.

'Uh Oh. Uh Oh!' the children chimed.

Hildy translated, laughing, 'They're singing 'Uh [Oh. We are going to crash into the oncoming car'.'

A scary prospect, indeed.

All seven children chanted in unison, in their ador[able] little high-pitched voices. I could only imagine how t[ired] the grandfather would be once the children were pu[t to] bed, later in the evening.

According to the signs, our lane had the right-of-[way]. An oncoming car closed the distance at speed, and ju[st as] a crash seemed inevitable, it pulled into a lay-by and [turned] off its headlights. As our bus thundered by, the chil[dren] squealed with delight. When we neared the end of the [tun]nel, the chant changed to 'No more tunnels!'

The children almost got their wish, but not in a g[ood] way. Exiting the cavern, at the narrow entrance of the [next] tunnel, a dark sedan overtook us quite irresponsibly, alm[ost] forcing our bus off the road and into the rock face. [Our] driver overcorrected as the children squealed with m[erri]ment, and then the bus plunged once more into a lu[minous] tunnel. The chorus began anew, as the irresponsible dr[iver] pulled away from us. I willed the bus driver to slow do[wn], fearing the sedan might cause a crash inside the tun[nel] further up ahead.

Finally emerging safely into daylight, our bus cross[ed a] low bridge, which brought us onto the island of Viðoy. [The] driver turned onto a ramp leading down to a harbour [with] a score of fishing boats at their moorings. A ferry with room for just four or five cars stood waiting for the bus to arrive, vehicles and other passengers had already boarded.

As the grandfather stood and looked despairingly at the pile of baggage blocking the aisle, I decided to go forward and help, and a few minutes later the assembly had successfully disembarked the bus and boarded the ferry, the grandmother leading her troop like a duck and her ducklings.

Throughout the entire delightful experience with the children, I had just one overriding thought. That regardless of how tired the grandparents looked, despite my depression and my reluctance to face my future, I would give anything for Hildy and myself to be in their shoes in the coming years. To have and to hold – grandchildren. Not just Sophie's child to be and her stepdaughter, no loads more. Perhaps this could be my vocation, but it would take some years to achieve and presupposed a certain willingness between my offspring and their current and future spouses, something I had no control over.

Hildy would make a wonderful grandmother, of that I was certain. And myself? Taking time to visit with my grandchildren, being there for them as they matured from toddlers to inquisitive youngsters, I could do that. I imagined myself as the patriarch of a family, a dynasty, or even a clan. The thought made me smile.

In a matter of minutes, the bus was back on a narrow road with lay-bys every fifty yards. We were the only remaining passengers. The driver shouted something and Hildy translated,

'This road is too dangerous in winter. They built a tunnel. We are coming up to the entrance in a minute.

Ahead of us, I could see the narrow road conti straight on, cresting the mountainside, a sheer drop on left. Instead, the bus veered right as the road forked we entered a modern, two-lane well-lit tunnel. Hildy forward to talk to the bus driver.

My phone rang. Maxwell.

'Hello, son, an unexpected treat, you so rarely call.

'You know how it is, Dad.'

'Of course, my boy, I've been there, myself. And n be in doubt, you make me so proud. My old regin even.'

'Dad, are you and Mum by any chance up on the Fa Islands?'

'How did you know?'

'I talked to Penny last week. She said you were on way, once you had visited mormor.' Mother's mothe Danish, they never said 'Nan'.

'Why do you ask, Max?'

'Dad, we're headed out of country. I just wanted to know.'

'Max, this is not a secure line. But yes, we flew up Friday and have visited your sister.'

'Okay, Dad, just asking. Give my love to Mum.'

'You could call her yourself.'

'No time, Dad. We're boarding in two. I'll call wh get back. Promise. Love you, Dad.'

My chest swelled with pride as it always did when hearing those words. From any of my children. It made me feel included in my family, worthy of their affection. Relevant.

Hildy returned to sit across the aisle from me.

'Max just called. I'm to give you his love,' I said.

'What did he say?'

'I'll tell you over dinner.'

'Alright, darling. The driver stays only ten minutes, then he returns to Klaksvík, this is his final run of the day. He says we can call a taxi when we want to go back, but it could take hours to show up. He thinks we should stay the night.'

'But we already have a room in Klaksvík, and all our things are there, including our toothbrushes and pyjamas.'

'Let's see how things pan out, darling. Perhaps you won't need your pyjamas,' my wife said with a mischievous smile. 'But first things first. We have time, we'll have dinner at Elisabeth's.'

'Elisabeth's?'

I was not planning on more family visits.

'You'll see,' Hildy replied.

As the bus came out of the tunnel, darkness was falling. Almost directly in front of us, on the far side of the valley, I spotted the chairman's house. Huge and sinister looking, it sat up on the cliff and looked nothing like normal Faroese dwellings. On the contrary, it looked more like a haunted mansion. I could see a dark car parked next to it.

Viðareiði itself was not a village proper. The thirt[y]
some houses were too far-spaced for that. Just two h[alf-]
mile-long streets connected by three short barren ro[ads,]
one in the middle, one at each end. The layout form[ed a]
digital '8'. Here in the twilight, the valley seemed plea[sant]
enough, the landscape promised to be outstanding, c[ome]
morning.

'Okay, let's take a room,' I relented, not adding [that]
sleeping in the nude sounded absolutely fine by [me.]
Provided the heater worked.

The bus driver headed across the valley and t[hen]
stopped in front of the Hotel Norden. As we got o[ut, I]
glanced up and saw one of the most curious geological [fea]tures, I had ever witnessed. Behind the hotel, the moun[tain]
rose dramatically towards the heavens with a profile s[imi]lar to gigantic steps, ascending from right to left. Plate[aus]
sharply defined, each above its predecessor, as though [they]
had been carved out intentionally.

Elisabeth's turned out to be a little guesthouse [a few]
houses down. We entered, dinner was still being ser[ved.]
Hildy ordered lamb for us both. The B&B was f[ully]
booked, so she called the hotel, and reserved a do[uble]
room. While we waited for our food, I went out into [the]
cold evening air to look around.

All was still, the silence absolute, save for the so[und]
of a single sheep bleating high up somewhere on the [hill]side. Looking across the valley, I saw headlights em[erge]
from the direction of the tunnel and race towards to[wn.]
An SUV, white perhaps. It was difficult to tell as the

flashed beneath the strung-out streetlights. The vehicle turned right and traversed the valley, before driving up the long driveway to the chairman's house.

Its headlights picked out the dark car parked there, then it disappeared around the side. I heard car doors slam and then nothing. Damn, if we were going to visit the chairman, I wanted to do so tonight, get it over with. However, now he had company.

I called Penny, there was still no answer. My concern for my daughter was on the rise. Most often, weeks could pass between speaking by phone or Skype. Normally, I would not have worried, but somehow, being in such close proximity to my daughter, seeing so much of her these past few days, it made me expectant, wanting to be able to contact her at will.

Feeling the cold, I once again entered Elisabeth's eatery. The warmth of her cosy, unassuming seating area hit me, as did the tempting smell of roast lamb. Elisabeth brought plates to our table, piled high and left us to enjoy our dinner. Thick succulent slices of meat, simple vegetables, potatoes, carrots, cooked plums with a thick brown gravy. Hildy drank water, she had ordered a Black Sheep beer for me.

Over dinner, I told Hildy of Max's call.

'I wonder where he is off to,' Hildy said.

'Dear, I might know. It was only hours ago, but I suggested to C the Brits, and the Danes do a joint exercise here on the islands. I think I might have stirred up a hornet's nest if things are moving this quickly.'

'But Max coming here, it's too much of a coincide[nce.]'
'Not really. It's your fault.'
'How so?'
'On holiday with you, he's visited the islands how m[any] times over the years? Ten summers?'
'Thereabouts.'
'When he joined up, he'll have listed the places [he's] been to. For the files. When they deploy units to s[ome] foreign land, they like to know if individual troopers h[ave] local knowledge. How many others in the Paratro[op] Regiment do you think have even been to the Faroes? [Let] alone ten times. Few if any. It would be an obvious ch[oice] for him to be in any advance unit. So it's your doing.'

'Will he be in danger?'

'I can't imagine so. It's just a precautionary measur[e.]'

After an excellent meal, Hildy settled the bill. A[s we] left the little restaurant, I told her about the white SU[V.]

'I still want to get this over with, we should go up t[here] tonight,' I said. 'Let's check into our room first. After t[hat] I suggest we take the scenic route, do some reconnaissa[nce] of the chairman's house and play it by ear. We don't w[ant] to walk in on him if he has a secret lover visiting.'

'Secret lover? Here on the islands? It wouldn't [stay] secret for long,' Hildy laughed.

The night manager was obviously glad to fill an o[ccu]pancy at short notice. I had requested a room facing [the] back of the one-story hotel. He was happy to oblige [and] handed over the key.

He did look at us sceptically.

'No baggage?' he asked.

Hildy explained we had missed the last bus and had decided to stay the night, a spur of the moment decision. The night manager provided us with disposable toothbrushes, a tube of toothpaste, no pyjamas and wished us a good night.

As I was using the toilet, Hildy called for me to hurry up. I thought she needed to use the facilities as well, but when I came into the room after washing my hands, the look on her face was ashen, one of utter horror, as she stared at the flat screen.

I turned and looked at the television not comprehending what was wrong. The picture showed two houses standing well apart, each house scorched and black. In the middle was a heap of rubble, small fires burning. Burnt houses on the news was not a novelty, I thought. Then I looked closer, the neighbouring houses seemed familiar.

Hildy's voice broke as she whispered,

'The newscaster is saying a gas explosion destroyed the house, there were no survivors. It's Sámal's house.'

# 29

The three men dined on grilled lobster and pink ch[am]pagne at London's premier fish restaurant, just off Re[gent] Street. The cream coloured walls were decorated [with] depictions of colourful seafood. Red velvet booths li[ned] the walls, matching chairs and white-clothed tables fi[lled] the room. All tables were taken, the ambience was hus[hed] and opulent. The restaurant was popular, bookings [were] normally required days in advance.

C pulled back the vacant fourth chair and sat d[own] uninvited.

'Good evening, gents, I have a proposition to m[ake]. Please listen carefully.'

The man sitting opposite C grinned and leant forw[ard] expectantly,

'This had better be good, sweetheart. Shoot.'

She too leant forward and in a conspiratorial ton[e of] voice, glancing to include the men on either side of [her,] she whispered,

'You are naughty, naughty boys. You have been [very] bad, and I am here to punish you.'

The man on her right grinned,

'I say, bring it on, baby.'

C found most bankers obnoxious, their air of sup[eri]ority and right of entitlement fully undeserved. Yes, would enjoy this, giving the three of them a spanking, but of a different sort.

'You will do precisely as I say, and if you behave yourselves and give me full satisfaction, I will let you keep your private parts. However, one false step and the last sound you'll hear will be snip, snip.'

The men looked uneasily at each other as if to say, 'Now, this is getting weird.' The American looked around for a waiter, they had all vanished on C's orders.

'You don't know who I am, do you?' she asked as she paused for effect. 'I'm the chief of MI6.'

From the smiles of astonishment on their faces, it was clear they did not know whether to laugh or cry. First, her enticing proposition, then a promise of punishment, now she wanted to play spies. The man on her left guffawed and then hushed himself as heads of other diners turned. C pulled from her clutch her ID and handed it to the American opposite.

'I'm sure you do not believe me. However, you are all smart men, despite being bankers. Take out your phones, look me up.'

C leant forward, picked up the full glass of ice water standing in front of the man to her right and took a sip while the men scrambled for their mobiles. A minute later, the American meekly handed back her ID.

'Good. Now that's out of the way, we can get down to business. You are here at my bidding.'

She looked at the American.

'Your chairman told you to take these gents to dinner only an hour ago, a spur of the moment thing, his own booking. It was my doing. I know about your little [plan] to defraud the Bank of England. I have known abo[ut it] for some time, but I've kept it to myself. Now I need [your] assistance, and you will give it to me unconditionally.

'I assume you are all aware of the situation on [the] Faroe Islands. Millions of dollars that little runt of a c[om]pany has borrowed in their hopeless endeavour to [find] oil. You will cancel what you are doing in the next [few] days. Here are tickets to Tórshavn leaving at eight o'c[lock] tomorrow morning, booked in your names. You will b[e on] that flight.'

After handing over three envelopes, she took ano[ther] sip of water.

'A senior civil servant from the Treasury will be [on] the flight with you. You will return to London on Fr[iday] morning. By five o'clock, Friday afternoon, you will [have] refinanced the loan and repaid in full the amount owe[d to] Eurodea Bank.'

'But darn, Ma'am, we can't do that. With that amo[unt] it's not our call. We'll never get credit approval for a b[or]rower that shaky, not in a million years,' the American s[aid].

'The Governor of the Bank of England will dis[cuss] this with your respective chairmen tomorrow. Your b[oard] of directors will approve whatever you recommend. [He] will work out the details and request any missing bits [and] pieces you need from Her Majesty's government. He[re is] an information memorandum with what we know at p[res]ent. You have the whole night to prepare. While you [are] in Tórshavn, you will take your direction from my m[an].

Frank Llewellyn. Do as he says, follow his instruction, and your secret is safe with me as long as you never bring your plans to fruition. And see yourselves lucky you can assist me. Otherwise, you would be looking at five to ten as Her Majesty's guests at Wandsworth Prison.'

C stood and made her way towards the exit as four men in dark suits detached themselves from the walls, and followed in her wake. Waiters suddenly reappeared amongst the guests, coming from the kitchen.

The American signalled for the bill, regardless the second bottle of champagne was still half-full, and they had yet to finish their lobster. They needed to be on their way.

Captain Schmidt of the futuristic-looking command ship, the Absalon, stood on the bridge and looked through his binoculars. The massive Russian warship loomed two kilometres ahead, it filled his view.

It had been a hectic departure. Earlier that morning, they had received orders to get underway and to catch up with the Russian convoy. In minutes, his officers had been on the phone cancelling all shore leave, the crew had one hour to get back to the boat, after that, the ship was leaving with or without them.

Schmidt was in nominal command of the task force since Denmark had sovereignty over Faroese waters. All direct communications to the Russian battleship would be

his responsibility. However, due to the nature of the th
the British Admiralty, acting on behalf of NATO, had o
all tactical command. The Admiralty HQ in Portsmo
the Danish central command in Århus and the other
face ships were wired in on a common frequency.

'Skipper, there is a joint call from the Admiralty. I
four,' the young female ensign said, she was his se
comms officer. Her post, when the ship was not at b
stations was on the bridge, right next to his captain's cl

# 30

In shock, I sat down on the bed and held my wife as I stared at the television screen. Last we spoke, Sámal had mentioned he and Hans would be going home for dinner. Now Sámal was dead along with his wife and children, dear old Hans as well.

I was deeply saddened, no survivors they said. I had only known the men for a few days, but we had bonded. Hans with his complaining attitude, Sámal, the righteous, ever-sceptical solicitor, and of course Sámal's family. This was terrible news.

'Frank,' Hildy said, through tears, her face in her hands. 'This thing about the chairman. Can it wait until morning? I'm not sure I am up to it. Those lovely, lovely people, how could something like this have happened?'

'Maybe it was no accident. It happened just after Sámal got himself appointed to lead the investigation, just after the news channel reported Hans would be giving evidence. I think, dear, it is more pressing than ever we get confirmation of what is going on. We owe it to them. But if you don't want to come, I fully understand, I'll go up there myself.'

'So, you've changed your mind. You do want to see this through. As do I. Just give me a moment,' Hildy said.

She sat clutching the remote control, then she loo[ked] down at it, pushed the button turning off the televis[ion] and pulled on her Timberlands. Without saying ano[ther] word, she rose from the bed and donned her sweater [and] raincoat. She was ready to go.

I was so proud of her.

I went over to my jacket, which hung on a hook by [the] door, and rummaged inside the sleeve. I pulled out a g[ut] knife in its sheath.

'Darling, where on earth did you get that?'

'An ornament from Elisabeth's hallway, I borrowed [it.]'

'Nicked it, rather. However, it's dark out, and as fa[r as] I know, there is no grind-killing happening. And if t[here] were, you would certainly not be permitted to join i[t. It] requires a special permit.'

'It's backup, dear. The chairman is going to tel[l us] everything he knows, and since you told me not to s[hoot] anyone, the knife will be a good incentive. Only if we n[eed] it. Come on, we're taking the clandestine route.'

I opened the window and climbed out.

Hildy turned off the lights and nimbly followed [me] over the windowsill. I knew she was in good shape a[fter] all those Zumba classes she attended. We set off, climb[ing] up the slope. In the moonless night, the only illumina[tion] came from the rear windows of the hotel and the close[st of] the village houses. I watched the ground, careful whe[re I] stepped, avoiding rocks identifiable only by their shado[ws].

We came to a wire fence and followed it to the r[ight] until we found a gate. Continuing up the incline, a c[

shape bolted into the night, giving me a start. I had the knife out of its sheath before I realised my mistake and smiled. We had disturbed a sheep. At the next fence, there was no gate.

'Darling, there will be steps,' Hildy whispered.

Sure enough, a short, broad triangular ladder allowed us to climb over the wire and down the other side. When I tried to help Hildy down, she batted away my hand. We crossed a final field as we approached the chairman's house from the side. In addition to a black Mercedes, two other vehicles stood parked, out of sight as seen from the village.

From our left, came the sound of crashing waves, and I could only imagine the spectacular view of the ocean the chairman's lodgings commanded in the daytime. The terrain dipped towards the cliffs, which, on this side of the house effectively made the cellar the ground floor. In the light coming from a single basement window, I could see that the SUV was indeed white. The other car was a dark sedan.

I turned towards Hildy and put a finger to my lips, a superfluous gesture I realised, it was not as if she was about to break out in song and dance, Zumba or otherwise. Motioning her to wait where she was, I approached the basement window. I did not want my face to suddenly appear framed in the light, so I retreated well back from the house and stayed out in the shadows. This meant I could not view the room in its entirety, only a bit at a time.

Well, well, well. The first thing that came into view was Baldy, Georgi, the Russian diplomat from Sumba in

his white shirt sitting at a desk in the far left corner. A  
lamp was turned on, and a pile of papers lay on the bur  
Next to the papers was a small plastic bag. It looked fa  
iar. Plastic ties?

As I moved further to my left, the next thing that c  
into view was a set of naked buttocks. Of all the thing  
might have imagined, this was not one of them. The m  
legs were bent beneath him, he was kneeling on a low   
form, his bare feet protruding. I deduced it was a shea  
table, the kind we had seen in Porkeri when Susanne t  
us to see the sheep shearing. There would be a stock at  
other end used to lock the sheep's neck in place. He  
assumed it was used to restrain a human head.

The soles of the man's feet and his buttocks   
pockmarked with small wounds and smeared with bl  
As I moved further left, a man's back came into view  
sat on a stool, a set of shearing scissors held high in his  
hand. He reached forward and jabbed the trussed-up   
in the butt cheek. The prisoner's body went rigid. F  
the tormentor's slight build and sparse hair, I was certa  
was Wet Lips, the smaller of the two men who we had  
the other night on the docks.

As the wounds began to bleed, Wet Lips's right h  
appeared, holding a clothes iron. He used it to touch  
skin with the triangular tip, cauterising the wounds, a   
of vapour rose from each contact.

I moved further left and could see into the far r  
corner. Oaf, the big man, stood over a person seate  
a chair, it was a woman. It seemed Oaf was fondling

breasts through her shirt. When the man moved a bit to the right, my head exploded. In rage. I clenched my jaw in disbelief at what I was seeing, I balled my fists, my whole body shook.

The woman tied to the chair was Penny.

I tried to control myself, I breathed deeply, and relaxed my tight grip on the grind knife as I opened my jaw. I would need my rage for later. For now, I had to remain calm, and think clearly. I snuck back to where Hildy stood, I refused to tell her what I had witnessed.

Instead, hiding the tremble in my voice, I said,

'There are three villains in the room, and they have hostages. We need a diversion. Do us a favour, go to the front door, ring the bell and ask if Eigil Jonasen is at home. That should get at least one of them out of the room. Play it by ear, and here, take this.'

I handed her the grind knife and the sheath.

Hildy gave me a solemn nod. As she disappeared around the corner, I took the Ruger from my pocket and moved back to a position where I could see the man fondling Penny. I waited, willing Hildy to hurry. Wet Lips was at it again with the shearing scissors and the clothes iron, he suddenly stopped and looked up. I moved closer to the window and saw the diplomat leave the room through the interior door. Oaf followed him out, and Wet Lips resumed his work.

Left of the window, at the cellar door, I slowly applied pressure to the handle. Locked, damn it. I backed away from the house. On the Faroe Islands, clumps of loose

basalt always lay around, I picked one up from the sh‑
ows, the size of a fist and went over to the window. I.
handed I threw the rock into the glass, shattering it.

Inside, Wet Lips jumped to his feet and tur‑
startled. His nose was smashed, his eyes blackened,
clumps of bloody cotton wool protruded from his nost
Seeing me, he put down the iron and changed his grip
the twin bladed scissors, from his left to his right har
raised the Ruger and stepped forward, my gun now in
the room, aiming at the man's head, just between his e
As Wet Lips took a step forward, a wicked grin on his f
I lowered the gun and shot him twice in the heart.

The bark of the pistol resonated off the concrete w
the cloud of cordite stung my nostrils.

My last-minute change of aim was deliberate. My h
had been shaking. It is easier to hit a torso than a crani
If I missed, I did not want bullets ricocheting around
room where my daughter sat. As the man collapse
reached down for a second piece of basalt, which I use
scrape away the shards of glass protruding from the
tom of the window frame. I got most of it, but not all.

Reaching inside the window, I bent over, placed
gun on the floor, and then I pulled the sleeves of my ja
over my hands. With my palms thus protected, I hoi
myself inside and retrieved the pistol. Looking up, I
my dishevelled daughter staring wide-eyed at me. (
tape covered her mouth, and plastic ties secured her to
chair.

As I took a step forward, Oaf appeared in the door

'Come in slowly with your hands up, or I'll shoot you, just like I did your friend.'

The big man glanced down at the body on the floor, an angry look crossed his face as he menacingly stepped forward.

'Don't do anything stupid,' I warned.

I knew from our last encounter the man spoke some English.

'Stop, or I will fire.'

My warnings had no effect. The man kept coming. I admit it, I felt panic, my heart thumped. I doubted the small twenty-two calibre bullets would be sufficient to stop this big man unless I went for a double tap to the head. There was a commotion out in the hallway behind Oaf.

When Baldy appeared, my stomach sank, 'What had they done to Hildy?' was my first thought.

I need not have worried. She was right behind the Russian.

The big man took advantage of my change of focus to launch his attack. As I stepped to my left and ducked under his swinging punch, I stuck my foot out and tripped him. Oaf fell forwards, hitting his head on the windowsill with a sickening smack. He collapsed to the floor and lay still amongst the broken glass.

'You have no right to do this. I have diplomatic immunity,' Baldy snarled.

Hildy prodded him forward with the big knife, her eyes widening at the sight, first of the inert Wet Lips on the floor and then of the naked trussed-up man in middle of the room. As she forced the Russian towards desk, I could see specks of blood on the back of his where Hildy had pricked him.

Stepping over to the bureau, I pocketed my pistol, I extracted plastic ties from the bag and quickly sec the diplomat's hands, and then did the same to the big on the floor.

Hildy sheathed the grind knife and turned around inspect the bound man. Only then did she notice Pe bound and gagged in the far corner. She gasped and str across the room to our daughter. Using the knife, she the ties holding Penny's arms to the chair. Penny put hands to her face, readied herself and then tore the from her mouth, gasping with pain. Both women crying as they embraced. Not used to seeing Hildy c had now witnessed it twice in one evening.

'Penny, dear, what are you doing here? We've phoning you all day,' I said.

'My charger broke, my phone went dead. I was or way to Sámal's place to visit Hans when those two stopped me on the street. Before I knew it, they had napped me and put me in their car. Somehow, they kn was Hans's assistant. The small man kept telling me he going to do the most horrible things to me. Just becat broke his nose.'

Held by her mother, Penny cried into her mot! shoulder.

# 31

I crossed the room, and we huddled around Penny. Once our daughter had calmed down, Hildy turned her attention to Wet Lips on the floor. She knelt, checked for a pulse and gave me a withering look.

'Darling, I distinctly remember asking you not to shoot anybody, let alone kill someone. We'll be in trouble if they find the body. You'll have to do something about it.'

A grunting noise got our attention. The man tied to the shearing table rocked back and forth, his head was locked in place, his hands bound in front of him.

I released Penny and pulled out the captive's gag.

'Thank God you come. You were at my house. My wife. Please, please,' the man said. I borrowed the grind knife from Hildy, and carefully sawed through the tie around the man's wrists and then undid the headlock.

'Penny darling, you need to help us.'

I wanted to give my daughter something to do, to get her mind away from the threats, which had scared her so. With me on one side, and Hildy and Penny on the other, we got the man up and off the shearing table. When his feet first touched the ground, he cried out in pain. We all looked away from the old man's nakedness as best we could, and held him upright while he got the feeling [back] into his legs and was able to support himself.

'Penny, you'll have to help your mother get him ups[tairs] and attend to his wounds. I'll be with you shortly.'

When they were out of the room, I manoeuvred [the] diplomat to the chair vacated by Penny and secured [him] with additional ties.

That done, across the room, I quickly leafed thro[ugh] the piles of paper on the desk. They were documents [of] agreement between FaroeFour and Eurodea Bank la[y on] the top of the pile. Beneath, a contract between FaroeF[our] and the Russian Federation. Checking the signature p[age] towards the back of each document, I saw they were sig[ned] by Eurodea Bank and the Russian Federation. Under [the] signature line for FaroeFour was printed, 'Eigil Jona[nsen, ] Chairman' and then 'Leif Olsen, CEO'. Only Leif O[lsen] had signed.

They were obviously Pdf copies, probably sent [by] email, not signed originals, but legally binding non[ethe]less. Somebody was in a hurry. Once the chairman sig[ned] the documents, they would be valid and final. At the [desk] stood a wheeled office chair, I sat down and scooted ac[ross] the room to face the diplomat.

'Georgi, Georgi, Georgi. It is Georgi, Georgi Ruzh[kov, ] correct? We do have to stop meeting like this. By the [way,] where are your eyebrows?'

I remembered his name from the diplomatic passp[ort,] which I stole in Sumba, the one I gave Sámal.

'I am a member of the Russian diplomatic co[rps] and currently stationed at the Russian consulate. I h[ave] diplomatic immunity. You have no right to do this to me. Release me at once, I demand it.'

I reached down, took the chairman's discarded gag and stuffed it into Georgi's mouth.

'Now, now. You can prove none of that, you don't have your green passport, do you? You and I are going to have a little chat, but first I have things to do.'

The clothes iron stood on the floor, the heating indicator clicking on and off. I bent down and pulled the plug from the wall socket. There was a pile of clothes in the corner, an empty shoe protruded from underneath.

In the hallway, I found the door to the bathroom. Searching for a receptacle, all I could find was the plastic bowl, which held the toilet brush. It would have to do. I decided to be nice and rinsed the bowl under the faucet before I filled it from the tap. Back in the room, I dashed the water onto the big man's head. Slowly, Oaf began to regain consciousness. I waited a moment, he groaned and rolled himself onto his back.

'What's your name?' I asked. I could not very well call him 'Oaf', and certainly not to his face. The man did not respond immediately, he seemed dazed. I slapped him a stinging blow across his unshaven cheek.

'What's your name?'

'Brian,' the man croaked.

'Okay Brian, this is how it's going to be. I've hurt you once, and I will do so again if you don't do exactly as I say. Do you understand?'

The man nodded. He probably had no recollection of me hurting him the first time, or of how he had ended up on the floor, with blood in his eyes, and probably a split headache to boot. I knew that being knocked unconsc[ious] often led to memory loss, people seldom remembered [any]thing from the time immediately prior to impact.

'Brian, in a moment, I am going to cut your ha[nds] free from behind your back. You will then hold them in front of you, and I will tie them again. Do you un[der]stand?' I received a nod.

I heard a yelp from upstairs and decided to checl[ on] the women before continuing with my plan. Out in [the] hallway, grind knife in hand, I bounded up the stairs [In] the sitting room, the FaroeFour chairman lay face d[own] on the sofa, his torso and legs covered with blankets, l[eav]ing his buttocks and bare feet exposed.

'We found the first-aid kit in the kitchen,' H[ildy] explained.

She and Penny were rubbing burn cream into [the] wounds, Hildy doing the buttocks and Penny, the fee[t. A] near empty whisky tumbler stood on the table next to [the] sofa. The chairman appeared to be in good hands. I sai[d not] much and headed back down to the basement.

After checking that the diplomat's bindings were [still] secure, I took an extra tie from the bag on the desk, m[ade] a loop of it, and then went over and knelt by Brian.

'As I said, I am going to cut your hands free f[rom] behind your back. You will immediately hold them ou[t in] front of you. If you don't do as I say, I will cut you [with] this. Do you understand?'

I held the imposing knife up in front of the man's face, doubting he could see much for the blood in his eyes. It came from a gash in his forehead.

'You have one second after I cut the tie to wipe your eyes, then I want to see your wrists held out together. Okay?'

I received a hoarse 'Ja, ja.'

The man did as instructed.

'Okay. I want you to get up.'

The man complied. He grabbed the windowsill for support. With a yelp, he jerked his bare hands away from the glass shards, fell back down, his head slapped against the concrete floor. After a moment, he tried again. This time, he used the wall to steady himself as he groggily got to his feet.

'Now pick up your friend.'

Brian picked up the body with ease and cradled it in his arms.

'Okay. Let's go for a walk.'

I intentionally kept things simple for the big bloke, he was clearly not the sharpest tool in the shed, and his recent head blows were not helping. I unlocked the back door and led Brian out into the night.

'Stop. Let your eyes adapt to the dark.'

'Adopt?'

'No, adapt. From the bright lights. Your eyes need to get used to the dark. Okay? Let's go.'

I led him by the elbow towards the cliff. We had just enough light coming from the house to see where the

ground ended, and the black void began. Below, by s
light alone, I could make out the ocean and the surf
crashed against the rocks.

'Brian, stop.'

I was in a dilemma. The question I asked myself
did Brian deserve to live or die? The man was stupid,
there was no doubt in my mind he had only been foll
ing orders from the smaller man. However, I had seen
fondling my daughter with my own eyes. Was that su
cient cause for taking a man's life? At that precise mom
I was angry enough to believe it was.

I took a step back.

'Now, throw him over the cliff. Give him a big he
I said, still thinking hard.

Brian stood at the edge, he flexed his body and to
his friend over the cliff. Before he could regain his
ance, I was about to plant a shoulder in the man's back
had second thoughts. You can always kill someone,
you cannot bring them back. I hoped I would not liv
regret my decision.

'Well done Brian, let's go.'

Returning to the bright lights of the basement, I u
ties to secure him, this time to a radiator. I noticed
bag was running low and hoped this would be our f
confrontation on the islands. Georgi made noises atter
ing to get my attention. I checked the diplomat's bind
once more and then went upstairs. The Russian could v

The chairman, now with an extra blanket cove
him entirely, lay snoring gently. A half-full tumble

whisky stood on the table beside him, he must have asked for seconds.

In the kitchen, the women had made tea. Penny had obviously used the bathroom to freshen up, the dishevelled look was gone, she looked tired, but was once again her beautiful self.

As Hildy got me a mug, I asked,

'Penny, I'm sorry, but I have to know. Did the two men hurt you in any way? Did they molest you? Just before I broke the window, I saw the big man leaning over you, groping you.'

'Dad, he wasn't groping me. He was buttoning up my shirt, whispering in my ear, telling me he would not let the other man hurt me. Assuring me, he would protect me. I trust him, Dad, he seems sincere. You didn't hurt him, did you?'

'And the other one?'

'I broke his nose when he grabbed me, when he tried to get me into their car. You know, the way Wilson taught us. He was a wimp. I could have handled him, I was just about to. A good swivel kick to the head would have finished him off, but Brian got between us.'

She may have been frightened, but I was proud of my defiant Penny and relieved. I had almost killed the big man, the would-be protector of my daughter. It would have been an unbearable mistake. With a deep sigh, I looked at my wife,

'Have you told her about Sámal and Hans?'

Hildy shook her head.

'What about Hans?' Penny asked anxiously.

I leant forward, put a reassuring hand on her arm told Penny of what we had seen on the news. When heard the words, 'no survivors', both she and her mo began to cry, holding each other for comfort. I alm joined in. However, tears were not my thing, at least for now. Crying released endorphins, which reduced p I did not want relief, I had work to do, and I needed rage, I needed to psych myself up for the interrogatio the Russian diplomat.

I wanted an explanation. Now I had the man in custody, I was going to get it, whatever it took. Grinc my teeth, my jaw set, I picked up the grind knife and v downstairs to get my answers.

# 32

Flicking the blade back and forth, swishing it through the air, I calmly crossed the room, taking my time. I bent down and put the clothes iron plug back into the wall socket. Those actions alone were enough to convince the diplomat to cooperate, he seemed eager to talk. I was relieved I would not have to torture him.

'I worked for Eurodea Bank, the New York branch. Just over a year ago, Moscow recalled me, instructed me to attend a meeting. I was nervous. I asked myself, what have I done wrong? It was the first time we met, Leif Olsen and I. There were two other men as well, the admiral of the fleet and another man in a white suit, he gave me only his first name. He asked me to call him Jay. They swore me to secrecy and then the admiral told me what was needed.'

Georgi was to come up with a plan. People could be removed and replaced. Bankers, consultants, and lawyers could be bought, threatened and coerced.

'All they required from me was the plan, others would execute it. It took me a month to develop. I hypothesised that for greed, people would do anything. The desire of the Faroese people for riches, for oil. But the first thing I needed was to put this man, Olsen, in place, he was crucial.

I needed him as the CEO of FaroeOil and FaroeFou[nd]... happened, I do not know the details.'

'I do, Georgi. They murdered the former CEO. He [had] two small children and a pregnant wife. You killed hi[m at] least indirectly. Afterwards, they probably coerced a h[ead]hunter to recommend this Olsen fellow. But carry on.'

'I arranged it so the Russian government would sec[retly] provide a full counter-pledge to an international in[sur]ance company. In return, the insurance company ga[ve a] guarantee to the banks. With that in hand, an Amer[ican] bank, IPFC, was only too happy to provide its services [to] arrange the syndicate. The banks were in fact not pro[vid]ing project finance at all, just a loan fully secured by [the] insurance company. Brilliant if I do say so myself.'

Georgi had set up the documentation, so Euro[pean] Bank could take over the whole facility. They had [used] the Americans to front the scheme. If it had been just [a] Russian lender from the outset, everyone would have c[ried] foul play when the loan went into default.

'There were two significant risks to my plan. One [was] that FaroeOil would actually find oil, which would a[llow] them to repay the loan. We approached an enginee[ring] company who acted as independent engineers for the ba[nks] and paid them bribes to produce a list of exploration [sites] different from the list made by FaroeOil's engineer. T[he] list was inserted into the loan document at the last mi[nute] and presented to the contractors who did the actual d[rill]ing. It worked, they found no oil. Can I have some wat[er?]

'When we are finished,' I said, noticing the toilet-brush bowl lying on the floor, ready and waiting. 'Keep going.'

'The second risk was if the Faroese government denied the Russian bank or the Russian Federation the right to develop the harbours after the default of FaroeOil. Therefore, the documents included a Faroese guarantee which allowed the banks to do whatever they wanted without government intervention.'

'But surely, zoning permits would be needed to make it legal.'

'The sites were already approved as harbours. Even for the storage of ammunition, although the government could never have expected ordnance of that size. Probably, just shot-gun shells and dynamite.' The Russian seemed to find his comments amusing.

'So why, Georgi, if you are so brilliant, and your job solely required you to come up with the plan, not to execute it, why are you here on the islands?'

'Things began to unravel when the company's engineer discovered the drillings were at the wrong coordinates, he threatened to tell the board. We always knew it was a risk, but until then Leif had falsified the coordinates on the progress reports. If someone discovered that he had arranged for the bogus sites, he would be accused of fraud, both towards his company and towards the Faroese government, which would allow them to renege on their guarantee not to interfere. The engineer was a problem we needed to solve.'

'So you were going to kill him. And what about assistant?' I asked, my anger on the rise.

'No, no, I received orders from home, from the ac ral. The assistant did not matter, Leif would take car her, get her reassigned. The engineer was to be kept a so he could help in getting the construction of the marine dock underway as soon as possible. We nec his data. But that fool, Leif Olsen panicked, he delet all from the computers, not just the files regarding th exploration, no everything. So we needed the archive Sumba.'

'You went to Sumba, you got the files, but you d have Hans, the engineer.'

'Correct. Except for your intervention when you cued him, all was going to plan. What happened to men?'

'I've no idea, keep going.'

'The default, the buyout by Eurodea Bank, the tal over of the development rights. My country was wel its way to getting the harbours we need. Until this a noon, when the Faroese prime minister revealed the ernment is consulting with the engineer. The govern guarantee might now be deemed unlawful and void if Dutchman talks.'

'Again. So why are you here?'

'I received orders from Moscow. Before the Far government can act, I was to get the immediate signa of the chairman on the hundred-year lease. Leif Olsen already signed. This would make the contract valid.'

'And then what, Georgi? You have a piece of paper. But you'll never be able to take possession.'

The Russian went silent, he gave me an obstinate stare.

'Come on, Georgi, we've come this far. Finish the story.'

When the diplomat did not reply, I stood from the swivel chair, stuffed the gag back in the Russian's mouth, and calmly went over and spat on the clothes iron, hearing, and seeing the sizzle. Setting the iron down on the floor next to Georgi's feet so he could feel the heat against his trouser leg, without further ado, I jabbed Georgi in the back of his hand with the knife and received a grunt in return.

'It's okay, Georgi, it will only bleed for a moment, then I'll use the iron to close the wound.'

The man struggled against his binds, his eyes roving frantically in their sockets, darting between the iron and the knife, beads of sweat appearing on his bald crown.

'Georgi, we could also leave it be, it's such a small wound, no need to use the iron. Instead, we could talk, is that what you want to do? Talk? Good, let me just pull the rag out of your mouth and turn off the iron.'

I was fortunate the man came to his senses.

'So tell me,' I said.

'There are marine landing ships on their way from Kaliningrad. Paratroopers will land in advance to secure the beachheads. Please, you must promise me. The Federation must never know I told you this. My father is high up in the military, and my mother, she will be punished as well.'

'But Georgi, you said it yourself. The drillings, documents, it's all fraud. Russia *has* no rights.'

'We have a signed statement from the enginee proves he is to blame. Therefore, the Faroese governn has no right to rescind its guarantee. Eurodea owns rights unless the engineer refutes his signature. It co not be allowed.'

'Not allowed, Georgi? What do you mean, not allow

'Leif Olsen found out where the engineer was stay Orders came. The engineer was to be silenced, but no me, I am not responsible. Olsen called his men. The Danes, that man and his partner.'

Georgi nodded towards Brian who patiently sat the floor, staring down at a puddle of blood, seemi enthralled by the occasional droplet falling from his b

'We were working out of the deserted FaroeOil bu ing. I left, we were supposed to meet here, they were l;

What happened in Tórshavn, Georgi did not kr As he attempted to convince the chairman to sign leases, offering money, the two Danes finally arrived. V Penny. On hearing that the chairman refused to cooper Wet Lips had gone to work on the old man. Then I shown up.

'Now I have told you all I know, you must let me g have done nothing illegal, and in any case, I have my lomatic immunity.'

'Georgi, you forgot to mention the Ocean Nemesi

'What about it? That had nothing to do with me.'

'Are you sure, Georgi?'

'The Faroese are responsible.'

'No, Georgi, you are. I saw you on the cruiser, standing by the railing, giving orders to the trawler's crew. Napalm, Georgi. Napalm for Christ's sake. Why?'

'We needed to disrupt the government, now we were so close. Two birds with one stone. The American banks, they refused to sell out to us, they gave a price, we agreed. Then they increased the price, they knew something was up. And they had no risk, they had the insurance company guarantee. We threatened the bankers and their families, we offered to pay bribes. Then one of the American banks decided to buy the others out, this was a few days ago. That would have been a catastrophe. We needed to stop them. The man called Jay, he controls a senator who got the sanctions passed in the US Congress in record time.'

'So Georgi, let me just get this straight. You nearly blew up half of Tórshavn and killed thousands of people to get sanctions imposed that would force the American banks to sell out to Eurodea Bank. And to stop the government from interfering. Am I correct?'

This time Georgi remained silent.

The diplomat spoke casually of mass murder. I felt like using the knife and the iron. But I refused to let my rage get the better of me, I would let the man stew. I went upstairs taking the pile of documents with me.

The chairman was now awake, and sitting up, albeit slumped.

'He is on a heavy dose of painkillers,' Hildy explai[ned]. 'Together with the whisky, it should numb his discomf[ort]. The poor man.'

I questioned the chairman and got confirmation. T[hey] had demanded he sign the documents. They had expla[ined] the contents. However, he had not read them himself.

'The Russian lawyer said, once we finalised the lease, banks would cancel all debt owed by FaroeOil and we, [the] owners, would receive money. I've put my entire savings [in] this venture, finding the oil, but I would rather lose ev[ery]thing before I become a traitor to my country. I refused. T[hen] the little man turned up,' the chairman said with a shiver.

'Russian lawyer?'

'The man downstairs.'

'He said he was a lawyer?'

The chairman nodded.

I heard the sound of an engine start outside the ho[use] and the wheels of a car crunching the gravel. At the [win]dow, I saw the dark sedan race down the driveway, the [head]lights streaked across the valley and reached the high[way]. A moment later, the car disappeared from view, heade[d in] the direction of the tunnel.

Pistol in hand, treading warily down the stairs [to] the basement I discovered the broken wooden chair [and] cut ties on the floor. The shearing scissors were g[one]. Remembering how quickly the three men in Sumba [had] liberated themselves, I decided plastic cuffs were no[t what] they were cut out to be. Too bad, I had wanted to ques[tion] the Russian further about the explosion at Sámal's hou[se].

Through the broken window, I saw the white SUV standing parked and went out to check, the keys were in the ignition. Back inside, surveying the basement, I knew I needed to erase the signs of the scuffle. Quickly, using a mop and bucket I found in a downstairs cupboard, I swabbed the blood from the basement floor down a drain. Brian had bled profusely, Wet Lips hardly at all. I emptied the bucket down the toilet, rinsed it and the mop and then decided I could do little more. I was certainly not going to install a new window.

Grabbing the pile of clothes from the floor, I went upstairs to the sitting room.

'We need to leave, we are vulnerable here. The others got away, we don't know if or when they will return. We also need to get Eigil to Tórshavn, they'll want to hear his story. Hildy dear, here are his clothes, see if you can get him dressed, I need to make a call.'

I went out the front door and standing under the stars, I called C, recounting for her what Georgi had told me.

'He said they have an invasion fleet on the way.'

'Yes, they were observed earlier today coming through the Oresund. ETA sometime tomorrow afternoon or early evening. We have deployed assets to handle them, but Frank, I need you to do us a favour. I need you to meet some bankers arriving tomorrow on the first flight from Heathrow. Twist some arms, do what it takes to have them take over that loan. Your thinking was good. And Frank, those bankers should be uncommonly accommodating, or I shall want to know.'

'Ma'am, my old regiment?'

'On their way, Frank. Greatly appreciated, we co not have done this without you.'

I could feel tears of pride swell at the corners of eyes.

# 33

Aboard the Hercules transport, as it flew through the night sky, second lieutenant Maxwell Llewellyn sat strapped in his seat.

He and his platoon were three hours into their mission. The briefing from his captain had been short and to the point. As the only junior officer who had actually been to the Faroe Islands, he would lead the advance troop. His mission orders were straightforward. Travel light, travel fast. His platoon had left a mere fifteen hectic minutes later, headed for the airport. The rest of the company would follow.

Based at Colchester Garrison, it had taken an hour to reach Southend Airport and their waiting transport. He and his men travelled as ordered, with only the one civilian boxed van. He had ammunition, Stingers and four BAT recoilless rifles, which would serve as his anti-tank capability, not that he expected any such targets. Rations would be supplied on-site. Smiling, he wondered what his men would make of the local cuisine. On the other hand, having been on training missions to remote areas throughout Asia and Africa, they were used to living it rough.

The male co-pilot came through from the cockpit and leant towards him.

'Mr Llewellyn, ETA in seven minutes. You are [welcome to] come to join us in the cockpit for landing.'

He looked forward to the day of his promotion f[rom] second to first lieutenant when it would no longer be '[...]' but 'Lieutenant' or 'Sir'.

Max shouted a warning to his men and then went [for]ward and strapped himself into the spare seat behind [the] co-pilot. The cabin's ceiling was lit like a Christmas t[ree,] buttons, switches and knobs in blues, reds and greens. [He] sat back to enjoy the rest of the ride. Some minutes l[ater] the female pilot put the plane into a sharp descent. A[s it] levelled out, the wheels bumped down on the tarmac, [and] he felt the aircraft brake.

He knew the abrupt landing was merely a precaut[ion.] The massive Hercules needed only seven hundred me[tres] to come to a complete standstill, the Vágar airport prov[iding] a kilometre to spare. The pilot taxied, passing the glass [ter]minal building, with its lights out, closed for the night.

The Faroese government had promised to pro[vide] covert transport for thirty-five men in two groups, [and] they were true to their word. In front of the main ha[ngar] stood an articulated lorry with a crane behind the c[ab] and a twenty-foot refrigerated container on its trailer.

An eighteen-seater blue bus stood waiting to [take] eleven of his men with their rucksacks and weapons [to a] tourist attraction, a rigid inflatable troop carrier, which [was] waiting for them fifteen minutes up the road. Their [des]tination was the high-ground around Sumba where [they] would reinforce the Danish Seals.

A second section of ten men would stay at the airport and crew the anti-aircraft battery.

As Max strode down the cargo ramp as fast as his short legs would take him, he thought it all very satisfactory. That was until his men opened the container doors, red interior lights came on, and the stench of fish hit him, this despite the interior having been hosed down. The inside was warm and damp, the humidity accentuated the smell. Not my problem, he thought with a wry smile.

Furthest in, Max saw cardboard and plastic boxes of food, canned meats, jars of pickles and other vegetables in Styrofoam packing trays, and boxes of fruit together with fresh bread. There were first aid kits and attached to the wall in the middle, a chemical toilet secured by fittings.

The Faroese were indeed treating them fine, Max thought, as he ordered his two final sections to mount up.

# 34

After we got the chairman dressed, Hildy and I he[lped] him down the hallway to the front of the house, each o[f us] supporting an arm. Eigil produced keys from his trou[ser] pocket and unlocked his Mercedes with a beep and a f[lash] as we came out of the door. With him installed on the [back] seat, Penny took the front passenger seat, and Hildy [got] behind the wheel.

I retrieved the pile of documents from the house [and] placed them in the boot.

'I'll lead in the SUV,' I said. 'We are not taking [the] tunnel. We are taking the high road. It's something I n[eed to] take care of. There should be guard rails all the way, [but] we would both do well to keep to the left, the side tow[ards] the mountain.'

'I'm good, I'll be careful,' Hildy said.

'Of course you will, dear.' I leant in and gave her a [quick] peck before closing the car door.

Across the valley, reaching the crossroads, I tur[ned] right onto the old road to Klaksvík, which curved [on] around the mountain. The night was pitch black, t[here] were no street lamps here, only my headlights on h[igh] beam and Hildy's lights on low beam behind me to l[ight] up the road ahead.

As I drove, I looked for a break in the guardrails and soon saw what I needed. Stopping the car, I signalled for Hildy to wait where she was. I then pulled the SUV forward, aiming for the opening where the ground began to fall away.

As I opened my door and stepped out, I watched the car roll over the edge and bounce down the near-vertical mountainside where it hit the surface with a mighty splash. I had left the headlights on. Fascinated, I watched as they continued to function while the car sank deeper into the clear waters of the fjord and then vanished altogether.

My reasoning was this. The white SUV must have belonged to Wet Lips. The Dane did not need it anymore, and I had seen the man's face up close before pulling the trigger. I wanted to make a clean sweep of things. If I could, I wanted to rid my mind of the man's existence. I wanted to forget the shooting, although I knew I never would.

Hildy drove up, and I got into the back. Eigil sat with a metal tumbler in his hand, a bottle of Maker's Mark between his thighs. He answered my questioning look,

'For the pain,' he said.

'I think I hurt my hand,' I replied.

Eigil passed the cup to me, and I took a healthy gulp, enjoying the rawness of the bourbon against the back of my throat. Handing back the cup, I sat back to enjoy the ride. The Mercedes was spacious, the seats comfortable. I was not overly concerned with Hildy's driving, which surprised me, taking into account the narrow roads and her

tendency to veer to the right. I put my trust in my v
and relaxed. Eigil's head lolled to one side. Just in tin
relieved him of the tumbler and the bottle, thinking
lucky I was to have a designated driver.

Passing the small sandy beach at the neck of Kollafjørð
lorry driver stopped short of the tunnel. Max's van pu
up behind it. He ordered his men to disembark from
container, and then the lorry driver pulled forward to
entrance of the tunnel. Illuminated by the van's headlig
Max could see a wrecked car parked by the roadside. It
chains around its chassis, meeting at the top.

The driver used his crane to lift the container off
bed of his trailer and placed it by the road, the doors fa
towards the mountainside. Next, at the driver's requ
Max ordered two of his men to insert the crane's hook
the chain around the car, and then the lorry driver li
the wrecked vehicle onto the roof of the container.

A single car, a dark sedan approached. Max and
men took shelter behind the container. Once the car
gone, they emerged from their hiding.

'Please sir,' the lorry driver said. 'Could you have
men release the chains and the sign?'

The banner attached to the container's top rolled do
the side, it had Faroese writing. The whole thing, the
tainer with the wrecked car on top and the sign loc

exactly like the other warnings against reckless driving Max had noticed on their way from the airport.

The driver pointed up the hill.

'The mountain is hard, you cannot dig in. So earlier today we blow holes, using dynamite, we marked them with, you know, reflective metal tags. Also holes at the other end of the tunnel. Enjoy your exercise,' the man said. He stuck out his hand, and they shook, then the driver climbed into his lorry and took off, headed in the direction of Tórshavn.

Looking around, Max had a sinking feeling in his gut. Even in the dark, he could sense the place was indefensible. Anyone higher on the mountainside would have a clear field of fire towards his positions. He made his decision. He would put troops at the very top, and by the tunnel entrance. He would defend only the Kollafjørð area, which had the best landing zone. When reinforcements arrived, his captain could decide whether to defend the other fjord as well.

Regardless, one thing was for sure, if the enemy came in force, fighting on the bare mountainsides was going to be bloody, for both sides.

He needed someone to liaison with the residents of the houses further up the inlet. They would need to evacuate if the Russians came, provided there was time. And he would need roadblocks to stop innocents from accidentally entering a war zone.

As if on cue, coming from the village across the fjord, an SUV drove towards him. It flashed its overhead blue

lights, slowed and stopped. A young police officer clim
out and said in English,

'Hello, I've been assigned to help you. How can
of assistance?'

Max told the young woman what he needed, but not

# 35

Sitting in the back seat, I woke with a start, and vaguely remembered Hildy paying the bill, me climbing the three floors to our hotel room in Klaksvík, retrieving our suitcase, seeing the unused bed and feeling sorry for myself.

I recognised familiar voices. Hildy's, whose sweet voice I had known for thirty years and another voice, a young woman,

'Jamen, kæreste Ida. Hvad laver du her?'

'Jeg blev overført her til morgen. Nogle mistænkelig polakker er blevet set og der har været en del indbrud, så vi har lavet en vejspærring. Flot bil i øvrigt.'

'Den tilhører Eigil Jonasen, han er medlem af Løgtingið. Han har fået lidt for meget, du véd hvordan det er. Men han skal ind til statsministerens kontor, det haster, noget med den der russiske bank, så vi har tilbudt at kører ham. Tror du de har åbent så sent? Eller skal vi vente til i morgen?'

It was Ida, the police officer from Suðuroy. She pointed a flashlight over Hildy's shoulder, into the back seat, illuminating first Eigil and then the light blinded me, as I grinned back at her.

'Good evening, officer.'

Ignoring me, Ida moved away with her flashlight.

'Lad mig lige tjekke med stationen.'

She disappeared into the darkness, I heard her key radio.

'What's going on, dear?' I asked.

'Ida says she was transferred over this morning, roadblock, it's something to do with break-ins. I explai[ned] we're taking Eigil to Tórshavn, she's checking if the pr[ime] minister's office is open.'

Regaining my night vision, I noticed we were stop[ped] at the entrance to the final tunnel before Tórshavn. T[here] was a new container standing at the mouth of the tun[nel,] I could make out the front of a van parked between [the] container and the hillside.

'The parliament is actually still in session,' Ida s[aid,] returning to the car, now in English, undoubtedly for [my] benefit. 'An emergency meeting, so you need their b[ack]ing, not the prime minister's office. Do you know whe[re it] is? In the middle of town? All right then, I'll tell the[m to] expect you. You all have a lovely evening.'

'And you, my darling, keep warm, don't catch c[old,]' Hildy replied and rolled up the window. It glided eff[ort]lessly up.

As we drove on, my heart felt heavy. I rememb[ered] what was in store for us in Tórshavn, what had happe[ned] to Sámal and his family, and to poor Hans.

'Hildy, we should wake them,' I said.

I saw my wife put her hand on Penny's shoulder [and] give it a gentle shake.

'Wake up darling, we're there soon.'

I shook the FaroeFour chairman awake. From the man's grunts, I guessed the painkillers were wearing off. He reached for the half-empty bottle, but I shook my head.

'Eigil, the Løgting is going to need you clear headed. You might be the only one who knows what truly has been going on. Because you need to know, Sámal Halvorson's house was firebombed earlier today. Your engineer Hans Klerk was staying with him. On the news, they said there were no survivors.'

Up front, Penny whimpered as I told the chairman of our discoveries. Of how we, with the assistance of Hans, had worked with Sámal to discover the Russian conspiracy. As I spoke, my daughter continued to cry. Hildy joined in, sniffling, I hoped she could see the road for her tears. When I finished, Eigil sat and looked out the window in obvious distress.

'Sámal, his wife and their children, I always liked the young solicitor. This is dreadful. And Hans, our engineer.'

As we neared Tórshavn, lights flashed by the car windows, and I saw tears running down the old man's cheeks.

Hildy pulled up in front of the glass-fronted parliament building and dried her eyes. When I helped Eigil out of the car, the chairman nearly collapsed on me. A guard, obviously forewarned of our arrival, hurried out to help. He came down the steps and took hold of Eigil's other arm as we half-carried the man into the vestibule, where we eased him onto a chair. Penny followed us in, carrying the pile of documents, the papers the Russian solicitor had demanded Eigil sign.

'Eigil. It's late. Where will you stay?'

'I will get a room at the Hotel Hafnia up the st[reet]. They always take good care of me. But thank you, I [will] forever be in your debt. Now I must get upstairs to [the] meeting and tell them everything.'

I leant in close and whispered in his ear,

'Eigil, you can't mention what happened in your b[ase]ment. I had to shoot that man, you realise that, don't [you]? We saved you, but I don't want to go to jail for it. M[um's] the word, okay?'

'Mums? What is this Mums?'

'Just don't mention it to anybody. And one last thin[g,] we return it tomorrow morning, would it be all right f[or us] to borrow your car? We're staying with friends in Hoy[vik.]'

'I will not need it the next couple of days, not unti[l my] feet have healed. Keep it, at least to the end of the w[eek.] And once again, thank you for everything you have d[one] for me. You saved my life.'

Penny and I went out to the Mercedes where H[eri] remained behind the wheel. I turned to my daughter,

'Penny dear, you've been through a lot. I think [you] should stay away from your flat for the time being. [The] Russian lawyer and the big bloke know you by sight, [they] might also know where you live. Wouldn't it be best if [you] come to stay with us at Knud and Oydis's house?'

'Yes, of course, Dad. We also need to talk. I've g[ot a] question or two about this stuff you've been doing, [run]ning around the islands with pistols and chasing pe[ople] with knives. And Dad, I saw you shoot a man.'

'As soon as we can get a private moment,' I promised.

Hildy took the coastal road, Yviri-við-Strond, and once it turned inland, she made a right, crossed a dark valley and headed up a steep road, which led up to the Hoyvík suburb and Knud's house.

To my surprise, when we arrived the lights were on, even at this late hour, it was approaching midnight. Hildy pulled into the driveway. We climbed out, and Hildy walked over to the front door and tried the handle.

'Locked dear? Doors were never locked in the old days,' I said.

She pushed the button, we heard the doorbell chime from within the house.

This was the moment I had dreaded, as I knew Hildy and Penny must have. Until now, I had somehow compartmentalised the fact that Sámal and his family were dead, along with Hans, because it was so unreal. Knowing in a moment we would stand face-to-face with Knud and Oydis, the tragedy hit home with full force. I felt the sting of tears in my eyes.

The door opened. Oydis, with Knud standing behind her. In tears, Hildy stepped forward and hugged Oydis. She released Oydis and stepped into Knud's arms, as Penny, crying, took her mother's place and embraced Oydis. Over Hildy's head, Knud looked questioningly at me, eyebrows raised.

Behind him, from the bathroom, we heard the toilet flush. A moment later, the door opened, and Sámal's wife emerged into the hallway. Hildy pushed Knud aside

and rushed forward to embrace her cousin, the crying
wailing reaching new heights.

I stood on the doorstep and said to Knud,

'We heard about the explosion, the destruction
Sámal's house. There were no survivors. We're so s(
but at least his wife was not home.'

Knud gave me a broad smile.

'Well, if we fooled you, our trick must have wor!
They were all out to dinner at the Angus Steakhouse d
by the harbour. It's quite good you know, they do a pe1
Rib-Eye, you should try it. And the shrimp cocktail…

'Knud, too much detail, what happened?'

As the women dried their tears, Knud explained
police had called and informed Sámal of the explo
while they were out eating. Sámal was adamant it c(
not be an accident. A qualified technician checked the
mains and the furnace at his house regularly.

'It seems Hans had spoken to his wife yesterday.
employers called her this morning asking his whereabc
they were trying to contact him. She thought it very stra
that the employers called her. 'Had he been fired and
he too ashamed to tell her?' she asked herself.'

She had told the man on the phone that Hans called
daily on a landline. He was staying with Sámal Halvo1
and had lost his mobile.

'Sámal is convinced the explosion was an attack
said so to the police. He got them to bring his family l
The TV station was asked to report there were no su
vors. If the explosion is indeed foul play, we do not v

the criminals to try again. Sámal has set the call tree in motion telling their relatives not to worry, the news story is a hoax. I'm afraid, however, the family's puppy died in the fire, the children are devastated. I hope they catch whoever did it.'

I somehow doubted they would.

The women took Penny upstairs to get her settled in.

'Where are Sámal and Hans now?' I asked.

'They are at the Løgting, a late-night session is about to begin. Now, Frank, you look tired. Klaksvík can have that effect on people. It's quite boring there, nothing ever happens except the rain. But my day has been very exciting. Let's go in, I'll tell you about it. Would you like a whiskey?'

'If I could bother you for an Ardbeg, please make it a large one. I want to do my bit in helping you rid yourself of that bottle.'

Ten kilometres north of Hoyvík, Max, his face painted in camouflage with smears of green and black, came down the hill to chat under the stars with the charming young police officer.

'All quiet?' he asked.

'Nothing to report,' she replied.

'We saw a Mercedes from our observation post. Nice car. Who has that kind of money up here?'

'You could see the car was a Mercedes? In the d[ark] from up there?'

'Sure, we have infrared goggles.'

'Oh, okay. I think it would surprise you. There a[re a] good number of very hard-working people. There is [a lot] of big money being earned in the fishing industry, e[spe]cially now the Faroe Islands can circumvent the EU [boy]cott of Russia, you know, fish exports. The Russians [must] like the Faroes a lot.'

'In more ways than you can imagine,' answered [the] lieutenant. 'So, you think the lady driving is wealthy?'

'You could see that? The woman?'

'Sure. When you used the flashlight.'

'Oh. Okay. No, I don't think she is rich, it w[as] her car. She was just driving a member of parliamen[t to] Tórshavn. He'd had a bit too much to drink and was s[leep]ing in the back seat.'

She snorted a laugh, Max found her charming.

Ida continued, 'The lady and her husband, he wa[s in] the back as well, they're just a sweet couple with an ove[rac]tive imagination. When I last met them on Suðuroy, [they] had crashed a car and thought gunmen were chasing t[hem] over the mountains. Here, on the Faroe Islands, can [you] believe it?'

'They're not normally that imaginative. Quite bor[ing] really, but I adore them.'

'What do you mean?'

'They're my parents. Max Llewellyn, at your servic[e.]'

'What a coincidence!'

'Not really, it's a long story.'
'Perhaps you could tell me sometime over dinner.'
'I'd love to. But I'll need a rain check.'
'Clear skies. Tomorrow, sunny…,'
'No, what I meant was…,'

# 36

The soft knock came just before seven o'clock Thursday morning. As I rubbed the sleep from my ey[es I] saw the door crack open, Penny peeking through, she w[ore] a pair of her mother's pyjamas and had a concerned [look] on her face. She beckoned me out into the hallway. In [the] TV room, on the sofa where she had spent the night, [she] tucked herself in under my arm, her legs curled up. I t[ook] her duvet and spread it over the two of us.

After a while, she whispered, 'I've hardly slept.'

'I understand, dear. A terrible experience, you m[ust] have been scared.'

'It's not that. I thought I knew my parents, then s[ud]denly you show up with guns and knives. You owe m[e an] explanation.'

'What can I say?'

'You're complete strangers to me. To all of us. Shoo[ting] people, rescuing people, climbing mountains with g[un]men in pursuit.'

'Well, hardly mountains. Hills more likely,' an in[ten]tionally flippant comment, this was not the talk I wa[nted] to have.

'Dad!' she hissed.

'Sorry.'

This was not supposed to be about me. I wanted to discern how my daughter was faring. Instead, she continued in this unwanted direction,

'Dad, I know how sad you were at being fired from the ministry. I guess that's okay, but running around, like secret agents? You and Mom?'

'I'm afraid one thing led to another, luv, I'm sorry. And I haven't been with the ministry of defence for years. I worked for MI6. It was they who fired me, I think unfairly.'

'So you were a spy and all this time, you never told us.'

'Not a spy, merely an intelligence officer, I was head of the Middle Eastern section, an analyst really, a strategy maker. I hunted terrorists, but only from a desk. And according to the Official Secrets Act, I'm still not permitted to tell you any of this, so you'll have to keep it to yourself.'

'The trips, Dad. I remember you were always so quiet when you got back.'

'Fact-finding missions, meeting contacts. Never anything dangerous,' I lied.

'But last night you acted so professional, so confident.'

'You can't imagine how frightened I was. But I felt rage, seeing my little girl like that.'

'You shot him, and we didn't call the police.'

'Would you rather I hadn't?'

She fell silent. Then,

'No, he was an awful person. He must be the one who blew up Sámal's house, and I saw him torture the old man. You did the right thing, and you know what? Thinking about it, I would have done the same for you and Mom, I'd had a gun, that is. Where did you get it?'

'It's illegal. It's why we couldn't call the authori[ties]. I would be in all sorts of trouble, and it wouldn't [have] brought him back,' I said.

'When I saw your face framed in the broken wind[ow], I couldn't believe it. And poor Brian, hitting his head [like] that. And then Mom shows up wielding a giant k[nife], sticking that man, taking charge,' Penny chuckled.

'She cooks at home, she's used to knives.'

'Dad, you're not listening.'

'I know, dear, but yes, she is quite formidable when [she] puts her mind to it. It's one of the things I've always lo[ved] about her.'

We sat in silence.

I spoke first,

'I need you to tell me you'll be alright.'

'You first,' my daughter countered. 'You've been so [sad] and I want you to be content. Promise me, Dad, prom[ise] you'll try.'

'I'm sorry, Penny, you don't know what it's like, bei[ng a] has-been, redundant. Most mornings, I've no reason to [get] out of bed. For the first time in my life, I'm well and t[ruly] afraid of living the rest of my life, existing in obscu[rity] without purpose.'

'You'd get up if I moved home, we could do this e[very] morning. But what you need is to find something to [do,] get a hobby, maybe you could take up pottery-making, macramé classes, watercolours or finer cooking.'

'Now it's you, who's not listening,' I laughed. 'And what's wrong with my cooking? But I promise to do as you say, I'll try, okay? In return, you have to promise to put all this behind you.'

'I'll do my best, Dad, you know I will. But it'll take time. That man was evil,' my daughter shivered.

'Penny, should we consider psychotherapy?'

'Good idea, Dad, in fact, it's just what you need. But not me, I'm made of sterner stuff. Mom says so. So don't worry about me, okay?'

'Alright dear. I just thought you would want to talk it through, get it out of your system.'

'No, not again, Dad.'

'What do you mean, again?'

'I spent time with Mom last night after you'd gone to bed. We had a good cry. Always helps.'

We sat in each other's company, in the still of the morning for what seemed an eternity, Penny snuggling under my arm, a single tear rolling down my cheek.

Hildy peaked into the room and smiled. She came over and crawled in under my other arm. Happiness filled my soul as I held my two girls, knowing how lucky I was to have them both in my life.

The spell was broken when Oydis stuck her head through the open door,

'You're all up. Jet lag, ja? I'll make coffee. See, I also make joke!'

She giggled infectiously.

I smiled.

# 37

I should have been satisfied. We had discovered Russian's plans, and I had given C the information needed to act. I had done my bit for Queen and Cou and was now working for C, not permanently, but still

Standing out by the airport next to the chairm Mercedes in my blazer, white shirt, and a red tie, v ing for the arrivals, I reflected on the events of the n before. What if I had given up while we were in Klaks or if, after hearing about Sámal's house, we had staye our room and put off visiting the chairman until the day. I shuddered at the thought and tried not to ima what could have happened to my Penny.

I wanted to say to myself 'all's well that ends v but it was no excuse. I had been impetuous, putting family and myself in danger twice, well three times if counted the Ocean Nemesis. Thankfully, all that was behind us, we were safe, and I was ready to go hom Guildford.

I had just one last task to perform.

Foiling the Russian's scheme was the end-game. Bri was counting on *me,* C had said so on the telephone. I could I refuse? I was also proud she had given me an cial codename, although Puffin? She had swept aside objections, me stating categorically that the alias was a bad omen with the birds facing extinction, and she not caring a damn.

When I told Hildy, she had merely laughed,

'Better than Guillemot!'

The passengers began to emerge through the revolving doors. The tall fit looking bankers in their Saville Row suits were unmissable as was the short, accountant-like Treasury man trailing behind. I stepped forward to greet them and felt an immediate dislike for their leader.

'Darn nice of them to send us a driver. Saves us the taxi fare,' the American joked to his colleagues, he had a Texan drawl. I stuck my hand out to shake. The banker looked at it and handed me his carry-on. I set it down, looked up at the man with a smile, attempting to hide my contempt and stuck my hand out once more. He could not avoid shaking hands, his palm was clammy.

'Frank Llewellyn, pleased to make your acquaintance. You've been told I'm in charge. Please put your bags in the boot so we can get going.'

I shook hands all around, lastly with the Treasury man, whom I in my mind dubbed 'Stubby'.

'Why don't you ride up front?' I suggested.

The bankers were forced to fold themselves into the back seat. I knew I was being petty, but I also felt the need to take charge. I climbed in behind the wheel, secretly thanking the chairman once more for the loan of his car, it made everything so much simpler.

I got us onto the highway.

On the ride out to the airport, I had kept my eye on mountain slopes, hoping to spot some military prese knowing that if the Paras were worth their salt, I need have bothered. Now driving back to Tórshavn, I cor ued to scan the hills, careful to keep an eye on the roa the same time. Approaching Tórshavn, a thought cro my mind. I had seen nothing. Could it be because Br had sent only a handful of troops? Readily concealable easily overcome? Well, there was nothing I could do al that now.

Parking down the street from the parliament build I led the others inside, the guard sent us up to a first-f conference room. Sámal stood waiting together with tall solicitor, Gov, the man who had taken my deposi regarding our Ocean Nemesis outing.

Hildy stood over by the windows. She turned, and face mellowed on seeing me, my heart melted as alw In bed last night, I had told her of C's telephone cal the need for me to lead the negotiations and arrange refinancing of the loan. Hildy had said she wanted to ticipate in the meetings as well, and then she had slip out of our room, obviously to have her mother-daug chat with Penny. It had not been my intention to end evening in such a manner. We had absolutely fine h rooms ready and waiting, standing empty in Klaksvík Viðareiði. Those were my last thoughts before I drifted to sleep.

'Right gents, phones off, let's get started,' I said, ( we were all seated around the conference table, me at end, Hildy at the other. On my left sat the bankers and Stubby. On my right, Sámal and Gov. Coffee, tea and ice water were on the table, we were in for a long session.

'First we need to agree on law and jurisdiction,' I said.

The bickering began. It lasted for a while.

The door opened and in came the recorder we had met at the police station the other day. He carried a pile of papers, which he placed on the table next to Gov, and then he came around and bent down to me.

'Sir, you have a call, they tried your cell. They told me to say it's urgent.'

'Not now,' I said. 'We're busy.'

'Sir, I was to say it is a Mrs Seabiscuit.'

That would be C. I rose and followed the young man out.

'Frank, how are the negotiations going?' she asked when I picked up the receiver in the adjacent meeting room.

'Enjoying my morning with bankers and solicitors, what could be better? Lots of discussions, but we'll get there.'

'The reason I ask is, things might come to a boil.'

'Land or sea?'

'Sea. The cruiser, the Pyotr Velikiy, is escorting a number of LST's as we speak. Frank, any ideas? NATO is considering going to DEFCON 2, the last time that happened was the Cuban missile crisis. It could get messy. One thing might lead to another.'

'How far out?'

'Approaching the Orkneys as we speak,' C said.

'Have the British tourists arrived here? Big group?

'Sufficient. Willing to engage if need be. A Cap Jenkins is in charge.'

'Okay, I'll need some time to think,' I said.

'We don't have much. Call me back if you have epiphany.'

As I opened the door to the conference room, the thing I heard was,

'Darn it, what if the Faroese government intention cancels the lease arrangements, throws the Brits off islands, then there will be no revenue. Y'all tell me, how we get our money under that scenario?'

The bickering continued.

Something nagged at the back of my mind.

# 38

'Boss, your son is on line three,' Defence Minister Rushkov's shapely secretary said, sticking her head through the open door.

He picked up the receiver and smiled with pride in hearing the voice of his one and only child. The line crackled, the connection was by satellite.

'Alexander, my boy. Good of you to give your old father a call.'

'Papa, did you know about this?'

'Know what?'

'You know.'

'Alexander, do I need to repeat myself? I don't know what you are referring to.'

'Papa, this line may not be secure. Still, I must risk it. I have been ordered to escort an invasion force to the Faroe Islands. We are in the North Sea as we speak.'

'Son, you must follow your orders.'

'They have authorised the nuclear option, Neptune, undersea detonation only, but still. I just got off the line with the admiral of the fleet, he made threats, Juliana, and the girls, your granddaughters. If I don't get through to the Faroes, there is no reason for me to come home. Papa, that's what he said. How can you do this to me?'

Oleg sat in shock. His lovely daughter-in-law and four little sweeties under threat, his son sent on a pote suicide mission. That bastard, the admiral.

'What are your chances of success?'

'Right now, ninety-nine per cent provided we have promised air-cover and submarine support. We are up against a single Danish corvette, which is trailing However, if contrary to the admiral's assurances, the I choose to engage, they have a destroyer in the vicinity have their radar signature. Also, they have their air b and perhaps submarines. We don't know, we are not p ing actively, it would be a declaration of aggressive int

'Alexander, I knew you were on your way up there, I had no idea of your orders. You must not start the sh ing, only defend yourself, and with a measured respo If you need to abort because of overwhelming odds, d And trust me, my boy, I will dispatch forces immedi to protect Juliana and the children.'

Oleg rang off. He needed a drink. He pushed the ir com button,

'My dove, vodka. Then get me FSB headquar Sankt Petersburg district, the commanding officer.'

HMS Artful had been on trials for the better part of weeks, sneaking in and out of sounds, shadowing ves running silent and participating in the occasional exe

or war game with other NATO ships. With her new crew, she invariably lost in all encounters.

They had been returning to Faslane, their base on the River Clyde, for more classroom education when the very-low-frequency signal, or VLF, came through, requiring them to send up a buoy and receive a data package.

Their new orders included a list of assets. Two destroyers, an American and a fellow Brit. Two attack submarines, their sister boat, the Astute, and a Yank to the north, and finally, his own command, the Artful to the south. An outstanding display of firepower was ready and waiting.

The Artful's skipper pondered his predicament. With a crew still classified as green, he could not risk mucking everything up. He had immediately advised the admiralty against his participation, stating his lack of readiness, but they were adamant. His boat was in the vicinity, and they needed every available asset.

With no other option open to him, he had therefore unilaterally decided on the only prudent strategy. The Artful would sit this one out. He would hide, he would not get in the way of his colleagues, and he would certainly not risk friendly fire. Not so much British and American ships shooting at him, but rather the genuine possibility of his crew, in this, their first ever weapons-hot encounter, making a hash of things and sinking one of Her Majesty's ships, or God forbid one of the Yanks.

On their starboard bow, the undersea cliffs of the island of Hollandstuon, the most northern of the Orkneys Islands, would hide his boat from sonar detection as the Russian fleet passed north of his position. If later on, the en began active pinging, the echo off his boat and the ne island would merge. Worst case, or rather the best case would be deemed a rock.

# 39

'Sámal, do you think we could have a word outside?' I asked.

Both Sámal and Gov rose from their seats.

'No, just you, Sámal,' I said.

I shut the door behind us.

'Sámal, I was sorry not to catch you last night or at breakfast this morning.'

'Yes, we made an early start. One moment the parliament wants to deal with the Russians, the next moment the prime minister gets an even better proposition from the British. Very curious.'

'The explosion, it's terrible, I'm sorry.'

'At least we are all safe. But our puppy, we are devastated. I hope they discover who did this. They say it could be a small man, our neighbours saw him hanging around with a rucksack.'

'Sámal, the reason I asked you to step out with me is, I think something terrible is going to happen, it's something we need to stop. Remember the Russian diplomat, we told you about? The man responsible for abducting Hans? I gave you his passport. He is also the one who took Eigil Jonasen prisoner last night.'

'Eigil has filed a complaint, he says they fled his h[ouse] when you and Hildegard showed up on his doorstep. T[here] is a warrant outstanding for the Russian's arrest, two o[ther] men, as well. And we heard about Peggy, is she alright[?]'

I was tired of correcting him, so I merely continue[d.]

'Yes, she'll be okay. But Eigil, I assume he told the [Par]liament everything last night. All the things we'd alr[eady] guessed. The Russians conspiring with Leif Olsen, [the] intentional default under the loan agreement, etcetera. [But] Sámal, there is more, things I cannot tell you.'

'Why not?'

'Because it's secret. Sámal, I used to work in the i[ntel]ligence community. So you'll have to trust me on this.[']

'Ah, that explains much. Here I was, thinking you [were] some ordinary tourist meddling in things, which were [not] your concern. And I did not understand why the ban[k] allowed you to take part in the meeting. Now I do, yo[u are] a secret agent.'

'Well, not exactly a secret agent, more precisel[y an] intelligence officer. I sat at a desk and studied reports.[']

'You are not fooling me, Mr James Bond. Is Hil[degard a] secret agent as well? Are you a husband and wife tea[m of] assassins? Is that why the men fled from Eigil's house [last] night?'

'Sámal, you're letting your imagination get the b[etter] of you. I need you to be serious. This Russian solicit[or, I] wonder if you somehow can find him for me. You hav[e a] picture from his passport, he's bald, shouldn't be har[d to] spot. Can you do this for me? This is important.'

'Mr Secret Agent, for you I will do this thing. I will call the police to see if they have caught him, and if they have not, I will set the telephone tree in motion, it works quite well here in Tórshavn. I will get it started immediately.'

As we broke for lunch, Sámal made another call, he nodded several times as he glanced towards me and on the way out of the conference room, he paused,

'He has not been caught by the police. The tree has had a chance to work. The last time anyone saw your friend was late last night, down by the harbour. He has a room at the Hotel Føroyar but has not been there since yesterday afternoon. He is not staying with any Faroese family or at another hotel. I'm sorry Frank, that's all we know. Now, come, it's Thursday, the cafeteria special is a marvellous steamed salmon with sauce Hollandaise.'

'Sounds good, Sámal. But first I need some fresh air.'

I looked down the corridor to where Hildy led the group, engrossed in conversation with the Texan.

'Hildy, dear, fancy going for a walk?' I called.

We left the building, passing the Faroes's one-and-only cinema. Turning right, we walked past the bookstore with its grass roof standing under the maple trees, and then down the stone steps to the West Harbour.

There were people about, it looked cosy, exactly as it had on our first day, the day we met Penny for coffee, the day this calamity began. Strolling arm in arm along boardwalk, I steered us towards the FaroeOil building

'Aren't you hungry?' my wife asked.

'We need to figure something out. C thinks it m come to a shooting war with the Russian fleet, so thing, which could escalate big time. The ships are at the navies deployed, there is not a lot we can do a that. But I was wondering if somehow Georgi can us de-escalate the conflict. According to Sámal, Ge was seen hanging around the harbour last night. He's been back to his hotel, so I thought we'd try and find here, at the FaroeOil building, or perhaps down by boatsheds.'

'We could ask one of the FaroeOil employees,' H suggested.

'I doubt anyone's about. The Russian bank is for the company into receivership, they will undoubtedly l sent the staff home.'

Sure enough, when we arrived outside the buildir tried the front door. It was locked, a paper sign, handv ten, hung inside the glass.

'Closed until further notice,' Hildy translated.

'Let's try around the back,' I suggested.

That door was locked as well.

I looked around. The back alley was deserted, empty save for bits of rubbish along the walls, s wooden crates and a stack of pallets. I stepped back looked up at the rear of the building. Beside the d above head-height, a frosted window was cracked ope difficult entry point, but not impossible. Under it, I leant a pallet against the wall, and then placed a wooden crate in front of it for support.

'Hildy dear, please try and hold it steady, as well as you can,' I said as I climbed up, slid my fingers into the space between the windowsill and the frame and pulled. The window did not budge. Running my fingers horizontally along the bottom rim, I felt the latch and pushed up on the metal bar. I felt it release, and the window swung down catching my fingers. Ouch. As I pulled my hands towards me, it swung shut. Damn it.

'Hildy, have you anything sharp in your bag?' I asked as I flicked my fingers back and forth, willing the pain to subside.

'I have this,' she said and took one of the chopsticks from her hair.

I used it to pry the window open and handed the chopstick back to my wife. I worked the frame up and down as I applied pressure, pushing it to my right. It suddenly became heavy as it came off its hinges.

'Can you take this?' I said handing the window down. 'Or is it too heavy?'

I need not have asked. Hildy lifted it to the ground as I prepared to hoist myself through the opening.

'Darling, just asking. Did you bring the gun? It could be dangerous, searching the building.'

'The metal detector at parliament would have picked it up, which would be awkward, and I did not want to leave it in Eigil's car. It's at home, locked in its box in my suitcase.

And didn't you tell me to leave it in the room and [shooting] people? You can't have it both ways, dear, [you] have to risk it.'

I did not mention the fact that I felt awkward hav[ing] the pistol in my pocket. Just the night before, I had us[ed] to kill a man.

Pulling myself up was hard work. Resting my st[om]ach on the windowsill, I found myself in the loo, h[ang]ing directly over an unflushed toilet bowl. The smell [was] devastating. I realised one thing was for sure, if I [was] not careful, it would be a while before Hildy kissed [me] again.

Once more, giving my silent thanks to Wilson fo[r] the agility training he put me through each week and [my] small athletic build, I held my breath and pulled m[yself] through the window, lowering my body until I had [my] hands on the cistern and then the seat. Then I walked [my] feet down the wall until I had reached the floor.

Cheeks bulging for want of oxygen, I opened the [door] and exhaled. The hallway was silent. I went throug[h to] the alley door and unlocked it. Opening it, I stepped [out] and inhaled deeply. Hildy watched me with a question[ing,] amused look on her face.

Putting a finger to my lips, I stood thinking until I [had] an idea. I looked around for a weapon, a piece of pip[e was] in the corner. If I hit someone over the head with th[at, I] might kill them. Not good. I opted for a piece of woo[d,] thick as my wrist, the length of a cricket bat.

I leant towards my wife and whispered in her ear,

'I agree, dear, searching the building is too dangerous. Do us a favour, go inside to the loo, it's just inside the door, and flush the toilet. Anyone hearing it will likely come to investigate. Then hurry back out and stand in the doorway. When somebody comes, lure them into the alley, then skedaddle. As soon as you are around the corner, there are people, you'll be safe.'

'What about you?'

'I'll be right on your heals if there is any danger.'

As Hildy disappeared into the building, I stood against the wall. The toilet flushed, then Hildy appeared holding her nose, she gave me an evil eye. I answered with a shrug and an innocent smile. She turned and looked into the building for what seemed forever.

'Hello,' she said, as she turned and hurried up the alleyway. The back of a bandaged head appeared, followed by a large torso. Brian, no doubt about it. Being right-handed, I took care to swing from above, so I did not hit the wall inadvertently and deaden the blow. I also aimed for the neck instead of his head.

Brian went to his knees and then fell flat on his face, I almost felt sorry for the man. To my right, I sensed someone inside the building. Georgi stood in the hallway with the shearing scissors in his hand, he looked surprised, and then he turned to flee.

I chased him through the building, into an office environment and caught up with the diplomat just as he fumbled to unlock the glass front door. The scissors were impeding his progress. I stopped six feet short of him.

'Georgi, my friend, seriously, we do have to stop m[eet]ing like this. Now turn around, relax, and drop it. I'm [not] here to harm you.'

The man spun around and struck out with the sciss[ors.] I swatted the Russian's hand with my stick, the wea[pon] went flying as Georgi yelped in pain.

'I told you, I'm not here to hurt you, please don't m[ake] me do that again.'

Standing patiently, looking at the man, giving hi[m a] minute, I saw the frantic look in his eyes subside.

'Georgi, I don't know if you are up-to-speed witl [all] that is happening. A consortium of British banks is pa[ying] back Eurodea Bank every penny owed. By the end of b[usi]ness tomorrow, the Russian Federation will have no ri[ghts] at all, not that they have any now, not with all the sw[in]dling, that's been going on. Your attempts have failed.'

'I have diplomatic immunity, you must let me go.'

'Georgi, you sound like a broken record. What I sh[ould] do is beat you to death, right here, right now. But I'm [not] going to do that. Instead, I want you to be a hero.'

'A dead hero, probably.'

'No, a hero of the Soviet Un…, uh, the Rus[sian] Federation. You see, the invasion fleet you mentio[ned,] we have ships, warplanes and submarines out there [with] orders to sink them.'

I did not know this for a fact, C had merely said as[sets] were in place. However, what other assets could there [be?]

'Georgi, if your friends attempt to force their [way] through, there will be a massacre, both sides will lose.'

'I'm sorry, I can't help you.'

'Georgi, I think you can. We can stop this together. The Pyotr Velikiy is escorting the Russian convoy, that's what I've been told.'

'Then..., what do I call you?'

'You call me Frank, just Frank.'

'Okay, Frank, maybe it is as you say, maybe I can help. Because one thing I did not mention. The defence minister of the Russian Federation, he is my uncle. He is also Alexander's father.'

'And Alexander is?'

'Vice Admiral Alexander Ruzhkov, commander of the Pyotr Velikiy. My cousin.'

I knew it.

# 40

Outside the FaroeOil building, the breeze blowing c[ool], the midday sun warmed my back. Next to me st[ood] a nervous-looking Georgi.

I asked my wife, 'Did you check on Brian?'

'Dilated pupils, definitely concussed. You have to [stop] hitting him like that.'

With a shrug, I took out my phone and called C.

'What's the latest, Ma'am?'

'They are still heading west. They're refusing to [take] our calls, they seem adamant, intent on reaching t[heir] destination.'

'The weather here can be awful, someone should [tell] them to stay home.'

'We've tried.'

'Well, I have an idea,' I said. 'Who better to trus[t on] such occasions than family? Are you aware of the skipp[er's] connections, his father?'

'We have been briefed. Almost royalty.'

'I have his cousin standing here next to me. He [has] agreed to have a word, he's the one who concocted [the] whole mess from the start.'

'That might work. You need to get him to somew[here] with secure communications.'

'It will be difficult. There is a warrant out for his arrest. So our first order of business must be making sure he doesn't get taken into custody. If you can somehow arrange that, I will get him to a radio. There is a coast guard vessel, the Brimil.'

I looked across the harbour waters and saw empty moorings.

'No that won't work,' I said.

'What other official buildings are there?' C asked.

'The parliament building where we are meeting with the bankers. I need to get back soon, the lunch break will be almost over. And there is the police station, but you'll have to hurry to stop them from detaining Georgi once we show up.'

'Leave that to me. Go there. They will have secure comms. Contact me when you arrive, and Frank...,'

'Yes?'

'This has priority. You need to get this done.'

'But the negotiations.'

'Is Hildy there with you? Yes? Has she participated in your detective work and the talks so far?'

'We've been together these last couple of days and at this morning's session, yes. Why do you ask?'

'Brilliant. Let her take over, she's a smart woman. Not to belittle you Frank, but the only thing those bankers need is continuous kicks in their buttocks. I'm sure she's up for it. After all, she runs three charities and raised four teenagers.'

'But...'

'No buts, Frank. Britain expects. I need you to st[o]
war. Get to the police station, and call me once you're th[ere]

She rang off.

I stood shocked at the enormity of what C had s[aid,]
the task I had been given. Excitement gripped my [
This was what I craved, to have a chance to make a di[ffer]-
ence, except I had never imagined a responsibility of [this]
magnitude. I could not help but smile. Yes! I would do [this]
thing, I would stop this war.

Hildy looked at me curiously, having heard only [one]
side of the conversation.

'Dear, you're not going to believe this,' I said.

I held the door for Hildy and followed her into the con[fer]-
ence room to find that the others had resumed their [dis]-
cussions. At each end of the table stood a plate of saln[on,]
asparagus and potatoes in a creamy yellow sauce.

Sámal interrupted himself,

'Frank, Hildegard, we couldn't understand where y[ou'd]
gone off to. I brought you lunch,' he said, his eyes wave[ring]
to Georgi who entered behind me. Hildy had gone aro[und]
to her end of the table.

All eyes were now on the diplomat, the men in [the]
room seemed mesmerised at the complete baldness of [the]
Russian, with even his eyebrows missing. I was hungry [I]
had nothing since breakfast, but I asked over my shoul[der]

'Georgi, when did you last eat?'

'Yesterday. Lunch. We were hiding.'

'Sit, enjoy,' I sighed, as I remained standing behind the Russian. 'Everybody, meet Georgi Ruzhkov, representative of Eurodea Bank. He needs to arrange for his bank's documentation, receipt of the repayment, etcetera.'

'Frank, we need to notify the police,' Sámal said.

'We are on the way over there, but first, he needs confirmation you will repay FaroeOil's loan in full before the weekend, including outstanding fees and interest.'

Now, this was important. Georgi had to believe his bank was out of it, that Russia no longer had any rights come Saturday. Sitting in front of me, he showed little interest in anything other than his plate, he wolfed down my food.

I looked around the table.

'Can you confirm this?'

'No, darn it. We can't...,' the Texan began, as he looked left and right for support from his fellow bankers.

'Yes, we can,' Stubby said and received a confirming nod from Gov.

'But, darn it...,'

'My boss in London told me no 'buts' are allowed,' I said. 'I believe you've met her, a tall woman with black hair.'

A look of fear crossed the Texan's face as he nodded his surrender.

'Right, just to be crystal clear. Are we in agreement?' I asked. 'Eurodea Bank has no claim to anything come end-of-business tomorrow, correct?'

I got a reluctant 'yes' from each of the bankers, wondered what kind of hold C and the Treasury had these surprisingly timid men.

'Georgi, are you finished eating? Was it tasty? G You got your confirmation, now we need to leave.'

'But Frank,' Sámal said. 'You can't go. We still delicate matters to discuss. We need your arbitration.'

'Sámal, I have received my marching orders. Hildy take over.'

The heads of the seated men swivelled in uniso face the opposite end of the table where Hildy sat smili thought it looked quite funny, similar to tennis spectat

Sámal responded,

'But…'

'No buts. She has been kicking my arse in discuss for years,' I said, the heads swivelling back to me, I ha stop myself from laughing. 'If you don't behave, I'm she'll kick yours as well. So Gents, make some prog Come on Georgi.'

I prodded the Russian in the shoulder. Georgi from his seat, plate cleaned and together we left the ro We departed the building and headed down the road around the block to the police station.

'Why, hello, Mr Llewellyn, how are you today?' the yo officer asked from behind the counter. I could see she

staring at Georgi's missing eyebrows, her colleague at a desk looking on, interested.

'Isn't he?' she asked.

'I'm fine, Ida, thank you for asking. And yes, he is. I think you have received orders to remand him to my custody.'

Ida turned to her colleague for confirmation, he nodded.

'Yes, they called from Danish Central Command in Århus,' Ida said, turning back to us. 'The chief is really pissed off, he doesn't like surrendering wanted criminals. We were also told to provide you with radio communications and to put you in contact with the command ship, the Absalon. I wasn't aware you were so important.'

'I'm not really, I'm just a nobody,' I said, realising how true those words sounded. Perhaps not under the current circumstances, but in general.

'I'm not sure I'm allowed to, but I should say hello from your son.'

I looked at her. 'Max?'

'I'm afraid you missed him last night when you were driving home. At the roadblock, where I stopped your car.'

I remembered waking up in the back seat, and the flashlight in my eyes.

'He's ever so dashing in his uniform and all. Perhaps I'll see him later. You should come out, they're on some kind of exercise out by Kollafjørð.'

'Oh, I don't imagine he wants his father hanging around, he'd take all sorts of ribbing.'

'Well, when I see him, I'll say hello, shall I? W agreed to stay in touch.'

I wondered if possibly, I was talking to my fu daughter-in-law. Max could do worse. I was also cur to know how many children she intended to have in course, but decided now was not the time to ask. It m convey the wrong impression.

She looked at her wristwatch,

'Central command advised of a radio confere beginning in ten minutes.'

'Okay Ida, we have time. First, the coffee machine then please show us to the communications room. you operate the equipment? And you have the NATO quencies? Splendid, then let's get to it.'

# 41

Georgi sat next to me, a cup of coffee warming both his hands. We faced a control console, a grey communications setup. Throwing switches, dialling dials, Ida's astute handling of the equipment was impressive.

'L16. L16. Come in, L16. This is Faroe Islands Police calling.'

'…receiving you loud and clear, Faroe Islands Police. The admiralty has advised us of your status, please confirm your participant, over,' the female voice said.

I leant forward, as Ida keyed the microphone. 'Frank Llewellyn here, together with Officer Ida...,'

'…Jensen,' she said.

'These comms are strictly top secret. Are there any other participants at your end, over?' the comms officer asked.

Ida was about to answer when I touched her arm and shook my head.

'Negative,' I said as she stared open-mouthed at me and then at Georgi.

I leant forward and whispered in her ear, she was wearing a delightful perfume.

'It's my responsibility, I'll tell you later,' I said.

'Affirmative, Faroe Islands Police. An all vessels b[riefing] is commencing in one minute. You need not con[firm] your identity when the call begins, you are in liste[ning] mode only, over.'

We heard sustained static, then,

'Commander Schmidt of the Absalon, joining the [call]' followed by a row of other sea and air force comman[ders] confirming their attendance.

'Standby for the admiral,' a voice said.

A moment later, there was a rustling sound, as if so[me]one had taken over the microphone and was getting c[om]fortable. Then a gruff voice,

'Good afternoon, gentlemen and ladies. What I [am] about to tell you has just been transmitted to the [sub]marines participating. This morning an encrypted s[atel]lite call from the Russian battlecruiser, the Peter W[ild] or whatever they call it, was intercepted. GCHQ and [the] NSA have been working furiously on cracking the enc[ryp]tion. Presently, all we know is, the word Neptune [was] mentioned. We know for a fact, this is the code use[d by] the Russians for tactical nuclear warheads.'

Georgi leant forward and listened attentively. [The] extent of NATO's ability to crack the Russian codes wo[uld] be a secret of the highest magnitude. I realised I woul[d be] in trouble for this, no doubt about that.

The admiral continued,

'Neptune for subsurface. We have no way of kn[ow]ing in what context this code was used. However, we r[ecognise]

assume the ship's commander was requesting added verification that such weapons were released to his discretion.'

The admiral paused, probably to let the information sink in.

'So we know what we are up against. The rules of engagement are therefore as follows. If the convoy reaches the demarcation line, one hundred and fifty nautical miles from the Faroes, the Dauntless and the Absalon will be ordered to destroy the transports without warning. That should take away their motivation for continuing or for using nuclear warheads to fight their way through. Until then, the Absalon's captain will do his utmost to convince the Russian convoy to turn back. Otherwise, you are ordered not to initiate hostilities. But you are authorised to retaliate in full against any aggression on target or missile launch by the Russians. If he shoots first, you will destroy the Peter Willy. Are there any questions?'

'Sir, this is the Winston Churchill. In this scenario, us engaging the Peter Willy after he fires, but before they reach the no-go line, what about the transports?'

'If possible, they are not to be harmed before reaching the one fifty mark. If they cross that line, I will give orders for their destruction. Further questions? No? You have her specifications. She will be a tough nut to crack, but I have every confidence in you. Gentlemen and ladies, I wish you good hunting.'

Our comms room went silent. I looked first at Ida who appeared stunned by what we had heard, then at Georgi.

He looked equally disturbed, beads of sweat forming his bald crown.

'Georgi. You own this,' I said. 'You started it. You it to all those innocent sailors out there. You need to this madness. They're talking nuclear for Christ's sake. please get me the skipper of the Absalon on the line.'

'Faroe Islands Police Station, I have Captain Schmidt you. With whom are we speaking, over?'

'Hello, captain, Frank Llewellyn here, formerly of Majesty's Secret Intelligence Service.'

I thought it sounded splendid, save for the 'formerly'

'I'm here with Russian diplomat Georgi Ruzh cousin to the admiral of the Pyotr Velikiy and nep to the defence minister of the Russian Federation. Central Command can vouch for me.'

'Mr Llewellyn, were you a party to the all-ships b ing which just took place?'

'Affirmative, captain.'

'And am I to understand you let a Russian governn official overhear that briefing?'

'Yes, Captain. I felt he needed to understand the se ity of the situation if he is to help us avoid disaster.'

'I take it you are aware of the consequences of abet a foreign national in espionage? You know I am oblig to report you?'

'Yes, Captain.'

'Mr Llewellyn, we are kind of busy here. I don't think we have any more to say to each other.'

'Please Captain, this will only take a moment, please hear me out. Georgi Ruzhkov has been heavily involved in this whole affair. According to Georgi, the Russians are convinced they have the law on their side, that they have acquired legal rights to certain land areas on the Faroes, and that they, therefore, have every right to take possession of that real estate. He is willing to persuade them otherwise, to make them back off. In order to do so, he needs to talk to the Russian admiral, his cousin, preferably not over an open line. Will you connect us?'

'Mr Llewellyn, I need to check with fleet command. In the meantime, I'll give you a passive patch to our comms with the Pyotr Velikiy.'

After a series of clicks, I heard a female voice,

'Russian warship, Pyotr Velikiy, this is Her Danish Majesty's ship, the Absalon. You are heading towards restricted waters. Please state your intentions, over.'

'Danish ship Absalon, this is the Pyotr Velikiy, please note these are international waters. We are on route to Murmansk, in escort of cargo vessels in ballast, over.'

'Russian warship, Pyotr Velikiy, if that is the case, you have strayed off course. Come starboard to a new heading, north-by-northeast, over.'

'Affirmative, Absalon, thank you for your assistance, over and out.'

'Russian warship, Pyotr Velikiy, we do not see changing course. Please come starboard to a new head north-by-northeast, over.'

No answer came from the Russian battlecruiser.

There were a couple of clicks.

'Mr Llewellyn, are you still there?'

'Yes, we are here,' I said.

'I wish to address Mr Ruzhkov directly. Am I on [y] loudspeaker?'

'Affirmative,' Ida said.

'Sir, I have been instructed by fleet command to [ ] you a chance to convince your cousin to return to Baltic or divert to Murmansk, whichever he chooses. have a translator standing by, we will know what you saying. If you deviate in form or substance from what have agreed upon, I will cut you off, and you will no given a second chance to save your cousin. Now, ur these conditions, are you prepared to proceed?'

'Yes,' Georgi croaked, clearing his throat. I could the seriousness of the situation had him rattled.

'Okay, the translation is on secure channel four-tw

Ida turned some buttons, threw a switch and han me a headset. I held it ready in my hand.

'Comms, patch him through,' I heard over loudspeaker.

Then the female voice again, 'Russian warship, P Velikiy, this is the Absalon. We have Russian diplo Georgi Ruzhkov for your admiral, please put him on line, over.'

The voice repeated the request, then,

'Danish ship, the Absalon, this is the Pyotr Velikiy. We wish to register a formal complaint against you holding hostage a Russian national with diplomatic immunity, over.'

'Mr Ruzhkov, the floor is yours,' I heard Schmidt say as I quickly donned my headset. With Georgi's muffled Russian in the background, I concentrated on the matter-of-fact female translator's voice.

'Sailor, this is senior diplomat Georgi Ruzhkov of the Russian Federation, and I object to your accusation I would betray my country, even under duress. Now, none of that 'over'...'

A pause. The translator made her decision. She decided to go for it.

'...shit. Get my cousin, Vice-admiral Alexander Ruzhkov on the line now, or I will have you court-martialled. This is a matter of national emergency.'

Another pause. Georgi was doing great, showing much more bottle than I had seen from him up until now. There was some more clicking, then,

'Georgi, you should not be contacting me like this.'

'Brother, you must turn back, we no longer control any lands on the Faroes. We have been outsmarted.'

I saw Georgi's gaze flick towards me, the confession must have hurt. He continued,

'I have just overheard a conversation between the NATO forces. They have submarines, planes and warships. Alexandrovich, they will destroy you if you continue. And if you do make it through, what then? It will be an inte[n]tional catastrophe. We have no rights, I assure you.'

'Georgiovich, you are the victim of a hoax, there [are] only two surface ships in the area. If they fire, I will o[p]erate them.'

'Brother, they know about the nuclear instructions[.]'

'What instructions? Again, it is a ruse.'

'Neptune. You received authorisation.'

The line went quiet, I wondered if we had been cut[.]

Then, 'Georgi, my friend, my brother, I do this [for] Juliana and the girls, tell them that.'

'Sir, the line went dead,' the comms officer said.

'Try and get them back online,' Schmidt's voice.

'Russian warship, Pyotr Velikiy, this is Her Da[nish] Majesty's ship, the Absalon, please respond.'

I heard the message be repeated in English, over [and] over. Then,

'Mr Llewellyn, Mr Ruzhkov, are you still there?' [the] captain asked.

'Yes Captain,' I said, with a heavy heart. I knew v[hat] was coming.

'Mr Ruzhkov, you kept your end of the bargain, [but] I'm afraid it did not work.'

'Captain, can we try again?' I asked.

'My orders were to give you one shot. You've ha[d it,] and besides, they're not responding. I'm sorry, it's not [my] decision. Now, Gentlemen, as mentioned, we are q[uite] busy. Mr Llewellyn, this changes nothing, I will stil[l be] reporting you. Now, good day to you both.'

I sat in shocked silence. This had been my final gambit. Or had it?

'Georgi, you need to call your uncle. They must recall your cousin. Can you convince them of that?'

Georgi took out his phone, swiped the screen and punched the glass with his index finger.

'Russian shit. Broken crap. Not always, only sometimes.'

'Do you see the number?'

'Yes.'

'Ida, can Georgi borrow a phone? But first the helicopter, we need to hire it.'

'They'll want to know which island is your destination. Suðuroy?' she asked.

'We need a three-hour charter, I'll pay whatever it takes,' I said knowing Hildy would be providing the dosh.

Ida reached for the phone.

# 42

'Frank, may I remind you, we are on an open line?' C[...]
'And just so you know, I was privy to the call. You did [...] you could.'

'Ma'am, I want to try again, but we need to be on [...] I need the coordinates of the Dane?'

'The Dane?' she asked.

This open communications thing was taxing.

'The Dane. You know, Schmidt.'

'You'll never make it in time by boat, and it's a n[...] zone. Things could light up sooner than we expect.'

'I'll chance it. There's a helicopter, I'm charterin[...] whatever the cost. My new friend and I are going for a [...] provided we can get the coordinates.'

'Alright Frank, you'll have an SMS in ten. Good lu[...]

The Faroese helicopter service was owned and ru[...] the national airline. Mostly, the helicopters transpo[...] hospital patients between the islands, rescued injured f[...] ermen from outlying trawlers, and did tourist char[...] The helipad lay just five minutes down the road, out [...] cliff overlooking the bay. Ida took us in a police car.

Arriving, I was disappointed to find the landing [...] empty. That was until I heard the distant throbbing of [...] aircraft. Coming into view from around the headland, it [...]

a relatively new machine, an Agusta Westland. Everything depended on the helicopter having sufficient range. As far as I recalled, this model was more than adequate.

We stood well back by the police SUV as the machine landed, Ida clamped her cap firmly down against the downwash. I led Georgi forward, but we need not have bothered. The pilot switched off the engine and the blades lazily rotated to a full stop. He opened his door and taking his time, he climbed out. The co-pilot stayed aboard.

I was getting hyper, knowing thousands of lives were at risk. I felt it was *my* responsibility to prevent this calamity. At the same time, I realised, if I told the pilot we would be flying into a war zone, in all probability, the man would decline my charter. Tact was needed. Or a perfect excuse, my mind raced to come up with one.

'We want to charter your aircraft. A friend, Sámal Haldersen, told us blue whales have been spotted. We want to go see them, I have the coordinates,' I explained.

'Sámal told you this?' the pilot asked. 'I think you have misunderstood, I'll just give him a call.'

I should have known better. Bugger. Everybody here knew everybody else, Sámal was probably the man's second cousin. A minute later, after some discussion in Faroese, the pilot handed me his phone.

'I pulled him out of some meeting. He wants to talk to you.'

'Frank, what is this?' Sámal said. 'We need you here, but instead you leave. Now you are going out into the Atlantic to look for whales. He says I told you about them, I never did.'

I walked away from the pilot and Georgi, covering
mouth and the phone with a cupped palm.

'Sámal, listen to me, this is secret, top secret. The s
people who put me in charge of the bankers, they told
to do this. There are Russian warships on their way to
Faroes. Georgi, the man who was with me, can stop th
But only if we get out there.'

'Frank, your imagination is truly amazing. We h
Russian warships visiting all the time.'

'Sámal, trust me, this time they are coming to stay.
an invasion force. If the pilot knows, he might refus
need you to confirm my ruse.'

'What is 'ruse'?'

'You need to confirm my story, that's what I mean
said, the exasperation creeping into my voice.

'Okay, give me back the pilot.'

A moment later, the pilot terminated the call
looked at me,

'Okay, Sámal, he confirms your story.'

I let out a sigh of relief.

'He says the Russians are coming to invade us, only
stand in their way. Get aboard, we must hurry.'

We lifted off, the pilot banking hard left, as he c
around in a half circle. Georgi and I were in the bac
the big helicopter, in window seats, sitting on either s
each donning a headset. I lifted the headphones from
ear to test the noise level, which was tolerable.

The pilot's voice came through, loud and clear.

'Mr Llewellyn, you should have told me the truth, to begin with. Blue whales. Ha!'

'Would you have believed my story of a Russian invasion force?'

'Normally not, no. But there is all this stuff in the media. And the Brimil has been, how do you say, like eggs, scrambled. The authorities have given orders to avoid the area, but no reason.'

'So you're willing to fly into the restricted area?'

'To save my homeland, yes sir. And it will be free of charge, but you will have to pay for the fuel.'

'Agreed. The Absalon is leading the operation, those are the last known coordinates, the ones I gave you. Can you find her?'

'If we have trouble I will contact the Brimil, Knud will tell us.'

'When do we get there?'

'We are flying at three hundred kilometres an hour, so just over an hour. But be aware, we can only stay airborne in the area for half an hour, then we must head back. Now sit back, enjoy the ride and thank you for flying Atlantic Airways.'

I took off my headset and scooted over to the other side of the aircraft, and motioned for Georgi to take off his ear protection as well. I raised my voice to be heard.

'What did your uncle say?'

Georgi told me about the threats made to the admiral's family, who were now being protected.

'He'll do what he can from his end. He says the re[st is] up to us.'

'Okay, Georgi. When all this is over, despite you b[eing] a right loathsome murdering bastard, I promise you [some]thing.'

'What?'

'I'll get you back your passport.'

'Not necessary. I have a new one from the consu[late.] And you can prove nothing.'

'Georgi, how about this then. If you stop this batt[le, I] promise not to throw you out of the helicopter on our [way] back.'

Georgi fell silent, and then he said, 'Deal' and pu[t the] headset back on.

As the helicopter raced across the North Atla[ntic,] infuriated by the man's casual attitude towards the cri[mes] he had committed, I wondered if I would hold up my [end] of the bargain.

# 43

It had taken some persuading to get the pilot to make the illegal distress call. We had flown the last many kilometres just above wave height, intent on coming in under the radar, then the pilot brought us up to a thousand feet, and I heard his exchange through my headset.

'Mayday, Mayday. Atlantic Airways, OY-HIH helicopter in distress. Mayday, come in anyone who can hear me, over.'

After that, it was all in Danish.

Looking past Georgi, I could see from our windows four sleek amphibious assault ships sailing behind the enormous battle cruiser, the Pyotr Velikiy. Green netting covered the landing ships' cargo decks. From the contours, I was in no doubt vehicles, maybe tanks stood concealed beneath the camouflage.

From the chatter back and forth, I assumed the pilot was doing a splendid job of sneaking us aboard, that was until I heard in my headset,

'They are going to report me for making a fake SOS, and they want to know the names of our passengers. Can I confirm?' a question to me. I gave my permission.

'Okay, we are cleared,' the pilot said. 'I've been told to fly over to the Brimil and wait there after I set you down.'

Schmidt was going to be busy reporting people, [...] vided we all survived the coming hours. We neared [...] Absalon, an ungracious design if ever there was one. [...] windows save for the bridge. No portholes, just a grey [...] of steel slapped onto a ship's hull, with bits and bobs [...] truding. 'L16' it said on the side, an encircled 'H' on [...] stern deck marked the landing zone.

Not since the Falkland's war, had I arrived by [...] copter on a ship. I had not enjoyed the experience t[...] I did not like it now. The helicopter bucked and swa[...] the deck below us rose and fell as my stomach turne[...] handful of crewmembers rushed out from a hanger d[...] which could have accommodated an articulated lorry [...] alone a helicopter. As soon as the wheels hit the deck, [...] helicopter's sliding door was pulled open.

Georgi and I were manhandled into life vests and [...] mets, and I was hustled towards the interior, a sailc[...] each arm, half-carrying me. Georgi and his escort were [...] far behind. I noticed they had pulled a hood over Geo[...] head and marvelled at where they had found one at s[...] short notice.

Our helicopter had hardly slowed its revs. The [...] thing I saw before the hanger door came down was our [...] home leaving the deck. Inside, the crew rushed us thro[...] the hanger, I had barely time to notice the helicop[...] standing there, then they hurried me through a bulkh[...] door and up a flight of stairs. We arrived only mom[...] later on the bridge where I stood winded, swaying with [...]

movement of the ship, the still blindfolded Georgi supported by one of the crewmembers.

The view was intimidating, the Pyotr Velikiy and the assault ships loomed not far up ahead.

A short and compact skipper loomed even closer.

'Mr Llewellyn, an unexpected pleasure,' a statement, dripping with sarcasm.

'Captain Schmidt, time is of the essence. Georgi here has spoken with the Russian defence ministry. As I mentioned, Georgi is the man who orchestrated this whole mess. Until yesterday, the Russian Federation truly believed it had the legal rights to develop naval bases on the Faroes, but no longer.'

'So what changed since yesterday, Mr Llewellyn?'

'The Russian bank who had the rights is being bought out by UK banks as we speak. According to Georgi, the Russian high command also threatened the admiral's wife and children to force him to continue at all costs. Georgi spoke by phone with his uncle, the defence minister, just over an hour ago. The admiral's family is now in protective custody. So you see, Captain, the admiral does not have any reason to continue. But he doesn't know it.'

'What do you propose?'

'We need to give Georgi another chance. If necessary, we have to land him on the Pyotr Velikiy.'

'Making an unauthorised landing with a helicopter is out of the question. However, we'll set up a translator and see if we can get them on the horn. Sailor, escort these men to the communications centre. Inside, Mr Ruzh need not wear the hood.'

'Are you sure they're safe?' the Pyotr Velikiy's comma asked.

We had been assigned neighbouring consoles, to the cute communications officer whose voice I k so well. She gave us different feeds through the head Georgi had the direct line, and I had the translator. appeared to be the first real opening from the Rus admiral. I felt elated. It was working.

'The Danish central command and fleet command also listening in,' the comms officer whispered to me.

Sitting enclosed in bowels of the rolling ship, liste to the exchange, I felt queasy and hoped I would not be all over the equipment. Would it short-circuit the radio ruin everything? Thousands of deaths caused by my vo

'And you are saying, Georgiovich, it would be an ill act of war for me to proceed? Why has the admiral of fleet not communicated this to me?'

'I told them only an hour ago. I called your father I got confirmation from the UK bankers. By this tomorrow, we have no more rights.'

'Could you have been tricked?'

'Alexandrovich, I will not dignify that question wi response.'

'So what is it, you as a diplomat, outside of my chain of command, are ordering me to do?'

'Divert to Murmansk or the Baltic, your choice. Or at least stop your forward progress until you can get confirmation to proceed.'

'So NATO can bring more assets into play.'

Georgi covered his mike and turned to me, 'What can I reply without them cutting me off?' he asked.

I shrugged. I had no idea. The captain's voice came through my headset, saving me from having to answer,

'This is Commander Schmidt. Admiral Ruzhkov, nice to make your acquaintance. Admiral, as you must have anticipated, we are listening in, and just so you know, we have overwhelming forces at our disposal, I think you'll agree. Three U-boats, two destroyers, my ship and three squadrons of Typhoons are at the ready, and that is just for starters. Although I in no way wish to show disrespect to your proud ship, our forces should be enough to convince your superiors that they have sent you on a fool's errand.'

This was even better. If only adversaries more willingly communicated with each other, so many conflicts could be averted. Now Schmidt and Ruzhkov were doing just that.

'Captain Schmidt. Yes, we speak at last, but I find it offensive you calling me a fool.'

Okay, all beginnings are difficult.

'Sir, with all due respect, it is just an expression. My meaning was they have sent you on an impossible mission.'

'I too have been promised air cover, it will ar shortly. And I have U-boat support, I am fully capabl fulfilling my objectives.'

'Admiral, NATO has denied the Russian Federa airspace over Europe for anything other than schedu Aeroflot flights. All military aircraft are being turned l as we speak. And there are no Russian U-boats with thousand kilometres.'

I reasoned air cover might be provided out Murmansk, way up north, but circumventing Nor would require aerial refuelling for the fighters. The Rus air force could never provide sufficient numbers of airc in such a fashion.

'Admiral, your cousin is advocating for you to halt y forward progress and await further orders,' Schmidt sa

I reasoned, taking things one step at a time was a sr move, instead of forcing the Russian admiral to adm face-losing defeat.

'Captain Schmidt, I will order my convoy to slow five knots while we seek clarification from Moscow.'

Hearing those words, a sense of relief washed ( me. I noticed my shoulders had tensed up, now I rela them. Smiling at Georgi, I patted him on the back, fea I might begin to like the bastard.

'Thank you, Admiral. Please keep communicat open,' Captain Schmidt said.

We waited for what seemed an eternity, but what in fact, a quarter of an hour. The comms officer nex me, wearing a pleasant perfume, shared some choco with us while concentrating on her headset. At last, she told her skipper something in Danish, I guessed it meant,

'Captain, the Russian admiral is on the line.'

I donned my headphones.

'Captains Schmidt, you will be happy to learn I have received new orders…'

I waited expectantly, hardly breathing, willing the admiral to say the words.

# 44

Aboard the HMS Artful, since sounding battle stations h[ours] ago, all was quiet. Anxiety had steadily been on the rise, since the Russian convoy passed north of the Orkney Isla[nds] coming within twenty kilometres of their position.

Only the chief sonar technician spoke in a subtle t[one] reporting the movement of ships. The skipper and his [crew] watched the glass battle board with the fluorescent ind[ica]tors showing the deployment of the NATO vessels and [the] steady progress of the Russian convoy.

The skipper had on several occasions consid[ered] bringing the boat up to periscope depth, but that w[ould] mean receiving orders, orders he did not want.

'Captain sir, the Russians are slowing down,' the s[onar] specialist said.

Thank God, the skipper thought. As soon as t[here] were clear signs that hostilities had been avoided, his [men] would be able to relax. He could feel the tension in [the] control room. He knew how taxing it was for his c[rew,] green as they were, to stay alert at battle stations for h[ours] on end. Especially his weapons team seemed jittery. Th[ey] had neither tea nor coffee for hours, lunch had been p[ost]poned, it would be good to stand down.

Fifteen minutes later, he heard,

'Skipper, the Russians are changing course, heading north.'

The situation was defused! He felt like instigating a cheer among his crew, something completely unheard of in a submarine. Instead, he decided he would wait no longer, it was time to go to periscope depth and receive new orders.

'XO, we can stand down and open the galley. Let's order up a nice cup of tea before lunch.'

'One or two, Captain?' The XO knew he sometimes took one lump of sugar, sometimes two.

'Launch one. Launch two, Captain.'

The control room stood in stunned silence. The skipper turned towards his weapon's chief.

'Torps, repeat that.'

'Sir, tubes one and two launched as ordered.'

In the captain's mind, he went over what had just taken place. 'Lunch' not 'launch'.

'Belay that. Commence self-destruct protocol. XO, bring us up to periscope depth, but not before both fish are destroyed. Otherwise, you might cut the cables. We'll get a true carpeting for this, no doubt about it.'

Murphy's law strikes again, he thought, hoping they had not just inadvertently started a war.

'Captain Schmidt, I have received new orders, we are changing heading to north-by-northeast...'

A short pause, then, 'Padla! You tricked me!'

In the background, the comms officer spoke urge[ntly]. I took off my headset.

'What's happening?' I asked.

'There is a launch, two torpedoes from the east, it's [the] Artful. We have no other assets in the area. It's a mist[ake],' the comms officer replied.

'Mistake?'

'Happens more often than you might imagine. [I] once had a harpoon missile take out an entire neighb[our]hood of summer cottages,' she said, too busy to give [me] her full attention.

I donned my headphones again.

'Admiral Ruzhkov, Schmidt here. Please be awa[re I] am in overall tactical command. I have given no orde[r to] fire. Admiral, I am putting my ship between you and [the] incoming ordnance, but please be advised you are at [the] outer range of the torpedoes. There's twenty minute[s to] impact, so we have plenty of time. Sir, please continu[e on] course north-by-northeast.'

I felt the ship accelerate and heel hard over. My st[om]ach contracted from seasickness or pure nerves. I [was] ready to spew forth the coffee I had drunk during the [day] and grateful Georgi had eaten my lunch. The yellow s[tew] would have been particularly embarrassing.

Fifteen kilometres north of the Absalon, HMS Astute cruised a hundred metres beneath the surface, running parallel to her American counterpart. She was returning down from periscope depth, having received a transmission burst, a SITREP.

'Skipper. I have the commander of the Illinois for you on line one.'

The underwater hydrophone transmission was possible over short distances only, no more than a few kilometres.

'Commander Carney,' the skipper said. 'We have just received revised rules of engagement. Orders are, we are only to fire if other allies fire first... hold on, launch from the Artful reported. They must have received orders to fire. We are engaging as well.'

'Captain Schmidt. This is vice-admiral Ruzhkov. Our sonar reports two sets of torpedoes in the water, fifteen kilometres north. Please advise. You lure us closer, then you fire from all sides. Is this your doing?'

I could hear the increasing defiance in the man's voice. Not good.

'The U-boats must have heard the torpedo launch from the east,' the comms officer said for my benefit. 'They think they are firing in self-defence.'

The Russian admiral continued,

'Captain Schmidt, my orders are to safeguard this ( voy and fire if fired upon. Please do not put your ship my cousin in jeopardy by shooting.'

'Sonar, use the emergency abort signal,' Schmidt over the open line. 'Admiral Ruzhkov, sir, I have ord the submarines to self-destruct their torpedoes. I beg not to retaliate. I am increasing speed and will take up tion due north of you.'

'Captain, what will that help? Your torpedoes are ] grammed to go after my engine signature, they will ( dive under your ship.'

'Admiral, sir, we are sending the acoustic abort si; as we speak. You may expect the torpedoes to self-dest any minute now. Please, sir, I beg you, hold your fire. if all else fails, my techy is reprogramming our nexies, decoys will emulate your ship's engine noise. Sir, you l my word, I will not let harm come to your ships.'

'Captain, I give you one minute. Then I must action. Goodbye.'

I was sweating, my armpits and forehead, my palm; were clammy. I was short of breath. This was the enc recent months, I had often thought life not worth livii had been depressed, thinking my existence was irrele to others, me having no work, no way of contributing.

Now, I realised how much I wanted to live.

I was in mortal peril, together with hundreds if thousands of seamen, all because the submarines taken it upon themselves to launch. Six torpedoes \

in the water headed for the Pyotr Velikiy, with Captain Schmidt manoeuvring to put the Absalon in their way.

In less than one minute, if the incoming torpedoes did not self-destruct, Ruzhkov would retaliate, perhaps with nuclear weapons, the killing would begin, and I would have failed.

How could this have happened? I was out here in the middle of the ocean, on the brink of being destroyed in a naval battle, I had done my utmost to prevent. Talk of being unlucky.

I bowed my head and began to pray to no one in particular, thinking of my dear Hildy and my lovely children, Sophie, Penny, Oliver and Max. With teary eyes, I said my silent farewells.

# 45

The generals said they wanted to wait it out in his off[ice] when in fact, Defence Minister Oleg Ruzhkov knew [they] were merely there to keep tabs on him. They did not t[rust] him, but they needed him. Oleg could only sit and liste[n to] their boisterous talk, he did not comment.

The military men were drinking vodka, counting t[heir] chickens, discussing how they would deploy their navy and which countries they would annex first. An i[nva]sion of the Baltic countries was in the cards.

A soft knock at the door, Oleg's first secretary, made her entrance. She walked across the room, her [sen]sual hips swaying. She stopped behind his shoulder, b[ent] down low, showing him and especially the others plent[y of] cleavage, and whispered in his ear.

The room had gone quiet, the military men seem[ed] stupefied by the sight of the young woman's body, acc[en]tuated by the tight-fitting red dress. She stood strai[ght,] thrust out her chest for effect, and left the room, head [held] high. The men's gaze followed her out. The door cl[osed] behind her. Ruzhkov was proud of his girls, his secre[tar]ies, they were by far the most spectacular of all the mi[nis]tries. With so little to occupy his defunct office, he had picked them for their clerical skills.

'Wow. Legs all the way up to her neck on that one,' the army general commented.

'What a fine piece of ass. How often do you do her?' Almazov, the chief of staff asked.

Oleg did not respond. Instead, he rose stiffly from his chair, put his tumbler down on the glass sofa table, stretched his stiff back and lumbered over to the red phone in the corner.

'I believe we have a call from the president,' he said.

He picked up the receiver.

'Mr President, to what do I owe the honour?'

'Ruzhkov. Those arseholes, Almazov and his gang of idiots. They did it again.'

'Yes, Mr President.'

'They exceeded their mandate.'

'Yes, Mr President.'

'Did you know about this?'

'No, Mr President.'

'So say something, for God's sake.'

Oleg was surprised by the president's choice of words. God had never existed under the old regime. Apparently, he was back.

'Yes, Mr President.'

'They are there with you.' A statement, not a question.

'Yes, Mr President. All but the admiral of the fleet whom we expect eminently.'

'That donkey. This time he's screwed things up royally.'

Apparently, the aristocracy was on the rebound as well.

'I take it you've seen the news.'

'News, Mr President?'

'It won't be on our networks, not yet. Not until cleared it with the censorship. Turn on CNN.'

'Of course Mr President. Right away, Mr President

'But before you go, Ruzhkov, afterwards this is v we are going to do…,'

A minute later Oleg replaced the receiver and shuf back to the sitting area. He took with him a fresh b( of vodka from the cooler and poured them each a dr spilling the liquid, his hand trembling and then he reac for the remote control.

The Danish prime minister was holding a p conference,

'…good sense prevailed. After the allied forces v forced to fire warning shots, the Russian fleet retre from Faroese waters and is now headed for Murma I want to thank all the men and women serving in NATO forces who stopped a tragedy from occurring, least, I wish to thank the captain and crew of the Absa

As he made this last remark, cheering erupted f off camera.

'At present, we are remaining calm. We consider actions of the Russians a misunderstanding, not an ac war…,'

Oleg turned off the television, took his glass, l back in his chair, and drained his drink. He looked aro at his stunned co-conspirators.

'This is not my fault,' Oleg began. 'You can't blame for this. I warned you. And now, my friends, I'm afra have other grave news for you. The President has ordered me to arrange with the FSB to have you all arrested. Then he wants my resignation.'

'Me too? I was not involved in the decisions,' the air force general said.

'The president did not mention any exceptions,' Oleg answered.

The army general was winding himself up. He slammed his empty tumbler down onto the table, Oleg checked to see if the glass top had cracked, it was still intact. The man's blood pressure was clearly on the rise, from the drink and from anger.

'We cannot accept this. This is not over. We still have the paratroopers. They are scheduled to land in a few hours. Almazov, your boy is in command,' the army general said.

'My son?'

'It is a delicate mission, seen perhaps by some as illegal. We need complete loyalty to our cause. I'm sure your son will do his father proud.'

'I agree, I thank you for honouring me,' Almazov said. 'I suggest we get some food in here and await events, it could take some time. Caviar and Pelmeni would be good. Once our troops have landed, we can decide what our next move shall be. Ruzhkov, your little assistant, if she's available, could I borrow her in your office?'

# 46

'So are you going to kill me? Throw me out of helicopter?'

The diplomat spoke over the engine noise as we r[a]covered the North Atlantic on our return journey.

I could not tell whether the Russian jested or spok[e] earnest, but I did not throw Georgi into the sea. Wher[ we] arrived back at the landing pad, Ida was waiting for u[s in] a police car. As we climbed in, she handed Georgi a w[hite] envelope.

'What is it?' I asked as the diplomat ripped it open[.]

'I am persona non grata, they expel me. I must l[eave] by tonight.'

As Ida got going, Georgi attempted to use his ph[one,] then, swearing, he gave up and returned it to his poc[ket.] Ida offered to take him to his hotel after dropping me [off.] After that, she was headed out of town, her evening w[atch] at the roadblock.

Outside the parliament building, I climbed out of [the] car. I did not bother to say goodbye to the Russian, in[ter]nally I said good riddance to the would-be mass m[ur]derer. I hoped it was the last I would see of the m[an.] Nodding to the by-now familiar security guard, I hur[ried] up the stairs.

As I opened the door to the conference room, I heard what sounded like a muffled gunshot. At the opposite end of the room stood the negotiators around Hildy, each smiling with a champagne flute in hand, Gov poured from a bottle.

'Frank, there you are,' Sámal said. 'You missed all the excitement. Here, take a glass, we are just congratulating your lovely wife on her arbitration. In all my years, this has been one of the more memorable negotiations. That story about you, yelling for everyone to duck, the wedding shotguns, we all laughed.'

I gave my wife a withering look, she smiled back, innocently shrugging her shoulders, the disarming gesture I adored. Even the American banker seemed more relaxed, he was obviously enthralled by Hildy. He leant close to her as if attempting private conversation, and I overheard the words, '...next in London, you must allow me to take you to...'

The man was hitting on my wife! My dislike for the Texan upped a notch. However, I was proud of her, and content. Hildy and I had done it. The battle avoided, the loan now in responsible hands, and Britain would get her submarine base. If I were lucky, given my contributions, C might take me back. Regardless of my decision to the contrary the day before, I knew in my heart, I would give anything for that, and I felt I had earned it.

'What's the plan, now?' I asked Sámal.

'The gentlemen from London had a reservation for tomorrow morning's flight, in case we needed to negotiate

into the night. They have rebooked, and we have a
arriving shortly to take them to the airport.'

Hildy broke away from her conversation with
Texan.

'Frank, Penny called. She's been through a lot,
wants to go to London. Can we take her to the airp
I said I would, but I'd also like to finish up here. Perl
you could fetch her while we say goodbye, you can pick
up afterwards.'

Dismissed by my wife, I left the group with m
feelings. The negotiations had been my doing, I shoul
the one celebrating. On the other hand, through neces
I had given Hildy the responsibility. She had done
rephrase that, she had been remarkable, and if she nee
ten minutes to bask in the limelight, I was happy to gi
to her, Hildy, the love of my life.

Outside darkness was falling. I found a slip under
windscreen wiper, two hundred kronor, £25. I laug
aloud, never having received a parking ticket that ch
not in the past many years. I climbed in and called
daughter, hoping her phone was working. It was.

'Penny dear, as ordered by the boss, I'm on my wa
to fetch you. Are you packed?'

She was. At the house, a going away party stood on
pavement. After hugging Oydis and the children, H
Sámal's wife and her children, all of whom had stayed
night in cramped accommodations, my daughter clim
into the car, I stowed her bag in the boot.

'What about the flat and all your things?' I asked.

'Oh, I'm not leaving, not altogether, not yet anyway. But after yesterday, I want to get away for a week or two, so I'm off to London for a friend's engagement party, and then I'll go visit Mormor.'

I ground my teeth. My daughter was going to stay with my mother-in-law for peace and quiet? Still, I could well understand her wanting to get away.

Returning to the parliament building five minutes later, Hildy stood waiting, she got into the back.

'What dear, you don't want to drive?' I asked.

'Darling, I'm exhausted. I have a splitting headache, and the champagne did not help. I've taken some painkillers, I'll be alright in a few minutes.'

I pulled away from the kerb and gave a silent salute as we passed the police station and the empty helicopter landing-site, the windsock discernible in the twilight and then headed out of Tórshavn. I drove fast, feeling good, we had succeeded, there was no more to be done, no more danger, I could relax.

'Dad, slow down, we have plenty of time,' Penny said, as we came around the headland and saw the fog coming in and taillights of a long line of cars queueing, probably all destined for the airport like us. I hoped we would not be late.

# 47

As the car in front pulled away, I inched the Mercedes forw[ard]

'Hello Ida, caught any bandits?' I asked.

'Hey, Mr Llewellyn, you can pass through. I just sp[oke] with you know who over the radio, he's at the other [end,] perhaps you can stop and say hello.'

'I'm not sure it would be appropriate, but thanks [any]way,' I replied.

I rolled up the window and accelerated down the h[igh]way and into the tunnel. Halfway through, I changed [my] mind. I mean, what harm could it do? The paratro[op]ers' mission was over, the Russians had turned back, [the] confrontation avoided, and it would be a nice surprise [for] Hildy and Penny. Also, it would give me the chance to [say] hello to Max's commanding officer.

As I neared the tunnel exit, through the dark m[ist I] saw another roadblock up the road, the headlights of a [few] waiting cars faced our way. I slowed and then crossed [the] oncoming lane and just past the container, I parked [in a] lay-by and doused the headlights.

'Darling, why are we stopping?' I heard from the b[ack.]

'Please bear with me, just stay in the car, Penny, you [—]'

I climbed out and shut my door. Looking up at [the] smashed car atop the container, I did a double take[.]

looked decidedly like Susanne's Toyota Camry with its open windows. I guessed we would be paying for a new car after all.

Going around to the rear of the container, the doors were closed, all seemed deserted.

'Captain Jenkins,' I called in a hushed voice.

A strange sight, one I had seen often enough on active duty, ages ago. Straight in front of me, a shadow, a soldier in camouflage dress seemed to come out of the ground, his face smeared with green and black.

'Hello, Dad.'

I stood speechless. Gulping, I worked hard to control my emotions. Ida had told me Max was among the troops, but seeing my son here in the field, in the flesh, in full battle dress, touched me in a way I would never have imagined.

'Ahem. Max, what a pleasant surprise. I suppose a hug for your old dad is out of the question.'

My son hesitated.

'Go on then,' came whispers from hidden figures. Max stepped forward and gave me a bear hug, the helmet's edge sharp against my brow. I held him for a moment, not wanting to let him go and then stepped back.

'Max, I'm afraid it's not just a social call. Is your captain here? Captain Jenkins?'

'How do you know his name, Dad?'

'Max, there are so many things I never told you, but for now, I need to speak to your commander.'

Minutes later, the captain joined us.

'Captain Jenkins, sir. This is my father, he says he n[eeds] to talk to you. I'm not sure why. He is on holiday her[e in] the islands with my Mum.'

The captain's expression was impossible to discer[n in] the darkness.

I stuck out my hand to shake.

'Nice to meet you, Captain. Frank Llewellyn, form[erly] of her Majesty's Secret Intelligence Service, now on t[em]porary assignment.'

It did sound grand, and technically, I *was* work[ing] for C.

Max stared at me, open-mouthed, his white teeth c[on]trasting his camouflaged face.

'I believe they have advised you of a codename. I[t is] the Puffin.'

I cringed saying it, but what to do?

'An unusual code name, Mr Llewellyn.'

'Agreed Captain. Be that as it may, it is I who reque[sted] your presence so we might pre-empt a Russian land[ing]. However, I'm sorry to have inconvenienced you. [The] Russian navy is on its way home.'

'So we've been informed, sir. Still, no trouble at all [Mr] Llewellyn, the lads need the training. But you being M[ax's] father, quite a coincidence, I'm curious to ask…'

'No, Captain, I'm sorry. Need to know. Now, ev[ery]thing seems quiet here. Anything to report?'

'There is one thing, sir. Not half an hour ago, a [per]son of interest trekked over the mountains, we've ta[ken] him into custody. Ukrainian passport, but we think he

Russian pathfinder. He had a satchel of infra-red homing-beacons on him.'

'May I see them?'

The captain opened the container door, emitting a red glow. Inside I heard a smack of flesh against flesh.

'My men are having a chat with him,' the captain explained.

Inside, held down by two troopers, his hands bound behind his back, the pathfinder was kneeling in front of a chemical loo, his hair was wet. I did not recognise him, although he bore some resemblance to the two young Ukrainian backpackers who had shared our taxi on that first day.

From a canvas bag, the captain withdrew a green metallic item with a red glass lid. I studied it for a moment and then handed it back.

'Did he have a radio?' I asked.

'Negative, sir.'

'Captain, please tell your men to concentrate on one question, only. What is the protocol for Russian paratroopers when there is no communication with the pathfinder immediately prior to their jump? Then, let's talk outside.'

I followed Max out to the fresh air.

'Dad, you never told me any of this. I thought you worked for the MOD, not that you were a spy.'

'I wasn't, and I'm getting fed up trying to explain it to people. I ran a desk, okay? Pff!'

I took a deep breath.

'Sorry Max, just letting off steam, not your fault. Now, come over to the car, I have your mother and Penny with

me. Your sister's off to England tonight, we're taking
to the airport. Your mother and I will be staying on f
few more days.'

Amongst catcalls, wolf whistles and chiding com
from the hillside, Max had a moment with his mother
sister. The women were back in the car ready to de
when the captain exited the container.

'He says, regardless there are no comms with the p
finders, they jump according to their coordinates and t
steer for the beacons. If no infrared is visible, they
their best judgement in landing. We would do the sa
But Mr Llewellyn, headquarters has advised us there i
longer a threat. We're ordered home tomorrow morni

'And I agree with that assessment, Captain Jenk
However, as a precaution, this is what I want you to d

I explained.

Max stood beside his captain, listening, saying n
ing. Now he did,

'Dad, we can't do that, it's tantamount to murder.'

I did not answer my son. Instead, I looked to
commander.

'Captain. The Puffin, you are to follow my g
ance. If need be, call it in. Again, this is just a precaut
Hopefully, you will have a peaceful evening. But we
not ignore the fact the pathfinder is here. Therefore,
must be prepared. If they do choose to come, they do s
their peril. Can I trust you to give the orders? Also to
troops on Suðuroy?'

'Yes sir,' Captain Jenkins reluctantly replied.

My son refused to look me in the eye.

So be it, some decisions were hard, especially the cold ones. For me decisiveness had come easier with age, weighing what needed protecting, what needed destroying. I just hoped for my sake and theirs, the Russians decided to stay at home.

Now it was off to the airport. As I got the car back on the highway, the women behind me engaged themselves in an animated discussion of how dashing Max looked. I agreed, hoping if the worst happened, my son would find it in himself to forgive me.

# 48

Befuddled, Oleg woke from his dream. What had they said? Assassination, a coup? A demonstration showing had the nuclear codes? No, not NATO. That would n retaliation. A non-member of the alliance then. The c of staff wanted to avenge his son. Revenge? Was he de

Almazov was speaking to Oleg in between gulp vodka, the general was drowning his sorrow.

'Ruzhkov, my boy, all of them, save a few, the l. ing was a disaster, we just heard. Now there is no g back. The president has declared war against us, his l command. We must retaliate. We need to eliminate before he has us arrested. He thinks his little love in the woods is unknown to us. He has little protec there, a handful of agents only. I will make the call. V use outside assassins, that Jay fellow can arrange it. But coup won't work unless we can prove we are in cha that we have the nuclear codes. And because we don't must act as though we do. We must make a demonstrat and avenge my son in the process. Ruzhkov, you will orders to your brother. Shall we say a coordinated eff 03:00 hours, our time?'

Oleg had never imagined it would come to this. F could everything have gone so wrong?

Very well, in for a kopek in for a rouble, Oleg reasoned. He could live with the outcome, it was not all bad. As the sole politician in the room, when they succeeded, he would become president, much better than the minister of culture. His wife would like that.

In his office, he dialled the number.

'Yes Pavel, I know it's late.'

Oleg caught himself whispering conspiratorially to his brother, the base commander of the 60th Missile Division. It would not do, he needed to sound authoritative, he raised his voice.

'This is urgent and highly confidential. Orders from the very top, confirmed by General Almazov, the chief of staff.'

'Oleg, you say 03:00 hours Moscow time. Is that launch time, or time of impact?' his brother asked.

'Time of impact.'

'Oleg, I find receiving such orders orally and directly from the Ministry highly unusual. These instructions should go through the proper channels, through headquarters at Strategic Missile Troops.'

'Pavel. Your superiors are under investigation, you might be next,' Oleg lied. 'As your brother, I beg you to follow orders. You must launch one of your RS-24's, at precisely 02:41 hours Moscow time. Coordinates will be sent to you thirty minutes prior to launch confirmed by the chief of staff, himself.'

'What is the target?'

Oleg told him. The line went silent. Then,

'You know Georgi is still up there, he phoned mother this morning. He is working for the Admir How can you do this to your own family?'

Oleg's mind raced.

'Shit. Shit. Brother, you must believe me. He called as well, but it had slipped my mind. I will contact him very minute.'

'Oleg, I will not murder my son. Unless I can r( him to confirm he has left the islands, there will be launch. Do you understand me?'

'Pavel, I promise, we'll get him off the...'

His brother had hung up.

# 49

Hildy and I stood inside the bay windows of the airport looking out into the night, towards the white airliner, starkly illuminated by floodlights. We had arrived in plenty of time for Penny's flight and were now in the sitting area of the small cafeteria, the attendant behind the counter was noisily closing up for the night.

Outside, Penny stood at the back of the short queue of remaining passengers, she turned and waved to us as the line inched forward and up the movable stairs.

It had been a busy day, and I had not eaten since breakfast, my stomach was grumbling. I considered getting something from the cafeteria but decided to save my appetite for a nice juicy steak at the restaurant Knud had recommended the day before.

'It's all so fascinating,' Hildy said. 'Tomorrow morning, the Løgting will meet in an extraordinary session to approve the arrangement, and the banks will get administrative approval by midday. The money will be transferred into Eurodea Bank's account before close of business.'

Hildy's headache was gone, she was full of energy, it had all been so new to her, but she had come through with flying colours. She was ecstatic with what she had achieved, and she had every right to be.

I saw the bankers in their expensive suits hurry ac[ross] the tarmac, the irritating Texan in the lead. They were [the] last passengers to board, carrying their bags of duty-[free]. Where they really that cheap? Well-paid bankers, [who] could easily afford the off-licence, but who chose ins[tead] to lug their spirits all the way to London just to save a [few] bob? I wondered if their gin had cost £60.

The bankers reached the queue. The Texan must h[ave] said something, because Penny turned around, smile[d at] him and then began an animated conversation as [they] ascended the stairs. I gritted my teeth.

Quick footsteps came from behind me, I turned to [see] Georgi come running lugging his carry-on, he approac[hed] the single security scanner, he would have to get a m[ove] on, the bankers were halfway up the stairs to the aircr[aft].

'Yes, of course, sir, we're just completing board[ing]. You'll need to go directly to the gate. Your boarding p[ass] please.' the lovely ground hostess said.

As Georgi reached into his pocket, I heard a ji[ngle]. Showing a raised index finger to the young woman, indica[ting] 'Just a moment', Georgi stepped away and swiped the scr[een].

I remembered Georgi complaining about his ph[one] not working and wondered how he had gotten a new [one]. The shops were closed when we arrived back from [the] North Sea outing. I willed the Russian to hurry, if no[t he] would miss his flight.

He spoke in what I took to be Russian, and nodd[ed a] lot. Only a few words were clear to me. 'Dah' and 'P[a]' the bald diplomat said them several times.

In our various encounters, I had never dwelled on whether the man had a family, although I vaguely remembered him mentioning his father was in the army and harm would come to his mother if I revealed what the diplomat had told me. Of course, the man had parents. In spite of his conniving, loathsome self, Georgi was a human being just like the rest of us. Well almost.

The call must have ended unexpectedly. Georgi looked at the phone, swiped up and down, and pushed the button on the side. No, not a new phone, just one, which occasionally was on the blink. The Russian looked up, noticed us and looked away, avoiding eye contact. Fair enough. I had bested the man in his evil endeavours, it must have been embarrassing for him.

I decided to rub it in, I could not help myself.

'Georgi, thanks for being such a good loser. You'd better hurry up, or you'll miss your flight,' I said, good-humoured. 'Goodbye and take care not to do this again. But if you ever want to defect, look me up!'

He smiled back, 'We will see who is the loser.'

My proposal got me thinking. I was in trouble for allowing Georgi to listen in on the secure communications amongst the allied fleet. Perhaps bringing Georgi in would give me some redemption. I filed away the thought as Georgi fumbled inside his beige coat pocket. He finally pulled out his passport, coloured red, not diplomatic green. Inside, his boarding card was sandwiched between the pages. He returned to the security checkpoint.

'Sir, the gate is closed, I'm sorry,' the ground hos[tess] told him. 'I did inform you, we were completing board[ing] but you refused to give me your boarding card.'

It was a first for me, I had never seen anything q[uite] like it. He lost it, there is no other word for it. The m[an's] face turned white in seconds, not in anger, no, Georgi [was] frightened. I could empathise with the man, having mi[ssed] flights in the past, but a night's stay at a hotel was ha[rdly] frightening.

'You have to let me through, you have no choic[e. I] am a Russian diplomat, persona non grata. I have b[een] expelled and ordered to take this flight.'

'Sir, I am sorry, we've completed boarding, the [air]craft is ready for departure, there's nothing I can do. [We] do have another flight to London in the morning. [The] Atlantic Airways ticket counter is across the hall, the[y are] just about to close, you should hurry.'

The ground hostess wore a sweet disarming smile, [she] must have used every trick she had learnt from the st[ew]ardess school.

'No, that will not do at all. I will pay you, ten thous[and] kronor, anything to get me on that plane. I need to ge[t on] this flight. Now let me through!'

'Sir, I told you we were closing the gate. You co[uld] have made the flight, but you chose to make calls inst[ead]. Now, if you insist on using aggressive language, then I [am] afraid I cannot help you. If you do not desist, I shall [call] security.'

'I don't see how my language figures into any of this. You were not fucking helping me before, and you are refusing to fucking help me now.'

Hildy stood shaking her head but said nothing.

The young woman dialled a number.

Bemused, I watched two men in blue uniforms approach and march Georgi towards the exit.

'I wonder what all that is about?' I said. 'I'm curious. Come on dear, let's go find out.'

Outside the revolving doors, having been released, Georgi looked to be in a panic. He was stranded, the last of the taxis were all gone, and the flight to London had been the airport's last departure of the day.

'Unfortunate missing your plane, Georgi. Need a lift?' I asked.

He looked at me, blinked hard as if taking a decision and strode over to us, appearing to want to hug me. Instead, he took my hand in both of his.

'Frank, I'm so happy you're here. We must work together, we must get off the islands. But first, I need to borrow your phone. There is still time.'

'Time for what, Georgi?' I asked.

'To avert a disaster. Please, may I borrow your phone?'

'What kind of disaster?'

'I need to stop it.'

'Stop what?'

'You would not believe me if I told you, now please, the phone.'

I handed it over.

'I hope it's a local call. Otherwise, you'll have to re burse me,' I said, knowing full well that, mine bei British number, the call would be international in any c

Georgi began to dial, then he stopped, and looked

'I don't know the number. I've never had to memo my father's telephone number.'

With shaking hands, he took out his phone.

'It's Russian-made, the encryption software is real s

He pushed the button to turn it on.

'Nothing. It's dead.'

'Georgi, take it easy. Is there a family crisis? You n tioned your father.'

'You don't understand. I don't have his number. It happen, but we are not too late to save ourselves. We l a few hours. We must get to Tórshavn, we must go to harbour. Perhaps a speedboat, something which can ge far enough away from here.'

I turned to Hildy with a raised eyebrow and rece one in return. We stood watching Georgi unravel.

'Georgi. Get a grip. What is going to happen?' I a:

'I will tell you only after we are in the boat. If we cr a panic, we will never make it.'

'Alright, Georgi. Hildy dear, you take him to the I'll be along shortly.'

Once again, Georgi grabbed my hand in both of Shaking it, he said,

'Thank you. Thank you. But we must hurry.'

Hildy led him away by the elbow.

I dialled C's number.

'Mrs Seabiscuit, just an update. The negotiations with the bankers went fine. It is all set for tomorrow. They decided to get an early flight out instead of leaving in the morning. They just left, headed for Heathrow.'

'Frank, where are you now?' C asked.

'Hildy and I are at the airport. There is a development I want to share with you. But why do you ask?'

'It's been a bit hectic here, I've not had time to properly thank you for all you've done in diffusing this crisis. It could have gone horribly wrong. So, good work. There *is* something else. Have you heard?'

'Heard what?'

'Let me ask you, when you left Tórshavn for the airport, did you see anything unusual on the way?'

'Well yes and no. We stopped and had a chat with Captain Jenkins. All quiet on the western front.'

'Frank, something terrible has happened. It will soon be in the news, we can talk openly. The Third Paras have taken a dozen or more Russian paratroopers prisoner. The Russians landed in force, or attempted to. Their aircraft had an Aeroflot transponder, it slipped through the NATO cordon. However, it seems Captain Jenkins had floated pathfinder beacons out into the fjord on Styrofoam trays, something to do with pickle packaging from some container. The ploy worked, the Russians, two hundred or more landed in the water and drowned, they'll be dredging

bodies for months. This is awful. I appreciate the need
our forces to defend themselves, but how they came u
such a ghastly ploy is beyond me.'

I chose not to comment. Instead I worried about v
Max would think, what we would say to each other w
next we met.

'Now, what did you wish to discuss?' C asked.

When I told her about Georgi's behaviour at the
port, she sounded concerned.

'Frank, the Paras are still there. I think you sho
hand your man over to them, let them sweat him. We r
to know what it is, he is so afraid of.'

'I could do it myself if I had a grind knife and a clo
iron.'

'Frank, just get him there, ASAP.'

# 50

Across the street from the Smyril Line terminal, Hildy and I had a table at the Angus Steakhouse for a late night supper. I had nearly finished one of the best Rib-Eye steaks I had ever eaten. Knud's recommendation had done the place justice. Feeling mellow, my bottle of Shiraz stood half-empty next to the candle.

I was content, truly happy for the first time in ages. The bankers had departed and would do their thing, and I had been instrumental in avoiding a major naval confrontation. Life was good.

We had delivered poor Georgi at the container, Max had taken custody of the struggling Russian as he, screaming Armageddon, became ever more deranged by the minute, finally shouting for all to hear, 'we must get off the islands!'

Max had said nothing to me about the many Russian deaths, he had avoided my eye. The place had been buzzing with activity, boats with searchlights out on the misty fjord. Hildy had commented on the spectacle, I had said nothing, I did not tell her of the events. It would ruin our evening. I was just happy Max was safe.

Hildy pushed her grilled salmon around her plate. She was not hungry after her substantial lunch. She even declined the salad buffet, and as the designated driver, drank water and just the one glass of white wine.

'Besides,' she said. 'The water here tastes better t wine.'

I, on the other hand, had gone all in with a shrimp c tail, the Rib Eye with baked potato, sour cream and ch and I still had room for dessert. The cheesecake looked g

During our meal, I told Hildy of my excursion on high seas, glad it was all over. I downplayed the dang had been in, being at the centre of a potential nuclear battle. And we talked about our son.

'I didn't recognise him at first, our Max,' Hildy laug 'I've never imagined him in camouflage makeup, and helmet seemed much too large for him. On our way b he did seem sad though, I wonder what was bothering h

Saved by the bell, my phone rang. The display sho 'Max', I went outside to take his call so as not to dis the other diners, and so, if he wanted to talk about paratrooper deaths, Hildy could not listen in. Without jacket, I shivered under the moonless sky blanketed stars. The night was silent save for faint disco thump coming from the direction of the West Harbour and ominous police siren in the distance.

I swiped right.

'Max.'

'Dad, where are you and Mum right now?'

'Max, we need to talk. I'm sorry about what happe but...,'

'Dad, I understand, I really do, no time for that now. Where are you?'

'We are having a splendid late-night supper at this marvellous steakhouse in Tórshavn. Just by the harbour. You should be here.'

The phone went silent, I could hear Max's heavy breathing.

'Sorry Dad, but no I shouldn't. Be there, I mean. And neither should you. That friend of yours, Georgi. The bastard, he finally cracked, but only after we took him to the old NATO bunker in the mountain. That's where we are now, at the entrance. Dad, it's all taken much too long. It seems he is the son of some general and the nephew of the Russian defence minister. He says there is a nuke coming our way. We've relayed the intel to HQ.'

Max stopped to let the information sink in. I could sense my son choking up.

'Dad, you and Mum need to evacuate. Come here to the bunker while there is still time.'

'Max, lad. I'm sure it will all come to nothing.'

'How can you be certain?'

'Max, rest easy. Why would anyone want to use an ICBM against the Faroes?'

'Okay, Dad. But just so you know, we're redeploying the company. Captain Jenkins will arrive shortly. I've got to go, take care, Dad. I hope you're right. Give my love to Mum. I love you Dad.'

Max's voice broke as he terminated the call.

My phone chimed again. I considered going insid[e] get my jacket. Any more of these calls and I would c[ause] my death. The display showed 'Michaels', MI6's directo[r of] operations. Curious, last I tried to contact him, the se[cre]tary said he was away. I swiped right.

'Shouldn't you be on holiday or something?' I aske[d in] greeting.

'They called me back in. Frank, we're not secure, [but] I want you to know. The father of your Russian fri[end,] he is reportedly the commander of the missile bas[e at] Tatishchevo. It has ICBMs, each carrying four multi-i[nde]pendently targetable re-entry vehicles, MIRVs. Flight t[ime] is just under twenty minutes. From radio intercepts, [we] think they are going to fire one at the Faroes.'

I caught myself in revealing Max's indiscretion.

'Michaels, why on Earth would they want to do th[at?']

'Ruffled feathers and to prove they have the nuc[lear] codes. From the chatter, GCHQ thinks a coup coul[d be] in the making. Satellite imagery has picked up a heat [sig]nature which shows an imminent launch, just the one [mis]sile, unscheduled. Frank, we've spoken with the Ya[nks.] They have a destroyer, the Ivanka Trump.'

'They have a ship called that?'

'I asked the same. It was the Winston S Churc[hill.] Apparently, it received orders only hours ago to chang[e its] name, their president didn't like having one of their [own] ships named after a foreigner. In any case, it is moving [into] harm's way. And Frank, just so you know, the only rea[son] they could get their destroyer into position was bec[ause] of you. Getting that Russian to the Paras, brilliant stuff. The Ivanka Trump should be southeast of Tórshavn as we speak. If you had an elevated position, you might even see it. However, it's not where I want you to be.'

I thought how fortunate we were with Max deep underground and Penny safely on her way to Heathrow. Already landed in fact. I refused to dwell on the consequences for Hildy and myself.

'Michaels, Georgi Ruzhkov was in a panic to call someone in Russia, it must have been to stop this. You said his father is the base commander. Georgi spoke to him from the airport. Surely GCHQ's listening station in Yorkshire can trace that call, you need to get Georgi that number, immediately.'

'It's in the works, Frank, but what I want now is for you and the wife to get out of there. The commander on the island is a Captain Jenkins, he has moved his men into some old NATO facility, which can withstand a nuclear strike. We have also contacted the Faroese government, and are urging them to get everyone into the tunnels as fast as possible.'

'Michaels, do we have hours? Because that's what it will take. They won't all fit in the bunker, and only the tunnels to Vágur and Klaksvík are deep enough to provide any real protection. There is no way they can evacuate the people of Tórshavn to safety, twenty thousand strong, along one road, it would take the rest of the night.'

Looking to the south, toward the old town and the city centre, I saw lights come on in the rows of houses

and blocks of flats. Looking up the hillside, I saw
same thing happening in the dwellings above me.
ominous sound of church bells began to toll throug
the town.

Michaels paused, seemingly distracted. Then,

'Frank. I am so sorry. NORAD and GCHQ have
just confirmed the launch of a single ICBM headed
If it's aimed at you, ETA will be in under twenty min
I have to go, Frank, good luck. If the worst happens
look you up in the Hereafter. Have a bottle of Laphr
waiting, you and the missus both.'

I could hear the emotion in his voice, Micha
throat constricting. I imagined the tears running down
younger man's cheeks as we rang off. They were runn
down mine.

With a surreal calm, I put the phone in my
pocket, dried my face and took out my wallet. I re-ent
the restaurant and walked straight past Hildy's uptu
questioning smile. At the cashier's counter, without
ing for the bill, I laid two five hundred-kronor note
the countertop and did not ask for change. Retrieving
coats from the hooks in the corner, I walked back to
table by the entrance.

'Hildy, we need to go.'

She would know immediately that this was a g
emergency. I always called her 'Dear', often 'Hildy d
but very seldom 'Hildy'. It had been that way ever sinc
first met thirty years ago.

She stood, and let me help her into her coat.

As I held the door, she preceded me out into the cold. I tucked her arm under mine and marched her across the street. In silence, we walked the fifty metres to the side entrance of the centuries-old citadel, the grass-covered fort 'Skansen' and then up the stone steps.

Turning left, we walked over to the rusty ancient four-cannon battery and sat down on the low embrasure, legs dangling over the edge. To the sound of ringing church bells and cars starting in the distance, I told her of Max's call and how much her son loved her. I then told her what Michaels had said.

After a moment of disbelief, she burst into tears. I joined in, I admit it. We sat holding each other tight, the cold seeping up from the rock on which we sat.

After a while, Hildy dried her eyes.

'Frank darling, it's not all bad. We've had a good life together, I've no regrets. Four beautiful children, they'll get on without us, they'll have to. I always wanted for us to grow old together as partners in life, but this is okay. We're with each other in the end, that's what matters, and we will be together for our new beginning. This way, neither of us will have to wait for the other,' she said, laughing through new tears.

I was too choked-up to reply. I sat, holding my wife, looking out over the waters. I was not afraid to meet my inevitable death, although the alternative was preferable. It was the thought of losing what we had together, losing the endless devotion I felt for my wife. I too had imagined us together, old and grey. Now I was helpless to save us.

And I was helpless to save all those beautiful pe[ople] who lived here on the islands, folks who, with their qu[aint] customs and honest attitude towards life and nature, [had] shown me such hospitality. Was this really to be the fa[te of] the Faroes? Destroyed in a nuclear holocaust? I felt a [pang] of sadness in my chest, a fist clenching my heart.

Looking out to the right of Nólsoy, beyond the [island,] I noticed the navigation lights of a ship moving [out.] Looking up towards the eastern sky, I saw a moving s[peck] of light among the stars, coming our way.

# 51

Aboard the USS Ivanka Trump, standing in the operations room, the skipper had received his written orders a half hour ago. He was to vacate his current position and head due west at flank speed. It came from the top, their second message from the president that day.

Further, he was to go to battle stations and have his full complement of anti-ballistic missiles ready to defend against a possible nuclear attack on the eastern seaboard of the United States.

His personal instructions from his admiral came separately. They informed him of the true reason for heading west. It was to save his ship from an expected nuclear attack on the Faroe Islands. The admiral would back him if he followed his conscience and chose to disregard the presidential orders.

'Sir. They're reporting a fault on the firing mechanism on the 61-cell launcher.'

Oh no. not again, he thought. During the past months, the system had unexplainably refused to function on several occasions. His sharpest electronics specialist, nicknamed 'Shorty' had tested every wire, every circuit board. Most times the system worked just fine and then suddenly

when the gunnery officer turned the key activating
launcher, the 'Systems Ready' light would go red.

'How many SM-6's do we have in the auxil
launcher? The '29'.'

'Eleven, skipper. Twenty-four in the main battery.'

'Get me Shorty on the horn.'

'Aye aye, sir.'

Sure, it would have been simple to obey orders
leave the islands undefended. However, he would n
again be able to face his wife and boys. He would n
be able to say he had done his best. His ship's motto
'In war: Resolution, In peace: Good Will', not 'When
chips are down, get out of Dodge'. The decision to
the president's orders had been easy.

'Shorty here, sir. We are still looking for the fault.
an idea it might be in the wiring boards which initiate
automatic targeting.'

'Shorty. Do your best, we don't have much time.'

In what seemed only moments, he had an exc
Shorty in his ear.

'Skipper, I found the fault, I can give you a tempo
fix.'

'Okay, Shorty. Great stuff. Be ready in two.'

He could sense the tense atmosphere aboard.
men and women in the operations centre had heard
all-hands briefing, as he addressed the crew over the sl
intercom. And they were well aware that their one pr
ous attempt at shooting down a mock ICBM had fa
miserably. This time it was the real thing.

'Skipper, automatic upload from NORAD to mainframe complete. We are tracking the target at fifteen hundred klicks, doing Mach 23. As it slows and releases the MIRVs, we are looking at seven minutes to re-entry.'

Then, 'Skipper, awaiting MIRV release from mother ICBM before individual targeting can commence. How many birds do you want in round one?'

'Gunny, let fly the full '61' complement. Use 'em or lose 'em.'

# 52

As the star rose higher into the heavens, the object fla[red] and a moment later, the light morphed into four shoo[ting] stars, each coming closer, getting brighter.

I felt the cold in my buttocks, a wonderful feel[ing,] the sense of being alive, being with my Hildy, a fee[ling] soon to be cut short. Looking up, I could see the shoo[ting] stars disperse marginally left and right. The four ho[rse]men of the Apocalypse. What were the Russians' targ[ets?] Tórshavn, Suðuroy, and Klaksvík? I wondered 'W[here] would the fourth one land?', and then caught myself. W[hy] did it matter?

Sitting beside me, Hildy jumped as a rocket shot [up]wards from where moments before, out to sea, there [had] only been navigation lights. Then another flame. Ro[cket] after rocket erupted from its silo, each launch illumina[ting] the ship's profile.

Minutes ticked by. High above, the four shooting s[tars] suddenly flared. They must be re-entering the atmosph[ere,] I figured, a swarm of fireflies raced up to greet them.

Then the fireworks began.

Two of the shooting stars disappeared in silent flas[hes.] A third seemed to change course and deflect north, a to our left. The fourth star just kept coming, and to be honest, I knew it really only took one.

'Skipper, two kills confirmed, a third diverted to the north. One still on course. Impact in three. Orders, sir?'

'Where is the expected impact of the one headed north?'

'Open waters sir. Maybe some fishing vessels. The Russian fleet is long gone.'

'Too bad. Okay, fire all remaining Sixes at the incoming MIRV.'

Not since the Iraqi wars had the ship fired in anger, and the skipper had never fired twenty-four missiles at four million dollars a pop. Almost a hundred million dollars of ordnance in thirty seconds. He got ready for another eleven missiles at forty-four million, wondering if his admiral would really defend his actions at the court-martial.

'Shoot when ready.'

The second, smaller, salvo was no less impressive, shooting into the night sky and then exploding in a multitude of airbursts and a single flash of light.

'I think it's over, dear, thank God. That was the one. We should be safe now,' I said.

We sat under the night sky. I felt somehow, we cheated death as Hildy whispered,

'Frank darling, will you pray with me?'

I bowed my head, folded my hands and whisp[ered] in unison with my love, 'Our Father who art in hea[ven] Hallowed be thy name….'

Then, with sudden apprehension, I looked no[rth] towards the invisible horizon, towards where a shoo[ting] star fell from the sky.

I put my hand behind Hildy's head and leant b[ack]wards, purposely toppling us to the flagstones, a fa[ll] just a couple of feet. My head smacked into the rock [with] a resounding crack, and the back of my left hand smashed between the stone surface and Hildy's skull, [sav]ing her from the impact.

'Darling, are you all right? You lost your balance,' [my] wife asked, out of breath.

I pulled her to me and smothered her face against [my] chest as I rolled both our bodies in against the rampa[rt].

The sky lit up as if it were noon on a bright sum[mer] day. We lay still for what seemed an eternity as dark[ness] slowly reclaimed us. I could hear a strengthening rur[nble] in the distance, the sound became a roar and then rece[ded] as a warm howling wind rushed over our bodies. [Only] then, did I release my hold around my wife's body. I c[ud]dled down and gave her a soft kiss on the lips feeling g[

to be alive. We remained there on the cold stones, holding each other tight.

'Darling. Have you any idea of what you've done?' my wife asked.

I felt her warm breath on my cold cheek.

'I've no idea what you are talking about, luv. I only acted as anyone else would in my situation.'

'No, that's not true, you did so much more. You saved me, you saved us all, and in the end, you even got the girl.'

'Didn't I always have her? But you're wrong, I did nothing. We did it, you and I, together.'

I held my wife and kissed her once more, with an affection deeper than I had ever felt, if that were at all possible. My phone jingled ruining the moment. It had slipped from my pocket when I tipped us off the wall. I dried a tear from my cheek as I scrambled onto my hands and knees and snatched the phone from the ground. Looking at the cracked display, I swiped right,

'Yes, we survived, as did my phone, well sort of. The EMP blast must have been too far away to do any damage. And you forget, it's Ardbeg I prefer. Yes, that should be possible, we'll be back next week. I'll look forward to it.'

I terminated the call.

'Darling, what was that about?' Hildy asked as we got up from the ground.

'Whiskey, and Michaels wanting to know if we were alive and if I was available to do some work, a job. He didn't go into specifics.'

'Oh, Frank, I'm so happy for you. You wanted bac[k] now they're giving you a chance.'

'Hildy dear, let's not get ahead of ourselves. I hav[e ]idea what he wants doing. We'll have to see.'

She gave me a hug and a long wet kiss on the lips, [and] a tingling in my groin.

'Well, while you were outside the restaurant and the telephone talking to Max, I booked us a room at Hafnia. Last minute decision before I emptied your b[ottle] and ordered another to go.'

'We might not have needed it, dear.'

'The bottle of wine?' Hildy asked.

'No silly, the room. We've made a custom of not u[sing] hotel rooms.'

'So let's break the habit. Come on double-o-puffin, getting cold.'

'What about the car?' I asked.

'Leave it 'till morning.'

'We'll get a fine, twenty-five pounds.'

'Darling, it'll be worth it, I promise.'

Together we marched off, arm in arm.

I leapt up and clicked my heels, a grin on my face.

# 53

London. Brook Street. The traffic was heavy, black taxis, cars and the occasional double-decker. The night was bustling outside the luxury hotel. Pedestrians, couples, inebriated groups walked by. Standing on the opposite side of the street, Hildy and I saw the two men arrive in their limo, right on time.

'Are you sure Hildy dear? You're not trained for this.'

'Darling, I was once, years ago, it'll be like riding a bicycle. And how difficult can it be? You say Michaels's Silver Foxes have made everything ready in our room.'

'But the consequences.'

'Frank, darling, you know what they did, and what they deserve.'

Hildy stood in the hallway, wearing a knee-length black dress with a white apron and white cotton gloves, a pair of chopsticks held her bun in place. She balanced a silver tray with a porcelain pot and cup.

She wanted to do this, she needed to. And she did not want Frank to bear the responsibility alone. Her darling, her loving Frank, caring father to their children, an h ourable man. Getting sacked had been bad, he'd b hurting for so long.

And the events on the Faroe Islands had taken t toll on him as well, she was in no doubt. He had ki a man in the chairman's basement, and something happened on Suðuroy in the fog, their pursuers had merely disappeared of their own free will, of that she sure. More weighed on his mind, things he refused to about. No, she would do this, while he was busy upsta

She knocked on the door.

'Enter!' An audible but faint shout. She could not, had no key-card, she knocked again.

The door opened wide, a broad-shouldered man hotel dressing gown, his hair cut short in military fash he stood barefoot in the suite's hallway.

'Good evening sir, your hot chocolate.'

'I not order that.'

Hildy had to think quickly.

'It's complementary,' she said and batted her eyes. worst outcome now would be the general simply clo the door.

He looked her up and down, mentally undres her. It was a long time since Hildy had last experier that from anyone but her Frank unless you counted charming banker from Texas. She could feel her ch blush.

'Put it in the bedroom,' the general ordered, a: turned his back on her and led the way into the suite. H bumped the door closed with her hip and then followed the man down the hallway, past the sitting room and into the bedroom. The ruffled bedclothes were pulled back, the only light came from the bedside lamp with its golden shade.

As the man took off his robe, revealing a wrinkled naked body, he sat down on the bed and then unabashed, swung his legs up.

'I stay here always, in London. But I not see you before.'

'No, sir. I am quite new. This is my first day,' Hildy said, averting her gaze.

'Shall I pour your chocolate for you, sir?'

She put the tray down on the bedside table, atop an adult magazine, and lifted the porcelain pot. She was careful not to spill a drop, even when the general's hand sneaked up under her skirt.

'Oh, sir!' she squealed joyfully, recoiling, feeling repulsed by the man's advances, his hairy body. By his very being.

'You know, I like young, but experience good too. You English, you're not 'sancha', a prude, are you?'

'No, sir. But the rules, it's not allowed!'

'Screw rules. Better, I screw you. At your age, we not need rubber. First, you give blowjob. Go to work.'

'Yes sir,' she said bashfully, 'I just need to freshen up. Perhaps you can drink your hot chocolate before it gets cold. I understand chocolate is a nice aphrodisiac.'

Hildy retreated through the side door to the en-suite bathroom hoping the worst would soon be over. She imagined the general taking a sip of hot chocolate and smacking his lips, there would be an aftertaste of almonds, they [no] way of hiding it.

She heard a grunt and went back to the room. The [gen]eral, leaning against the pillows, looked at her with p[ain] in his eyes, his hands at his chest.

'Please, I have pain, call help,' the man whispered [with] desperation in his voice.

She looked him in the face and said through clenc[hed] teeth, 'You attacked my people, the Faroe Islands. [You] would have killed them all. You may beg forgiveness f[rom] Our Lord, but you shall have none from me.'

The general's lips moved, but no sound came. [His] body went rigid in pain and then relaxed.

She watched the general die, feeling no remorse [or] pity. This man would have seen thousands die in his g[reed] of ambition. She thought of the small children on the [boat,] Oydis, Knud, Sámal and his wife, and their children. [She] thought of all the wonderful people at the party and s[weet] Susanne in Porkeri. And her lovely Frank, all of wh[om] would have perished if it were up to this man. No, it se[rved] him right.

She used a serviette from the tray to close the m[an's] unseeing eyes, and then she dried a trickle of choc[olate] from the corner of his mouth. Carrying her loaded [tray] into the corridor, Hildy closed the door behind her. D[own] the hallway, back in their room, after thoroughly w[ash]ing the thermos, the pot and the cup, she left the w[hite] apron and the serviette on the floor for the Silver F[ox] to collect.

Hildy donned her coat, pulled the new broad-brimmed hat down over her head and left the room. She descended the stairs to the lobby, slipping out through the main entrance, taking off and pocketing the white gloves in the process.

She turned left, crossed the intersection and walked up Brook Street, looking straight ahead, not glancing in the shop windows as she normally did. She got into the passenger seat of her Jaguar.

# 54

In my dark suit and white cotton gloves, I looked left
right, making sure the corridor was empty, and th(
rapped my knuckles against the door, holding the tray ᵥ
the bottle of cognac and a single snifter carefully balar
in my left hand, the silenced pistol beneath, covered
cloth napkin.

When there was no reply, I knocked again, this t
louder, willing the occupant to open up before any
showed themselves in the hallway or arrived by lift, fur
down the corridor. There was a noise from within, t
the door glided open, revealing a dishevelled heavy
man in a hotel dressing gown who looked at me quest
ingly, his comb-over standing on end. It was mesmerisi
I had only ever seen the phenomena in windy weather

'I'm sorry if I woke you, sir. We're running a bit
Your complimentary bottle of Cognac, Remy Martir
said.

Ex-Defence Minister Oleg Ruzhkov, a man nov
exile, stepped aside for me to enter.

'Yes alright, bring it in, put it in sitting room.'

I walked down the suite's hallway, hearing the o
door close behind me. Ruzhkov followed me into
lounge and dumped himself heavily onto one of the s(

I placed the tray on the side-table, and then lay my gun wrapped in the serviette beside it.

'Shall I open the bottle, sir?' I asked over my shoulder and received a 'Dah' in reply.

I removed the aluminium wrapper, twisted off the top and poured a healthy splash into the balloon. Turning around to serve the drink, I found myself staring down the barrel of a pistol.

'So, this is who they send to kill me. Some Arab who speaks fancy English. They not even find a decent white Russian,' the man laughed. 'You get it? White Russian? Like cocktail?'

'Sir, I have no idea what you are talking about,' I said as I edged my way back towards the sideboard. The minister held what looked like a nine-millimetre Makarov, a silencer attached. I was heavily outgunned.

'No, no, not that way. Stay where you are. Better yet, come over, put drink on table, no fast moves. Good, now sit on sofa,' he said, waving the gun.

I obliged, there was little else I could do. I sat down across from him.

'So tell me, my little Arab, why they send you?'

I considered keeping up the pretence, but then thought, what was the point?

'Minister Ruzhkov, I believe your president gave you his word, if you left the country, he would not seek revenge.'

'As he gave others, we expect him to keep promise if we hold up our end of bargain.'

'Which is?'

'We keep mouth shut.'

'Yes, that is my understanding as well.'

Ruzhkov leant forward, lifted his glass, sniffed aroma of his drink and took a sip.

'Then why you here?' he asked.

'You may not have heard, Minister, about the adm and the generals. They died in a plane crash this morn It seems a Georgian fighter-jet ordered them to land when they did not adhere, they were downed by a mis It would appear the Georgians were willing to do president a favour. As is the British government.'

'And is that why you here, little man?'

'Yes, so you can join your four deceased friends.'

'You mean three friends. General Almazov very m alive.'

I studied my watch.

'I'm afraid not, Minister. He passed away some n utes ago.'

I did not know this for a fact, but I trusted my Hi

He stared at me for a moment, through half-cl eyes.

'You say I die. Why? None of what happened my fa

'Your nephew says differently. You would have k him as well. He's working for MI6 now and says 'hello', that he knows we're meeting. Just something, he said w last we met. If you see my uncle, tell him, 'bashue nal or something like that.'

The minister put back his head and laughed.

'Little man, it is 'bashule naboo', up yours, fuck yo

'Sir, I'm sure he meant it with the utmost respect.'

It got me a smile but no laugh.

'So little traitor told you everything. You know it was he who develop plan?'

'Yes, but not to invade, not to launch nuclear bombs.'

'No, not good that. Invasion not my doing, but the military does what military does.'

'And the missile?'

'Orders. Military want new fleet. President stand in way. Nuclear demonstration needed for coup to succeed, but was not personal.'

'Minister Ruzhkov, it was personal to me.'

'Why you say that? We shoot missile at Faroe Islands, not London.'

'I consider them my family, the Faroese people. That is why I am here to kill you.'

'But little man, you fail.'

'Do I?'

The ex-minister looked at me, eyebrows raised.

'Your president has fabricated compelling evidence proving your son, Alexander, took part in the coup,' I said. 'That he intentionally withdrew his command from the area, knowing you were about to launch the missile. When this information is released to the FSB, your son will be prosecuted and hanged. They have fabricated emails between him and his wife. She too will be brought to trial and end up in a gulag. Minister, only you can stop it from happening. Now, I am going to stand up, get the bottle, and then I am going to pour you another drink.'

I wondered what to do if Ruzhkov refused to coo
ate. I had to assume the Russians would make good
their promises, that they would persecute the ex-minis
family. This was as much to save them as it was for
Well, almost. Standing over the ex-minister, I poured
glass half-full and said,

'Minister, drink, bottoms up. Make your peace
the world, and give me your decision. Either you use
gun and pull the trigger yourself, or you ask me to kill

I sighed, as I climbed into the driver's seat.

'I'm glad it's over and done with. How did yours
I asked.

'Without a hitch darling. Such a revolting man, he'l
much nicer now.'

'I'd say the same about the defence minister, now
done. But dear, no remorse?'

'He tried to obliterate my father's homeland and
family. I think I'm on firm ground here, I've no reg
But you, darling, do you feel bad about it?'

I turned away, hiding my emotions.

'Yes, a first, in cold blood after talking to the n
after letting him make his peace. But as you say,
deserved it.'

I breathed deeply, calming myself, willing my hand
stop shaking, and then I started the car.

'Right then,' I said. 'Too bad about the room, we can chalk down another empty one. Paid for, free minibar just so you know. Still, it'll be good to get home.'

When I received no reply, I looked over at my thoughtful wife.

'Frank, darling. We did what Six asked of us. I'm sure Michaels will soon be giving you more to do. I've just one request, a demand actually.'

'And that is?'

'In the future, I've decided, you're not going on missions on your own, call them intelligence gathering, if you must. I told you after the blast, you got the girl. Now I'm afraid you're stuck with her. Darling, from now on, I'm coming with you.'

## THE END

# AUTHOR'S NOTE

I hope you enjoyed Puffin. When I began writing, goal was to write novels that were intelligent, poss and entertaining. I will leave it to you to decide if my attempt, Puffin, meets those expectations.

I would like to thank the many kind people I l met on the Faroes for their gracious hospitality and many who have given their input making this novel sible including, Cat Skinner, Swati, Chuck, Niklas, Tór Tine, Bjørn, Jens C, Kristin, Trúgvi, Laurits, Anne M Kris, Paul, Hans Hjørleivur, and my loving wife.

For anyone wanting to visit the Faroe Islands experience its truly unique nature and wonderful peo I would recommend a four or five-day trip, and that treat yourself to the flexibility of a rental so you can low in Frank and Hildy's footsteps. Alternatively, the service is great, beware of the Sunday schedules. Belo the address for the Faroese tourist bureau.

http://www.visitfaroeislands.com

Although the characters in this novel are fictional, Elizab eatery in Viðoy does exist and in my view is a must-experience. Remember to book a table at the tourist in mation in Klaksvík.

For those of you who found a Russian nuclear attack on the Faroe Islands a bit farfetched, I suggest you search the internet for those four words 'Nuclear attack Faroe Islands'. It will surprise you. And Russia, and the Faroe Islands? Russia has great ambitions for their navy, they are in desperate need of ice-free ports for their new aircraft carriers and battlecruisers, and they seem to be getting a new port in Syria in exchange for services rendered. So who knows?

T. K. Louis

If you would like to join Frank & Hildy's readers club, so I can tell you when new titles are available, and so you can receive FREE background stories for Puffin, please visit the link below.

http://www.tklouis.com/freestuff

# AUTHOR'S BIO

After nearly four decades of financial wizardry worl
with innovations in the wind power industry, and 
ship and corporate finance, as an investment bank
treasurer, a CFO, a CEO, and a ground-breaking 
sultant, T. K. Louis is now doing his damnedest to v
exciting, intelligent fiction. Puffin is his debut novel.

Living in a suburb to Copenhagen, he has two gr
sons, a brown Labrador and a wonderful wife.

This is an indie book, privately published on Ama
without the horde of editors, publishers, and agents,
who accompany traditionally published novels. There
be mistakes, I hope, few and far between. They are m
but should you wish to bring them to my attention, you
welcome to leave a message at

http://www.tklouis.com/contact

To receive FREE background stories for Puffin, pl
visit the link below.

http://www.tklouis.com/freestuff

Printed in Poland
by Amazon Fulfillment
Poland Sp. z o.o., Wrocław